"THAT BLOW SHALL COST YOU DEARLY!' CRIED THE FARMER."

THE
SPIES OF THE SCHOOL;

OR,

Peeping Tom and Knowall Dick.

BEAUTIFULLY ILLUSTRATED.

COMPLETE.

LONDON:
"BOYS OF ENGLAND" OFFICE, 173, FLEET STREET, E.C.,
AND ALL BOOKSELLERS.

THE SPIES OF THE SCHOOL;

Or, Peeping Tom and Knowall Dick.

"THE MAN STRUCK JACK A BLOW ON THE HEAD."

No. 1.

THE SPIES OF THE SCHOOL;

OR,

PEEPING TOM AND KNOWALL DICK.

CHAPTER I.

HOME FOR THE HOLIDAYS—A PERFECT TORMENT—JACK AND HIS CHUM, HARRY.

"OH, what have you been doing?" cried Marian Spencer, a girl of fifteen, to her brother, who was two years her senior.

"Nothing much," replied Jack. "Don't get excited. That's the worst of you girls."

Jack Spencer was the son of a well-to-do farmer, living at the Home Farm, near Clare, in Suffolk.

He had been one quarter at Stingwell Hall School close by, under the strict discipline of Doctor Birchoften, and was home for a week's holiday at Easter.

"You are a perfect torment!" continued Marian.

"What have I done now?"

"I wonder you are not ashamed to ask."

"Now, Mary Anne, don't go piling up the agony too strong. Everything in law has got to be proved, and where are your proofs that I did it?"

"My name's Marian," she said.

He knew that nothing annoyed his sister so much as to be called Mary Anne, and that was why he did it.

"It isn't what you were christened, anyhow," he retorted; "but let me look at the pretty thing you are nursing."

Marian had a pet rabbit in her arms. An hour ago it had been white as snow.

Now it was a deep crimson.

Jack had brought a bottle of red dye from school, and the temptation to operate on the rabbit was irresistible.

"The creature isn't hurt," continued Jack. "It is something out of the common. If I were you I'd hire a caravan, and show it about the country. A red rabbit would be sure to draw."

"I'm glad you have only got a week's holiday," said Marian. "Cook says you have been in the dairy, dipping in all the cream on the milk coolers. I'll tell of you."

"My dear girl," replied Jack, with an air of superiority, that brothers are apt to assume, "you can please yourself about that, but—"

He paused abruptly, and gave her a significant look.

"What?" she demanded.

"I was going to tell you something."

"Some rubbish, I expect."

"To you it isn't, Mary Anne—not by a long way."

His provoking manner made her all the more curious to know what he had to say.

"Well," she replied, "I will look over your behaviour this time, and make no further remark about it, only to add that I am sure your chum, Harry Rawlings, would not have done such a thing."

"That's just where you are wrong."

"How so?"

"Harry held the rabbit while I transmogrified her."

"You are a pair of wretches, and it will be a long time before I speak to him again. Where is he now?"

"Hiding in the barn. He's your sweetheart, you know, and he's afraid to see you after dyeing the rabbit; but it was about him I was going to tell you. He's going back to Stingwell Hall School with me."

Harry Rawlings was about Jack Spencer's age. He was an orphan, living with Mr. Burns, at Five Oak Farm. His father had been very rich, and had resided at Hurst Castle close by.

His mother died at his birth; his father did not survive her long, and his uncle, Mr. Simeon Rawlings, came down, produced a will, leaving everything to him, took possession, and put Harry out to board at Burns' farm. Since then he had taken not the least notice of his nephew.

Some said, under their breaths, that the will was forged.

As Home Farm adjoined Five Oak Farm,

it was quite natural for Jack and Harry to be chums.

It was equally natural that Harry should fall in love with Jack's pretty sister.

"Who's going to pay for his schooling?" asked Marian.

"You can make a very safe bet that his uncle is not going to do so," replied Jack. "That very necessary part of the business is to be defrayed by Mr. Burns."

"I'm glad of it, for Harry's sake, though I shall miss him."

Going into the barn, Jack found Harry Rawlings lying very comfortably upon a truss of sweet-smelling hay.

"Hullo, Jack! what did she say?" asked Harry. "I suppose I am in for it, through being an accomplice in the fell deed?"

"She went on as all feminines do. Called me names, threatened to report me to my maternal relative, and declared that you were unworthy of future notice."

"She'll soon get over it. There's no harm done. Come for a walk, and tell me all about the school."

"Very well. We'll cut across country towards the castle," replied Jack.

"I'm not allowed to go within two miles of my uncle's place," said Harry. "He told Mr. Burns so."

"Not having seen you since you were quite a little chap, I don't suppose the squire would know you."

"Anyhow, I'll chance it."

"Is it not strange the squire should be so hostile towards you?"

"Mr. Burns says that my father and my uncle both loved my mother; that is why they quarrelled. But I don't want to talk about him. Tell me about the school," exclaimed Harry.

They had got out of the yard, and were now walking across a meadow.

"First," said Jack, "I must mention Doctor Birchoften."

"That is a very suggestive name," remarked Harry. "Does he act up to it?"

"Yes, I am sorry to say he does. There are sixty boys in the school, and I don't think one has escaped."

"How is that?"

"There are two spies—little fellows, but sharp, cunning, and impish. Their names are Tom Harris and Dick Wilkins."

"The spies of the school!"

"Exactly," answered Jack. "We call them Peeping Tom and Knowall Dick. They are great favourites with Mr. Dobby, the second, and Mr. Caner, the third master."

"I should pay them out."

"We are afraid of them. Even Clayton, the captain of the school, dare not say much to them."

"Aren't they hated?"

"I should just think they were. The doctor is unmarried; his house is managed by his sister, an old maid, Miss Martha. She is spiteful and vindictive, and encourages the spies. Then there are two fellows who make things lively."

"Who are they?"

"Wildash and Pranks. They are always getting into scrapes, for the simple reason that they don't seem to be able to keep out of them. Then there is Warner, the bully, and little Kennedy, who is everybody's victim."

"Are those the principal characters?" asked Harry.

"They have made more inpression on my mind than any others; but we must try to get rid of the spy system. The doctor has, every morning, at ten o'clock school, a report handed to him by Mr. Dobby."

"What for?"

"It is called the 'Black List,' and if there is not some unfortunate fellow's name down in it for punishment, you can see a look of disappointment come over his face. When it is full his features light up."

Suddenly their conversation was interrupted by the barking and yelping of dogs.

"Look out!" cried Harry Rawlings; "it's the hounds."

"Hurrah!" replied Jack; "we shall see them go by."

The next moment a fine large fox glided by them.

There was a hole in the hedge near where the boys were standing.

Regardless of their presence, he made for it, went through, and disappeared in the adjoining field.

There had been a heavy dew during the night. The scent lay well, and the hounds were after him in full cry.

CHAPTER II.

THE SQUIRE OF HURST CASTLE.

In a few minutes the pack burst into full view, and after them came the hunters.

Some took the hedge in a flying leap; others went through a gate hard by.

Not long was it before the entire field was past..

"That fox will lead them a dance," said Jack; "he is full of wind and go—not a quarter spent yet."

Before Harry had time to make any reply, the thud of a horse's hoofs was heard on the damp ground behind them.

Turning, they saw a tall, well-built man on a powerful black horse.

He was covered with mud from head to foot; his hat was smashed in; his face streaked with blood, and he had the appearance generally of having been thrown.

Reining in his horse he beckoned to Harry, who did not move.

"Come here, you young vagabond!" cried the gentleman.

"Why should I?" asked Harry, who was of an independent frame of mind.

"Because I order you."

"I'm not anyone's lacquey."

The stranger bit his lips, and his face flushed with anger.

"Which way has the fox gone?" he demanded. "My horse refused the last jump. I had a bad fall. Where is the hunt? Make haste! I'm all behind."

"If you want to know, find out for yourself," answered Harry.

"What?"

"If you had spoken civilly to me at first, I might have told you."

The man raised his whip with a threatening gesture.

"It is easy to see you are a young scamp," he exclaimed, "and I have a good mind to thrash you soundly."

"Try it!"

"Don't bandy words with me. Open that gate!"

"I shall not."

"You won't?"

"No!" replied Harry Rawlings.

Jack Spencer was standing by, with his eyes twinkling; he enjoyed the scene, for the rude, imperious manner of the stranger did not entitle him to any consideration.

The huntsman sprang from his horse, and striding towards Harry, seized him by the collar.

"Now, my lad, I'm going to teach you a lesson," he said.

"You sha'n't touch him," cried Jack.

"Who is to prevent me?"

"I am going to have a try."

"You!" was the contemptuous reply.

Turning his whip, the man struck Jack a blow on the head with the handle.

It caused him to reel into the hedge half stunned.

Then, in spite of Harry's struggles, the huntsman administered blow upon blow to him.

The castigation would have continued longer had not Jack recovered himself, and, tearing up a hedge stake, attacked the man.

He was obliged to quit his hold, and retreat to his horse, which he mounted with the skill of an experienced rider.

Harry sank to the ground writhing with pain.

"Coward!" exclaimed Jack.

"Do you know who I am?" asked the stranger, savagely.

"No, but I will find out."

"I am Squire Rawlings, of Hurst Castle."

"Then the boy you have so cruelly ill-used is your nephew. Are you not ashamed, coward?"

The squire elevated his eyebrows.

"My nephew! I have no nephew—he is disowned. I do not recognise him," he said.

"What harm has he done you?"

"I would give five hundred pounds to hear of his death."

"That is a cowardly thing to say," cried Jack. "I am his friend, and shall not forget it. If it is in my power, I will make you repent it when I am older."

"It's little you can do to injure me. Who are you who speaks with such insolence?"

"Jack Spencer."

"Ah! Your father rents his farm from me. It is my land. His lease is nearly run out. He shall suffer through you."

The squire laughed harshly as he said this, touched his horse with the whip, took the gate flying, and galloped away.

Jack assisted Harry to rise.

"Are you much hurt?" he asked. "Cheer up, old fellow."

"I ache a bit," answered Harry.

"Did you hear what the squire was saying?"

"Every word. Fancy his declaring that he would give five hundred pounds to hear of my death! How he must hate me!"

"Fear is at the bottom of it. He is afraid of you."

"What for?"

"The will. There is forgery in the matter, or I am greatly mistaken. Hope on! It will all come out in your favour some day; then it will be your turn," replied Jack.

There was a rustling in the hedge.

"Did'nt you hear something?" asked Harry.

"Yes, and I'm going to find out what it is."

He ran to the hedge and looked into the ditch which ran alongside it.

"Harry! here—quick!" he shouted.

"I'm coming."

"Run hard!"

"What is it?"

"The spies of the school. They live in the town, and I'm blest if they aren't hiding in the ditch, and have been listening to everything we have had to say."

Harry had gained his side by this time, and looking into the ditch, which was a deep one, saw two small boys.

They looked up at him with grinning faces, which had a good deal of the expression of the monkey about them.

CHAPTER III.

THE TWO SPIES—DUCKED IN A HORSE-POND.

IT was a most extraordinary thing to Harry Rawlings to find Peeping Tom and Knowall Dick in such a place at such a time.

Not so to Jack Spencer.

He was used to it at school.

The two spies were always lurking where one would never dream of looking for them.

"Get out of that!" cried Jack.

"We're all right," replied Tom, opening his ugly mouth wider than ever.

"Very comfortable ditch this," answered Dick.

"Come out, I say."

"Not yet. We heard the hounds were going this way, so we came out to see them."

"Been here long?"

"'Bout an hour," said Knowall Dick. "My eye! didn't the squire give it to your friend Harry."

"And didn't he talk?" put in Peeping Tom.

Then they looked at one another, and burst out laughing with irrepressible glee.

"If anything was to happen to you—" began Dick.

"And it might, you know," said Tom.

"Oh, yes; and I was to tell him you were dead, he'd give me five hundred pounds—"

"Us," corrected Tom.

"Certainly. We always share, we do."

"Always."

"You'd better hold your tongue about what you've seen and heard!" exclaimed Jack. "If I catch you blabbing, it will be the worse for you."

"We never tell, do we, Dick?" said Tom, with a wink.

"Never," answered Knowall Dick, making a grimace, which put him on a level with a chimpanzee.

"If you don't come out of that ditch, I'll make you!" cried Jack.

"You want it yourself," Tom answered.

"You want a jolly good hiding, and you'll get it!"

"What have I done?"

"A lot. I owe it to you, my boys. You are not at school now. This isn't Stingwell Hall. You can't run to Doctor Birch-often and Miss Martha."

Peeping Tom put on an air of injured innocence, and looked at Knowall Dick.

"Did you ever hear such a thing?" he asked.

"No, I never," replied Dick. "What will folks say next of us?"

Jack reached over, and getting hold of Tom's ear, pulled him out of the ditch.

Animated by this example, Harry tackled Dick in a similar manner.

Soon the two spies were standing on the bank.

"Oh, my ear! Let go!" whimpered Tom. "It ain't injun rubber."

"Nor mine ain't putty," whined Dick.

Their captors released their hold.

Instantly the spies turned like two sprites in a pantomime, and dropped into the ditch again.

They crouched at the bottom.

"Well, I'm blessed!" cried Harry. "Look at them; they've put on that everlasting grin again."

"I'll make them grin on the other side of their faces before I've done with them!" replied Jack. "What do you mean by this, you wretched little sneaks?"

"Ain't it funny?" said Peeping Tom.

Jack began to grow angry.

"Stop your chaff!" he exclaimed. "You're volunteering for a good dressing, and you'll have it."

"Pelt them out," said Harry; "here is plenty of ammunition."

He pointed to a heap of mangolds and turnips, which the farmer had carted there for the sheep.

The best had been picked out by the sagacious animals.

What remained were in a more or less advanced state of decomposition.

Each seized a missile, and cast it with unerring aim at the spies.

Peeping Tom was about to remonstrate, when a very squashy turnip blocked up his capacious mouth.

A jellyfish kind of wurzel made an intimate acquaintance with Knowall Dick's nose, much to his disgust.

The spies quickly evacuated their position, and sprang on to the bank like the Bounding Brothers of the Balkans in a circus.

"Hi! stop it!" cried Tom; we're not vegetarians."

"I like my vegetables a little bit fresh," said Dick.

"You've got to take them as we like to give them to you," replied Jack.

"Drop it! We'll go home."

"Not yet, my little joker."

"Why not?"

"Because we haven't done with you. Harry, seize your prisoner!"

In a moment Harry Rawlings had Tom by the arm, and Dick was made captive by Jack.

"This is an outrage!" cried Tom.

"I thought we lived in a free country where law and order are respected?" remarked Dick.

"Why don't you tell Miss Martha?" sneered Jack.

"Wouldn't be so mean. We never tell, do we, Dick?"

"Oh, no, never!" Dick replied, solemnly.

"You haven't got the chance, or else you would. But you shall have something to talk about when you get back to school."

"You misjudge us; we never tattle, do we, Dick?"

"Never."

"Shut up!" said Jack. "Do you see that horse-pond over there?"

They both strained their eyes in the direction of the middle of the field.

"I certainly do see a pond," replied Peeping Tom; "but regarded as a pond simply, I don't notice anything remarkable about it."

"Nor I," said Knowall Dick. "It is rather a mean-looking kind of a pond."

"Just so," added his chum. "I have seen many better. Is there anything else in the landscape you can ask us to admire?"

"Only a weeping willow tree close by," answered Jack. "When I have ducked you in the pond, I shall hang you up to dry."

The spies drew rather a long face, but their captors gave them no further time for talk and remonstrance.

They were ruthlessly dragged across the field to the pond, which was not very deep.

Jack was well aware that they could both swim, so he was not afraid of drowning them.

Much out of breath, they were halted at the edge.

"Allow me to protest," said Peeping Tom.

"I join in the protestation," cried Knowall Dick. "Bathing at this time of the year is somewhat unseasonable; besides, I do not stand in need of a bath."

"My clothes," added Tom, "will prevent my skill in swimming being seen to proper advantage."

"The water has a decidedly stagnant appearance," continued Dick.

"It's good enough for you," responded Jack.

"My family doctor advised me to give up cold water bathing," said Tom.

"My physician did the same thing," remarked Dick. "He told me my system was not strong enough to stand the shock."

Harry burst out laughing.

"I feel sorry for you; but I am persuaded there is nothing like the cold water cure!" he exclaimed. "That is, for sneaks."

The spies shivered.

"In with them!" cried Jack.

There was a sudden propulsion.

It was as if a steam pile driver had struck each of them in the small of the back, and at the same time a catapult seemed to have come into contact with their necks.

Over the bank they went.

There was a splash, a rise of water, and the spies vanished.

"They are a couple of cool fish," said Harry, "and ought to be in their element."

"I'm enjoying it. You don't know them so well as I do," Jack replied. "If ever two fellows deserved ducking they do, and more than that."

The day was mild, the water was not very cold, and when the spies came up they were not much the worse for their immersion.

They puffed and spluttered as if they had swallowed more water than they were in the custom of taking.

But they soon swam to the shore.

They were allowed to land.

Directly they had got ashore, they ran, one up to Jack, the other to Harry, before the chums could divine their intention.

They threw their arms round their necks and embraced them in a cordial manner.

"Bless you!" said Peeping Tom; "you are my best friend."

Jack quickly threw him off sprawling on his back.

"Oh, thank you!" said Knowall Dick, rubbing himself against Harry. "I have enjoyed myself."

Harry cast him after his companion.

The spies rolled on the grass over and over, like dogs drying themselves, and laughed and chuckled as if it were a huge joke.

"Confound the fellows!" exclaimed Harry. "I'm all over duckweed, and the new cravat your sister made me a present of is ruined."

"I'm wet through," cried Jack.

"Kick the beggars!"

"No. Pull down some of those willow wands from the tree. We'll leather them."

"That will do fine."

Harry Rawlings went to the tree, while Jack Spencer shook himself, and began to pull down a bough.

Some few minutes elapsed before he could get it down.

When he had succeeded, Peeping Tom and Knowall Dick were halfway across the field, running as if for their lives.

"You see," exclaimed Jack, "that I have not in the least exaggerated about those young plagues."

"Not a bit," replied Harry. "What a comparative paradise the school would be without them."

"It is the exact reverse with them. Suppose we go down to the 'Cricketers' Inn,' and treat ourselves to ginger beer?"

"Capital. I feel so sore with the thrashing my uncle gave me, that I should like to sit down."

"Really! I should have thought that was an operation you could have readily dispensed with for a time."

Harry attempted to smile at this joke, but failed dismally.

"I'll say to rest, then," he replied.

They went in the direction taken by the spies, which led to the road, that being about a mile off.

The "Cricketers" was a solitary roadside inn.

Looking up at the parlour window when they arrived, Harry fancied that he saw the face of Peeping Tom.

It was but a momentary vision.

"I thought I saw one of the spies!" he exclaimed.

"Where?" asked Jack.

"At the parlour window."

"If so, we will soon have him out."

Going inside, they spoke to the landlord, drank their ginger beer at the bar, and then walked into the parlour.

There was nobody there.

"You were mistaken in your supposition," remarked Jack.

"So I perceive," replied Harry.

There was a good fire in the grate. Pulling two chairs up to it, they sat down, Harry Rawlings making a grimace as he did so.

It was a plainly furnished apartment.

The floor was sanded, a few sporting sketches hung on the walls, a stuffed pike was displayed in a glass case over the mantel, some fishing rods were in one corner, and a heap of old sacks in another.

By the door ticked solemnly an old Dutch clock.

"Half-past one," observed Jack. "I must be home by three."

"What's up?" asked Harry.

"Didn't I tell you?"

"Not a word."

"Well, I meant to. An important event is going to happen. The great Doctor Birchoften is going to honour us with his presence at dinner to-day."

"Never! What brings him your way?"

"Father has offered to supply Stingwell Hall School with milk and butter, and the doctor is coming to settle the terms of the contract. It will be a good thing for father if he can arrange it at his price. So immense preparations are being made in the eating line—a turkey, a haunch of mutton, fowls, ham, all kinds of pastry, and I don't know what else. Mother and Marian were hard at it all day yesterday."

Harry looked up with a twinkle in his eye.

"Jack," he said, "an imperative duty devolves on you."

"How so?"

"You ought to organize a reception for the doctor."

"In what way?"

"I will be cautious and speak in whispers, for walls, they say, have ears."

Bending his head and lowering his voice, he communicated something to his chum.

"Glorious!" cried Jack, laughing.

"You grasp the idea—do you like it?"

"Immensely."

"Will you do it?"

"Yes."

Of a sudden, Harry saw a movement among the old sacks in the corner.

"'MY DEAR SIR,' SAID THE FARMER, 'I CANNOT FIND WORDS TO EXPRESS MY REGRET.'"

Rising quickly, he took up the butt of a fishing-rod and approached the spot.

Jack regarded him with astonishment.

What could it mean?

Before he had time to ask any questions, Harry began to poke the sacks vigorously.

Loud cries proceeded from underneath.

Jack ran to the door and put his back against it, determined that there should be no escape.

Meanwhile Harry lifted up some of the sacks.

Like two Jack's-in-the-box, Peeping Tom and Knowall Dick popped up.

Not in the least disconcerted, they dis-distended their mouths with their accustomed impish grin.

"Here they are again!" cried Harry.

"What were you fellows doing?" asked Jack, sternly.

"Trying to get dry," replied Tom.

"Went to sleep," said Knowall Dick.

"That's not true," remarked Jack. "One of you saw us through the window, and you hid as usual. Now I'll serve you out for it, my boys."

Peeping Tom looked at him in a malicious manner.

"If you do anything to us," he exclaimed, "we'll tell the doctor."

"Tell him what?"

"That you are going to give him a reception."

"Oh, that's what you call sleeping, is it?" replied Jack.

"They are like weasels," said Harry; "they sleep with one eye open and both ears on the alert. What shall we do to them?"

"We will put them in sacks, and make them run a race up the road."

"Bravo! that will be royal sport."

The spies' faces began to grow elongated.

From each the grin died away, and they looked as if they were preparing to go to a funeral.

"We'll tell on you," said Knowall Dick.

"That we will, as soon as we get out of the sacks," cried Peeping Tom.

"You don't know much to sneak about," answered Jack, "and I don't imagine you will get out quite so soon as you think."

"Don't be afraid of them," said Harry. "I'm with you."

"Not I. Put Dick into a sack, and I'll do ditto with my facetious friend Tommy. We will keep behind them with sticks, just to stimulate their exertions when they flag," replied Jack.

The spies saw that it was useless to argue the point.

They, therefore, submitted with a bad grace.

Made to lie on the floor flat on their backs, they were put in the sacks feet foremost.

The sacks were then drawn up to their necks, where they were tied.

Very comical they looked when they were stood upright.

"A few words before the show begins," exclaimed Jack, "may not be out of place. The life of a spy is not all honey, nor do sneaks always lie upon a bed of roses."

"Our turn will come," said Peeping Tom, viciously.

"When?"

"Wait till we all get back to school."

"Yes; you'll know why it is called Stingwell Hall then," cried Knowall Dick to Harry.

Jack and his chum did not condescend to reply to this threat.

They took up the top joints of two fishing rods, and striking the spies smartly on the back, made them jump.

"The procession is about to start," said Jack.

"The games are going to begin," chimed in Harry. "All the fun of the fair for one penny. March!"

Thick though the sacking was, the spies could feel the blows they had received, and endeavoured to walk towards the door.

It was hard work.

They had to go very slowly, to avoid falling.

Their tormentors guided them into the road, steadying them until they were ready to start.

When the landlord saw what was going on, he laughed until his sides shook.

When the spies were in position, Jack gave the word to start.

There was a turn in the road about a hundred and fifty yards higher up, and when they reached that, the race was to be considered over.

If they did not do their best they were to look out for the stick, which would be applied without reserve.

Away they went.

The first to stumble and go down was Peeping Tom.

He fell right in the track of Knowall Dick, who fell over him.

They rolled about for some time, and, with some difficulty, got on their feet again.

It was a succession of tumbles, rolls, hops, and jumps, until the goal was nearly reached.

Then an unexpected incident arose.

A farmer was driving a flock of over a hundred sheep to market.

They crowded the road.

Behind them was the farmer, his shepherd,

and a dog, who barked loudly at the stragglers.

On pressed the sheep, keeping close together, huddling, crowding on.

The spies saw them coming, but were unable to move on one side.

In consequence of this they were pushed down, and the whole flock of sheep rushed over them. It was not very pleasant.

They felt as pulpy as if they had been through a paper mill.

Their eyes were full of dirt; their mouths stuffed with wool and mud, and it was with pain that they gasped for breath.

Jack and Harry laughed until they cried, and their cheeks positively ached.

The spies sat up in the sacks, but did not attempt to move. They intended to stay where they were until someone rescued them.

This was effected by the landlord later on.

Jack and Harry did not stay to have any hand in it. Work of a different kind claimed their attention.

They had served out Peeping Tom and Knowall Dick.

Never had the spies of the school been treated in this way before.

It was a lesson to them. Yet it did not mend them. It only served to make them more bitter against the authors of their humiliation.

In less than a week school would begin again.

Then they reckoned they would have their chance of revenge.

Jack was anxious to get back to the farm in time for the three o'clock dinner, as he had undertaken to give Doctor Birchoften, his father's guest, a reception.

What this was to be will be related in the next chapter.

CHAPTER IV.

DOCTOR BIRCHOFTEN MEETS WITH A RECEPTION HE DID NOT EXPECT—BUT FAILS TO BE FLATTERED BY IT.

THE principal of Stingwell Hall School was a tall, portly man of nearly sixty years of age.

His manner was bland; his demeanour gentlemanly; and had it not been for his fondness for inflicting punishment, corporeal and otherwise, he would have been liked.

Stingwell Hall was only three miles from Home Farm, and an hour before the time appointed for dinner, he mounted a safe old nag, and ambled along the road.

The spring air made Doctor Birchoften hungry.

The reins hung loosely on the horse's neck; his spectacles—for he was very near-sighted— were suspended by a piece of ribbon from the button-hole of his coat.

When he reached the gate of a path, which led through two fields to the farm, he encountered two boys.

They were Jack and Harry. Opening the gate for him they touched their caps.

"Good morning, sir," exclaimed Jack; "we have come to meet you."

The doctor shaded his eyes with his hand.

"Ah, good-day, John, I thank you," was the reply. "Who is your companion?"

"Harry Rawlings, your new pupil, sir."

"Good. I have heard of Henry. So you have come to meet me, and thus show respect to your master?"

"That is it, sir."

"Good boys. Lead the way. I appre-ciate this. Are we to be gay and festive to-day, John?"

"Very much so, sir."

"What are we to have for dinner?"

"Turkey, ham, fowls, haunch of mutton, sweets—a regular bang up set out, sir," replied Jack.

"Ah," said the doctor, smacking his lips, "all in my honour. I ought to be grateful. What wines, John, may I ask?"

"Sherry, champagne, claret, port. Father is sparing no expense. It's all done regardless of that."

"Very kind of him, I am sure. Anybody else invited John?"

"No, sir. You're the only one."

"Better still. Henry, how do you think you will like coming to school?"

"I can't tell until I get there, sir."

"A very sensible answer. I am sure you will like Stingwell Hall. My sister, Miss Martha, and I are so attentive to the boys under our charge, are we not, John?"

"Oh, very, sir—very," rejoined Jack, with a tinge of sarcasm in his tone.

The boys themselves were very attentive to the doctor on this occasion. The old horse was led over all ruts and holes.

Harry, when not observed, cut the ribbon of the spectacles, and put them into his pocket.

This was a great loss to the doctor, as he could not see six feet beyond his nose.

Conducting him into the yard, they halted the nag in front of the barn.

This was cut off from the house by a belt of trees and laurel bushes.

No one had seen the arrival.

Mrs. Spencer and Marian were busy in the kitchen; Mr. Spencer, with the help of Turmuts, the yard man, was decanting the wine.

"Where are we now?" inquired the doctor, blandly.

"We have the lavatory out here, sir," replied Jack. "Come in with me and wash your hands, while Harry puts the horse in the stable."

"Certainly. I thank you. Henry."

"Yes, sir."

"Be sure to give my poor beast a plentiful supply of oats," said Doctor Birchoften.

He was anxious to get his horse a good feed on cheap principles.

"I'll see to that."

"Always be kind to dumb animals. I thank you. Now, John, your hand, if you please."

While Harry took charge of the horse, Jack assisted his preceptor to alight.

The latter searched for his spectacles.

"Dear me!" he exclaimed, "where are my glasses? Can you see them, John?"

"No, sir."

"I could declare I had them when I left home. How tiresome. They must have dropped on the road."

"Perhaps you left them behind."

"It may be so. Humph! I can smell the dinner. Roast turkey—I think you said roast—is so appetising."

"I hope you will have a good tuck in, sir."

"If by that you mean a repletion, I shall, for I feel to want my dinner. The inner man cries cupboard, John."

"This way, sir. Lean on me."

"I must perforce, for, without my glasses, I am a poor creature. Lead on, John."

Opening the small barn door, Jack led the schoolmaster inside.

In the middle of the floor there was a deep pit, in which was shovelled the corn after being thrashed with the flail.

This was about half full of corn at that moment.

"Dear me, how dark it is," remarked Doctor Birchoften, "I can't see where I am going."

"This way to the lavatory, sir," said Jack.

"What a strange place to have it."

"No room in the house, sir; all the latest improvements here, by the most eminent sanitary engineers from London."

"I should not have thought it."

"Nobody believes it until they see it. Now, sir, step over this hole. Lift your foot and mind your eye."

"All right. I thank you. Ah!"

The doctor put his foot into vacancy.

Jack drew away his arm.

With an awful idea that he was rushing into eternity without any warning, the doctor dropped into the hole.

He had only about ten feet to fall before he touched the corn, into which he sank up to his waist.

Not in the least degree hurt was he.

Only a little shaken, and a good deal frightened.

He could not believe it was done on purpose.

Surely it was an accident, owing to the imperfect light.

Who would dare to play a practical joke on his sacred pedagogic person?

"John!" he exclaimed, "there is some opening here, into which I have inadvertently fallen."

He received no answer.

"I pray you, good John, to rescue me with a rope or ladder, for I am in no way injured or hurt."

Still no reply came.

"John, you must hasten, or the good dinner will be spoilt, and your worthy father will be apt to take offence."

Jack was stuffing his handkerchief into his mouth to smother his laughter.

Again the doctor raised his voice—

"I am in a pit! It behoves you to get me out quickly. A plague on the boy! Is it a planned thing? Am I to be left in the lurch? Impossible!"

Jack could not stand it any longer.

He was obliged to run out, locking the barn door after him, and putting the key into his pocket.

Joining Harry in the stable, he rolled on some clean straw, and nearly went into a fit.

"Is the fell deed done? But I need not ask," said Harry Rawlings.

"Oh, oh, oh!" laughed Jack.

"Where's the old man?"

"In the ho-ho-hole. I shall bur—burst! It's so awfully funny."

At length Jack's merriment subsided, and he got up.

"You should have seen him go!" he exclaimed. "Such a flop! And then when he asked me to get him out! Ha, ha, ha!"

"Doesn't he want his dinner?"

"The worst way. I shall take you in to fill his place. The governor won't wait more than a quarter of an hour for any-one."

"Off we go, then," said Harry. "Mind, not a hint about our conspiracy."

"Is it likely?"

"What shall we do when the cat's out of the bag, and it is sure to be when old Turmuts goes into the barn to look round?"

"He can't get in. I've got the key," replied Jack. "We will have our dinner, and if you don't mind, I'll spend the night at your diggings."

"With the greatest of pleasure."

"Father keeps a switch, and he likes to use it when he has sufficient provocation."

"That is settled, then. Come on. We will drink the old boy's health."

"Certainly. Schoolmaster can't hurt; he's got plenty of corn to satisfy his hunger. Ha, ha!"

"Oh, oh!" laughed Harry, as they quitted the stable together, and walked to the house.

Two lambs could not have looked more innocent.

Mr. Spencer was standing at the door, looking anxiously down the field.

"Where have you been, my lad?" he asked.

"Out to see the hounds with Harry," Jack replied.

"Good-day, Harry. You are in time to have a bit of dinner with us if you like."

"Thank you, sir."

"Did you see anything of Doctor Birch-often, Jack?" continued the farmer, "he's late. I sha'n't wait for him."

"He is rather uncertain in his movements," replied Jack. "Sometimes when he gets interested in a Greek or Latin book he forgets to come into school, and either Mr. Dobby or Mr. Caner, the ushers, has to go and remind him of his neglect of duty."

"Mother!" shouted the farmer, "serve up the dinner."

His will was law.

No member of his household ventured to dispute it.

Mrs. Spencer and her daughter felt annoyed at preparing a feast for a guest who did not come, but they made no complaint.

Turmuts brought in the good things, and waited at table.

It was like a family party on Christmas Day.

The two bottles of champagne and sherry were consumed, and when the sweets were served, Turmuts went away to attend to his duties in the yard.

"I could have enjoyed myself better," exclaimed the farmer, "if the doctor had been here. As for the contract, I suppose I must go and see him about it to-morrow."

"He might have had the civility to send us an excuse," said Mrs. Spencer.

"Perhaps he knows Jack's a bad boy, and is afraid to come," remarked Marian.

"Who asked you to speak?" cried Jack. "I'm no worse than other boys."

"What did you do this morning?"

"Silence!" said the farmer. "We are all disappointed; but I'll have no snarling to mar the harmony of the occasion."

Just then Turmuts came into the room scratching his head.

"There be summut in the barn, zur," he exclaimed.

"Of course, there is. I've got a good sixty quarters of wheat there," replied Mr. Spencer.

"It's alive, for it do be making a queer noise, to be sure."

"Why don't you go in and ascertain what it is?"

"I do be mortal afraid, zur. And more'n that, I can't find key."

Jack fumbled in his pocket.

"Dear me," he said, "I think I have it."

"Give it to the man, and go with him to see what's got into the barn," replied the farmer.

"Yes, father."

Very glad was Jack to have the chance of getting away.

Harry slipped out with him at the same time.

The discovery of the doctor was now a question of a few minutes only. And then—

They hardly liked to think of the probable consequences.

Jack handed the keys to Turmuts, who was trembling violently.

"I say," whispered Jack to his chum, "hadn't we best hook it out of this?"

"To make ourselves scarce at once is my advice," replied Harry. "I should have liked a slice of that pudding, and a few tarts, but no matter."

"The murder's out now."

"Yes; and we shall catch it hot! Come up to my crib, and lie low till the storm is over."

"Thanks. I accept," answered Jack.

With them discretion was the better part of valour.

Summoning all his courage to his aid, Turmuts lighted a lantern, and armed himself with a pitchfork.

Bravery was not one of his qualities.

He imagined that some tramp had got shut up in the barn.

Several outrages and robberies had lately been committed in the vicinity.

Turmuts dreaded lest he might be attacked.

Opening the door cautiously he stopped, holding up the lantern,

"Whoever you be," he cried, "I warn you to come out quietly, with all due respect for law, or I'll crack 'ee on th' 'ed wi' pitchfork.

"Ah!" replied a sepulchral voice, which seemed to emanate from the depths of the earth, "heaven be praised, you've come at last."

"Who be 'ee?"

"Doctor Birchoften, of Stingwell Hall, my friend."

"What, schoolmaster?"

"The same. I am in a sorry plight, being up to the middle in corn. Stuck fast in a dark pit. I have bawled myself hoarse."

Turmut's mouth distended into a broad grin.

Then he burst out into a loud guffaw.

The facts of the matter began to dawn on his bucolic mind.

"Ha, ha! Oh, oh, oh!" he roared.

"Restrain your merriment, my worthy fellow," said the doctor. "It is not seemly, nor befitting the occasion."

"Dang it, I can't help it."

"Get me a ladder. Extract me, and I will give you a crown."

"Gi'e me a crown! I'll soon have 'ee out, measter; but how in the world did 'ee get in?"

"The youths, Spencer and Rawlings, beguiled me with the ready falsehood that this was the lavatory."

"Worn't 'ee expected to dinner?"

"I was, indeed."

"Hey, but turkey's gone; fowl's all eat; wine drunk. Man alive, ye've missed your chance," cried Turmuts.

The doctor groaned deeply.

"Of a verity thou art a harbinger of bad news," he said.

"I never see two boys put away the food as they did, measter."

"Alas! I am in evil case, but their backs shall smart for it."

"My word, I be main sorry for 'ee. Hold on while I get the ladder."

Turmuts went out for this purpose.

In the yard he met Mr. Spencer, who had come from the house, being curious to know what was the matter.

The man told his master in a few words.

Very wrath was the farmer to hear that his son had played such a trick on so distinguished a guest.

In vain he called for Jack. That young gentleman was fairly on his way to Five Oak Farm with Harry Rawlings.

Hastening into the barn, the farmer aided Turmuts to extricate the schoolmaster from his deplorable position.

"My dear sir," he exclaimed, "I cannot find words to express my regret at this unfortunate occurrence."

"I have no blame for you," replied the doctor; "but I pray to have something wherewith to recruit my strength."

"Certainly."

"My throat is sore with calling for aid, and my heart faileth me for faintness."

"There is plenty left, though it is getting cold, I am afraid. The port and the claret are not touched."

"Lead on, friend Spencer. I am in your hands."

"Rest assured I will punish Master Jack."

"If you don't, I shall. Leave him to me," answered the doctor, in very decided tones.

He was conducted to the house, much to the surprise of Mrs. and Miss Spencer, who, when they heard the story, were loud in their censure upon Jack.

After all, the doctor managed to make a very good dinner. The home-brewed ale was in fine condition, and the port wine worthy a connoisseur.

The afternoon was pleasantly spent. Before dark, Doctor Birchoften mounted his nag, and, accompanied by Turmuts, he returned to Stingwell Hall.

CHAPTER V.

AT SCHOOL—THE DOCTOR DOES NOT FORGET—A FIGHT WITH A BULLY.

DING dong! Ding dong!

It was six o'clock, and the school bell was clanging out its noisy summons.

Harry Rawlings and Jack Spencer were asleep in No. 2 dormitory, which contained four other boys.

They had arrived at the school on the previous evening. The sound was something entirely new to Harry.

He thought it was an alarm of fire.

Springing out of bed, he stood shivering in the chilly morning air.

The other boys were old stagers.

Although they heard the bell, they did

not so much as open their eyes, or make the slightest movement.

The bell always rang at six, but the boys were not required to be in school till seven.

They were allowed an hour to dress, wash, and look at their lessons.

The old stagers, who took things easily, ran over their lessons the night before.

They could dress in ten minutes, so the bell did not disturb them much.

Harry experienced that sense of desolation that every boy falls a prey to on leaving home.

He awoke in a strange place among strangers for the first time.

Sitting down on the side of his bed, he rubbed his eyes.

In the bed, on his right, was Jack, comfortably curled up like a dormouse in winter quarters.

On his left was a burly boy, a year older than he, with a ruddy face.

This was Warner, the bully; but Harry did not know that, as he was not acquainted with anyone as yet.

Ding dong! Ding dong! continued the bell.

"I say, Jack," cried Harry, "who's kicking up that shine, and what is it all about?"

Jack had gone off to sleep again, and made no answer.

He repeated his question just as the bell stopped, and aroused the wrath of Warner.

"Hold your row!" cried the bully.

"I wasn't speaking to you," replied Harry. "Jack, old man, will—"

"Shut up, you new fellow!" interrupted Warner.

"I certainly shall not, unless you tell me what that bell is ringing for."

"It isn't ringing—it's stopped."

"What *was* it ringing for, then?"

"Find out. Fish for information if you want it. Let a man sleep, can't you? I suppose you think you've got a monopoly of this room? If I hear any more from you, I'll get out and give you a jolly good hiding."

Harry thought he was being rather roughly treated, but he did not want to have a fight if he could help it in the bedroom on his first morning at school.

So he got into his warm bed again, watching the course of events.

Exactly at ten minutes to seven, an alarm clock, which stood on Warner's washstand, rattled off with a loud noise.

In a moment the boys jumped up, and began to get their clothes on with all conceivable expedition.

Harry followed their example.

"I wonder if the doctor will remember the reception we gave him?" remarked Jack to him, as they were going downstairs.

"Possibly not; it was done out of school," replied Harry.

"He seems very friendly with father, who has got the contract for the butter and stuff, which a good many were after."

"Let us hope for the best."

"We will," said Jack.

They now entered the schoolroom.

The school was divided into three classes —the first, second, and third—the first being the highest.

Harry had been informed that he would take his place in the second with Jack, and they sat on the same form.

Doctor Birchoften taught the first; Mr. Dobby the second; and Mr. Caner attended to the studies of the third.

Whatever Doctor Birchoften's deficiencies might be, a bad memory was not one of them.

Before dismissing the boys to breakfast, he rapped on his desk with a ruler.

"Spencer and Rawlings will remain!" he exclaimed.

The others trooped out of the room.

Jack and Harry sat as if rooted to the form.

The doctor and the ushers then went away, it being the custom at Stingwell Hall to leave culprits alone for a quarter of an hour before punishment.

This gave them time for consideration, and the suspense they were kept in was anything but agreeable.

"We are in for it," remarked Harry, with a lugubrious air.

"Safe as houses," replied Jack.

"Will no apology satisfy the doctor?"

"Not it."

They looked sadly at one another.

Presently Clayton, the captain of the school, entered, and unlocking a cupboard, produced a couple of birches.

These he placed on the doctor's desk.

"What have you fellows been doing?" he asked, in a kindly tone.

"Only having a bit of a lark with the old man," replied Jack.

"You are a new fellow," said Clayton, looking at Harry.

"Yes; this is my first half."

"Have you been birched before?" continued the captain, addressing Jack.

"No," was the reply.

"Well, look here, according to the rule of the school, and custom from time immemorial, you can plead 'first fault.'"

"What does that mean?" they asked, in a breath.

"Simply that he can't flog you. The

doctor is bound to let you off," answered Clayton.

Their countenances brightened directly.

"Thank you for the information," cried Harry.

"I sha'n't forget your kindness," said Jack. "Will it work?"

"Of course it will. It always has. I have been here six years, and they can't make an exception against you if you claim the privilege."

In a few minutes Doctor Birchoften made his appearance, wearing his academical cap and gown.

His lips were puckered up, and his wizened countenance wore a hard severe look.

"Spencer and Rawlings!" he exclaimed, "you made yourselves facetious at my expense a short time ago. The sword of Damocles, in olden times, was suspended over offenders. Here, it is a simple collection of twigs tied together, which is called a birch. This instrument of correction has been in use at our public and other schools for centuries. It will be used on you to-day, and I think you will admit justly, for you have grossly insulted the person of your head-master."

"I will admit we were wrong, sir," replied Jack.

"It is too late for excuses."

"But, sir, I want to say one word."

"Make haste! Breakfast awaits me."

"We both claim 'first fault,' according to the custom of the school."

The doctor's face was a study.

He had entirely omitted this from his calculations, and he reddened with rage.

Throwing down the birch, he exclaimed—

"You are correct. I had forgotten that. The traditions of the school must be respected; but—"

He paused, and raised his hand warningly.

"Beware of the second offence," he added.

Then, with the air of a tiger baulked of its prey, he swept from the room, and loudly banged the door behind him.

Clayton, who was a good-natured fellow, could not help laughing.

"I got you out of that," he remarked.

"What return can we make you?" asked Jack.

"Practise all the cricket you can. We have several fixtures for matches. I want to get up the best eleven I can this year, and if you show good form, I'll put you in."

"But I am a new fellow," said Harry.

"That does not matter. I show no favouritism when I make an eleven," answered Clayton.

The bell, which had so startled Harry earlier in the morning, now rang for breakfast.

At ten o'clock lessons began, continuing until twelve, when the boys were at liberty to do what they liked in the playground till two, which hour brought dinner with it. At three school began again, and continued up to five.

The playground consisted of a yard and a five-acre field, at the bottom of which ran a narrow river.

Jack took Harry at once into the field to show him about.

They passed the two spies in the yard, who grinned at them, but said nothing.

As they got into the field they heard someone cry out with pain.

Looking round, they saw a thin, delicate boy rubbing his leg; a dozen yards off was Warner, the bully.

"Throw up that ball!" cried Warner.

"Please, don't!" said the little fellow.

"Don't do what?"

"Hit me again. You're always hitting me with that ball."

"Throw it up, I tell you!"

Jack touched Harry on the arm.

"That's Kennedy," he said. "Warner's always bullying him."

Kennedy picked up the ball, threw it to Warner, who deftly caught it.

Kennedy was walking off.

"Hold hard!" cried Warner, "I want you."

"Oh, please, don't! I'm sore now," replied Kennedy.

"Nonsense! Touch your toes."

Kennedy bent his body, and put his hands on his boots.

Thus he presented an excellent target.

Warner threw the ball at him, and struck him sharply on the back.

"Good shot!" he said, clapping his hands.

Kennedy jumped half a foot in the air, and began to cry.

"Once more, throw it up!" cried the bully.

Harry Rawlings did not exactly want to make himself the champion of the oppressed on first coming into the school, but he did not like this.

"Go away!" he said, on the impulse of the moment. "I'll see that he doesn't hit you again."

Kennedy looked up in astonishment.

Nobody had ever taken his part before.

"Don't interfere," whispered Jack.

"Why shouldn't I?" asked Harry.

"He'll give you a thrashing."

"Will he?"

"Yes. We call him the cock of the school."

"'BOY,' CRIED MR. DOBBY, 'HOW DARE YOU?'"

"I don't care," replied Harry. "This kind of thing is new to me, and I don't like it."

Warner had, by this time, stepped up close to him with his hands clenched.

"What did you say?" he demanded fiercely.

"Simply, that you shouldn't bully that little fellow if I could help it," replied Harry.

"Take that for your pains."

As he spoke, Warner struck him between the eyes, and knocked him down.

"Fair play," said Jack. "Let him get up. Never strike a chap when he's down."

"Who's going to?" asked Warner.

"You looked as if you would."

"Not I. If he wants a mill, he can have it fair and square."

For half-a-minute Harry did not move.

Then he got up, looking rather dazed, for the blow had taken him unawares.

But the pluck was not knocked out of him.

He had plenty of fight in him, as Warner was destined to find out before long.

"You evidently want to have a row with me," said Harry, "because I am a new fellow, and you think I can't fight."

"I mean to have one anyhow," replied Warner.

"Why?"

"Because you don't know enough to mind your own business."

"It is anybody's business to interfere when he sees a big fellow bullying a weak, inoffensive boy."

"Shut up, or put up!" cried Warner.

"What do you mean?"

"If you don't shut up your mouth, put up your fists."

"Oh, I'm ready for you."

"If you are not, I'll soon knock you down again. I'm a regular auctioneer at knocking down."

"Perhaps you will get knocked down yourself."

"You can't do it," sneered Warner.

"I'll have a try at it," replied Harry.

He took off his coat and vest, and turned his shirt-sleeves up to his elbows, an example which was quickly followed by his opponent.

There was a tree close by, growing near the wall, and they went under this.

They were not likely to attract attention here.

"Are you ready?" asked Warner of Harry.

The reply was in the affirmative.

Harry deftly struck out.

The blow hit Warner on the side.

It made him gasp for breath.

Jack clapped his hands.

"Wasn't that a rib-roaster!" he cried.

"Who asked you to speak?" demanded Warner, savagely.

"Hit him hard, Harry. Get first blood if you can," cried Jack, jubilant.

Warner had dropped his hands for a moment, but he soon put himself on the defensive again.

The battle now waged fast and furious.

Warner was stronger, bigger, and more scientific than his adversary.

After several hits on both sides, Harry received a blow which sent him rolling to the grass.

"First blood to me," exclaimed Warner. "I've tapped his claret. How's that, umpire?"

Jack assisted Harry to rise, and gave him a handkerchief to stanch the blood, which flowed freely.

There was plenty of fight left in Harry, and after a brief breathing spell, he faced his antagonist a second time.

This time Warner forced the fighting.

He rained blows on Harry, who, in vain, endeavoured to ward them off.

His guard was broken down, and he was hit all over the head and body.

A second time he fell on his back.

Nor was he more successful in the third round.

One of Warner's eyes was closing up, and a blow under the ear made him feel dizzy, but he had the best of the encounter.

At last he managed to strike two blows in quick succession, and down went Harry again.

"Hurrah!" said Warner; "that's what I call the postman's knock—one, two. I'll bet you he won't come to time."

Nor did he.

"Get up," urged Jack; "you are not beaten, surely?"

"I've had enough of it," rejoined Harry. "It's no use. He's too much for me."

"Have another go at him. Where's your pluck?"

"It is not a question of that. I am beaten as much as Napoleon was at Waterloo," Harry replied. "Someone's got to be thrashed in a fight. Both can't win."

"That's true," said Jack. "Stay where you are. You'll be all right presently, when you get your wind."

Warner had picked up his vest, and was about to put it on.

"Stop a moment, if you please," cried Jack.

"What for?" asked Warner.

"I mean to have a shy at you myself."

Warner looked astonished.

"Oh, yes, I am. I'll soon be ready," cried Jack, taking off his things. "You've got your steam arm wound up, you know, bully Warner, and it would be a pity to let it run down."

"I have no row on with you."

"Rawlings and I are chums. If anybody offends one, he provokes the other. Anybody in this school has got to count on both of us. Harry's down, but I am up, and I'll take the conceit out of you."

"But I don't want to fight you."

"Whether or not, you must, or I'll kick you round the field. You think you are the cock of the walk, and that you can knock anyone about, if it pleases you."

"Certainly not; only I can't stand cheek from a new fellow."

"Nor I from an old fellow. Besides, Rawlings did not cheek you. He merely took the part of that little chap you were bullying."

"I see; I have Kennedy to thank for this," said Warner, bitterly. "Won't I take it out of him!"

"No you won't, bully Warner!"

"Who's to stop me?"

"I will."

"Oh, come on. If I've got to fight you, let's have it out. Don't stand there jawing all day. You're worse than a sheep's head."

"I'm your humble servant," replied Jack.

"I'll polish you off as I did your friend, in a brace of shakes."

"If you can spell 'able,' my intelligent friend."

"I am able to fight you and thrash you," retorted Warner; "and I'll do it."

He was getting into an ungovernable rage.

Flying upon Jack he hit out right and left, but his opponent, acting on the defensive, parried his blows.

His policy was to let him exhaust himself.

The fight was a long and severe one.

Jack did not escape punishment; but, in the end, he defeated Warner, who was finally knocked down by the side of Harry.

He showed no inclination to get up.

"Have you had enough?" inquired Jack.

"If I hadn't, I should be a glutton," was the faint reply.

"Is that a fair and square confession of defeat?"

"It is this time."

"Get up, then, and we will shake hands all round just to show there is no animosity."

"Not I," hissed Warner. "I'm not that kind of chap. I shall hate you to the day of my death."

"Will you?" returned Jack, carelessly. "Oh, well, I daresay I shall be able to survive the infliction. Anyhow I'll try hard."

Harry and Warner rose to their feet at the same time. The bully's bruised face was disfigured by a malignant scowl, which made him look positively ugly.

"You had best keep your mouth shut about this affair," said Warner, "because the masters don't like fighting. If it is found out, you are sure to get a hundred lines, if not something worse. I shall say I was practising at the high jump, and came a cropper over a hurdle. You can cook up your own story if questioned.

"You forced the quarrel on us, so you are to blame," replied Harry.

Warner did not deign to make an answer. He put his hands in his pockets, and went off whistling, but he soon left off, as his mouth was very sore and swollen.

"What fun we are having," remarked Jack.

"It seems we are not making friends at this school," answered Harry. "What shall we do now?"

The boys were playing cricket at the other extremity of the field, and did not appear to have noticed that a fight had been going on.

"We must say we were bird-nesting, and fell out of a tree, owing to the breaking of a branch," remarked Jack.

"That will do as well as anything else," said Harry. "I'm very much obliged to you for taking my part. It is lucky the spies of the school were not about."

"Very. I don't want to get into trouble."

"Nor I. Let us make up our minds to be extremely good."

"If we can," replied Jack, laughing.

He noticed that the tree by which they were standing was a chestnut, and its pretty white flowers were already in bloom.

Inspired by that instinct, which all boys possess in a larger or smaller degree, that induces one to knock something down, he took up a stone.

Throwing it at a flower he missed his aim, but was surprised to hear a sharp cry.

It came from inside the dense green foliage.

"Did you hear that?" he queried.

"Yes, by Jove," replied Harry, "there is somebody up the tree."

"That's a sure thing," cried Jack. "I say, up there, if you don't come down in a jiffy, I'll throw some more stones, and make you."

This threat had the desired effect.

There was a rustling among the leaves, and a shaking of the branches. Then two boys, one after the other, came sliding down the trunk.

They were the two spies, who looked rather sheepish at being found out.

"Well, I'm sure!" exclaimed Jack, "what were you doing up that tree?"

"We've got a kind of arbour there. I nailed a board across some boughs for a seat," replied Peeping Tom.

"So that you can see what is going on in the playground, without being seen yourselves?"

"Oh, no," said Knowall Dick; "we would'nt be so mean as that."

"You would'nt? Of course not," cried Jack, sarcastically. "I never saw such fellows in my life. I'm blest if anyone can tell where you will be next."

"If we were to go to the moon in a balloon," remarked Harry, "they would be there to meet us on our arrival."

The spies grinned in acknowledgment of this compliment, for as such they undoubtedly regarded it.

"Did you see the fight?" inquired Jack.

"What fight?" replied Peeping Tom, innocently.

"When Rawlings and I had a mill with Warner."

"Really! What was it about?" asked Knowall Dick.

"He was bullying little Kennedy. But, come now, you must have heard the row, if you did'nt see the fight."

They shook their heads.

It was evident the spirit of mendacity was very strong within them.

"I was asleep," said Peeping Tom. "The fact was, I had a bad night, and I am—oh, so tired now."

"And I was getting up my lessons," replied Knowall Dick, taking a book from his pocket.

The one yawned as if he wanted to catch all the flies.

The other earnestly scrutinised the sky, as if he were on the point of discovering a new planet.

"You'd better not sneak about it," continued Jack.

"Not for worlds," answered Tom.

"Too much the gentleman," remarked Dick.

"If we get into trouble we shall know whom to blame."

"Don't worry your dear self. You won't come to grief as far as we are concerned," replied Peeping Tom.

"Ta, ta, see you later," added Knowall Dick.

Linking their arms together, they walked away down the field.

A crowd in one corner, and loud shouts of laughter, had attracted their attention.

Something unusual had occurred.

Their curiosity was aroused, and they were eager to see what it was.

"We're in it—fairly in it," remarked Jack, gloomily. "Those fellows are sure to split."

"I should like to pulverise them," muttered Harry.

CHAPTER VI.

HOW THE SPIES MANAGED THEIR BUSINESS—AN EFFIGY—MR. DOBBY'S RAGE.

THE bottom of the playing field was shut off from the river by a high wooden fence. The river was not of great width, but flowed between high banks, and in some parts was deep.

Near the palings a score of boys had assembled to look at something that Pranks was doing.

We have alluded to Pranks as an extremely mischievous boy.

This statement does not in the least degree exaggerate his character.

If there was any larking going on, Pranks was sure to have a hand in it if he was not the originator.

On this occasion he had cleverly dressed up a dummy figure, which he had placed against the fence in a position indicative of intoxication.

It was stuffed with hay. The mask was well put on, and the tall hat was cocked on one side. The head inclined a little to the left shoulder, the necktie awry, but the frock-coat was scrupulously buttoned over the high clerical vest, and the check trousers came over the well-cleaned boots.

There would not have been anything extraordinary in this, had not the effigy been the exact counterpart in size and appearance of Mr. Dobby.

The mask had been carefully selected as bearing a close resemblance to his long, hard features.

But the cruellest part of the joke was the attitude of inebriety.

It was well known that the second master was fond of his glass, and he had frequently been seen asleep in the parlour of the "Cricketers."

On these occasions he would be snoring

loudly, and have a jorum of punch before him.

When he returned home his gait was always unsteady.

Just as the spies of the school arrived, Pranks was making a speech.

"Boys!" he exclaimed, "allow me to present to your notice an old friend."

"Dobby, Dobby!" shouted the boys.

"Yes; it is Mr. Dobby. He is represented as you sometimes have seen him in life, after having had a drop."

The boys roared with laughter.

"You will naturally wonder how I came to get the clothes?" continued Pranks.

"Yes, yes. How?"

"You recognise them as his very ownest own?"

"We do," was the cry.

"Well, I'll tell you in confidence. Dobby's got a new suit. These he made a present to Miss Martha, our mean old housekeeper, whose wig I should like to burn."

"Hear, hear," said one boy.

"Groans for old mother Martha!" cried another.

The doctor's sister, Miss Martha, was no favourite with the inmates of Stingwell Hall.

She did not administer the domestic affairs of this classical and commercial academy to their liking.

"Hearing that she had got them, I—I borrowed them," Pranks went on. "If I have been fortunate enough to give you some amusement I am satisfied. What do you think of it?"

"Capital. Stunning. First-rate," was the reply.

"I think it comes pretty near Dobby."

"It's he to a T."

The spies were horrified to witness such a scene.

They did not stay to hear or see anything more. It was quite enough to know that the sacred person of the second master had been burlesqued in this dreadful way.

Off they started to acquaint Mr. Dobby with the tremendous fact.

"Ain't it horrid?" said Peeping Tom.

"Awful!" replied Knowall Dick. "I wouldn't have believed it. What will Pranks be up to next?"

"He would'nt mind making a guy of the doctor."

"Not he; but he'll smart for this," answered Dick. "Let me see, as the blind man said, we've got to report this to Mr. Dobby—and the fight."

"Oh, yes; we mus'n't forget that It's Warner, Spencer and Rawlings. I hate them all three. Don't you?"

"Can't bear the sight of them."

"Won't we make it hot for a few, eh!"

"Rather."

They rubbed their hands with glee, and looked as pleased as if they had found a five-pound note.

"I particularly detest that new fellow, Rawlings," continued Peeping Tom; "he has such a disdainful way of looking at you."

"Just as if we were not good enough for him. I have noticed that," said Knowall Dick.

"Exactly. He must be closely watched, and brought down a peg. Don't fellows look small when they have been to see the doctor privately?"

"None of them like being birched," replied Dick. "But, I say, do you recollect what we heard the squire say about Rawlings?"

"Do you mean that he would give five hundred pounds to hear that he was dead?"

"Yes; that is it."

"Such a thing might occur. Accidents will happen in the best regulated families," said Peeping Tom.

"Fifty pounds is a lot of money," Dick remarked, thoughtfully.

"I should like to have it, I know. I'd buy a new bat and a set of stumps, and some pads, and I'd swim in ginger-pop and tarts."

"I would buy a boat, to go on the river, and have a sailor's suit, and some new Sunday-going clothes."

"If I saw a chance—" began Peeping Tom.

"Of what?" asked Knowall Dick.

A sinister look crossed Tom's features, but whatever he had in his mind he did not say it.

His quick eye caught sight of the second master, who was walking towards them.

"Hush!" he whispered; "here is Mr. Dobby."

"Well, my little man," said the usher, smiling, "does the little busy bee improve each shining hour, as the poet says?"

"He always does, sir—at least, we do," replied Tom.

"That is right. I call you my busy bees, you know. Have you any report to make to me?"

"Yes, sir; there has been a fight. I may call it a pitched battle."

"Between whom?"

"Warner, Spencer and Rawlings. Warner had to fight the two latter, one after the other, and got the worst of it."

"That is grave. I cannot overlook fighting. It is not allowed. If boys cannot settle their differences, they should come to me. In this case who were the aggressors?" replied Mr. Dobby.

"Spencer and Rawlings, sir, unquestionably," said Peeping Tom.

"You saw it all?"

"Oh, yes," answered Knowall Dick. "Spencer especially would not leave Warner alone, that I can swear to."

"They shall be punished," exclaimed Mr. Dobby. "Now what else have you to tell me? I can see there is something more coming."

"Yes, sir; and it is very important. I know you will be in a great rage."

"Never mind that. Speak out, and fear not."

"Did you not give Miss Martha a bundle of old clothes to sell?" continued Knowall Dick.

"Certainly; this very morning. I bought some new ones during the holidays. What of them?" asked Mr. Dobby.

His lean, cadaverous face grew longer and hollower.

"They have been taken away and made into an effigy—a regular first-class guy, as like you as two pins."

"Ha! a guy," ejaculated the master.

"It is down at the bottom of the field, sir," said Dick.

"Who has dared to do this infamous thing?"

"Pranks. I think Wildash helped him, but of that we are not sure," Tom replied.

"Like me, is it?"

"The very image; and—I'm ashamed to say it, sir—the head is on one side, as if it were drunk."

Mr. Dobby drew a long breath.

His little eyes rolled with indignation, and he trembled with rage.

"It is a rascally trick," he exclaimed. "I shall hit that Pranks, I know I shall. It will be impossible for me to keep my hands off him."

"He deserves it, for the guy looks awfully drunk, sir," replied Peeping Tom.

"Take a cane or stick, sir," said Knowall Dick.

"I can't wait for that. I see a howling mob of boys round the disgraceful figure. I hear their derisive shouts and jeers. It is more than I can bear. Flesh and blood won't stand it. I'm off."

Mr. Dobby did not walk.

He was so excited by the insult which had been offered him that he ran.

He could not get there fast enough.

Well he knew that his presence would strike terror into the hearts of the evildoers.

Pranks had no idea that anyone had gone to inform about him.

All the boys had their backs turned to the school, and were intensely enjoying the comicality of the vivacious Pranks.

He was exerting himself to be as funny as he could.

Rolling up a cigarette, he put it in the mouth of the effigy.

"You will please take notice," he said, "that the great classical scholar is about to smoke a halfpenny geranium. It is rather bad form in his condition; but, as the song says, he really cannot help it."

"Burn him!" cried Wildash.

"That might attract attention," replied Pranks.

"Sell him for a scarecrow, then."

"I'd rather send him up to the waxworks in London. He'd do for the last awful murderer, or the newest burglar swell."

"Well," replied Wildash, "if you think he would be an addition to the Chamber of Horrors, let him go."

"There is a great moral lesson to be learnt from this figure of old Dobby, boys," exclaimed Pranks. "I like to point a moral. If—"

At this crisis his eloquence was suddenly and most unexpectedly interrupted.

The usher had halted on the edge of the admiring crowd.

He had heard some of the disparaging remarks made about himself.

Seizing Pranks by the collar, he held him tight.

"Boy!" he cried; "how dare you?"

Pranks turned as white as a sheet.

"It is only a lark, sir," he stammered.

"A lark!" replied Mr. Dobby, with his thin lips quivering. "I'm in the habit of smoking halfpenny geraniums, am I?"

"No, sir."

"I'm to be held up to derision, and sold as a scarecrow! That's your idea of a lark, is it?"

"It wasn't meant for you, sir," said Pranks.

Mr. Dobby gave him a shaking.

It was like a terrier giving a rat a reminder that he had teeth.

"Don't tell me any falsehoods, it only aggravates the offence!" he exclaimed. "So there is a great moral lesson to be learnt from me? Oh, you young scamp."

"I hope so, sir," answered Pranks, with a subdued grin.

"How? Why?"

"That's what you are here for, isn't it? What else does the doctor pay you your salary for?"

"No quibbling. I won't have it!" screamed Mr. Dobby. "Oh, you viper! I have been kind to you. So you would send me to a waxworks exhibition? That is my reward. You would class me with the vilest of mankind? Take that, and that."

Two blows in quick succession fell upon Pranks' face.

He began to see stars, but making a desperate effort, he broke from the usher's grasp, and ran. The others made a bolt at the same time, and did not stop till they had gained a safe distance.

Then they stopped and watched Mr. Dobby's proceedings.

These were of the most eccentric kind.

He strode up to the counterfeit presentment of himself, and glared at it in a fiendish manner.

Then he hit it savagely with his fist until he knocked it down, whereupon he kicked, jumped on, and otherwise maltreated it.

When he had exhausted his passion on the inanimate thing, he took up the fragments, and threw them over the fence.

Seeing that he was preparing to return to the school, the boys scattered in all directions.

No one intruded upon him, and with a majestic air for a little man, he walked across the field.

His purpose was to seek Doctor Birchoften, and complain of the treatment he had been subjected to in effigy.

Had he been a sensible man, less sensitive and narrow-minded, he would have overlooked the matter altogether.

But to him it was a monstrous offence.

He thought it subversive of all discipline in the school, because his self-esteem was wounded.

Doctor Birchoften did not spend much time in the open air. When not in school, he was engaged in writing a book.

This was, in his fond hopes, to place him on the pinnacle of fame.

It was called "A History of Romulus and Remus; or, the Foundation of the Roman Empire, with some account of the Sabines."

For seven years he had been hard at work on this great book, which was to be published in five octavo volumes, four of which were completed.

He was seated in his study when the usher entered. Books of reference were piled on the table before him, and he looked up with a troubled air.

"Ah, Dobby," he said, "I am glad you have come, for I am perplexed. Do you think the Roman boys flew kites? I like to be precise on these points."

"I cannot say, sir; but I feel sure that they did not make effigies of their masters," was the reply.

The doctor laid down his pen.

"What do you intend to convey?" he asked.

"I have been insulted, mocked, and made a laughing-stock of."

"Explain, for I am in the dark."

Mr. Dobby did explain, much to the doctor's annoyance; for he felt that such a deed as the usher described, was a grave blow at all authority. The usher also mentioned the fight.

"Very good," exclaimed Doctor Birchoften. "We may say, with the fowler, that we have set our net and caught our birds. Pranks shall be taught to play no more pranks. I itch to whip Spencer and Rawlings. Summon them all into the schoolroom at once, and I will attend to their cases. You shall be amply vindicated."

"Thank you, sir; that is all I ask."

Saying this, Mr. Dobby departed with a light heart, and, going into the yard, sent messengers to summon the three delinquents.

They were soon found, and with downcast heads, wended their way to the schoolroom.

The doctor, in cap and gown, was awaiting their arrival.

He made a few observations on the enormity of Pranks' offence, and upon the sin of fighting.

Mr. Dobby and Clayton held the unfortunates while they received their castigation, which was administered without stint.

When it was over, Jack and Harry were burning with pain, shame, and mortification.

Full of angry thoughts they passed into the yard, not knowing where else to go.

They thought it unfair that Warner should have been let off.

Pranks passed them laughing.

"You will soon get used to it if you stop at this school," he remarked.

"It is not fair," replied Jack.

"We only took Kennedy's part," said Harry.

"That is nothing. The doctor only heard half the story, I suppose? If you are bullied in future, put up with it. I deserved what I got, but I had my joke at Dobby's expense; though how he found it out, I can't tell."

As he went into the field the boys gave him a hearty cheer, and crowded round him.

He was the popular hero of the hour.

To add to their irritation, the friends, as they walked sulkily to and fro, were met by Warner, who had heard all about their misfortune.

News travels quickly in a small private school.

"'YOU'VE BEEN AND GONE AND DONE IT THIS TIME!' CRIED CORKS."

He burst out laughing, evidently in an intentionally provoking manner.

"So you got in for it sooner than you expected?" he exclaimed.

"Did you split about it?" asked Jack, with flashing eyes. "If you did, I'll fight you again now, and chance the consequences."

"No," replied Warner; "I don't do that sort of thing, nor do I like those who do. I have a sense of honour, and that is more than sneaks have."

"Although we are not friends, I'm glad to hear you say that."

"It is the truth, and I am not afraid of you!" exclaimed Warner, as he went on.

This declaration convinced Jack and Harry that they had to thank the spies for what had taken place.

It made their resentment against them all the more bitter.

They determined to get even with them at the very earliest opportunity.

Before the school-bell rang, Kennedy came up to them. There were tears in his eyes. He seemed much grieved.

"Excuse me," he exclaimed, "but I am so sorry to hear that you got into trouble on my account."

"Don't mention it," Jack replied.

"Another time, do not interfere. If Warner hurts me it can't be helped," Kennedy added.

The little fellow sighed.

"Indeed, it can," cried Jack. "If you are put upon again, come and tell me; or, if you can't find me, tell Rawlings."

"I would much rather not."

"You must! I insist!"

"If you are in earnest, I can't refuse," replied Kennedy. "Yes; I will tell you. It is very kind of you, for I am not strong."

"Have you no father and mother?"

"Oh, yes."

"Why do they not remove you?" asked Jack.

"Doctor Birchoften is an old friend of my father, who is not well off; and the doctor takes me at half price," answered Kennedy.

This explained why any complaints he made would not be attended to.

The bell now rang, and they were all obliged to hurry into the schoolroom.

CHAPTER VII.

MISS MARTHA'S KIND ATTENTION—REVENGE IS SWEET—THE SPIES FIND THEMSELVES IN AN AWKWARD POSITION.

JUST before dinner, for which meal Jack and Harry had an excellent appetite, they were accosted by the page, whose name was Tuffins.

He was a very fat boy; and although he waited at table, cleaned knives, forks, and boots, doing the rough part of the school work generally, it did not seem to reduce his size at all.

"If you please," he said, "Miss Martha wants you in the housekeeper's room."

"What for?" inquired Jack.

"I don't know. This way. Follow me."

He led them through a passage to the room, which was on the ground floor, the window overlooking the playground.

Miss Martha was standing at the table, mixing some compound in a couple of basins.

Her age was probably fifty; her face suggestive of vinegar. She wore a wig of corkscrew ringlets, was as lean as a lath, and had a squeaky voice.

Seated at the table, with a basin before him, was Pranks.

He was consuming some sticky substance with a spoon, and making horrible faces.

"When boys have been punished," she said, "it is not customary to allow them any dinner. They have bread and water."

This announcement came like a sudden chill upon the boys, for a delicious smell of roast mutton was wafted from the kitchen.

"But," she added, "as this is the spring season of the year, I will treat you to brimstone and treacle. It is very wholesome, and good for the blood. Pranks is already enjoying his. Are you not, my boy?"

"Yes, ma'am," replied Pranks.

"Sit down. I will give you yours in a moment," said Miss Martha, with a patronising smile.

Tuffins was at the door.

He looked at the young gentlemen, winked, rubbed his chest significantly, and with a grimace, made his exit.

The boys sat down with an ill grace. The basins of brimstone and treacle were put before them.

"I will return in half-an-hour, to see if you want any more," exclaimed Miss Martha.

"Don't trouble yourself, ma'am," replied Jack.

She went away, shutting the door after her.

"I say," cried Jack, "this is a surprise. I can't tackle the stuff. I'd rather go without anything."

"I am doing the best I can with my dose," answered Pranks. "Bread and water is always the rule here after interviewing the doctor. They think they save on the meat and vegetables—at least, Miss Martha does."

"Can't we throw it out of the window?" asked Harry.

"She'd find it out, bless you," said Pranks. "She's got an eye and a nose for everything."

"Really."

"Very remarkable woman is Miss Martha. Pitch in. You've got to do it. Better regard it as the boy did the peas-pudding: very filling at the price," continued Pranks.

Jack laid down his spoon, so did Harry.

"I can't do it," said Jack.

"Nor I," supplemented Harry.

Suddenly they saw two grinning faces at the window.

These belonged to Peeping Tom and Knowall Dick.

They moved their arms as if conveying spoons to their mouths, and, just as Tuffins did, made faces.

Actuated by a sudden impulse, Jack rose. ran to the window, threw it up, jumped out, and seized Tom.

Harry followed him, and did the same with Dick.

Before the spies could say anything, they were hauled into the housekeeper's room, and thrown on to the floor by their captors.

Never were two boys so completely surprised.

"I say, what are you up to?" asked Peeping Tom.

"Give us an explanation of this extraordinary behaviour," said Knowall Dick.

Jack shut the window.

"Certainly," he replied, blandly. "We have had a little lunch provided for us through the kindness and forethought of Miss Martha."

"Well?" ejaculated Tom.

"Seeing that you looked hungry, we thought we would ask you to partake, as we really have more than we can eat ourselves. Pray be seated," added Jack.

Pranks, with difficulty, suppressed his laughter.

He saw the joke now, and began to enjoy it.

The spies rose to their feet with a ghastly grin on their pale countenances.

It was a hollow mockery of mirth.

They were far from feeling at their ease.

"I thank you kindly," replied Peeping Tom. "But I am afraid the lunch would spoil my appetite for dinner."

"As for me, I assure you I don't need it," said Knowall Dick.

"Don't be bashful, dear boys," continued Jack. "It is a great deprivation on our parts to give it up, but we don't mind it."

Pranks had some of his left, and he divided it equally between the two basins.

"There is nothing mean about me," he remarked; "so I will contribute my mite."

If there was one thing the spies detested more than another, it was the horrid vicious compound known as brimstone and treacle.

But they quickly saw that their tormentors were in grim earnest, and that it was of no use to resist.

Jack and Harry forced the spies to sit down.

"Open your mouths," cried Jack. "If you refuse to partake of the splendid lunch we have provided for you, or make a noise, you will be thrashed within an inch of your lives."

Peeping Tom groaned in anguish of spirit.

Knowall Dick made a hideous face.

Their mouths opened, and their captors at once proceeded to feed them.

"Oh, dear, I shall choke!" gasped Tom.

"Again!" exclaimed Jack.

They had another dose, and so it went on, the contents of the basins gradually diminishing.

"What an interesting sight it is to see the animals feed," observed Pranks.

The spies gave him a vindictive look.

At length their nauseus meal was ended. Jack and Harry gave them the last spoonful.

Having accomplished their task, they were anxious to get rid of them.

Miss Martha might return at any moment.

It would not do for them to be found there.

"Gentlemen," said Jack, "we are very fond of your company, but we will not detain you any longer."

"Bless you, my children," exclaimed Harry, with a paternal air, "you may go."

The window was opened for them.

As they stepped out, they were as white as sheets, and looking very ill.

Turning, Peeping Tom remarked—

"Good old joke, isn't it?"

"So glad I'm alive," observed Knowall Dick, "because you will hear more of this."

"There is ingratitude for you!" exclaimed Jack.

"Awful!" answered Harry. "Oh, for the depravity of human nature!"

The dinner-bell now rang.

Alas! the spies had no longer any appetite for roast mutton.

They leant against the wall, and were dreadfully ill, after which they went into the wood-shed, and sank, limp and ghastly, upon a heap of sawdust.

"Bravo!" said Pranks, as the window was closed once more; "the enemy is routed."

"I think we scored that time," replied Jack.

"It shall always be so," said Harry, "so long as they interfere with us. Let them keep their noses out of our affairs."

"That's more than they can do," answered Pranks. "Peeping Tom and Knowall Dick ca'nt let anybody alone."

Just then Miss Martha entered.

"So," she exclaimed, "you have cleared up your basins?"

"It is all gone ma'am," Jack replied.

"Good boys. You can go and play now, and mind you keep out of mischief in future."

"Thank you, ma'am. We will be extra good."

"You will not want anything to eat until tea-time. What you have had is highly nutritious, as well as satisfying. By the way, I suppose you have heard that the doctor made an announcement at dinner to-day?"

"No, ma'am. How could we?" answered Jack.

"Certainly not. I forgot you were not there."

"We could not be in two places at once, ma'am."

"You are right, Spencer."

"I was enjoying the nourishing food you gave us, ma'am—a perfect health restorer, I call it," said Harry.

"Worth a guinea a box," remarked Pranks.

"When you ask for it see that you get it." cried Jack.

Beware of spurious imitations!" said Harry.

Miss Martha smiled.

"Really you boys are very funny," she exclaimed. "I have put you on the usual punishment diet, and you thank me."

"Never ate anything so delicious in my life," replied Jack. It is more tasty than chocolate cream, cocoanut ice, and all the other sweetstuff."

"Can't beat it," said Harry. "I shall always ask for the old original."

Miss Martha frowned.

"Was that remark intended to apply to me?" she demanded.

"By no means, ma'am," replied Harry.

"What, then, did you mean?"

"I was simply referring to the brimstone and treacle, ma'am, of which you seem to be the only reliable purveyor. I may say, without flattery, that you are the champion contractor."

"Rawlings!"

"Yes, ma'am."

"For a new boy, you allow yourself a strange freedom of speech; but, perhaps, you do not know any better."

"Pardon me, but I came here to be taught."

"That is true, but I came here to tell you that my brother, the doctor, has given the school a half-holiday."

"Hurrah!" cried Jack.

"Bravo!" shouted Harry.

Pranks stood on his head against the wall.

Miss Martha felt scandalised at this behaviour

"Do for goodness sake conduct yourself properly," she exclaimed.

Pranks rolled over, and resumed his seat.

"I don't know how, ma'am," he replied.

"You are the worst boy in the school," said Miss Martha.

"That is what everybody tells me."

"So you are."

"Why do you keep me? Perhaps my money is as good as anybody else's."

"You shall not participate in this half-holiday."

Jack and Harry began to laugh.

"Nor you, Spencer; nor you, Rawlings!" cried Miss Martha. "I am as much master here as the doctor."

"Please, ma'am," said Jack, "I haven't done anything."

"You laughed at me."

"No, ma'am. I laughed at Pranks; he's such a comical fellow."

"I did'nt do anything either," exclaimed Harry.

"You, Rawlings, are as bad as Spencer. All of you will stay here until it is tea-time. I will give you an imposition to occupy your time."

"Can I see the doctor?" asked Jack.

"No, you cannot. He is going to be busy on his great work, which is nearly ready for the press. Seven years has he been engaged on this labour; but it will make his name. He will be famous."

"What is the book called?" asked Pranks.

"'A History of Romulus and Remus; or, the Foundation of the Roman Empire, with some account of the Sabines.'"

"Whew!" whistled Pranks. "That is a large order, isn't it?"

"What do you intend to convey, sir, by that remark?"

"There's a lot in the title. How much is there in the book?"

"It is in five volumes, and fifteen hundred pages of brevier type."

"Who is going to read it?"

"Millions! It will go all over the civilised world!"

"Then it will be translated into every language?"

"It will, indeed," said Miss Martha, who was a firm believer in her brother's genius, if no one else was.

"It is a big thing," replied Pranks, thoughtfully.

"The work of a lifetime. It will be read in the Choctau language, as well as the Cingalese and the Timbuctoo."

"Stick-jaw language!" cried Pranks. "Is that brimstone and treacle loud talk?"

"Pranks," said Miss Martha, holding up her finger, "you are incorrigible; but I will punish you this afternoon. While your companions are enjoying themselves, you will be at work."

"Don't be so hard on us," said Jack

"I go to Mr Dobby, who will prepare your tasks for you. In half-an-hour or less, expect me back."

"Please, ma'am—"

"Move from this room if you dare!"

With these words Miss Martha walked away, with the air of a tragedy queen.

She had a slight squint in her left eye, and, when in a passion, it became intensified.

She seemed to look round the corner and then all over the room at once.

"Beloved eye!" remarked Pranks. "If I had a squint like that I think I'd order my funeral."

Harry and Jack laughed at this sally, though they were far from feeling in a mirthful frame of mind.

They were very hungry, and very sore from the effects of the castigation they had received.

It was a beautiful afternoon, and they would have greatly enjoyed a country ramble.

Suddenly Pranks got up and put on his cap.

"What's up now?" asked Jack.

"I'm off," replied the irrepressible Pranks.

"You'll get into a row."

"I'll be content to chance that. The weather is so very tempting. I can't be kept in just to satisfy the spite of that old hag. Good-bye."

Pranks opened the door and disappeared in the passage, leaving Jack and Harry with a strong inclination to follow his example.

"Shall we do ditto?" queried Jack.

"I don't want to get into trouble again so soon after this morning," replied Harry, "although if you mean to go I sha'n't stay alone."

There was a knock at the door as he finished speaking.

Thinking it was Miss Martha, he politely opened the portal.

What was his surprise to see the page, Tuffins, with a tray in his hands, on which were two plates of meat and vegetables.

"What, Tuffins!" exclaimed Jack.

"Yes, sir," was the reply. "I've brought you some dinner, hearing that you and Master Rawlings was on what Miss Martha calls punishment diet."

"How did you get it?"

"It was cut off for Harris and Wilkins."

"The spies!"

"That's them. Somehow they never turned up to dinner," continued Tuffins, "which is a very peculiar circumstance."

"Why?"

"They are in general mighty particular to be on hand. Two more reg'lar eaters I never see."

Jack exchanged glances with Harry.

They could guess why the spies had not made their appearance at dinner.

Tuffins put the plates on the table, and urged the boys to set to and finish before Miss Martha returned.

He was running a great risk in bringing the dinner to them.

If caught, there was no telling exactly what Miss Martha might do.

Like her brother, she took a pleasure in the severity of the punishments she inflicted.

"How do you find it eat?" asked Tuffins.

"First-rate," replied Jack. "It's cut rather thicker than usual. Who carved?"

"Dobby presided to-day. The doctor's got a working fit on his book. I hope you're enjoying of it?"

"Don't fret about that, my friend; but I say, Tuffy, what made you think of us?"

"Last half you gave me half-a-crown."

"Did I?" said Jack. "I'd quite forgotten it. I suppose you thought you might get another."

Tuffins grinned, opening his capacious mouth to its fullest extent.

"I ain't above accepting of it, sir," he replied.

Jack good-naturedly put his hand in his pocket, and producing half-a-crown, made him a present of the coin.

The page seemed to be highly delighted. He was not a spending boy; he was a genius for saving; he got a good many tips from the boys, and carefully put the money in the post-office.

"What do you do with your money?" inquired Jack.

"I saves it up for a rainy day," was the answer.

"How much have you got?"

"Close on fifteen pounds. It soon mounts up when you keeps on putting away. **Peg** into the vittles, sir, in case the missis turns up."

Both Jack and Harry had soon finished; but before Tuffins could pack up the plates, the catastrophe he dreaded happened.

Miss Martha walked into the room.

When she saw the tray she held up her hands in astonishment.

"What!" she gasped. "How dare you defy my authority in this way?"

"Tuffins thought there was no harm in—" began Jack.

Miss Martha would not listen.

She rushed upon the page, and seizing him by the hair with one hand, began to box his ears soundly with the other.

Tuffins struggled desperately, but he was unable to escape from her clutches.

Seeing this, Jack determined to interfere.

Going behind her, he put out his foot and tripped her up.

She fell on her back, and Tuffins, with a desperate effort, escaped, leaving a handful of his sandy hair in her grasp,

"Help! help!" she cried. "I'm being murdered."

Frightened almost out of his life, Tuffins ran away and hid himself in the boot-cleaning room.

"Let us make a bolt," said Jack.

"All right," replied Harry. "It is getting rather hot. The old dragon will be on to us next."

"I'm not for it. Come on."

Leaving Miss Martha in an hysterical state, shouting and screaming, they hastened out of the room.

Getting their caps, they ran from the house, and were soon in the fields, going in the direction of the "Cricketers' Inn."

This was a favourite resort with both of them.

CHAPTER VIII.

THE SPIES DO NOT SPEND A VERY COMFORTABLE HALF-HOLIDAY.

A BRISK walk brought our boys in half-an-hour to the comfortable, old-fashioned hostelry.

Going into the parlour, with the intention of ringing the bell and ordering some drink, they found Mr. Corks, the landlord, laying the cloth for two.

"Good-morning, gentlemen," said he, with a pleasant smile. "So you've got a half-holiday."

"How do you know?" asked Jack.

"A little bird has flown over and told me."

"Are you preparing for a dinner party?"

"Roast fowl and sausages for two, potatoes, and bottle of Bass."

"Very good tack. Shouldn't mind it myself. Who are the guests?"

"Two of your boys," said Corks.

"What are their names?"

"Master Harris and Master Wilkins."

Jack threw his cap into the air, and Harry smiled.

"By Jove!" he cried, "isn't this fine? Peeping Tom and Knowall Dick are going to have a little feed on the quiet."

"They must be hungry, as they had no dinner," replied Harry.

"Where are they, Corks?" inquired Jack.

"Out in the yard, playing with the dogs, sir."

"Nice boys!"

"Wasn't that a trick you played them last week," laughed Corks, "when you tied them up in the sacks and the sheep walked on them?"

"It wasn't bad. We'll play them another to-day."

"Will 'ee?" grinned Corks. "Who's to pay I for the dinner if they be driven away?"

"I will. When will it be ready?"

"'Bout twenty minutes. I was to call them when it was served up."

"Very good. Mind the fowl is not cooked too much, and have the sausages properly browned," said Jack.

"What a chap you be to be sure, Master Spencer!" exclaimed Corks.

"Why so?"

"You're up to one of your larks, I know. Howsomever, it don't matter to me, so long as I get my money."

"We don't like Harris and Wilkins," replied Jack. "They are spies and sneaks. Only this morning they got us into serious trouble."

"Then I don't blame 'ee for paying of them out."

"Nobody can. What fun, to think they should have come down here."

"Retribution is swift," remarked Harry.

"The way of the transgressor is hard," answered Jack. "Let us go and see these interesting youths."

"Fancy what long faces they will pull when they see us."

"Rather. They will think there is some more brimstone and treacle coming. Ha, ha!"

"Ho, ho!" laughed Harry.

Arm in arm they sauntered into the yard, at the entrance to which were two dogs, chained to their kennels, one on each side of the gate.

These were two large retrievers.

Their names were Gip and Carlo.

Peeping Tom and Knowall Dick were engaged in the pleasing pastime of pelting the dogs with stones.

It was not in their nature to be kind even to dumb animals.

They appeared to be in high spirits, having evidently recovered from their sickness.

But a change came over the spirit of their dream.

When Jack and Harry entered the yard, they started and turned pale.

"Glad to see you are amusing yourselves in a congenial way," cried Jack.

The dogs were crouching and yelping, for they had been hit several times with the stones.

"You here?" stammered Peeping Tom.

"The place is as free to us as it is to you."

"There are plenty of other places to go to."

"Shut up!" exclaimed Jack. "What are you shying at the dogs for, eh?"

"For fun."

"Fun! How would you like it? They have done you no harm."

"It's only play. The dogs don't mind it," said Knowall Dick.

"You are a couple of vicious little scamps, without an atom of principle in you."

"Leave us alone," cried Dick.

"They are not your dogs," said Tom.

Jack laid hold of him by the arm, and Harry did the same to Dick, although he did not know what his friend was going to do.

That was a matter for conjecture.

He had not to wait long, though, before he found out.

They were all three speedily enlightened.

"Let go of me!" exclaimed Tom.

"Not much," replied Jack.

"It's a shame we should always be bullied by you!"

"I'm going to put you in the place of the dogs."

"Do what?"

"Chain you up."

"You daren't do it," cried Peeping Tom.

"We ought to have the protection of the law," said Knowall Dick.

Jack made no answer.

He dragged his captive to Gip's kennel, undid the dog's collar, and fastened it round the boy's neck.

Harry imitated him exactly with regard to Dick.

Then Jack cut off a piece of cord from a drying line, and tied Peeping Tom's right arm tightly to his side.

He could use his left arm, but was unable to undo the collar, which was securely buckled at the back of his neck.

"Now," said Jack, "you've got what I may call three legs."

"You will repent this," replied Tom.

"Down, and crawl into your kennels," said Jack.

"But, look here—"

"Down, I say."

Peeping Tom sank on to his knees and his left hand.

So did Knowall Dick, who had been treated in a similar manner.

They were burning with rage.

"Will you tell tales of us again?" asked Jack.

"As if we ever did such a thing," answered Tom, indignantly.

"It isn't in us," said Dick.

"Don't stoop to falsehoods."

"Let us go. We have got a bit of dinner cooking."

"And we mean to eat if for you."

"Eat our dinner?"

The look that crossed the faces of the spies was a study.

They were very hungry, and had been looking forward to something nice to eat.

"Get into your kennels," continued Jack.

"Don't make fools of us," pleaded Tom.

"Shy a stone at your dog," said Jack. "Don't be afraid of hurting him."

Harry picked up some pebbles and threw them at Knowall Dick.

He was struck three or four times.

The pain made him quickly hobble into the wooden box, howling, and dragging his chain after him.

When similar attention was bestowed on Tom, he, too, clanked his chain, and went in.

As they could not turn inside, they made their way backwards.

It was very comical to see them hopping along.

Both crouched down, peeping out of the kennels.

Jack and Harry burst into uncontrollable fits of laughter.

"Spencer," pleaded Tom, be a Christian."

"That's what you never were."

"Let us out, and we'll try and do better."

"Yes," cried Knowall Dick; "let us go, and we'll never sneak again."

"Oh, you admit that you do sneak?"

"Yes."

"That's enough. You stand convicted on your own confession."

"Won't you let us go?"

"Not yet. We are going [for a little walk," replied Jack.

The [dogs, delighted at being let loose, were bounding and gambolling about, and barking loudly.

Attracted by the noise, Corks looked out of the kitchen door.

When he saw the state of affairs he roared with laughter.

"What's the matter, you old picture card," asked Jack.

"You've been and gone and done it this time."

"How?"

"Oh, aren't 'ee a fair caution?" said Corks.

"What!"

"If ever there was a cough drop, you're one. Ha, ha! new breed of dogs, ain't they?"

"Yes," replied Jack; "that's the spy dog."

"Oh, oh! Ha, ha!"

"Is that dinner nearly ready?"

"We'll dish up in ten minutes, sir."

"Very well. Then I shall walk down to the river. Don't you interfere with my spy dogs."

"Not me, sir."

"Hi, Gip! Hi, Carlo!" cried Jack.

Gurgling with laughter, Corks went back to the kitchen to assist his wife, and Jack, with Harry, proceeded to the river, which was only a little way off.

"What are you going to do with the dogs?" asked Harry.

"Give them a swim," was the reply.

"And then?"

"Send them into their kennels."

"You think Peeping Tom and Knowall Dick might be getting too comfortable?"

"That is it," said Jack.

"I declare that those fellows deserve all they are getting from us," remarked Harry.

"Yes, and more, too."

"It is open war between us."

"And always will be, my boy."

Reaching the river Jack picked up some sticks, which he threw in for the dogs to retrieve.

In a couple of minutes the animals were thoroughly soaked with water.

This was all Jack wanted.

Calling them to his side, he returned to the yard of the "Cricketers' Inn."

Peeping Tom and Knowall Dick had crawled out into the yard.

They were sitting on the stones, with the collars still round their necks.

Directly they saw Jack they scrambled back into the kennels, afraid lest they might be stoned again.

"Gip! Carlo!" said Jack. "Good dogs. Go to bed. In with you—quick!"

The dogs bounded into their kennels.

Peeping Tom and Knowall Dick were covered with the dripping water.

Pushed on one side, they were squeezed up against the wood, and had to share the kennels with the dogs.

It was not a pleasant companionship by any means.

Tom poked his head out.

"I'm wet through," he said, plaintively. "Haven't you done enough to us?"

"Not quite," replied Jack.

"If the doctor knows this he will go on awfully."

"Let him. If you like to sneak, so much the worse for you."

"I never met such a fellow as you are."

"You feel as if you had burnt your fingers, don't you, my boy?"

"Something of that kind."

"I am an awkward sort of chap to tackle," said Jack; "but if you will let me alone I won't hurt you."

Corks came out.

"Dinner's ready, gents!" he cried.

"So am I," answered Jack. "Open the beer. I'll be there in a moment."

Peeping Tom uttered a low wail.

Knowall Dick groaned in a dismal manner.

"Won't you give us a bit?" asked Tom.

"Not a smell," rejoined Jack. "But, I say!"

"What?"

"You shall have the bones."

"Thank you for nothing."

"Good-bye."

"Call the dogs off before you go."

"Oh, no; couldn't think of it. Ta, ta!"

Saying this, Jack took Harry's arm and went into the inn, leaving the spies to shiver in company with the wet dogs.

The fowl was excellent, the sausages were done to a turn, the potatoes floury, and the beer was foamy and brisk.

Although Jack and Harry had eaten one dinner, they were quite ready for another.

This one they enjoyed exceedingly.

"What a day we are having," said Jack.

"Splendid! If we don't catch it when we get home we shall be all right."

"Miss Martha can't say much. She had no right to keep us in."

"Perhaps the doctor will back her up."

"If he does, I'll speak plainly to him," replied Jack.

"THE NAUSEOUS STUFF WAS POURED INTO PETER'S MOUTH."

No. 3.

"What will you tell him?" asked Harry.

"Simply that I will write to my father. All we want is justice."

"Are you going to give our spy dogs the bones?" asked Harry.

"No. That was only a joke of mine. We will be off now. I'll pay Corks, and he can let the spies loose when he likes."

"I hope we sha'n't get into a row."

"So do I," replied Jack.

Corks was speedily settled with. He was laughing still. Being told that he might release Peeping Tom and Knowall Dick from their thraldom, he promised to do so.

The fine weather had suddenly changed. Clouds rolled over the sky obscuring the sun, and rain began to fall as soon as the boys left the inn.

They did not cut across the fields, but took the high road; it was better walking, and did not make much difference in the distance.

The rain fell more heavily every minute.

A quarter of a mile up the road was an old cottage, which had long been without a tenant.

It had once been occupied by a ratcatcher, and was known as "The Ratcatcher's Cottage."

A fire had taken place in it, burning it out, but the four walls were standing, and part of the roof remained.

The landlord did not care to repair it, and the ratcatcher had gone elsewhere.

Coming to this cottage, Jack and Harry thought they would shelter for awhile.

The shower could not last long.

Accordingly they went inside, but no sooner had they entered, than they were surprised to see a boy bending over the hearth, which was paved with red bricks.

As he heard their footsteps, he sprang up in a flurried manner.

It was Pranks.

"Holloa, old fellow!" cried Jack, "what are you doing here?"

He looked nervously at them.

All the blood seemed to leave his face.

"I might ask you the same question," he replied.

"We are taking shelter from the rain."

"So am I," said Pranks. "It's a heavy shower, and just as I got in, I dropped a shilling out of my pocket."

They believed his story, though his manner was strange.

The bricks of the hearth were loose, as if they had been recently moved.

Had he been hiding anything?

"We've had such a lark with Peeping Tom and Knowall Dick" remarked Jack.

"Have you?" replied Pranks. "Tell me about it."

Jack did so, and Pranks, who looked very serious, conjured up the ghost of a laugh.

"A good many in our school want serving out," he said, "from the doctor, down. I'm not going to be sat upon."

"What has ruffled your feathers?"

"That old cat, Miss Martha, for one; and I am no friend of the doctor. He won't perform on me for nothing!"

"He must preserve discipline!" observed Jack. "It is rather a serious thing to ridicule the masters."

"He's sorry for punishing me by this time."

With these words, Pranks took his departure.

"He's a curious chap," said Jack.

"I think he is revengeful," replied Harry. "There was an awfully vindictive look on his face."

"Let us look for his lost shilling."

"Go ahead."

Harry approached the hearth, and began to make an examination. Some loose earth was thrown into the fireplace.

It looked as if it had just been dug out.

"These bricks are loose," cried Harry.

"Take them out, then," said Jack.

It was not a difficult task to do this.

At length an oblong cavity was revealed.

In it was a pile of foolscap paper, amounting to several reams.

Harry took it out. It was quite dry, which showed that it could not have been here long.

"What in the world have you unearthed?" queried Jack.

"A pile of manuscript," answered Harry.

On it was written "A History of Romulus and Remus; or, the Foundation of the Roman Empire, with some account of the Sabines. By Doctor Birchoften."

It was the doctor's great work.

By some means Pranks must have got possession of it.

Whether it was only a trick to cause annoyance for a time, or dire revenge, was a question difficult to solve.

The doctor had been labouring at this production for seven long years.

The book was like a favourite child.

"I say," cried Jack, "it is lucky we dropped in here. This is a very serious matter. Pranks has evidently stolen it."

They stood looking reflectively at the precious manuscript.

"I should return it to the place where we found it," said Harry, at length.

"Honesty is the best policy," answered Jack.

"But it is not a question of our honesty. We have had nothing to do with it."

It was a difficult position in which to be placed.

The doctor would be dreadfully upset when he discovered the loss of his MS., which, no doubt, he had done by this time.

"We must think this matter over, and decide what is to be done about it to-morrow," said Jack.

"Heigho! more trouble ahead."

They quitted the cottage in a perturbed and melancholy state of mind.

They would have been more uneasy in their mind if they had seen two evil faces peering in at the cottage window.

Peeping Tom and Knowall Dick were outside.

Corks had released the spies, and on their way home they had been attracted to the cottage by the sound of voices.

These were familiar to them.

Of course they listened.

They heard little to enlighten them as to what was going on, but they saw the MS. put under the bricks.

That was enough for them.

As soon as Jack and Harry had cleared out of the cottage, they entered and raked up the papers.

A glance at the title made them jump for joy.

"Now we've got them," exclaimed Peeping Tom. "It is the doctor's book. They have stolen it."

"Yes, and hidden it for revenge," replied Knowall Dick.

"Isn't this a grand find?"

"They will be expelled."

"Serve them right, too, for putting us in sacks."

"And giving us brimstone and treacle," said Dick.

"Yes, and eating our dinner, and making dogs of us," added Tom.

"We will take the manuscript straight to the doctor."

"Wasn't it lucky we stopped to look in at this window?"

"I always like to look in at windows."

"And listen at doors, eh?"

"Yes; hide and peep and listen. That is the way to find out things."

"Ha, ha!" laughed Tom. "There isn't much that goes on that we don't know."

"You can bet there isn't."

"We shall be in prime favour for restoring this manuscript."

"Of course, we shall. Hurrah!"

"Come on, I'll put it under my arm. Up and away. Perhaps we shall be invited to tea. Miss Martha always has eggs and muffins."

"Don't," said Knowall Dick. "I'm so empty and hollow. I'm like a drum."

"Cheer up," answered Peeping Tom; "there is a land before us flowing with milk and honey. We've struck it. Hurry up."

Taking the MS. with them, they made all haste back to the school.

"If I were only big enough," remarked Peeping Tom, "I'd give Spencer a thrashing. We used to have it our own way before he came to the school."

"Perhaps it is want of pluck. I don't think we're very plucky," replied Dick.

"What's the use of it? If you fight you get hurt. Cunning is the thing."

"And yet you said—"

"That's how I feel," interrupted Tom.

"I like to be artful," answered Dick. "That is the way to best everybody. I would listen to a fellow talking in his sleep, and make something out of it.

"I'd pick torn-up letters out of a dustbin and put the pieces together. There is nothing like being cunning."

Peeping Tom thoroughly coincided with this opinion. They hastened along, much elated at the rich discovery they had made.

It was close upon six o'clock, and the evening was beginning to draw in.

They had just time to reach school before the tea-bell rang.

CHAPTER IX.

JACK AND HARRY GET INTO UNDESERVED TROUBLE.

DOCTOR BIRCHOFTEN's private study was not very far from the housekeeper's room.

When Miss Martha began to scream murder, and shout for help, the worthy man heard it instantly.

He had his manuscript paper spread out before him; his books of reference ready to his hand.

The work he had accomplished during the past seven years was in a pile on the table, and occasionally he would refer to it, and make a marginal note.

Hearing his sister screaming, he felt annoyed at being disturbed.

As it went on he became alarmed.

What could the matter be?

Rising, he strode to the door.

"Martha," he cried, "what are you doing?"

"Help! help!" she vociferated.

He felt compelled to go to her assistance.

Something very unusual must surely have happened.

Striding along the passage he entered the room, and promptly assisted her to rise, after which he led her to a sofa.

It was while he was doing this that Pranks, who was prowling about full of mischief and bad feeling, looked in at the study door.

Nobody there.

The manuscript was on the table.

Surely this was an opportunity that he ought not to neglect. Striding gently in, he took up the papers like a thief in the night, and hurried away.

What he did subsequently with them we already know.

It was some time before Miss Martha became calm enough to relate the story of her woes.

Of course, she represented the conduct of the boys in as black a light as she could.

"As they have all run away, I can do nothing to them at present," said he; "but when they answer to their names at six o'clock roll call, I will attend to them."

With this promise Miss Martha was obliged to be content.

The doctor retraced his steps to his study, and she solaced her outraged feelings, and steadied her shaken nerves with a glass of wine.

Suddenly she was startled by hearing a terrible noise in her brother's room.

He was calling out "thieves" as loud as he could.

The loss of his book had just been discovered by him.

It was her turn to be frightened, and go to his assistance.

His face was a picture of stony despair.

"My book is stolen!" he cried. "The labour of a lifetime, I may almost say, is gone in a few minutes."

"Gone!" she repeated. "Where?"

"How should I know? It was here. When roused by your clamour, I went to your room."

"Who could have done such a wicked thing?"

"Some villain!" said the doctor. "Ah, he has stabbed me in my tenderest part. Money I could have spared without a sigh; but the loss of my book is irreparable. Look at the days and nights of labour I have given to it."

The tears forced themselves into his eyes.

"Do something," he went on, desperately. "Search the house. I am stunned and incapable of action."

He sank into a chair, scarcely capable of speech or action.

"My poor brother," exclaimed Miss Martha, with a more sympathetic tone than anyone would have given her credit for, "believe me, I feel for you, and will do my best to clear up this mystery."

He thanked her with a look.

She left him to prosecute her researches, and when alone he covered his face with his hands, while the tears trickled through his fingers.

As may be imagined, Miss Martha made no discovery.

It being a half-holiday, all the boys and the masters were out.

The house was empty, in fact, with the exception of the cook, the housemaid, and Tuffins.

Very imprudently the latter happened to pop his head out of the pantry to see how the land lay, when Miss Martha was passing.

He had reason to regret this before long.

"Ha!" cried Miss Martha, as her lynx-like glance caught sight of him, "there's the villain!"

Tuffins shut the door quickly.

"She's spotted me with her swivel eye," he muttered. "Oh, wouldn't I like to give her a dab in it."

The next moment the door opened, and Miss Martha loomed on the horizon.

Tuffins felt afraid of her. She looked so gorgon-like.

He crawled under the table.

"Ha," screamed Miss Martha, "that's a sign of guilt."

"What is?" asked Tuffins, tremblingly.

"Come out, you rascal!"

"I ain't no rascal. Who are you calling names?"

"You've done it. Oh, you monster, to try to break your poor master's heart. You ingrate!"

"What are you talking about?"

"You warmed-up viper. Come out!"

Very much alarmed, Tuffins emerged from his place of concealment.

Miss Martha at once faced him.

"Now, where is it?" she said, pantingly. "What have you done with it, you base, bad boy?"

"What?"

"Confess that you've got it, and put us out of this misery."

Tuffins stared curiously at her, thinking

she had gone out of her mind, and did not know how to answer her.

"Will you speak, or shall I have to make you?" continued Miss Martha, desperately.

At length Tuffins recovered himself sufficiently to speak.

"What's the caper?" he asked, in a faint voice. "I believe you have gone a bit off, ma'am, or you'd never go on to a poor chap like this."

"The book my brother is writing has been surreptitiously removed from his study within the last half-hour," replied Miss Martha.

"Is that all?"

"All!"

"I thought you had lost your cash-box, or the bank had gone broke, or the house was set afire by some malicious person."

"Miserable creature!" ejaculated Miss Martha.

"Don't get flustrated over a trifle like that."

"You call it a trifle?"

"Whoever's got it can't eat it," argued the philosophic Tuffins; "consekvently, it's sure to turn up."

Miss Martha eyed him keenly.

"Do you think so?" she said.

"I'm sure of it, miss. P'r'aps the one as took it will hold back for the reward."

"You are very confident," Miss Martha exclaimed. "Both your words and your manner convince me that you have got the manuscript. Now, will you give it up at once?"

To emphasise her words, she took him by the ear.

Tuffins uttered a yell, and broke away.

"I ain't going to stand no more of it," he cried, as he gained the door.

"Come back this instant!" she shouted.

"Not me. It's ag'in' natur' to do it."

She made a cat-like spring in his direction; but he saw her coming, and snatching up his cap, ran out of the house.

Reaching a field at the back, he sat on a stile, and began to whistle.

Every now and then he turned his head to see if Miss Martha were coming.

He did not want to be taken in the rear at a disadvantage with a broomstick.

"She's a wicious cat," he muttered, "and capable of any willainy."

This declaration of his opinion somewhat relieved his feelings.

In his pocket he found a cigarette and a match.

A smile crossed his features, and he lighted up the cigarette, but scarcely had the fat page done so, than he was surprised to see a boy in livery approaching the stile.

On his arm he had a basket. He was a tall, slim youth.

His face fell when he saw Tuffins on the stile.

There was no way of getting to the house, except past him, and he and Tuffins were mortal enemies.

His name was Peter, and he was the doctor's boy. On the present occasion he was bringing some medicine for one of the scholars.

Their enmity at first had been signalised by fights, but Tuffins was the master, and Peter was obliged to acknowledge it.

"Oh, isn't this spiffing!" thought Tuffins. "I was just wishing I could take it out of somebody."

He wanted to relieve his mind.

"I say, Spider," he continued, addressing the lanky one, "does your mother know you're out?"

"Oh, yes," replied Peter, who was not in a good temper that day. "She gave me tuppence to buy a donkey. Are you for sale?"

"Really," said Tuffins, "I wasn't aware she'd sold her mangle."

They looked at one another with no friendly eyes.

"He's inclined to be imperent," reflected Tuffins. "I shall have to take some of the cheek out of him."

"Will you let me get over that stile, please?" said Peter.

"Presently," replied Tuffins. "I want to enjoy your society a little first. It is not often we meet now."

"That is not my fault, Mr. Tuffins. You should come more into the town."

"Last time I showed myself there, you and some friends of your'n set a dog on me," said Tuffins, reflectively.

"Not I!" cried Peter.

"Time before that," continued Tuffins, "I was set upon at the corner of the street, and chucked into a horse trough."

"Not by me."

"Oh, no, you wouldn't. You ought to get on. You do try."

"I know nothing of it," protested Peter.

"None of your crammers!" cried Tuffins. "I've heard all about it. It was you who gave Joe Buggins and Tom Heaver two pots of four-'arf to do it."

Peter began to tremble.

There was an old-time look in Tuffins' eyes which he did not like.

It was useless to make any further denial of the grave charges brought against him, for Tuffins would have no disclaimer.

"What have you got in that basket?" continued Tuffins.

"Some physic for one of your young gentlemen," answered Peter.

"Bring it here."

Reluctantly the doctor's boy did as he was told. Tuffins examined the bottles with a critical air, and read the label.

"Black draught in one," he remarked, "paregoric in the other. Very nice is both of them in the spring time. Isn't they, Peter?"

"I don't know much about drugs myself," replied Peter, faintly.

"Then you ought, being a doctor's boy. I'm ashamed of your ignorance; but your master wouldn't send them out if they wasn't proper?"

"Certainly not."

"Very good; that is what I wanted to be sure in my mind about. I'm sorry to say, Peter, that you don't look well."

"Me!" cried Peter, turning an ashen grey. "I was never better in my life."

"You deceive yourself," said Tuffins. "You want medicine badly."

"If you think so," replied Peter, with a sickly smile, "I'll take some when I get home."

"No, no; you will take it now. Which will you have first—the black draught or the paregoric?"

"You aren't in earnest?"

"Very much so. I've forgiven you the dog, and forgotten the horse trough, and I'm really concerned about you. Here, take the draught. Open your mouth."

Peter did not at once comply.

Seeing his hesitation, Tuffins doubled up his leg-of-mutton-like hand in a way that was desperately suggestive.

With surprising rapidity, Peter's mouth opened.

"Throw back your head," said Tuffins. "Let it all go down."

The cork was drawn, and the nauseous stuff poured into his mouth.

When it had been duly swallowed, the paregoric followed.

Peter turned green. He put his hands on his chest and moaned deeply, as if the two drugs were not agreeing with him.

His internal economy was painfully affected.

"Oh, dear," he said, clutching desperately at his basket, "I think I'll go home."

Tuffins smiled sweetly and serenely.

"Drop us a line to tell us how those medical fireworks agreed with yer," he cried.

With a very crestfallen air, Peter wended his way back to the town, registering a vow that he would rather throw up his situation than go to the school again.

But if Tuffins dared to venture into the town, dire results would follow.

Vengeance would tread upon the heels of hate.

Scarcely had Tuffins done chuckling at the discomfiture of the doctor's boy, than Peeping Tom and Knowall Dick came up to the stile.

"What's the news, Tuffy?" asked Tom.

"There's a big cricket match going on in the field between Mr. Clayton's eleven and another chosen by Mr. Warner," replied the page.

"I don't care about leather hunting," said Tom. "Anything else to tell us?"

"The doctor's dreadfully upset."

"Ha! What about?"

"Somebody has stolen the papers of the book he is writing. Done it for a lark, I suppose. But he is going on, and so is Miss Martha."

The spies regarded one another pleasantly.

"I think we can supply some much needed information," observed Peeping Tom.

"Don't talk too much," replied Knowall Dick, "let us tell our own story."

"Quite so. Come along."

Tuffins got off the stile to let them go over.

"It seems to me," he observed, "that what you two don't know isn't worth knowing."

"We make it our business to learn all we can," answered Peeping Tom.

"Ain't you got nothing else to do?"

"Nothing half so pleasant."

With this reply, they left Tuffins wondering what pleasure they could find in spying; and when they had entered the house, and hung up their caps, they proceeded at once to the doctor's study.

He had shown symptoms of being very ill, and Miss Martha, who was with him, had more than once thought of sending for the doctor.

The spies knocked at the door, and Miss Martha opened it.

"Who is it?" asked Doctor Birchoften.

"Harris and Wilkins."

"What do they want?"

"Please, sir," replied Peeping Tom, "we have found your book, and brought it back."

The doctor jumped from his chair, ran to him, seized the book, examined it, found it perfect, and his face became radiant.

It was like the waving of a magician's wand, which had suddenly transformed a howling waste into a beautiful garden.

He shook them both by the hand, and exclaimed—

"Heaven bless you!"

Then he questioned them as to where and how they had found it.

They told him without any reserve.

The natural conclusion that he came to

was that Jack Spencer and Harry Rawlings must have stolen it out of spite, and concealed it where it was found.

They had been punished and kept in, going out before they had obtained leave to do so; and while his back was turned, they must have perpetrated this mean revenge.

He at once put the manuscript under lock and key, resolved that it should never be left unguarded again until it went to the printer.

Peeping Tom and Knowall Dick were rewarded with half-a-sovereign each, and, as they expected, received the honour of an invitation to tea with Miss Martha.

They were evidently in high favour.

The doctor sent for Mr. Dobby, who was closeted with him in close conference for half-an-hour, when the usher departed to the dining-room.

All the boys were present, having nearly finished their tea.

Mr. Dobby called Jack and Harry into the passage.

He informed them of what had taken place, and of the accusation which Peeping Tom and Knowall Dick had made against them.

"Now," he concluded, "I am willing to hear your account of the matter. What have you to say in your defence?"

The two friends were almost dumb-founded.

They had not expected this sudden and heavy blow.

"It is quite true, sir," said Jack, "that we went into the ruined cottage to seek shelter from the rain, but there was somebody there before us."

"Who was that?"

"Pranks. We saw him bending over the bricks on the hearth. He left in a hurry. When he was gone, we dug up a brick or two, and found the doctor's book."

"Why did you not bring it home?" asked Mr. Dobby.

"I wanted to, but Rawlings said we should only get into trouble, and had best leave it where it was."

"Is this true, Rawlings?"

"Perfectly, sir; on my word as a gentleman," answered Harry.

"You acted very foolishly. If Harris and Wilkins had not looked in at the window, the MS. would not have been discovered, and you can imagine the doctor's distress of mind. I shall call Pranks."

He did so, and Pranks came into the passage, looking rather pale, but preserving a confident and somewhat defiant air.

Being told of the charge against him he laughed.

"That is one way of getting out of it," he said.

"What do you mean?" demanded Mr. Dobby.

"Putting the blame on my shoulders to save their own backs," replied Pranks, boldly.

"Do you deny their statement?"

"I do, most emphatically, sir. I was not in the cottage to-day, and I will defy them to prove it."

Jack and Harry were very indignant at this audacious assertion.

"What a barefaced falsehood!" cried Jack.

"It is simply monstrous!" said Harry.

"Oh, you can bluster as much as you like," exclaimed Pranks; "but I stand on my rights, and stick to my guns. I was not in the cottage. I never saw or spoke to you there. I know nothing about the book."

Mr. Dobby looked angrily at Harry and Jack.

"I am bound to believe Pranks," he exclaimed; "and I think it is a very base thing of you to endeavour to saddle him with the fault."

"Pardon me, sir—" began Jack.

"Silence!" Mr. Dobby interrupted; "not another word! You are only aggravating your offence."

"I should like to have my father sent for."

"Nonsense! At school you are removed from his authority. If not, what are you sent here for?"

"It is all very unfair. Pranks has spoken falsely."

"Silence! You two will be confined in the strong-room, on a diet of bread and water, for seven days," replied Mr. Dobby.

"I protest."

"Silence, I say! At the end of that period we shall decide what further punishment shall be awarded you for this cruel trick."

Pranks smiled in a provoking manner.

"As if I would do such a thing. Absurd!" he exclaimed.

"You can go," said Mr. Dobby.

Pranks walked gaily away, and the usher marched Jack and Harry to a small room at one end of the passage. It was built of stone; the door was heavily barred with iron; a small skylight admitted a little light; the walls were whitewashed, the floor was uncarpeted.

Two small iron bedsteads, two chairs, and a deal table constituted all the furniture.

This was known as the strong-room.

"THEY GOT PRANKS UP. HE GROANED HEAVILY AS THEY LIFTED HIM."

It had always been a place of confinement for desperately unruly boys.

Taking a lamp from a table, and a key from his pocket, Mr. Dobby unlocked the door.

The room had not been used for some time, owing to the intervention of the holidays.

Many of the boys, however, had spent weary days and nights in it.

A damp, mouldy, unwholesome smell arose.

"I will allow you the luxury of a light, so as to enable you to get acquainted with your prison," said Mr. Dobby, "until your bread and water is brought you; then solitude and darkness will be yours."

The boys entered sullenly.

It was perfectly useless to resist.

Force would have been used if they had tried to rebel.

"It isn't fit to put a dog into," replied Jack.

"Who asked you to speak?" rejoined Mr. Dobby.

"Have I no right?"

"None whatever. While at this school you must submit to its discipline. Your masters know what is best for you."

He gave Jack a push, which made him fall against Harry, and they both rolled over on to one of the beds.

"Don't do that again," cried Jack.

"If you don't like it," replied Mr. Dobby, "apply to your parents or guardians to take you away. The school existed before you came, and I will venture to say it will survive your loss."

Saying this in a callous, unsympathetic tone, he went away like a gaoler, and locked the door behind him.

"This is a particularly nice state of things," remarked Jack, as he sat on the bed.

"I don't know how it is," replied Harry, taking a place by his side, "but we seem to get into all sorts of unmerited trouble."

"We must take the bitter with the sweet, I suppose."

"How is our innocence to come out?" asked Harry.

"That is more than I can tell. Isn't it a shame of that fellow Pranks to say what he did?"

"Yes; but is it not more extraordinary that Peeping Tom and Knowall Dick should have passed by the cottage when I was handling the MS.?"

"That beats everything," answered Jack.

"Pranks will stick to it. You see if he doesn't."

"Of course he will, and we shall be the victims."

"It is too bad. We cannot clear ourselves."

"I can't blame Peeping Tom and Knowall Dick so much this time," continued Jack. "They did not see Pranks. Anyone, under the circumstances, would think we were the guilty parties."

"Still, it is extraordinary how the spies are always on our track."

"They are everywere; but they owe us an especial grudge for what we have done to them."

Harry laughed in a half-hearted manner.

"We have got the best of them generally," he said. "Don't be down-hearted."

"Who can help it?" asked Jack. "Seven days on bread and water! It's horrible!"

"At least, we have the consolation of each other's company."

"That is something, certainly."

"We must pray and hope that we shall be cleared of this horrible charge."

"Heaven send it may be so," answered Jack. "If we had only grappled with the difficulty, acted boldly, taken the bull by the horns, and carried the book to the doctor, this would not have happened."

"True. I was wrong."

"You admit it?"

"Frankly," replied Harry, "and I am very sorry for my weak judgment; but you must allow it was a difficult fix to be placed in."

"So it was, old fellow," said Jack, heartily.

They felt very gloomy.

At nine o'clock Mr. Dobby visited them again.

He placed a jug of water and a loaf of bread on the table.

Then, without uttering a word, he took up the lamp, leaving them in the dark, and locked the door.

They undressed themselves, got into bed, and went to sleep.

CHAPTER X.

A SINGULAR FATALITY—THE TRIUMPH OF JUSTICE.

THE day after the incarceration of Jack Spencer and Harry Rawlings in the strong-room, nothing was talked of in the school but that event.

Jack and Harry were generally condemned.

The attempt, as it was considered, to shift the blame on Pranks' shoulders, was held to be very mean.

Warner, who hated the two friends, congratulated Pranks on his escape.

"It serves them jolly well right," he said, "I never thought much of those fellows."

"They are rather too cocky," replied Pranks. "I vote we all cut them."

"By all means send them to Coventry. If I can help it, no one shall talk to or play with them," added Warner. "I feel sorry for you, for they tried hard to get you into a row."

Pranks winced a little.

He felt very mean, and his face began to grow red.

"Never mind, old boy," Warner went on; "everyone knows that you wouldn't do such a thing."

"Not for worlds," replied Pranks. "I'm fond of a lark, but I wouldn't do what they have done."

He did not like to prolong the conversation.

His guilty conscience pricked him.

Instead of Jack and Harry being in solitary confinement in the strong-room, he knew very well that he ought to be there himself.

Saying he was going for a walk, he strolled into the fields.

In reality, he felt too miserable to join in the games of his companions.

His secret weighed very heavily on his mind.

Do what he would, he could not help thinking of the two prisoners in the strong-room.

It was not at all probable that the secret would never be known; but if it were, how ashamed he would be!

The exposure would bring him into contempt with everybody.

It was a beautiful morning. The sun rode high in the heavens, clear, warm, and bright. A balmy air blew from the west.

Buttercups, daisies, cowslips decorated the fields. In the hedgerows violets and blue bells raised their pretty heads.

The white may already adorned the hedges, and the birds sang their simple notes.

In a tree, which overhung an old disused saw-pit, he noticed a bird's nest, which looked to him like a wood-pigeon's.

He had a collection of birds' eggs at home, but he had not one of the kind in the nest he now saw, so he determined to get one.

He threw up a stone, and the pigeon, which was sitting, flew off the nest.

In a moment he began to climb up the tree trunk into the branches.

One of these to which he clung was rather more fragile than he imagined.

It broke off short under his weight.

There was a crash, and, with a wild cry, he fell into the old sawpit.

His leg got twisted under his body, and was broken.

Instantly he was in terrible pain.

Unable to move, he screamed aloud in his agony.

At the bottom of the pit, who could see him?

He might linger there for days until he died of exhaustion and starvation.

It was an awful prospect!

A few short minutes before this unlooked-for accident, he was well, strong, and safe.

Swift, indeed, was the retribution which had overtaken him.

He looked upon it as a direct punishment for his wickedness.

A horrible fear of death took possession of him.

He groaned dreadfully, and sobbed aloud.

Suddenly he heard a voice exclaim—

"Hullo! what's the matter down there?"

Looking up with as much pleasure as would be expressed by a shipwrecked mariner, who is snatched from the waves at his last gasp, he beheld a dark gipsy-like face peering at him.

It was that of a boy about sixteen years of age, who had a hump on his back.

"I have fallen into the pit, and my leg is broken," replied Pranks.

"How did that happen?"

"In trying to get a bird's nest; the bough snapped."

"I don't know how to hoist you up."

"For Heaven's sake try! I am in such pain."

"Where do you belong?"

"To the school up yonder—that big white house," said Pranks.

"I see it," answered the boy with the

hump. "My time is valuable; but I suppose I shall have to go and tell them about you."

"Please do. I must have help."

"You see, I'm travelling with a caravan," explained the boy. "My name's Charlie, though it's something else in the bills, and my governor, Mr. McNab, is a very hot-tempered kind of gentleman."

"What do you do?"

"I'm a snake charmer," replied Charlie. "We go to fairs and races, and the charge is threepence to come inside and see me. Old McNab plays the flute, and I manage the snakes."

"Are you an Indian?" asked Pranks, forgetting his pain for a time.

"That's what they call me, though I'm as white as you are. I'm stained."

"Well, Charlie, or whatever you are," exclaimed Pranks, "get me out of this, and I shall be eternally indebted to you."

"Have you got any sof?" asked the boy.

"What's that?"

"Money. I like to be paid for what I do."

"About seven shillings. It's all my pocket money; but you shall have it willingly if you will go up to the school and bring help."

"That's good enough," and with a nod, the boy with the hump trotted off to the school.

It was truly fortunate for Pranks that he had happened to come by when he did.

Had it not been so, he would have soon succumbed to his injuries.

Charlie, the snake-charmer, hastened to the school.

He had not a bad face, but his hump made him look very ungainly, while his brown skin did not improve his appearance.

The front door was open. Entering, he went into the hall. There was nobody there. He opened the first door he saw. It was that of the drawing-room; that, too, was empty.

On a table was Miss Martha's watch and chain alongside of a basket containing four silver spoons and forks, which had been cleaned that morning.

Charlie looked round carefully to see that no one was watching him.

Then followed a most extraordinary proceeding.

He took off his jacket.

The hump on his back was made of wood, like a hollow box, with an opening at the top.

This deception was effectually hidden when he had his jacket on.

No one could suspect such a cunning, clever impostor.

A cord, attached to each side of this mimic hunch, was tied around his chest to keep it in its place.

With a celerity, almost amounting to sleight of hand, he snatched up the watch, chain, and silver plate.

These he dropped into his hump, and slipped on his jacket again.

The boy had evidently been trained by his master and employer to be a thief.

This cunningly contrived hump was only a means to an end.

Scarcely had he executed the manœuvre we have described, when Miss Martha appeared in the doorway.

She uttered a wild cry.

Who and what was this brown, ill-shaped, strange-looking creature?

"Please, ma'am, it's all right," said Charlie.

"All wrong," she replied, missing the valuables. "The plate! My watch! Thieves! Help! Fire! Murder!"

Mr. Dobby heard the noise in the school-room, and hastened at once to her assistance.

He had been correcting Latin verses, and wondered greatly what was the matter.

"Robbery!" cried Miss Martha. "A watch! Spoons! Forks! That misshapen piece of humanity has done it!"

There was a tinge of gall in her voice, with an infusion of wormwood.

"Search me!" exclaimed Charlie. "I'm willing!"

Mr. Dobby proceeded to do so without any delay.

All the boy's pockets were emptied; but, of course, nothing was found upon him.

"It must be a mistake," said the usher.

"The property is gone, and what is he doing here?" replied Miss Martha.

"I came to tell you something, you folks at this school, and all the thanks I get is to be accused of robbery!" exclaimed Charlie

"What is it?" asked Mr. Dobby.

"It's very important."

"Speak!"

"It's life and death—that's what it is."

"Dear me, what does the strange creature mean?" queried Miss Martha.

Charlie rubbed his knuckles into his eyes, and began to shed tears.

"I'm an honest chap, I am," he whispered.

"What did you come here for?" pressed Mr. Dobby.

"I'm poor, but I'm honest." replied Charlie.. "A poor boy has nothing but his name to protect him, and you want to take that away from me."

"Will you disclose your errand?"

"You've got a boy named Pranks in your school, ain't you?"

"Yes, certainly. What of him?"

"Well, he's fallen down the old sawpit in the close, and broke his leg bad. I happened to be passing by, and heard him groan. He'll die soon if you don't get him out."

"Is this true?" asked Miss Martha.

"Let the gentleman come with me, and see if it ain't," replied Charlie.

"You will conduct me to the spot?" said Mr. Dobby.

"That's the ticket for soup, master," answered the boy with the false hump.

They left the room together. Miss Martha was greatly upset about the loss of her valuables, and began a useless search for them in every direction.

For two generations they had been in the family, and they were as precious to the old lady as if they were her eyes.

It is true that the watch would not go, and the pattern was nearly worn off the forks and spoons.

Still, that made no difference in her veneration for these family relics.

Mr. Dobby followed Charlie over the field, feeling greatly concerned about Pranks. He had no positive liking for the boy; but he was warm-hearted enough to feel for his misfortune.

Passing by the place where Clayton, Warner and others were playing cricket, he informed them of what had happened, ordering them and two more to get a ladder and a hurdle.

These they were to bring to the sawpit as rapidly as possible.

When the scene of the accident was reached, Mr. Dobby had ocular demonstration of the truth of the story.

Charlie, who could climb like a monkey, dropped into the pit.

"The gentleman's come—give me the cash," he said.

"I am very much obliged," replied Pranks, faintly. "Put your hand in my pocket."

This was quickly done, and Charlie climbed up again.

"Now I'm off. Good-day," he exclaimed.

Giving Mr. Dobby a nod, he walked off at his best pace, and was soon halfway across the field.

"My poor fellow," said the usher, looking down, "I am sorry for this. Are you much hurt?"

"Dreadfully, sir," answered Pranks, who had quite lost his presence of mind. "I believe they will have to cut my leg off, and if they do, I know I shall die."

"Don't think that."

"It's a judgment upon me. Oh, this pain. How can I bear it? I shall go mad!"

"How is it a judgment? I do not understand that," exclaimed Mr. Dobby.

"I have been very bad, sir; but I am anxious to make amends."

Mr. Dobby was somewhat puzzled.

What could the boy mean?

"Your mind is a little excited," he replied. "If you allude to burning me in effigy, say no more about it. You have been punished for it, and have expiated your offence."

"It isn't that," said Pranks, sorrowfully.

"Keep quiet. You really must not distress or vex yourself. Clayton and some others of your schoolfellows will be here anon with appliances to remove you."

"I must confess."

"Well, if you have anything on your mind, and you think that a confession will relieve it, by all means tell me."

"Spencer and Rawlings are not guilty."

It cost Pranks an effort to say it; but he felt better after he had done so.

"Is it possible?" cried Mr. Dobby.

"I took the MS. Why, I do not know. Some bad impulse made me, I suppose. I hid it in the cottage."

"Then you were there?"

"Yes, sir; Spencer told the truth. I spoke the lie, and I am sorry for it now."

Mr. Dobby was astonished.

"Are you sure that your mind is not wandering?" he asked.

"Perfectly. Please acquaint the doctor."

"I will at once."

"Peace and I will be strangers till Spencer and Rawlings are set at liberty, and justice is done them by the boys."

"You have made reparation. That is the only atonement in your power. I am glad that your sense of right has asserted itself," answered Mr. Dobby, gravely.

"What will Doctor Birchoften do to me?" asked Pranks.

"You must wait till your leg gets well. Perhaps what you will have to suffer will be enough. Disgrace will follow pain."

"He won't send me away from the school?"

"No, I think not. Indeed, I am sure of it," replied Mr. Dobby.

The doctor, he knew, never resorted to expulsion, because he would have lost a pupil, and he was too fond of money.

The more quarterly bills he and his sister, Miss Martha, could send out, the better they were pleased.

To punish a boy was one thing, to get rid of him another.

Clayton and the others who were

requisitioned, now appeared upon the scene with a ladder and a hurdle.

They got Pranks up. He groaned heavily as they lifted him, and when they put him on the hurdle he fainted.

"Off and away, boys," said Clayton.

The sufferer was quickly conveyed to the school, put to bed, and the doctor sent for to set the leg.

On his arrival he made an examination, declaring it to be a compound fracture, which would take some time to get well.

There was no danger, and with rest and quiet, he would recover.

Mr. Dobby communicated Pranks' confession to Doctor Birchoften, who was very much annoyed to think he had punished the wrong parties.

There was no reason to doubt the truth of the statement which had been made; but the doctor visited Pranks personally.

He repeated what he had said to the usher.

Jack and Harry were immediately liberated and conducted to the schoolroom, where their innocence was made known to their companions.

A revulsion of feeling at once took place. They were loudly cheered.

Clayton shook hands with them, and his example was followed by all those who were in the upper division.

There were only three boys who were disappointed at this manifestation in their behalf.

These were Peeping Tom, Knowall Dick, and Warner, the bully.

Little Kennedy was profuse in his congratulations.

"We've got out of it, old fellow," Jack remarked to Harry.

"Yes," replied Rawlings; "and now we will keep out of it."

"If we can."

Harry laughed lightly at this observation.

"Perhaps that is well said," he exclaimed. "Boys will be boys, and we never know what is going to turn up."

"Anyhow," rejoined Jack," we will be as good as we can."

CHAPTER XI.

THE RACES ARE TALKED ABOUT—ALSO CHARLIE, THE SNAKE-CHARMER—MORE BULLYING.

JACK SPENCER'S father had a very fine greenhouse, in which he grew grapes, pine-apples, and early strawberries.

His sister made up a hamper of these good things, including a veal and ham pie, a chicken, and some store apples, and sent them to the school.

When they arrived, Jack opened the hamper in the servants' hall in the presence of Harry and Tuffins.

The delight of all three was unbounded.

In the hamper was a note signed "Marian," which said—

"Give Harry some."

"Bless her little heart!" cried Harry; "your sister's a duck."

"Is she?" replied Jack. "I never saw her swim, or heard her quack."

"You know what I mean."

"She isn't so bad, as girls go," said Jack. "I've met with worse, but all the same, I don't take much stock in her."

Harry held up his fist playfully.

"If you say a word against Marian, I'll hit you," he cried.

"Mary Anne—"

"Don't call her that; it's Marian. Provoke me not, or I will wade knee deep in your gore," cried Harry, assuming a tragedy air.

"Take your fate!" said Jack, throwing a slice of pine-apple at him.

It missed the mark, and struck Tuffins on the nose.

The page boy was busily engaged in devouring an apple at the time.

"Drop it, gents," he cried.

"It wasn't meant for you."

"But it came home all the same."

Harry threw a small bunch of grapes at him.

Tuffins very neatly dodged this favour, and they made their mark on the wall.

"Look here," exclaimed Tuffins, "if you've got more than you know what to do with, I'll tell you—"

"Give it to you, I suppose?" remarked Jack.

"Send it into the schoolroom for the fellows to eat, eh?" observed Harry.

Tuffins shook his head gravely.

"It is far from me to recommend a course of conduct like that," he rejoined, with a lofty air.

"What, then?"

"Oh, no; not by a jugful. You may

think me a strange chap, but I've got a heart."

Harry laughed.

"I wonder it doesn't burst the buttons of your uniform," he said.

"It's big, and perhaps it will some day," replied Tuffins.

"Big as a bullock's, and tender as a sheep's."

"No matter. If it bu'sts my buttons—"

"The doctor will have to buy you a new suit," cried Jack.

"Hold on," replied Tuffins. "What I was going to say was this: We all ought to return good for evil. We are taught to cultivate the milk of human kindness."

"What kind of a cow does that come from?"

"I'm interrupted, but I will keep on. Clamour shall not put me down. I was going to suggest that some of this fruit and stuff would be very acceptable to Pranks."

"Isn't Miss Martha attending to him?" asked Jack.

"She!" said Tuffins, derisively, as he started on another apple. "She! What do you take her for?"

"A mule," replied Harry.

"A camel," answered Jack.

"More'n that. I never see one; but I believe solidly she's a dromedary. All she's given him is one mug of gruel since his leg's been set."

"Really!"

"Give him some of your good things, and you won't miss it," concluded Tuffins. "He treated you badly, but he's met with his reward. It was a strange thing about that boy with the hump finding him in the sawpit."

"I heard something about it," said Jack. "Who is he?"

"Nobody knows," replied Tuffins. "I have been talking to Master Pranks, and he tells me that he travels in a caravan, and is a snake-charmer. It looks as if he stole the watch and the plate, though nothing was found on him."

"Where is he now?"

"Somewhere near. He and his employer are going to the races, which takes place the day after to-morrow."

"I should like to go," said Jack, "if it is only for a couple of hours."

"So should I, dearly," added Harry. "My uncle, Squire Rawlings, always runs a horse every year."

"I have heard," replied Tuffins, "that the doctor does not mean to allow any of the young gentlemen to go to the races this year."

"Perhaps some of them won't ask permission," Jack rejoined.

"There is such a thing as taking French leave," observed Harry.

Tuffins made a grimace.

"And don't it hurt afterwards?" he remarked.

"Silence!" said Jack; "we give you too much liberty."

"Yes," added Harry; "familiarity breeds contempt."

"Is that what I've got?" asked Tuffins.

"Yes."

"What is good for it?"

Jack was a little irritated.

He thought that Tuffins was going too far.

Raising his foot he gave him a kick, which made him roll over two chairs, and lie down in a corner of the room.

"That's the only remedy I know of for cheek like yours," cried Jack.

"Oh, dear," moaned Tuffins, "you've knocked the breath out of me."

"Serve you right!" exclaimed Harry. "We will take something up to Pranks, Jack, as suggested, and have a chat with him. I think when a man's ill, it does him good to have someone come and see him, and be talked to kindly."

"Rather," replied Jack. "I've been ill, and I know it is better than medicine."

"I've forgiven Pranks," added Harry.

"Have you?"

"With all my heart. I never bear malice."

They got a big dish, and piled up many of the good things for Pranks.

Harry carried the dish.

They left the room, not taking any notice of Tuffins.

No sooner did he see the backs of them, than he got up, and, ransacking the hamper, began to eat all he had a mind to.

When Pranks saw them come into the room, where he was lying on his back with his leg in splints, he felt inclined to pull the sheet over his face.

He thought they had come to reproach him for his meanness.

All day he had been very miserable, for Miss Martha had not given him anything to read.

It was terrible to be left alone with his thoughts.

In an illness of that kind, books and papers, and a little company occasionally, would be very agreeable.

"Well, old man," cried Jack, cheerily, "how are you by this time?"

Pranks averted his face.

"I'm very sorry," he said.

"What for?"

"You know, I—"

"Don't say a word—that is forgiven," replied Jack.

Pranks looked earnestly at Rawlings.

"And forgotten," said Harry.

At this Pranks drew a great sigh of relief.

"It's very good of you—very," he exclaimed. "I did not expect it; in fact, it is more than I had any right to expect."

Harry now produced the dish heaped up with good things, and put it on the bed.

"What do you say to that?" he asked. "There's something good for you. Jack's had a hamper sent him."

Pranks' eyes sparkled.

"Oh, thank you, so very much," he cried.

"What good fellows you are. When I get over this, I'll be your true friend. I'll stick to you through thick and thin."

Harry promised to bring him some papers and books to read, at which he renewed his thanks.

"I don't know what made me take the MS.," he remarked. "It was a sudden impulse."

"It ought to have been resisted," said Jack.

"I did not mean to destroy the MS., and to ruin the doctor's work, but I was vexed at being kept in."

"There was no harm done," remarked Harry. "You will soon get better, I hope, and what I can do for you I will."

"I am very grateful," replied Pranks. "The doctor says I shall have to keep my bed for many long weary weeks."

"You will not go to the races?"

"Not much. I should have liked to go if it was only to renew my acquaintance with the young snake-charmer, who found me in the sawpit."

"The boy with the hump?" Jack said. "I have heard of him."

"He stole the silver spoons," observed Harry.

"Very likely," answered Pranks, "though I have my doubts about it, as he was searched, and nothing was found on him. He talks a good deal, and told me that he was not the Indian he appeared to be, but that his face was stained."

"We mean to go to the races," replied Jack.

"Then you will see him and his snakes."

Having done all they could to make Pranks comfortable, they took leave of him.

Harry went to his locker to procure some books, by means of which he could beguile the tedium of the boy's illness.

Jack went back to his hamper fearful lest Tuffins might take too great liberties with its contents.

When halfway down the stairs he heard voices.

He stopped and listened.

Mr. Dobby was talking to Peeping Tom.

"The races are coming on," said Mr. Dobby, "and Doctor Birchoften is going to issue an order that none of the boys are to leave the playground on that day."

"Some of the daring ones will, sir," replied the spy.

"That is what I think."

"What shall I do?"

"Wait a moment, and you shall hear. I want you and Wilkins to go into the town and report the names of all our boys you see there."

"I understand, sir," replied Peeping Tom.

"Your evidence will be quite enough. I can always rely on you and Wilkins," added Mr. Dobby.

"Will you give us some spending money, sir?"

"Money to spend? What for?"

"We shall have to go into the shows."

"Very well. You shall have half-a-crown each."

Jack heard no more, because the usher and Peeping Tom moved on.

He had gained some important information, however.

Doctor Birchoften was going to prohibit the race meeting, which was a thing he had never done before.

The spies of the school were to go on the course, however, and tell if they saw there any one they knew.

Jack strolled along towards the room where he had left his hamper, and seeing that it was all right, went into the yard.

Here there was a giant-stride, hanging to one of the ropes of which he was surprised to see Kennedy.

Standing by was Warner, who had a stick in his hand.

Every time Kennedy came round he gave him a sharp cut on the legs.

"Keep it up!" cried Warner.

"Leave off!" pleaded Kennedy.

"Stick to it!"

"I can't. I shall fall off!"

"Nonsense! You are shamming."

"Indeed, I'm not!" said Kennedy.

He spoke in heart-rending accents.

Anyone but a born bully would have taken pity on him. Not so Warner.

He had no more feeling than a post.

Jack felt his blood beginning to boil.

He determined to interfere.

Kennedy was running round, and swinging on the giant-stride as well as he could.

He was trembling in every limb, and his nerves were stretched to their utmost capacity.

His strength was nearly exhausted.

Perspiration streamed from every pore, and he panted for breath like a hunted hare.

"' HOLD HIS ARM, HARRY!' CRIED JACK."

No. 4.

Each time he passed Warner he received a cruel blow from the stick, but he was afraid to let go lest he should fall on his face.

It was as bad a case of bullying as Jack had ever seen.

If the spies had told the masters of anything like that he would not have objected —in fact, he would have been the first to applaud them.

But Peeping Tom and Knowall Dick did not report this sort of thing.

"I say, Warner, leave off!" cried Jack, stepping up to his side.

The bully turned fiercely on him.

"What has it to do with you?" he asked.

"We had a row about this kind of thing before."

"And we can have another."

"Oh, yes," said Jack; "as many as you like. I'm agreeable. You will have to leave off assaulting Kennedy, or I'll make you."

"Not I."

Without any further parley, for he saw it was useless to waste words upon him, Jack dealt him a blow in the face.

It struck him with such force that it knocked him clean off his legs.

He fell half stunned.

At the same moment little Kennedy, thoroughly exhausted, dropped from the stride, and slid along on his side on the gravel.

His face was scratched, his ear commenced bleeding, and he lay on the ground sobbing and moaning.

In less than a minute Warner was up, holding his hand to his face.

"What did you do that for?" asked he.

"Why didn't you do as I asked?" replied Jack.

"You took me unawares."

"No I didn't. You might have known from experience that I was not to be trifled with."

"I believe you have seriously injured me!" grumbled Warner.

"If you want to fight, I'm ready to give you satisfaction," said Jack.

He quite expected Warner to take up this challenge.

The bully, however, did not do so.

In fact, he had got quite as much as he wanted in the last fight they had had.

"I'm not a champion pugilist, thank you," he sneered.

"Nor am I," said Jack. "What do you mean by that slur?"

"You seem ambitious of obtaining the reputation of one."

"Coward! You dare not fight! All you can do is bully. Look at that poor little fellow."

Jack pointed to Kennedy, who was now sitting up, wiping the blood from his scratched face with his pocket-handkerchief.

"He daren't sneak about it, because he knows if he did I would half kill him!" answered Warner.

"Perhaps *I* shall."

"If you do, I will work you some injury. Mark me well," said Warner, savagely.

"Who's afraid?" laughed Jack.

"I am of a very revengeful disposition. There is more bad than good in me, I can tell you."

"Aren't you ashamed to say so?"

"No. I don't know what shame is, or remorse either. I was never sorry for anything I did in my life."

He assumed a defiant, boastful air, which made him look like a very commonplace kind of ruffian.

"At all events, my boy," exclaimed Jack, "if you have no moral sense, you have the sense of touch and feeling. So just be good enough to get on that stride and go round as you made Kennedy."

"Do what?"

"Sauce for the goose is sauce for the gander. Up with you."

"You'll have to make me!"

"I'll knock you down again and thrash you afterwards if you don't obey orders."

Warner raised threateningly the ash plant he had used on Kennedy.

"Oh, that's your game, is it?" cried Jack.

"I'll hit you if you attempt to touch me," answered Warner.

With a rapid movement Jack snatched the stick out of his hand.

This act rendered Warner defenceless.

A look of intense hatred crossed his face.

Jack gave him a smart cut across the legs, which made him jump.

"Mount! Get up! Show your agility!" exclaimed Jack. "Put some steam into your movements, and don't leave off till I tell you to stop."

Very reluctantly Warner laid hold of the handle at the end of the rope, and began to run and swing round.

It went against the grain with him.

Each time he passed the spot where Jack was standing, he received a cut with the ash plant, well delivered.

This made him redouble his exertions, but he could not escape the blows which fell on him, with remorseless regularity, every time he went round.

He could now realise the nature of the torture to which he had subjected Kennedy.

After he had gone round about thirty times Jack relented, and told him to stop.

Warner did so, and stood still, trembling, but with a savage expression on his face, which showed that it was distorted with passion.

He was decidedly conquered, but not subdued.

As soon as he could steady himself, and his head ceased whirling, he shook his fist at Jack.

"I'll pay you for this!" he hissed.

"When you get a chance, eh? Perhaps I shall not give you one," replied Jack.

"You will be caught tripping some day."

"Go away, or I'll put you on the stride again."

Warner retreated towards Kennedy, who had risen to his feet.

"You're the king of the school, I suppose, in your own estimation?" Warner remarked to Jack.

"Of course. That is stale news. Tell us something we don't know."

"I'll be revenged."

"So you were kind enough to say before, bully Warner."

"I hate you!"

"Do you? I'm sure I don't want your love."

Warner gave Kennedy a spiteful kick on the shin.

"This is all through you, you little wretch," he cried.

Then he ran off as fast as he could before Jack could catch hold of him, or he would have undoubtedly been thrashed again.

Kennedy approached Jack nervously, with tears in his eyes.

"Are you much hurt?" inquired Jack, kindly.

"Nothing the matter much. My face will be well in a week," replied Kennedy.

"Warner ought to be reported."

"Please don't say anything about it. I shall only get it hotter. It will be all the worse for me."

There was a look of intense and earnest pleading in the boy's voice.

"Oh, very well," replied Jack, rather disgusted. "If you are such a milksop as all that, I sha'n't take any more interest in you."

"Don't say that."

"Have a little pluck."

"It's been all knocked out of me, if I ever had any."

"Which I doubt."

"Perhaps you are right," said Kennedy, with a sigh. "Compared with other boys, I'm a poor, puny, miserable fellow. All the same, I am sincerely grateful to you."

Jack did not know exactly what to make of him.

"I have done the best I can for you," he observed.

"Again I thank you from the bottom of my heart."

"Don't let that chap Warner kill you."

"If he did, I should be no loss. Who would miss me?" answered Kennedy.

"Well, I don't know. You are a funny fellow."

"May I tell you something?" said Kennedy, earnestly.

"Certainly. Speak out."

"In the night-time I lay awake often, and I see white-robed spirits standing by my bedside."

"Do they say anything to you?"

"No. Angels never speak, but they look so sweet and kind. They beckon me to come up into the sky with them; and I shall some day. Don't trouble about me."

Saying this, Kennedy walked slowly away.

There was a hectic flush on his cheek, and a far-away look in his eyes.

"I don't fancy he's all right in his head," muttered Jack, as he walked down the field.

He was met by Clayton, the captain of the school, who had been playing cricket.

"We are making up the first eleven, Spencer," he said.

"I suppose it is about time," replied Jack. "Do you think it will be a strong one."

"That is certain."

"Who have you put in?"

"All the best; and I want to know if you will take a bat? Your form is very good. It is not usual to offer a bat to a new fellow; but I am determined to get all the best men."

Jack naturally felt highly flattered.

It was a great honour to be asked to play in the first eleven.

"Thank you very much," he replied.

"Will you take a bat?"

"With pleasure."

"That is settled, then. We shall want you every day for practice, as we are making arrangements for a lot of matches this year," said Clayton.

"You can rely on my best endeavours," rejoined Jack.

Clayton shook him cordially by the hand, wishing him every success.

Jack felt he had achieved a position in the school.

To be in the first eleven is to be somebody, and it was more than Warner could boast of, with all his swagger.

CHAPTER XII.

THE RACES—EXCITING ADVENTURES—HARRY'S SUCCESS.

IT happened that the race day fell on the doctor's birthday.

This was always celebrated as a whole holiday.

It was a great blow to the more adventurous spirits, on the preceding night, to have a notice read out to them prohibiting anyone attending the races.

After breakfast away ran the boys, some to play cricket, others to row on the river, some to bathe, others to fish or enjoy themselves in any way they thought best.

Jack Spencer and Harry walked up and down the yard in rather a disconsolate state of mind.

"I want to go to the races," Jack said, "for I heard father say that he was going to run his horse, Stonecrop, in the Welter Handicap."

This intelligence did not interest Harry much.

He knew nothing about racing, and did not care for it.

"Will your sister, Marian, be there?" he asked.

"Sure to go with father, so is mother. They will drive over in the wagonette."

"I vote we go and chance it," exclaimed Harry.

He wanted to see Marian Spencer.

"If we do, the spies are sure to observe us," answered Jack.

"The course is a big place, and they may not see us."

"It isn't much that Peeping Tom and Knowall Dick miss."

"Never mind. I'll go if you will."

Jack was undecided for a moment.

"Let's toss up," he replied.

"All right."

"I'll spin a shilling in the air. If it comes down head we will go. If it is tail, we won't."

"Agreed. Where's the coin? Spin it," said Harry.

Jack flipped a shilling off his thumb, and it spun up in the air, falling with a clink on the gravel.

They both ran to the spot, and stooped to see what had turned up.

"Head, by Jingo!" Harry cried.

"We are in for it," said Jack, "and we declared we were going to be such very good boys."

"If we could. That was the reservation."

"Then it is our fate."

"Kismet, as the Turks say—decidedly Kismet," replied Harry.

"Then all I can say is, I hope most fervently that Kismet will not get us into trouble."

"Think of the fun we shall have: the races, the shows, the lunch with your people in the wagonette."

"Don't you mean to come back to tea at six?"

"Oh, bother tea! In for a lamb—in for a sheep," laughed Harry.

"I can see how it will be," sighed Jack.

"How?"

"We shall sleep in the strong-room to-night, and be birched by the doctor to-morrow."

At this moment Tuffins came towards them.

"I've done it!" he exclaimed.

"Done what, my gentle Tuffins?" asked Jack. "That remark conveys nothing to my mind. You are always doing something."

"That's what I'm engaged for."

"Certainly. When you are not eating bread and butter, you are cleaning knives and boots."

"I try to get as much into my daily life as possible," rejoined Tuffins.

"Into your interior, you mean. You ought to be called Stuffins."

"If I am fat, I can't help it. It's my misfortune, not my fault. I'd be ashamed to taunt a poor boy with his corpor—his corpor—corporation, don't you call it?"

"I'd call it corpulence, but no matter. What have you been doing, my Tuffins?" Jack inquired.

"Had the reward bill printed, and given it to the bill-poster to post all over the town."

"What reward bill, may I make bold enough to ask?"

"Miss Martha has offered £5 reward for information that will lead to the recovery of the watch, spoons, and forks she thought the boy with the hump stole; also to the conviction of the thief," said Tuffins.

"Are you going to the races, Tuffy?" inquired Jack.

"You bet," replied Tuffins. "I shall be there as soon as I have cleared away the dinner things. I ain't a schoolboy."

With a defiant snort Tuffins walked off.

"Cheeky brute," cried Jack. "Have you got a fives ball?"

"One in my pocket."

"Give it to me."

Jack took the fives ball, and threw it after the page.

It was an unerring aim, for it hit him under the small of the back with considerable force.

He clapped his hands behind him, and gave vent to an unearthly yell.

"Good shot!" cried Jack.

"Ball, please. Thank you," said Harry.

Tuffins, however, did not condescend to throw up the ball. He ran away as hard as he could, amidst jeers and laughter.

"Them schoolboys is suffin' cruel," he murmured.

Jack and Harry went to the cricket field for a little practice before dinner. They had made up their minds to have the dinner, if they did play truant afterwards.

It was a great pleasure to Harry to hear that his friend was in the eleven, although the same distinction had not been extended to him. The time soon passed.

Dinner was enjoyed. Mr. Dobby made a speech, the doctor's health was drunk, and Jack and Harry started for the race-course, which was not far off.

They got there at two o'clock, just after the first race had been run.

There was a fair sprinkling of carriages, men on horseback and spectators, for a small country meeting.

Booths, roundabouts, cocoanut shies, organs, niggers, and shows of various kinds mustered pretty strongly.

They went into a booth to get some lemonade, and there saw Peeping Tom and Knowall Dick.

"The two spies are here," whispered Jack.

"Let us go back," said Harry.

It was too late.

The spies of the school had seen them, and came forward with their usual malicious grin.

"Oh, won't you catch it if anybody sees you," cried Peeping Tom. "Mr. Dobby is coming to look out for the boys, and we are dodging him."

"Keep dark! We won't tell," said Knowall Dick.

Jack turned away.

"I don't want to speak to either of you," he exclaimed.

"Why not?" asked Tom.

"Because I know you to be a couple of rank humbugs! You are sent here for a special purpose."

"It is unkind to say that," replied Dick.

"How we get misjudged," Tom remarked.

Taking Harry's arm Jack walked away, leaving the spies chuckling at having seen them.

As he was passing the counter, Jack took up a bottle of ginger beer, which happened to be well up.

Cutting the string, he went behind Peeping Tom, and held the neck of the bottle near his ear.

Pop went the cork.

Feeling a sensation of a very painful nature, Tom turned sharply, only to get a flood of the ginger beer in his face.

It deluged him, spoiling his collar and shirt front, and going down his neck.

"That will teach you to laugh at me," cried Jack.

"Hang you, Spencer!" said Peeping Tom; "that is not the way I take my ginger beer."

"It is an external application, intended to promote civility. Tell that to Mr. Dobby."

"I'll tell him more than that."

"Do your worst, you little sneak."

"Perhaps you won't be so cocky to-morrow," replied Tom.

Jack paid for the bottle, regarding the spy with a contemptuous look, and quitted the booth with Harry.

They had not proceeded far before they met Mr. Spencer, who was walking towards the stables, where the horses were stalled before racing.

His face wore an expression of anxiety and annoyance.

"Hullo, my lads!" exclaimed the farmer. "I did not expect to see you here. How did you get away from the school?"

"We took French leave, father," replied Jack.

"That's bad; but your mother and Marian will be glad to see you."

"Where are they?"

"In the wagonette over to the right there. The lunch basket will be opened after this next race is run."

"Thank you; that's jolly. Have you got a horse entered?" asked Jack.

"Yes; my Stonecrop. It is in the Welter Handicap. Squire Rawlings runs his bay, Chancellor. I have backed mine for a lot of money, so has he his; and, dang it, I'm afraid I shall lose my money, which I can ill afford."

The look of annoyance on his countenance deepened.

"Why so, father?" inquired Jack.

"My stableman has just been to inform me that Tiny Tim, the jockey I had engaged, is taken very ill in the harness-room. If so, he cannot ride. I shall have to scratch my horse, and drop my money."

"Can't you get somebody else?"

"Impossible! I want a little chap because of the weight."

"Shall we come to the stable with you?"

"If you like. It's deuced annoying, 'pon my word it is. In a quarter of an hour the race begins. You will hear the saddling-bell in a minute or two, Won't Squire Rawlings have a chuckle! He never did like me," replied the farmer.

"He does not like anyone, sir," remarked Harry.

"And you may add, nobody likes him," said Mr. Spencer.

The stable was soon reached.

In the harness-room were our old friends, Turmuts and Tiny Tim.

The latter was rolling on the floor, pressing his hands to his chest as he writhed in pain.

"Are you very bad?" Mr. Spencer asked.

"Awful!" replied Tim. "I can't keep still with the pain."

"What have you been taking?"

"I only had a glass of Champagne, sir, on the course an hour ago."

"Who with?"

"Squire Rawlings, sir. I was passing his carriage, and he asked me to take a drop. Oh, dear, oh! what shall I do?"

Turmuts scratched his head, which was a way he'd got when an idea entered it.

"My opinion is, sir, as how the lad's been hocussed," he said.

"You are right," replied the farmer. "The Squire has given him something so that he shouldn't ride. It is plain as daylight."

"Ain't it a shame to nobble a boy in that way?"

"I wish I could prove it. He should pay dearly!"

"Shall I die, sir?" asked Tim.

"Not you. It will go off soon," said Mr. Spencer. "In the meantime, I suppose you can't get into the saddle?"

"I could'nt sit on the 'orse, sir."

"Then Stonecrop can't go to the post. I shall lose five hundred pounds when I expected to win five thousand."

"It is very provoking," said Jack.

"I call it maddening. Won't the Squire laugh in his sleeve! He thinks he's done it this time."

The saddling-bell now rang loudly.

Mr. Spencer bit his lips with vexation.

Suddenly an inspiration struck Harry's mind. He was just about Tim's size, and a good rider.

"Couldn't I take Tim's place, sir?" he exclaimed.

"You!" cried Mr. Spencer. "Stop a moment. Off with your jacket and waistcoat. Jump on those scales. We will see what you weigh."

Harry did as he was told. His weight was just what was required by the rules which governed the handicap.

"Bravo! you will do," said the farmer.

"Then I will ride for you. It will be a pleasure to me to beat my uncle. I owe him something."

"Take the things off you have on, and get into the colours. Here they are. Quick! No time to be lost."

Nor was there.

When Harry had the silk jacket and cap on, he looked every inch a jockey.

"Now, Harry," exclaimed Mr. Spencer, "listen to me: If you win this race, I'll make you a handsome present."

"I'll try my hardest," was the reply.

"The course is a mile and a half. Stonecrop can stay the distance; but I would not force the pace. Come with a rush at the finish, and don't spare whip or spur."

Harry nodded.

"I understand," he said.

Turmuts had gone to saddle the horse. Tim was lying on his back, very faint and groaning,

In a few minutes the horse was brought out, the farmer gave Harry a leg up, handed him his whip, and walked with him to the starting post.

The other horses, seven in number, were already there.

Getting into line, Harry looked at Squire Rawlings' bay, which was a well-built, powerful-looking animal.

His uncle's horse was the one he had to be afraid of.

The flag soon fell, and they were off to a good level start, the Squire's horse making the running.

Harry kept close behind him.

It was a novel experience to be rushing along like the wind. He heard the cheers of the crowd; but he looked to neither the right nor the left.

His eyes were fixed on the bay in front of him, which was leading by about a length, the others being behind.

As the winning post was being neared, the shouts grew louder, and Harry saw that he would have to make his effort.

Giving Stonecrop the whip, and digging his spurs into its sides, he got level with the bay.

A tremendous race now took place.

Neck and neck they sped on to the finish.

As they passed the judge's box, Stonecrop shot forward, and secured the verdict by half a length.

Squire Rawlings was defeated. Mr. Spencer's horse had won.

As Harry pulled up, the Squire, who had been waiting to hail his jockey as the victor, came to him.

His face was livid with rage, for he had lost heavily.

"What!" he cried. "You! Is it you?"

"Yes, uncle," replied Harry.

"What do you mean by it?" continued the Squire. "Confound you, I won't pay another shilling for you at school!"

"But——"

"No words. Henceforth you shall be a beggar, and get your living the best way you can. By heaven, you shall bitterly repent this!"

Harry felt his heart sink.

After all, he was entirely dependant upon his uncle.

He had not thought of this when he so readily consented to ride the horse.

"What did you do it for, you—you reptile?" continued Squire Rawlings.

He spoke in a low voice, leaning one hand on the horse's crupper.

The crowd, which had gathered round, thought he was talking on some matter of business.

Not for a moment did they think there was an altercation going on.

"I did it to oblige Mr. Spencer," replied Harry.

"It's an infamous lie!" cried the Squire. "You did it to spite me!"

"No, I did not, uncle."

"I'll ruin you for it! You haven't a friend in the world."

"Perhaps one will turn up."

"Do you defy me, you ingrate, when I have paid for your bringing up, and am now paying for your schooling? You shall suffer for this, you viper!"

Squire Rawlings flew into an ungovernable temper.

He completely lost all control over himself.

Grasping his nephew by the leg, he dragged him off the horse.

In spite of his struggles he struck him, and would have beaten him badly had not Mr. Spencer and Turmuts come on the scene.

"Oh, that's your game, Squire, is it?" cried the farmer.

Jack had gone to the wagonette by his father's instructions, and was helping his mother and sister to get the lunch ready.

Turmuts took hold of the horse and led it away.

Squire Rawlings turned furiously upon the farmer.

"He's my nephew," he replied, "and I can do what I like with him while I keep him."

"A fine keep yours is," laughed Mr. Spencer. "I should be ashamed to talk of it when all the money you've got is his by right."

"But not by law."

"Let him alone. You are only savage because he won the race for me, after you felt sure of it, through your meanness in hocussing my jockey."

The Squire savagely struck Harry on the side of the head.

"That blow shall cost you dearly," cried the farmer.

He dragged Harry away from him.

The crowd of people were rapidly growing impatient and indignant, for they now saw there was something wrong going on.

Loud murmurs arose.

"The Squire's beating the lad because he's won the race for me!" exclaimed Mr. Spencer. "You all know me, and you all know him."

Threatening gestures were made against the Squire.

The mob had surrounded him.

In vain he endeavoured to escape.

He was far from being a popular man.

Suddenly an ugly, vicious rush was made upon him, and he was borne to the ground.

When the police arrived on the scene, he was glad to be carried to his carriage, and driven home.

For fully a fortnight he was unable to leave his bed.

When he was being carried off the field, Mr. Spencer led Harry in the direction of the weighing-room.

"Shall I change my clothes?" asked Harry.

"You've got to weigh in first. What a chap that uncle of yours is, to be sure."

"He declared he would not pay for my schooling."

"If he won't, I will."

"I have no claim on you, sir."

"Yes, you have. You won me a good bit just now, and I'll see you are cared for; besides, you are a chum of my son, and I think a deal of Jack, I can tell you," replied the farmer.

This assurance was extremely gratifying to Harry Rawlings.

If deserted and thrown on the world's mercy by his unnatural uncle, he would not be friendless.

Mr. Spencer had promised to pay his school bill; he would have a home at his house during the holidays, and in a few years he would begin to earn his own living.

The weighing in was accomplished to the judge's satisfaction, and the race, with the stakes, awarded to Mr. Spencer.

When Harry had changed his clothes, he proceeded to the wagonette.

Mrs. Spencer, Marian, and Jack received

"THE SHOWMAN THREW UP HIS ARMS, WITH A WILD, UNEARTHLY YELL."

him very cordially, for they had seen him win the race.

The basket was unpacked, and lunch began without any further delay.

Marian pressed his hand affectionately.

"I like you more than ever for winning so cleverly," she whispered.

"I tried hard, because I knew you were looking," replied Harry.

The champagne corks popped merrily, and the pigeon pie, the chickens and the ham disappeared as if by magic.

All at once Jack saw two long hungry-looking faces at the end of the wagonette, watching the feast.

It was the spies of the school, who were hungry and thirsty.

"Give us some," exclaimed Peeping Tom.

"Just a snack," said Knowall Dick.

"Not a bit," replied Jack, slicing a fine ox tongue.

"Couldn't think of it," answered Harry.

The spies slunk away, with their faces full of venom and spite.

"Were those boys two of your schoolfellows?" asked Marian.

Jack replied in the affirmative.

"And you would not give them some lunch?" cried Marian.

"I should not have believed it of Jack," said Mrs. Spencer. "He used to be so very generous."

"Those two are the spies of the school," replied Jack. "You don't know them."

"They are always getting fellows into trouble," remarked Harry.

"We shall be reported for being here without leave, and catch it to-morrow," continued Jack. "No dirty trick comes amiss to their minds."

As he spoke a bag of flour, thrown by Peeping Tom, struck him on the side of his face.

It covered his hat and jacket, making him as white as a miller, and also bespattered Marian.

A somewhat similar piece of attention was paid Harry by Knowall Dick, only, in his case, it was a bag of red ochre.

Marian could not refrain from laughing.

As soon as the mischief was done the spies took to their heels, fearing they might be pursued.

The ochre spoilt the provisions, and the lunch was brought to a premature conclusion.

"What little torments," cried Marian. "Who would have thought it?"

"Did I not tell you so? It is just like one of their monkey tricks," answered Jack.

Another race now took place, and the boys left the carriage to see it better.

When it was over, they strolled about among the booths, had a ride in the steam roundabouts, and fired at glass bottles.

At length they came to a caravan, on each side of which was painted a most terrifying and alarming combination of snakes.

These were of all breeds, sizes, and colours.

On a canvas was written—

"Walk up, and see the Oriental Serpent Enchanter, from the Court of the Shah of Persia. The Boy Snake Charmer. Admission, Threepence each. Walk up! the Greatest Show on Earth. Patronised by all the Crowned Heads of Europe. Now's your time. Don't miss this. MacNab, sole registered Proprietor. See the Great Boa, Draco."

"This must be the show Pranks was telling us about," said Harry.

"If the boy with the hump is here," replied Jack, "the articles stolen from Miss Martha cannot be far off."

"I wish we could find them."

"So do I, by Jove! We should get the reward of five pounds Tuffins spoke about, and nothing would be said about our playing truant this afternoon."

"Shall we go in?"

"Certainly. I wouldn't miss it for the world," said Jack. "We may discover something. Walk up, and 'ank down your merry little sixpence."

"All right," answered Harry. "I'll treat you to threepennyworth of snake-charming."

CHAPTER XIII.

THE YOUNG SNAKE-CHARMER.

THE boys walked up the steps.

MacNab, a tall, stout, rough-looking, middle-aged man, was standing inside the open door. He did not appear to be in a very good temper; his face was red and flushed as if from drinking.

Business had been bad all day. The attractions of the racing had kept people away from the show.

When the racing was over, he hoped to do better; but, as yet, he had taken only one shilling, which, as he said, was not enough to pay for the oil in the lamps, with which the van was lighted inside.

There was standing room for twenty people at each performance, which would realise five shillings; and as the charming only took about a quarter of an hour, MacNab could do very well when busy.

"Ain't there no more coming up?" said the showman. "It don't pay me to play to two; however, I'll break the rule for once, just for the sake of something to do."

The boys passed in. Halfway across the caravan was a curtain. Going behind this, MacNab left them by themselves, the door being closed behind them.

In less than a minute the curtain was drawn on one side.

A small space was disclosed, lighted by three lamps, with powerful reflectors.

Charlie, the boy with the hump, was seen in a suit of spangles, something like the tight-fitting dress of a harlequin.

He was standing near several wooden boxes in which the snakes were kept, and MacNab was sitting on a stool with a flute in his hand.

"Bring on Draco," said he.

"I don't want to touch him," replied Charlie. "He's done nothing but hiss all day. Let me have some of the smaller ones."

"If you don't do as I tell you," cried MacNab, "you'll get a thrashing as sure as you've got a hump on your back."

"I'm afraid."

"Humbug! Haven't you handled him hundreds of times?"

"That's true; but—"

"Out with him, or I'll give these young gents back their money, and then I'll have a little performance of my own with you."

Charlie still hesitated.

"Are you going to bring him out or not? I want Draco, and I'm going to have him, or I'll know the reason why," cried MacNab, with drunken obstinacy.

He was determined to have his own way.

Charlie was evidently frightened, but he opened a large box in which, lying on a blanket, was a large boa-constrictor.

Directly it was at liberty to move, the snake crawled out of its nest, and began to hiss in an alarming manner.

Its forked tongue darted in and out.

The eyes scintillated and dilated.

Its length was about twelve feet, and owing to the thickness of its body, it was a very dangerous reptile to handle.

MacNab put his flute to his lips, and played a plaintive, soothing air in a creditable manner.

The snake coiled itself on its tail, and swayed its head to and fro.

Charlie sat down by its side, and passed his hands over its body.

For a minute or two, the boa allowed him to touch it, and drew its head over his shoulder.

The menacing gleam in its eyes, however, continued to increase.

Suddenly it withdrew to some distance, and then flung itself round the boy.

It was just as if a whip-lash had got round a post.

Charlie fell to the ground in the coils of the monster.

"Help! help!" he screamed.

Jack and Harry were almost paralysed with horror.

This could not be a part of the usual performance.

They had not come there to witness a ghastly tragedy.

MacNab threw down his flute.

He rushed on the snake, and seized it with both hands by the neck, just below the head.

With all his strength he tried to pull it off.

He might as well have tried to drag down a brick wall.

"Lay hold of his tail, you chaps!" he shouted, "but don't hurt the snake."

He seemed to think more of his serpent than of the boy.

The latter was panting for breath.

Draco tightened his coils.

"Oh, heaven, save me!" moaned Charlie; "he will break my back!"

The serpent was, in fact, pressing against his wooden hump, which his master made him wear for purposes of his own.

The hump, in its turn, was brought tightly against the boy's back, causing him acute pain.

At the same time his ribs were being crushed, and every moment were in danger of cracking.

Jack saw that the compression would increase rather than decrease, for MacNab was not strong enough to uncoil the reptile.

The death of the boy was only a question of time.

On the floor Jack saw an iron bar, which was used to fasten the door at night.

Stooping, he seized it without hesitating a moment.

Rushing to the spot where this fearful contest was going on, he raised it to strike.

MacNab divined Jack's intention.

"Mind the snake, you fool!" he cried.

"Look out!" replied Jack.

"Don't hurt my boa."

Jack's only reply was to deal the serpent a blow with the bar of iron, which had the effect of paralysing its action, and causing it to relax its terrible muscles, which were slowly crushing the young charmer to death.

The reptile fell to the ground, writhing in horrible contortions.

It was powerless for further evil.

Charlie began to breathe again in quick, short gasps.

The rage of MacNab knew no bounds.

"Hang you!" he exclaimed. "If you don't pay me for my loss, I'll tear you limb from limb."

"I had to save the boy's life," replied Jack.

"What's his life to you?"

"Simple humanity—"

"Stop your preaching. I want my money back!" shouted MacNab.

"You won't have any from me."

"Then I'll make you suffer, my pippin!"

He made a grab at Jack, but the latter neatly dodged him.

Seeing that the man meant mischief, Jack raised the iron bar, and dealt him a blow on the shoulder.

MacNab drew a knife.

There was murder in every gleam of his eye.

"Hold his arm, Harry!" cried Jack.

Harry got behind him just in time to prevent the knife being buried in his friend's heart.

Then Jack struck him again with the iron bar, this time on the head.

The burly ruffian sank senseless to the floor of the van, groaning heavily.

As he did so he knocked against a locker, the door of which flew open.

Some silver articles, flashing in the lamp-light, attracted Jack's attention.

He looked closely at them, and saw, to his great surprise, but unbounded delight, the doctor's crest and initial B on some spoons and forks.

Close by was Miss Martha's watch and chain.

"You took these from our school," said Jack to Charlie, who was now on his feet.

"He made me do it," replied Charlie.

"Who did?"

"The governor, as is lying over there. I'll tell you all about it if you will let me go with you."

"Where?"

"Anywhere for an hour or two, until he gets over his temper. He's been on the drink. When he is like that I have to run away. He misses me; so when I come back, he goes on a bit, but is quite friendly like after."

"Very well; you can come. How do you feel now?"

"Awful sore, master."

"What made the snake so savage?" asked Harry.

"It ain't been fed for a week. I can do what I like with him when he's full; but MacNab was sulky, and wouldn't go to the expense of a rabbit for him," replied Charlie.

"I shall confiscate these things," Jack observed.

He put the purloined articles into his pockets.

"It don't matter to me what you do with them, so long as you don't split upon me," answered Charlie.

"I ought to say where I found them."

"Then I shall be arrested, and I ain't done nothing to you," whimpered Charlie.

"It would be a charity to take you away from that ruffian."

"I don't want to go."

"And yet he ill-treats you?" said Jack in surprise.

"He ain't a bad sort when he's sober," cried Charlie. "I like him, and I like the life well enough. I ain't got anywhere to go."

MacNab moved uneasily.

It looked as if he were coming to his senses.

"We must get out of this," exclaimed Jack. "Come on."

He and Harry got out of the caravan as quickly as they could.

Charlie was close at their heels.

He had two objects in sticking close to them for a time.

The first was, he wanted to get away from MacNab until his fit of passion had cooled down.

Secondly, he wished to get an assurance from the boys that they would not inform the police of his theft at the school.

It was growing late now.

The last race was about to take place. Many people had already left the course, others were going.

It was scarcely worth while for Jack and Harry to return to Mrs. Spencer and Marian in the wagonette.

Instead of doing so, they went into a refreshment booth, and sit down at a table to have a cup of tea and some bread and butter.

Charlie was invited to participate. He had hastily thrown a long coat over his spangled dress as he left the van, so that he did not attract any attention.

He looked up anxiously at Jack, in whose hands he evidently considered his fate was lying.

"You won't give me away to the police, master?" he exclaimed. "If you mean to, you might tell a chap, and give him time to bolt."

"How did you manage to get away with the things?" asked Jack.

"That's my secret."

"I'm bothered if I can make it out. They say at the school that they searched you all over."

"So they did."

"Well, how on earth did you do it?" Jack continued.

"If I tell you," replied Charlie, "will you promise not to hand me over to the police? I am only a poor boy, but—"

"It seems to me that you are a young rogue!" interrupted Jack. "Anyhow, I don't want to be hard on you. Tell me your secret, and I will return the plate and the watch without compromising you."

Charlie held up his head and smiled.

"That is what I call generous," he cried. "I think you are a proper sort of chap. If ever I can do anything for you, I will, though we shall move on with the van to-morrow, and perhaps we shall never meet again."

Then he told them about his false hump.

"That is the best thing I ever heard of," said Jack.

"Are you really not a hunchback?" Harry asked.

"No more than you are," was the reply.

"How long have you worn it?"

"It's three years now since MacNab hit on the idea. It was what he called a stroke of genius," said Charlie, "and he's often laughed since, and said he would take out a patent for it. Keep it dark, won't you?"

"My word is as good as my bond," answered Jack.

"And t'other one?"

He jerked his thumb towards Harry.

"Oh, he will do as I do."

"That's enough, gents; I'm satisfied. Thank you for me. I'll go now and hang around the van. That clip on the head you gave the guv'nor will want seeing to."

"Stay a moment," exclaimed Jack. "How long have you been with him?"

"Ever since I was four or five years old."

"How did he get you?"

"Stole me one day when I was out in the fields playing. I lived in a fine house then. Servants waited on me," said Charlie.

"What else can you remember?"

"Not much. Mother must have been dead; but I can recollect father, because he used to beat me. I should know him again if ever I saw him."

"What's your name?"

"Charlie is all I can recall. It was Charlie then, and has been ever since."

"Perhaps your father paid MacNab to take you away?" suggested Jack.

"He might have done so, for he was awful severe on me, but MacNab always says he stole me. I've got a fixed idea though, somehow, that he and my father will meet again some day.

"I wish you luck," he added. "If I had been a schoolboy like you, with kind friends to look after me, I might have been different."

All at once a large cobra crawled out of his coat-pocket on to the table.

Jack and Harry shrank back with horror.

Laughing, Charlie took hold of it, fondled it, and put it back again.

"Don't be afraid," he exclaimed; "its poison fangs are drawn. It must have crawled out of its box, and got into my coat. I've generally got one about me somewhere. Good-bye."

Nodding cheerfully, he took his departure. The others were not long in imitating his example.

The racecourse was now deserted; but in the meadow, where the swings, roundabouts, and shows were, a number of people had congregated.

Naphtha lights flared in all directions; music mingled with hoarse shouts, the beating of drums, loud laughter, and rough voices.

The fun of the fair had now commenced in earnest.

They carefully avoided that part of the field where MacNab's caravan was, as they had no wish to renew their acquaintance with that gentleman.

He might pay them attention of an unpleasant nature if they fell into his clutches.

They stopped at a large barrow or stand, with a target at one end, at which one could shoot for nuts.

The guns were loaded with darts.

"Will you have a shot, Hal?" asked Jack.

"I don't mind," replied Harry.

The man in attendance handed each of them a gun, and at this moment Jack saw the two spies going by arm-in-arm.

They were laughing and talking, and appeared to be in high spirits, as if they were enjoying themselves.

"I say," cried Jack, with a mischievous twinkle in his eye, "there are our friends. Shall we pot them?"

"Oh, yes; do."

"Very well. You take Dick. I will concentrate my skill on Master Tommy."

They turned half round, and aimed at the spies' backs.

It was more of a snap shot than anything else, as they had no time to take a careful aim; but they hit the mark.

The darts struck both the spies under the jacket.

Uttering fearful yells, Peeping Tom and Knowall Dick clapped their hands behind them, and made a quick rightabout-face turn.

Jack and Harry broke into an uproarious shout of laughter.

So did the surrounding people, for they divined the joke and appreciated it.

The spies noticed their enemies, and turned livid with rage.

"It's a shame!" said Peeping Tom; "but I'll pay you out for this."

"So will I," cried Knowall Dick. "Oh, you brutes!"

They extracted the darts, and rubbed themselves vigorously.

"How do you like it?" asked Jack.

"Not at all. How would you?" replied Tom. "I suppose we've got feeling as well as you?"

"Did it sting?"

"You wait till you've interviewed the doctor to-morrow, and I will ask you the same question."

"Go home," laughed Harry. "If you aren't off, I'll fire again."

"Oh, don't flatter yourself," said Knowall Dick. "We do not want to stay; your society is not so very fascinating."

"I'd rather make friends of a sweep," remarked Peeping Tom.

"Certainly. Just what I thought. That's about your mark. Sheer off," exclaimed Jack.

With indignant glances, the spies walked away amid the jeers of the spectators.

"Let us follow them without being seen, and have another lark with them," said Harry.

"I'm agreeable," replied Jack.

They gave the man sixpence as compensation for his darts, and pushing through the crowd, managed to keep Tom and Dick in sight.

"Do you think we shall get into any row when we get back to school?" asked Harry.

"Not now I have recovered the spoons and things," replied Jack.

"What will you say?

"That we acted on a clue given us by Pranks. I won't claim the reward, and that will be in our favour, as the doctor likes money."

"Then we shall beat the spies, after all?"

"Of course we shall; and it's two to one we get off scot-free," said Jack.

Harry rubbed his hands with glee at this encouraging prospect.

He had felt rather low spirited at the chance of being punished. It had damped the enjoyment of the races.

The spies halted in front of a canvas booth, before which was a large poster, informing the public that a dog named Towser would worry twenty-five rats in two minutes and a half by the watch. The admission was six pence.

After considering the matter for a time they decided to go in.

This show was repeated every half-hour, and as one lot of spectators had just gone out, there were only half-a-dozen inside, including the spies.

Jack and Harry did not hesitate to go in.

In the centre of the booth was a square wooden pit, about four feet high, and within this were the rats.

When the booth was full of spectators, crowding round the pit, the dog was put in, and the work of slaughter began.

Peeping Tom and Knowall Dick were leaning over the sides, watching the rats dart about, and make fruitless efforts to climb up.

They would get up a foot or more, and then fall back.

So intent were Tom and Dick on watching the long-tailed rodents, that they were totally oblivious of the presence of their foes.

"Don't they look happy, as if they were having a day out, and were thoroughly enjoying themselves," whispered Harry.

"Wasn't there a Roman emperor who used to give men to lions in the arena on public fêtes and holidays?" asked Jack.

"Several. It was a custom. For centuries, men were butchered to make a Roman holiday."

"Why shouldn't we give the sneaks to the rats?"

"Do you mean it?"

"Most decidedly."

"Ha, ha!" laughed Harry. "I'll manipulate Dick. He's my pet aversion."

"So is Tommy mine."

"Give him a good hoist."

"I will."

They crept up behind the unsuspecting spies, who had leant their arms on the edge of the pit, and were craning their necks.

No suspicion of evil crossed their minds.

Jack thought of the flour and red ochre, which had spoilt the lunch in the wagonette.

He panted for retaliation.

Revenge was within his grasp, and he meant to have it.

Peeping Tom and Knowall Dick were seized simultaneously by the left leg and the nape of the neck.

Up they went.

There was no means of escape from the retribution which had come upon them.

After they had gone up they went down. Both were very neatly pitched into the pit.

They fell on the sawdust upon their hands and knees.

The rats squealed, running over them, and, in their blind terror, biting them, before they could get up.

Never were a body of rats so scared before.

It was as if two big dogs had been dropped amongst them, and, by instinct, they began to defend themselves before they were attacked.

As quickly as possible the spies clambered to their feet, with a sensation of horror creeping over their bodies.

It was long before they forgot that night.

Their consternation changed to anger when they saw the faces of Jack and Harry looking at them.

Each wore a broad grin.

The rats kept on making charges at their legs, climbing up a little way, giving a bite, and slipping down again.

Peeping Tom and Knowall Dick made a plunge at the side of the pit, hauled themselves up, and got out.

"I'll have the law of you for this," cried Tom.

"As for me," said Dick, "I'll ask the judge to give you three years."

"I've got two ears; that's quite enough for me," laughed Jack.

"So has every ass!" retorted Tom.

"Ah, but mine are not long enough for a donkey like you!" said Jack.

"I'm bitten all over," continued Peeping Tom. "But I'll be even with you yet."

"You'd best let me alone."

"Never!"

"Up to the present I reckon I've scored oftener than you. Go home and get to bed."

"When it suits us," replied Knowall Dick.

Taking Harry's arm, Jack left the tent, satisfied with this last piece of revenge on the spies of the school.

He determined to leave at once.

By doing so, he would cut the ground from under their feet, see the doctor first, make his peace with him, restore the stolen property, and be happy.

He had not miscalculated at all.

When they reached the school, Tuffins let them in at the back door.

"Oh, my!" he exclaimed; "won't you catch it!"

"Shall we? Perhaps not," answered Jack.

"I was home before tea-time, and when you two didn't answer to your names at roll-call, the doctor told Mr. Dobby to send you to him as soon as you made your appearance."

"Where is the learned man?"

"In his study, a-going over the accounts with Miss Martha. I wouldn't be in your shoes for somethin'," continued Tuffins.

"Come on, Harry," cried Jack, "we will go and see the chief. As for this ignoramus, he can keep on grinning like any other clown."

Boldly they repaired to the doctor's study. Knocking at the door, they were told to enter.

The head-master and his sister were seated before a bright fire, enjoying a glass of wine.

"Ha, you boys!" exclaimed Doctor Birchoften, "where have you been?"

"To the races, sir," replied Jack.

"How dare you disobey my commands?"

"We had an object in going, sir. From information I received from Pranks, I thought I could recover your lost property."

"Have you done so?" asked the doctor. "If you have, as this is my birthday, I may be induced to take a lenient view of your offence."

"If I could only have my watch back, I would forgive them anything," cried Miss Martha. "'Tis an heirloom."

Jack's only reply to this was to take the articles he had recovered from his pocket, and place them on the table.

"Now, I suppose, you want the reward?" exclaimed Miss Martha, with an eye to business.

"No, ma'am."

"You can't have the five pounds reward, and be let off, too."

"I'll waive that, ma'am. I'm sure Rawlings and I are only too glad to have got you back your property."

"How did you do it, Spencer?"

"All I am at liberty to say is, that I got it through the boy with the hump."

"Ah, the little rascal!" said Miss Martha. "I knew he was the thief, but how he concealed it, I am unable to guess."

The doctor waved his hand.

"You can go," he exclaimed. "I forgive you for playing truant, but don't do it again."

"Shall we have to come and see you privately to-morrow morning, sir?"

"Not this time."

"Good-night, sir; thank you. Many happy returns of the day," said Jack.

"The same from me, sir," chimed in Harry.

This touched the doctor so, that he gave each of them a glass of his best port.

"What do boys want with wine?" they

heard Miss Martha ask, as they quitted the apartment.

"My dear," answered the doctor, "this is a high day or holiday—an occasion that only comes once a year."

About half-an-hour after Jack and Harry had joined their companions in the school-room, where "prep." was going on for the morrow. The spies of the school arrived in a somewhat dilapidated condition.

Mr. Dobby was in a room set apart for the accommodation of the assistant masters, and known as the masters' room.

There was a speaking-tube connecting it with the doctor's study.

Through this tube Mr. Dobby had been duly informed of Jack and Harry's return, and their pardon.

Peeping Tom and Knowall Dick did not meet with such a gracious reception as they had expected.

They entered the room, thinking to be encouraged, thanked and rewarded.

But they had made a mistake.

"We have come back, sir," said Peeping Tom, "after having a hard time of it."

"Awful hard!" added Knowall Dick.

"But we've done our duty," Tom added, with a self-satisfied air.

"I don't mind suffering in a good cause," said Dick.

Mr. Dobby looked at them with indifference.

"You should have been back long ago—hours ago," he exclaimed.

"Couldn't possibly be done, sir," rejoined Tom.

"On no account whatever," said Dick.

"Your appearance is very dirty and disreputable," remarked Mr. Dobby.

"All on account of Spencer and Rawlings, sir. We tracked them from place to place. They saw us, and we were subjected to insult and injury. We—"

Mr. Dobby held up his hand.

The garrulity of Peeping Tom was cut short in a premature manner.

"Go into the schoolroom," he interrupted. "I don't want to hear anything about it."

"What!" ejaculated Tom.

"Oh, dear!" gasped Dick.

"Spencer and Rawlings have been excused by the doctor. I have nothing more to say," replied Mr Dobby.

The two spies looked the image of despair.

Slinking into the passage, they stood and stared blankly at one another.

This reception was like a death-blow to them.

"I wouldn't have believed it," Tom said. "I'd just as soon have believed you if you had told me you had seen a crocodile sitting up shelling peas."

"They've got the best of us," answered Dick. "It makes me feel like—like—"

He paused for a simile.

It would not come to him, however.

"Like what? Speak out!" cried Peeping Tom.

"Like—like a fellow who's had an unexpected cold shower-bath in the middle of winter," returned Knowall Dick, desperately.

"I don't want any supper." said Tom.

"Nor I."

"Let us go to bed, or we shall get chaffed to death in the schoolroom."

"Good."

They went to Tuffins, who gave them a bedroom candle, and then glided up the stairs, ghost-like, to their dormitory.

The spies were allowed to sleep in a little room, where they were not in the track of the big boys.

They soon went to sleep, and were not interrupted during the night, which, all things being considered, was, perhaps, more than they deserved.

CHAPTER XIV.

A STRANGE MEETING.

WHEN Charlie, the young snake-charmer, went back to his master's caravan, he saw MacNab sitting on the steps, with a strip of calico bound round his forehead.

The outside lamp had been extinguished—all was dark.

It was a decided case of no show.

"I've come back, governor," said Charlie. MacNab looked up.

"It's lucky for yer ye have," he replied. "I'd have scoured the world for you, if you hadn't."

"I always do come back, don't I, after I've given you time to get over your temper?"

"You know you've got to!"

"Are you much hurt?" asked Charlie.

"What's that got to do with you? Do you suppose a chap can be floored with a bar of iron, and not feel it?"

"Was it my fault?"

"Yes; it's ever your fault! If it wasn't for opening the show, and some business I want you to do to-night, I'd knock the life out of you!"

"WORKING LIKE TROOPERS, THEY SOON MADE A LARGE SPACE."

"It's a good time now. We shall rake in the money," said Charlie.

"Fancy losing that fine boa," added MacNab; "and more than that, them boys stole the things out of the locker."

"Why didn't you feed the snakes?"

"Mind your business! I feed you, don't I?"

"The boy only saved me from being crushed to death!"

"Good thing if you had been! I don't know what use you are to me, or anybody else!" snapped MacNab.

"What do you keep me for?"

"Heaven only knows! I don't. Get up and light that lamp. I'll beat the gong. We'll have a show, and I will tell you afterwards of what I've got for you."

Charlie entered the van, took off his coat, set the flaring lamp going, and soon plenty of people came up.

While Charlie went inside the van to get ready for the performance, MacNab rattled away at the gong, as if he wanted to get rid of some of his superfluous energy.

It was what he called letting the steam off.

When he had attracted a crowd, he began his patter.

"Here, zar," he shouted, "young Nouweddin, the only original and unique boy snake-charmer, formerly with the Shah of Pershaw, now with me!"

Bang! Bang!

"Walk up! The price of admission is only thruppence! We've performed before all the crowned heads in Yourope and the Heast!"

Bang! Bang! Bang!

"Don't be shy or afraid. The serpents is perfectly under control, and there ain't no sort of danger. Walk up! Children half-price. No charge for babies."

Bang! Bang! Bang! Bang!

"It's the chance of a lifetime. The free list is entirely suspended. This way for the young Nouweddin, the only boy snake-charmer in the world. Walk up! Walk up!"

So strong were his lungs, and so persuasive was his eloquence, that a crowd soon entered the caravan.

Charlie fearlessly handled the snakes. MacNab played plaintive melodies on his flute, and everything went well.

At ten o'clock the people began to go home. It was impossible to get an audience after that time, so MacMab closed the show.

Some bread and cheese and beer provided him and Charlie with a substantial supper; and while they were eating it, MacNab told the boy what he wanted him to do that night.

"Did you notice particularly," he asked, "a large white painted house we passed on the road yesterday?"

"Was it lying a little back?" queried Charlie.

"Yes."

"You halted the van and went in to beg a drink of water?"

"Right; but that was only a pretence," said MacNab. "I wanted to see what kind of a place it was."

"What did you make of it?"

"I found out by putting a few simple questions to the servant gal, that it belongs to Squire Rawlings, him who ran a horse in one of the races to-day, and got illused by the crowd."

"I didn't see that bit," remarked Charlie.

"That's no matter. You've got to go to the Hall to-night."

Charlie's countenance fell.

"Don't ask me to do that," he replied.

"What do you mean?" cried MacNab, fiercely.

"Don't I work hard enough for you as it is?"

"No; we don't draw in enough coin," said MacNab. "I want to take our show over to the Continong, and to do this I must have money. If you refuse, I'll thrash you till you are nearly dead."

"It's very hard, and I can't do it."

"Don't I feed you, and keep you, and clothe you? Ain't I a second father to you?"

MacNab asked these questions with an air of injured innocence.

"I won't say you are bad when you're sober," returned Charlie; "but when you are drunk, you're a demon."

MacNab put his hands to his sides, and laughed loudly.

"Bravo! that's me to a dot, my boy," he exclaimed. "Rub me the right way, and I'm soft as silk. Rub me wrong, and I'm a hedgehog, all spikes and bristles."

Very bitter were Charlie's feelings, but he did not dare to disobey his hard taskmaster.

The last words of MacNab were—

"If you're not back soon, I shall come after you."

*   *   *   *

It was a dark, cold night.

All the lights were out in the Squire's mansion, except in a bedroom, where the owner was sleeping, or rather, trying to sleep, for he had been a good deal bruised by the rough usage he had received from the mob on the racecourse that day.

He was suffering considerable pain; in vain he sought solace in reading. Book after book was discarded, and he gave himself up to bitter reflection.

His hatred for his nephew, Harry, had been intensified by recent events, and he vowed again to have revenge.

He would not be satisfied until Harry was made an outcast and a homeless wanderer.

Charlie having effected an entrance, the light shining under the Squire's door attracted him.

He crept forward and pushed open the door.

The Squire was wide awake. He saw the boy enter, and wondered what he was about.

He always kept a loaded revolver under his pillow, and no sooner did the conviction flash across his mind that something was wrong, than he drew it from its hiding-place.

Springing out of bed, he placed his back against the door to prevent escape, at the same time presenting the pistol at Charlie.

"Hullo, you!" cried the Squire; "what are you doing here at this time of night?"

Charlie turned pale under his dark skin, and trembled.

His eyes, however, were firmly fixed upon Mr. Rawlings, as if he had seen his face somewhere before.

Evidently his mind was going back to the dim and misty past, and he was trying to recall something.

"Oh, sir," he replied, "please let me go."

"You misshapen hound! make a full confession; it is your only chance," said the Squire. "Hesitate, and it will be the worse for you."

"Charlie began by saying that he was stolen from a good home when quite young, adding that his captor, MacNab, had made him work at snake-charming, concluding by taking off his ingeniously contrived hump, and stating that his face, hands, and neck were made dusky by the old rascal with the stain of walnut juice.

This narrative very much surprised Mr. Rawlings.

"It is a strange story!" he exclaimed.

"It is every word of it true, sir," replied Charlie.

"But why do you stare at me so fixedly?" continued the Squire, with a strange, wild look in his eyes.

"I cannot help it," replied Charlie. "You are like what I remember of my father."

"Your father!" cried Mr. Rawlings, who became greatly agitated.

"Yes, sir; his face has never been absent from my mind, sleeping or waking."

"There is something in this. I had a son who was stolen from me. This is not a mere accidental meeting. The finger of Fate is in it; but the question can soon be settled. A servant, who had been an old sailor, tattooed a cross, an anchor, and a heart on my boy's left arm, and underneath the letters C. R. for Charles Rawlings.

Quickly, Charlie turned up his sleeve.

There, on the arm, were the very marks in question.

Faith, Hope, Charity, and the initials.

There could not exist the shadow of a doubt that the father had found his son.

Mr. Rawlings was not a man to give way to emotion; but he was visibly affected.

He had mourned his boy as one dead, and to see him now was a genuine surprise.

Tears of expectation trembled in Charlie's eyes. Would his father acknowledge him?

Or would he hand him over to the law to be rigorously dealt with, repudiated, and disowned?

All doubts were quickly dispelled.

Mr. Rawlings took him by the hand and regarded him as kindly as his stern hard face would allow.

"My boy," he said, "for your mother's sake, I will acknowledge you. Say not a word about your past to anyone. Be affectionate and faithful to me, and you shall have your reward. There has been a void in my heart. You have come to fill it."

Charlie could only cry.

Such a sudden change in the condition of his life he had not dreamed of. To have a father, a rich and comfortable home, instead of being like a strolling gipsy, liable to be beaten brutally at any moment, was more like a fantastic fancy than reality.

The Squire put on a dressing gown, stirred up the fire, and asked Charlie a variety of questions about his life with MacNab.

Gradually he recovered himself. Neither had any inclination to sleep.

It was a rough night. A storm of wind and rain had come on. The heavy drops splashed against the windows; the wind raged and howled under the eaves.

Charlie enjoyed the comfort of the handsomely furnished bedchamber, contrasting it with the squalid poverty of the caravan.

He was in luck at last; his miserable way of living was over; fortune smiled on him.

"You shall be a gentleman," exclaimed the Squire. "I will engage a tutor to teach you."

"Should MacNab come, you will not let him take me away?" said the boy, with a shudder.

"I will soon settle his business. The fellow has no right to you. Hark! what was that noise at the window?" asked Mr. Rawlings.

They both listened intently.

"Was it only the wind, father?" asked Charlie, looking up startled.

"No; it sounded as if someone without were trying to open it."

As he spoke, the Squire seized his pistol, which he had placed on a table.

He was not a moment too soon.

The window was suddenly pushed up, and a man's face appeared, framed, as it were, in the casement.

Charlie, with a sickening feeling at his heart, recognised the features.

It was his persecutor, MacNab.

The showman had become alarmed at Charlie's prolonged absence, not that he cared for the boy, or what became of him in the least. It was his own ease and safety he consulted.

If Charlie had been captured, the chances were he would tell about the one who had sent him, and the police would come to the van.

It was best, he thought, to see if anything had happened; so in spite of the wind and rain, he started for the Hall.

A ladder, used by some workmen, who were repairing the roof, stood against the wall.

He climbed up, and looking under the blind, saw Mr. Rawlings and Charlie seated together.

There was clearly some mystery, which, with his usual recklessness, he determined to solve. Boldly throwing up the window, he revealed himself as we have described.

"MacNab!" cried Charlie, starting up in horror.

"Ha!" said the Squire, "is that the rascal? He has rushed on his fate! His blood be on his own head!"

Raising the revolver, he fired point blank at the showman.

The latter threw up his arms, and with a wild unearthly yell, disappeared in the darkness.

He had fallen mortally wounded from the top of the ladder to the bottom.

The report had alarmed the house, and when the servants went into the garden, they discovered MacNab, dead.

The bullet had pierced the heart.

As soon as it was light the police were communicated with, and took the body away to await an inquest, at which the Squire was acquitted of blame, for an open knife was found in MacNab's hand, leading the police to think he intended murder.

To account for Charlie's presence in the house, he stated that the boy had come to warn him that an attempt would be made to rob him during the night.

In return for this he had determined to adopt him as his son.

It did not take long for the stain to wear off Charlie's skin, and when he was well-dressed, no one would have recognised him as Nouweddin, the young snake-charmer.

One day, in conversation, Mr. Rawlings said—

"When my brother died, and I came into this property, he had a son named Harry, who is at a school near here. I dislike that boy, who has always been a thorn in my side."

"Why so?" asked Charlie.

"I have my reasons. I have heard it said that a will was made in his favour, but that will has never been found."

"If it were to be—"

"We should be kicked out, and have nothing," hastily interrupted the Squire. "I wish Harry were dead. Though he is your cousin, if you should meet him, have nothing to say to him."

"Not I."

"Remember he is my enemy, and yours, too. Doctor Birchoften's school is not far from here. You may meet."

"Who pays for him?"

"I have been fool enough to do so, but I shall not any longer. He shall be what you were, a waif and a stray."

Charlie had the same vicious temper as his father.

"I'd make him bitterly repent it if he interfered with me!" he exclaimed.

"Hush! do nothing rash. Perhaps, after all, there is nothing to fear from him."

"He shall never take my place in this beautiful house," cried Charlie. "I would lay him dead at my feet first!"

"Again, I say, be not hasty. Keep him at a distance," replied the Squire.

"I'm no fool, father, and I know when I am well off. No interlopers for me."

"I don't know how it is," mused Mr. Rawlings, "but I dread that boy somehow. He has worked me harm already, and I fear he is destined to bring trouble on me."

"I will rid you of him, father."

Before the Squire had time to make any reply, a servant brought him a letter.

It was from Farmer Spencer, and ran as follows—

"DEAR SIR,—Hearing casually that you have written to Doctor Birchoften to the effect that you will not be responsible for the school money of your brother's son, Harry Rawlings, after this quarter, I beg respectfully to inform you, that I will undertake to support him. In future you need not trouble yourself about the poor lad, who, I must say, deserves better treatment at your hands.

"I have the honour to be, Sir,
"Your obedient servant,
"JOHN SPENCER."

The Squire stamped his foot on the floor with rage. He tossed the letter to Charlie.

"Thwarted again," he cried, "Read that."

Charlie did so, with a vexed expression on his face.

"He has friends," he remarked. "You won't get rid of him so easily as you think."

"No. Perdition to this man Spencer. If he had not a lease, I would turn him out of his farm. It expires soon, though. Let him beware!"

"If Harry were to fall into the river, and be found drowned, would it not be an accident?"

The Squire looked curiously at his son.

"What do you mean?" he asked.

"Oh, nothing," carelessly replied Charlie.

"But—"

"Such things have occurred, father. By the way, do you happen to have a photo of him?"

Mr. Rawlings went to an album, and took out a carte of Harry.

"There is your cousin," he replied.

Charlie started.

"That! Why, I know him. We met on the racecourse," he cried.

He walked towards the door, with his hands in his pockets, whistling.

"Where are you going?" inquired the Squire.

"Out for a walk," was the reply.

"Don't get into any mischief."

"Not me."

Charlie put on his hat, and walked into the garden.

In a few minutes he was crossing the park in the direction of Doctor Birchoften's school.

CHAPTER XV.

A DAY'S FISHING—THE OLD MILL—IN DANGER.

SPRING had given place to the beautiful summer time, which, to schoolboys, is the most enjoyable part of the year.

Twelve o'clock struck, and the boys bounded out of school full of life and animal spirits—some to bathe, some to play cricket, others to go into the hayfield, and roll upon the heaps.

The two spies, about five minutes after school was out, met in their favourite place at the corner of the wood-shed.

"Such a lark!" exclaimed Knowall Dick. "Miss Martha has been making lemon cheese cakes, and the cook has just taken a tray with two dozen out of the oven."

"How do you know?" asked Peeping Tom.

"I looked through the kitchen window, which is open. More than that."

"What else?"

"Miss Martha and cook have gone into the housekeeper's room," continued Knowall Dick. "If you like cheese cakes—"

"Don't I just—that's all."

"Now's your chance, then. Come on."

"All right. Six for each of us, eh?" said Peeping Tom.

"That's about my share. We will bring them into the wood-shed and eat them. No one will see us there, and the crumbs won't tell tales."

"Who shall we say did it if we're asked?"

"Put it on Kennedy. No one believes what he says. Everybody makes him a scapegoat."

"That will do, first class. Hurry up, or we may be too late," said Peeping Tom.

He began to smack his lips at the anticipated delicacy.

They hastened to the kitchen window, which was on a level with the yard. Two legs of mutton and a quantity of shelled peas were on the table, to be cooked for dinner. The cheese cakes were on the dresser.

Miss Martha and the cook were still in the housekeeper's room, going through some accounts, for Miss Martha checked the bills every week.

She was dreadfully afraid of being cheated by the butcher or the baker.

"We will put them in our caps," Tom suggested.

"That's business," answered Dick.

Getting in at the window they soon helped themselves, and retreated to the wood-shed.

For the next ten minutes they were busily engaged in eating the succulent morsels which Miss Martha had prepared for the doctor's special delectation and her own.

As it happened, Tuffins' evil star led him into the kitchen for a glass of water.

He had a sweet tooth.

The savoury smell of the tarts assailed his nose, and, following it, he was led to the dresser.

"Ah, cheese cakes all 'ot!" he remarked. "This is crummy. Cooky won't miss one."

Better would it have been for Tuffins had he restrained his dishonest promptings.

The fat page opened his capacious mouth. He raised the tart to his lips, and took a bite. He tasted, and breathed a sigh of satisfaction.

The lemon flavour tickled his palate, and he finished the cheese cake.

"That goes down good," he muttered. "If I have another there will be ten left. I'll chance it."

The wretched youth laid his purloining hand on a second cake, but, alas! for human aspirations.

He was not permitted to enjoy it.

At that critical moment Miss Martha, followed by the cook, returned to the kitchen.

She saw Tuffins at his nefarious work, and made a rush for him.

There was an avenging gleam in her eyes.

The miserable delinquent found himself seized by his hair, and was pulled round into the light.

The cake dropped from his hand.

"What!" cried Miss Martha, "fourteen cheese cakes gone at one fell swoop?"

"No, no!" replied Tuffins; "I've only taken two, and one's on the floor, ma'am."

"Oh, you awful gorger! No wonder you're so fat! Fourteen tarts! It's horrible! Incredible!"

"Only two, as I'm alive."

"Don't tell me any falsehoods!" screamed Miss Martha. "Oh, you gormandiser! You—you cormorant!"

"I ain't."

"Where do you put them? It's my belief you would eat sardines by the box, and tarts by the bushel. To think I could not leave them for a minute!"

"I didn't take 'em, ma'am, I—"

"Hush! You shall suffer for this."

In a vigorous manner she proceeded to box his ears, and, as usual, he only managed to escape from her clutches by leaving a handful of hair behind him.

He ran to the window and sprang out.

"Ain't you a fair caution?" he said.

"I discharge you," Miss Martha yelled. "Miscreant, go!"

This was nothing new to Tuffins.

As a rule, he was discharged twice a week, but he did not go.

"I'd like to pay for your funeral," cried Tuffins.

"If I can get hold of you, I'll—I'll scalp you," screamed Miss Martha. "Fourteen tarts! Awful!"

"Keep on," cried Tuffins; "it's quite a treat to hear you."

"Base creature, begone!"

She took up a basin and threw it at him.

It went through the window at the top, breaking the glass.

There was a dreadful crash.

"Good shot," said Tuffins, mockingly.

Miss Martha sank hysterically into a chair.

"Don't take on so, ma'am," said the cook, soothingly.

"He'll be the death of me," wailed Miss Martha. "Fourteen tarts! Did anybody ever hear of such a thing?"

"He's a bad, wicious boy," replied cook. "I should like to limb him!"

Tuffins did not stay to hear any more. He thought it quite time to make himself scarce until Miss Martha cooled down.

Walking across the yard he met Peeping Tom and Knowall Dick, who, having finished their repast, had emerged from the wood-shed on hearing the crash of falling glass.

Tuffins was rubbing his crown; his face was red from the ear-boxing, and he was much upset.

The spies were wiping their lips.

"What's up, Tuffy?" asked Tom. "Anything wrong?"

"I'm tired of my life in this crib, and that's a fact," replied Tuffins, in a lachrymose tone.

"Somebody trod on your worst corn?"

"This is a wale of tears. The only consolation I've got is that so long as I keep this place, I shall never want my hair cut."

"Why?"

"Because that old dragon, Miss Martha, keeps on a-pullin' of it out."

"Have you offended her?" queried Dick.

"She's given me the sack as usual; but I shall stay on to spite her."

"But what for? Can't you tell a chap?"

"Just for cribbing a couple of cheese cakes, and she vowed I'd eaten fourteen."

"That's good goods."

"I didn't do it," cried Tuffins. "As I'm a living sinner, it wasn't me. She's gone wrong, I tell you."

Peeping Tom looked significantly at Knowall Dick.

The precious pair could scarcely refrain from bursting into a roar of laughter.

It was exquisitely amusing to them to think that the page should be accused of doing what they had done.

"Oh, Tuffy," exclaimed Peeping Tom, "if you go on like this you'll burst, and then what will become of you?"

"He'll come to a bad end," said Knowall Dick, shaking his head.

Tuffins stamped his foot, and got redder in the face than ever.

"Hang it all," he cried, "I never ate them tarts! Do you want to madden me?

If you do, keep on. I'm a wictim, I tell yer. A living wictim—that's what I am."

Tom looked at him compassionately.

"Poor fellow," he said, "how you must suffer!"

"My sympathetic heart bleeds for him," remarked Dick. "I hope all those cakes won't disagree with him?"

"Gluttony's a sin."

"Yes. Tuffy, I'm ashamed of you!"

Unable to stand their chaff any longer, Tuffins ran out, as hard as he could, into the field, hoping that he might meet the doctor's boy again.

It would have been a supreme satisfaction to him to be able to "take it out" of somebody.

"Oh," he groaned, in anguish of spirit, "I could kick a dorg!"

But there were no doctor's boy and no dog to be seen; so to relieve his feelings, he chased butterflies.

In the meantime Peeping Tom and Knowall Dick were plotting together. They did not care for playing cricket, or joining in the sports of the other boys; but, nevertheless, they were far from idle.

"I want to tell you something which we may turn to our advantage," said Peeping Tom, confidentially.

"What is that?" asked Knowall Dick, who was still giggling, as he thought of how Tuffins had suffered for their fault.

"Jack Spencer and Harry Rawlings are in high favour now with the doctor."

"They won't be so long."

"Not if we can help it, of course," replied Tom.

"That is understood. What are they going to do?"

"Just what I am coming to," answered Tom. "They have obtained permission to have a day's fishing at the old mill on the river. You know the mill-stream? It is full of trout and other fish. They are to take some sandwiches with them, and need not come back till tea-time."

"That is a concession that I should like to have, although we have got roast mutton and green peas for dinner."

"Isn't it a pity that they should enjoy themselves so much?" added Tom.

"Who's to stop them?" enquired Dick.

"We can, if we are bold enough."

"How?"

"You know what the Squire told us—if he heard of Harry Rawlings' death, he would give the one who told him five hundred pounds."

Peeping Tom lowered his voice, as if fearful that somebody might hear him, though no one was near.

"What is your idea?" asked Dick.

"The mill-race runs swiftly. They will borrow the old punt from Corney Grain, the miller. If they were to get swamped—"

"I see!" hastily cried Knowall Dick. "Have they started?"

"Not yet. I saw them digging in the garden for bait," replied Tom. "If we could get there before them and take the plug out of the bottom of the punt, I'll bet they would never reach the shore after they had launched themselves on the stream."

"They can swim."

"That would not help them in the least, for the force of the current would carry them right down to the wheel, and then—"

He paused.

It was unnecessary for him to say more, for Dick knew the spot as well as he did, and was well aware that when Jack and Harry were once in the current they could not successfully struggle against it.

They must be carried down to the wheel and crushed in its ponderous folds.

"I'm on, if you are," said Dick. "Let us run down to the mill, get there before them, and fix the plug in the punt so that the water will run in, then we can hide behind the bushes and watch the result."

"That's the way to talk. We must mind the miller does not see us."

"Not he," cried Dick. "Won't he be busy inside the mill?"

Without another word they started for the river to carry out their nefarious design.

Squire Rawlings was more to blame than they were.

Had it not been for his words, they would not have thought of such a thing.

As they passed the garden, they saw Jack and Harry digging for bait.

The spies were unnoticed by the two friends.

Little did they dream of the plot that was being hatched against them.

The mill was half-an-hour's walk from the school, and prettily situated on the river, which widened at that spot.

It was fringed with trees and bushes, beneath which lurked the trout, the barbel, and, here and there, a grayling.

For the consideration of half-a-crown, Grain, the miller, would lend anyone his punt, and allow them to fish.

When the spies reached the mill-stream, they looked carefully around to see that there was nobody on the watch.

Not a soul was to be seen.

All was silent as the grave, save the rush of the babbling water, and the occasional cry of a heron.

The punt was moored to a willow tree.

"You get in and do the trick," said Dick; "I'll keep watch."

"'I HAVE KILLED HIM, WITHOUT MEANING TO DO SO,' SAID WARNER."

Peeping Tom pulled the punt towards him by the painter, crept in, and looked for the plug.

This was a round piece of wood like a bung, inserted in a hole in the bottom.

When it rained the punt got full of water, and the miller, hauling it on shore, pulled up the plug, and let the water run out.

This saved the trouble of baling.

The spies were well acquainted with this fact, for they had several times fished at the old mill.

When Peeping Tom found the plug, he loosened it so that the water would ooze in gradually.

Having accomplished this fiendish task, he rejoined his companion.

"Now let us hide," he said.

"Is the deed done?" asked Dick.

"You will see how well I have done it, in a short time," was the reply.

A group of alder trees, under which the rank grass grew high, offered them a promising place of concealment.

They repaired thither, and, crouching down, waited.

The dull thud of the mill-wheel, and the roar of the water behind it in the fall, were distinctly audible.

To their ears it was like the knell of their enemies' doom.

Close by, rose the old mill, white with flour, and bathed in a flood of golden sunshine.

Suddenly Tom uttered a deep groan, and pressed his hand to the region of his chest, while his face was drawn down as if by a spasm of pain.

"What's the matter now? You look as if you had sat down on a tin-tack, or a pin." said Dick.

"Really, I can't help it."

"Keep quiet, can't you? They will be here directly. Oh, dear, I've got it now, I do believe," cried Dick, doubling himself up on the grass.

It was the quantity of hot pastry they had eaten, which was giving them such inward qualms.

For some time they suffered great agony, turning white as ghosts and perspiring in every pore; but they were obliged to endure it in silence, for Jack and Harry were seen approaching.

They were laughing and talking merrily, as if they were looking forward to a good day's sport.

The spies watched them narrowly from their place of concealment.

They put their fishing apparatus at the bottom of the punt. Harry sat down, and, slipping the rope, Jack pushed off.

He punted to a certain spot, and fixing the pole in the sandy bottom, moored the boat to it.

Then, for the first time, he remarked that there was water in the punt.

"Dash it all!" he cried, "the old tub lets water."

"By Jove, yes," answered Harry. "She's leaking like a sieve."

He was right.

The motion of punting had removed the plug altogether, and the water was rushing in.

"Open that locker," said Jack, "and see if there is a bowl there."

Harry lifted up the locker lid, but there was not one there.

"It will be a case of swamp if we don't look out!" exclaimed Jack. "What are we to do?"

Harry looked blankly at him.

He had nothing to suggest in this unexpected emergency.

"I'll try and punt back to the shore, where we can investigate the cause of this sudden inundation," Jack went on.

He heard the roar of the water, and the dash, dash of the mill-wheel.

Casting an uneasy glance in the direction of the old mill, he endeavoured to pull up the punt pole.

Before them was the flat, regular side of the mill, made of boards; under this ran the mill-race, which turned the wheel.

The entrance to the mill faced the road, so that, situated as they were, if any accident happened, no one could see it, unless it was somebody on the bank.

It was hard work to get the pole up, as the punt careened with its weight of water.

At last the pole came up with a jerk.

As it did so, Jack lost his balance, and fell head-first into the stream.

"Help!" he cried, as he came up.

Harry stretched out his hand, and, with a desperate effort, Jack caught it, but it only had the effect of making Harry follow suit.

He was literally dragged out of the swamping half-submerged punt.

They were now both struggling in the water.

The spies had watched the whole affair, and forgot their pain in their glee at the success of their stratagem.

It seemed as if nothing but a miracle could avert Jack and Harry from falling a prey to a cruel death.

They breasted the stream as well as they could, swimming side by side, but surely and slowly were they drawn towards the mill sluice.

Jack took a look over his shoulder, and saw that this was the case.

"Shout with all your might, Harry," he

cried. "It is our only chance, for the miller to hear us."

"That's a poor look-out," rejoined Rawlings. "It is all up with us, I fear. Heaven help us!"

Both of them shouted as loudly as the strength of their lungs would allow, but the rush of the water effectually smothered their voices.

As far as the miller was concerned, he heard not a sound.

Exhausted with their exertions, the two friends, whose day's fishing had turned out so disastrously, resigned themselves to their fate.

A look of despair settled on their pallid faces.

Still they continued to swim, and so put off the evil moment as long as possible.

It was only a question of a few minutes. Then they would be sucked into the great sluice, and the huge mill-wheel would soon thrash the life out of them.

Yet the two spies made no sign.

They had been witnessing the gallant fight for life during a quarter of an hour, which, to those concerned, seemed an age.

Two of their schoolfellows were drowning before their very eyes, and they were such craven wretches that they would not uplift their voices to save them.

"Good-bye, Jack," cried Harry.

"Good-bye, old boy," replied Jack, in short, quick gasps. "We've done our best, as English boys should."

Just at that critical moment, a small fellow appeared on the path leading round the stream.

He had wandered from the high road to gather some flowers, which grew on the margin.

Jack gave one last shout.

"Help! In heaven's name, help!"

The little fellow was no other than Kennedy.

He heard the faint, despairing cry.

He saw two human beings struggling, and in imminent danger.

Quick as lightning he dashed back into the road, and rushed into the mill.

Grain, the miller, was putting some corn into a hopper.

"Stop the wheel!" screamed Kennedy, wildly.

The miller looked at him in astonishment.

There was no mistaking the expression of that white, terror-stricken countenance.

Danger was lurking somewhere.

"Stop the wheel!" cried Kennedy again.

The miller stretched out his hand to the pulley which let down the iron door at the mouth of the sluice.

All at once the noise, the splashing, dashing and grinding ceased, as if by magic.

The wheel was stopped.

Then Kennedy sank against the door, muttering—

"Saved! Saved!"

Grain was quite in the dark as to what had really happened, though he made a shrewd guess that someone had fallen into the mill-race.

Going to the wall, he opened a door, which had a wooden ladder attached, leading to the water.

Clinging to the bottom rung were Jack and Harry, who had drifted to the first support they could get hold of.

The reaction had set in.

So bereft of strength did they feel that they could scarcely save themselves from sinking into the depths.

"Schoolboys," muttered Grain. "They've had a narrow shave, and no mistake. I only shut down just in time."

He went down the ladder and assisted them up, one after the other.

A glass of spirit revived them, and they told their story.

"I never knew the plug come out of the old punt afore," said the miller.

"How did you know we were in danger?" asked Jack.

"You've got to thank that young gentleman for telling me."

They had not hitherto noticed their little schoolmate, who was modestly standing in the background.

"Kennedy," cried Jack and Harry, in a breath, "how can we thank you?"

"I did not know it was you," said the boy, with a smile. "I only heard your cry, saw you in the water close to the sluice, and I ran to the mill. You were, indeed, near death.

"You have often taken my part," went on Kennedy. "You know the fable of the lion in the net, and the mouse helping him. A good action is never thrown away. I'm only too glad to think I happened to stroll down this way to-day."

The miller recognised Jack and Harry as the ones who had engaged his punt for the day's fishing.

Not liking them to be baulked of their sport, he offered to go into a little skiff he had to the punt, bale the water out, and get it ready for them.

Their tackle was not lost, and all should be made right in about an hour, which time he advised them to employ in taking a short rest.

At the top of the mill was a loft where a quantity of old sacks were kept.

It was very warm up there. They could

lie down on the sacking and dry their clothes while they were resting.

To this they at once agreed, and climbed up the ladder; Kennedy continued his ramble, and the miller went to look after the water-logged punt.

Kennedy felt delighted to think that he had been able to be of use to his friends.

But the spies of the school—what did they think of it?

Their hearts were filled with rage to find that their intended victims had slipped through their fingers.

They had watched the whole affair from beginning to end, and Peeping Tom had looked in at the mill, and seen Jack and Harry go up the ladder.

When they did not come down again, he concluded they had gone to have a rest.

He rejoined Knowall Dick.

"Isn't this disappointing?" he exclaimed. "I made sure of a double funeral."

"So did I, till I saw the mill wheel stop," answered Dick.

"We must try again."

"Of course. Where are they now?"

"Gone upstairs to sleep in the loft."

"We sha'n't get the five hundred pounds from Squire Rawlings this time," said Dick.

He bit his lips with vexation.

"It isn't our fault," replied Tom.

"Not it."

"We planned to rid the Squire of Harry Rawlings, but it did not come off—that's all."

"Next time will settle it," said Dick.

The words were scarcely out of his mouth before a well-dressed young fellow stepped from behind a tree trunk.

He had been listening to all that was said.

Toying with his heavy watch chain, and displaying on his finger a stone of price in a gold ring, he raised his hat slightly.

"Pardon me," he exclaimed; "if I have overheard your conversation. it is not altogether my fault."

Peeping Tom and Knowall Dick began to shake.

Their faces became elongated, and their knees knocked together.

What they had been saying was nothing more nor less than a confession of an attempt to murder.

They had admitted that they had made the attempt on the life of Harry Rawlings.

His name had been distinctly mentioned.

They had also declared that they would try again, and hoped to succeed next time. The stranger had overheard them.

Here was a dilemma to be placed in.

How were they going to get out of it?

CHAPTER XVI.

THE DESTRUCTION OF THE OLD MILL—THREATENED BY THE FLAMES.

SEEING their evident discomfiture, the young stranger could not help smiling.

He hastened to put them at their ease.

"I mean you no harm," he said. "You were speaking of Harry Rawlings, the nephew of the Squire. I am his son."

"Oh, if you are the Squire's son, it is all right," replied Peeping Tom.

"Perfectly," observed Knowall Dick.

They felt immensely relieved.

The declaration of his identity took a great weight off their minds.

Still they had a lurking doubt.

"I never heard that Squire Rawlings had a son," continued Knowall Dick, "though I do not presume to doubt your word for a moment."

"Oh, no!" added Tom; "not for worlds."

"When I say I am his son, I mean his adopted son," responded Charlie. "Now who are you, and what did the Squire say about Harry?"

"We are boys from the school," said Peeping Tom. "I'm Tom Harris. This is my chum, Dick Wilkins."

"It is very nice to chum up, and feel that you have got someone you can trust and confide in," observed Dick.

"Very. Proceed."

"We heard the Squire say, on one occasion, that he would give five hundred pounds to hear of Harry's death."

"Ah, I begin to understand," exclaimed Charlie.

"I hope we are not betraying a secret?" Tom continued. "It is true, and to-day we tried to—"

"No, no," interrupted Knowall Dick; "that is going too far. It was quite an accident."

"Well, so it was, now I come to think of it."

Charlie began to grow impatient at this circumlocution.

"Come to the point," he cried. "Don't beat about the bush."

"All right," resumed Tommy. "This

fellow Harry, and his friend Spencer, whom we hate, were going fishing in the punt. Somehow the plug got out of the hole in the bottom, and they were swamped. If it had not been for the miller being told of their peril, they would be dead now."

Charlie laughed.

"Very good," he answered. "You are a very promising boy."

Tommy took this as a compliment.

"Thank you," he said.

"Where's Harry and his friend now?" asked Charlie.

"Up in the loft, at the top of the mill, asleep on some sacks, restoring their nerves, and drying themselves."

Charlie regarded the barn-like structure critically.

"It looks very old," he observed.

"Oh, it is; hundreds of years, they say," replied Tom.

"Wouldn't it burn like tinder?"

"Rather!" ejaculated Peeping Tom.

"There would be a terrific flare up," said Knowall Dick.

"Where is the miller?"

"He's been baling the punt out; but I think he has gone inside the mill again to have his dinner. Perhaps he'll sleep for half-an-hour. It's very hot, and he isn't busy."

"How do you know?"

"Oh, we know everything, don't we, Dick?" said Peeping Tom, with an air of complacency.

"I should say so," replied Knowall Dick, proudly.

"Never miss an item, do we?"

"Never."

Charlie gave each of them a sovereign.

"It is nice to have some spending money," he said. "Enjoy yourselves with that."

Then he lighted a cigarette, and handed the box of matches to Peeping Tom.

"I don't smoke," observed Tommy.

"It doesn't matter," returned Charlie, carelessly. "I don't want them, and I thought you might find them useful."

"What for?"

"Oh, I don't know. It would be a dreadful thing if this old mill was to catch fire while the miller was napping after his dinner, and those two boys were fast asleep in the loft."

"Awful!" said Peeping Tom.

"The slightest spark would do it, and it would be reduced to ashes in half-an-hour," continued Charlie.

Tom and Dick indulged in one of their fiendish grins.

The hidden meaning of Charlie's words now dawned upon them.

He was doing nothing less than asking them to set fire to the mill.

For a certain purpose, too, which was to kill Harry Rawlings.

"I'm fond of playing with fire," said Peeping Tom. "It is awfully dangerous, though. Once I set a hayrick on fire. Didn't it blaze, though it was only a little one!—just the same as I was at the time— and the farmer nearly killed me with an ash-plant when he caught me."

"I lighted some gunpowder once," remarked Knowall Dick, who was not to be outdone by his companion, "and it blew me on to the roof of a house. The whole fire brigade of the town had to come with ladders to get me down."

There was no truth whatever in these assertions; but they made them for the purpose of looking big.

"Be very careful, now, what you do with those matches," continued Charlie.

"I'll throw them into the water when you are gone," rejoined Peeping Tom; "they are no use to me, are they, Dick?"

"None at all."

"Well, I am very glad to have made your acquaintance. Come and see me at the Hall," exclaimed Charlie.

"Thank you, very much."

"I will entertain you as well as I can with the best the house affords."

Saying this, Charlie shook hands in rather an effusive manner, and walked rapidly away.

He was quickly lost to sight among the trees.

"That's a cool fish," observed Tom. "I never saw his equal. He did not tell us to do anything, and yet he put an idea in our heads."

"Who could mistake his meaning?" replied Dick.

"He might have given us more than a sovereign each."

"Perhaps that is all he had with him, and we shall get some more if—"

Dick did not finish the sentence.

What he had in his mind was too dreadful even to be talked about in the open air.

"You lie down in the grass again. I'm going to take a little walk," said Peeping Tom.

He had set his thin white lips firmly together.

"Are you—" began Knowall Dick.

"Don't ask any questions," interrupted Tom.

His friend was silent, and he glided along to the mill like one who is afraid that his shadow will be seen.

The road was deserted.

Stealing into the mill with all the caution of a watchful Indian on the war-path, Peeping Tom looked around him.

As he had surmised, the miller, overcome by the heat, was reclining in a well-shaded spot.

Some shavings were lying in a corner.

Striking a match, Peeping Tom set fire to them.

Instantly a dense smoke arose; this was followed by a brilliant red flame, which began to lick the dry wood of the wall.

Going away as noiselessly as he had come, the incendiary regained the spot where he had left Dick.

Putting his finger to his lips to enjoin the necessity of silence, he beckoned him to hasten away.

It was unsafe for them to remain any longer in the vicinity.

Were they to be seen by anybody, the finger of suspicion would point to them.

The miller, Jack, Harry and Kennedy were all ignorant of their presence on the scene.

They did not stop until they had got some distance away, when they had recourse to one of their favourite devices.

They climbed up a tree, and sitting on high branches, watched the progress of what was to be a serious conflagration.

The secret of those wretched boys was safe; yet they pushed aside the verdant leaves, and peered out with scared faces.

They were afraid of their horrible work, for their consciences could not acquit them.

Ten minutes elapsed, and then a burst of flame broke out of the mill.

It seemed to rival the splendour of the sun.

On such a bright day it was a ghastly mockery, however.

We must leave the spies of the school, and return to the mill, where Grain was at last roused by the suffocating smoke.

He had fallen into a heavy sleep.

At first he could not understand what had happened, but he soon recognised the fact that the mill was in flames.

Although water was so near at hand, no appliances were kept for extinguishing fire.

His first impulse was to rush out into the road, and he did so, darting through the blinding, choking smoke, and the hissing, scorching tongues of fire.

The mill was now well alight, and the blaze was terrific, for everything there was of a highly inflammable nature.

Suddenly he thought of Jack and Harry.

"Oh, heaven, the boys!" he gasped

It was impossible to re-enter the mill, for to do so, would have been to court instant death.

He was almost at his wits' end.

There was a window in the loft, which looked out on to the road.

Picking up some stones, he began to throw them with frantic force and haste at this window.

The glass crashed.

Jack and Harry luckily were aroused by the noise, and jumped off the sacking.

"Somebody throwing stones," said Jack, sleepily.

"I'll go to the window and see who it is," replied Harry, adding, "by Jove, old fellow, there's a smell of smoke."

"What is it?"

"I don't know. Hark! Do you hear that roaring noise below?"

"I hope there's nothing wrong!" replied Jack.

He went quickly to the ladder. The flames were running up it.

"The place is on fire! Our retreat is cut off!" he shouted. "Good heaven, what shall we do?"

More stones came through the casement.

They both went to the window, and saw the miller gesticulating like a madman in the dusty road.

"Fire! Fire!" he yelled. "Hasten, or you will be burnt to death!"

"We can't get down," answered Jack. "What are we to do? Have you a ladder?"

"No," was the despairing answer.

To jump into the road would be certain death.

If anything was to be done, there was no time to be lost in considering.

Jack saw a hatchet lying on the floor.

He seized it with his usual presence of mind, and running to the wooden wall, on the water side began to chop with all his might and main.

Harry asked no questions.

He divined what he was about to do.

As Jack made a hole in the wall, his friend seized the boards with his hands, and pulled at them for dear life.

Working like troopers, they soon made a large space, and extended it to a level with the floor.

The smoke and flames were now roaring up the ladder hole.

In a few minutes the whole upper part of the fabric would be ablaze.

Casting away the hatchet, Jack looked at the stream below him.

It was a giddy height where he stood.

His brain reeled for a moment, but he quickly recovered himself.

Fortunately the miller had not started the wheel again, and the water was calm.

They knew it was very deep.

"Now for it," exclaimed Jack, in a voice hoarse with excitement.

"Are you going to jump?" asked Harry.

"There is nothing else to do."

"Will you take a header or a footer?"

"Feet first. Keep your legs tight together. You go first," replied Jack, always self-sacrificing.

"No, you."

"Go, I tell you. I'll wait till you come up. For heaven's sake, don't stand there. The flames are coming up under my feet. Do you want the floor to fall in?"

"All right."

Harry set his lips, and, drawing a deep breath, let himself fall.

It was not a jump, but a quiet drop.

He did not turn over, but went down into the water like a stone.

For a minute he was lost to view.

How the fire raged and crackled! It came up the chinks of the floor, and the smoke was as mephitic as that of the bottomless pit.

"He's up," muttered Jack.

Harry swam away to give his friend a wide berth.

Inflating his lungs, Jack took the perilous leap, and went down—down till his feet touched the bottom of the river.

The shock shot him up like a cork.

Imitating Harry's example, he struck out vigorously, and swam towards the shore.

The air was filled with pieces of burning wood, which sank hissing into the water.

At last they reached land, and crawled on to the bank to watch the progress of the fire.

It was, indeed a grand sight.

The fire demon had it all his own way.

There was none to dispute his will.

"My word," said Jack, "it was a lucky thought of mine to knock down the wall with the hatchet. If I hadn't, we should have perished."

We are not born to be drowned or burnt," replied Harry.

"What inference do you draw from that? Are we born to be hanged?"

"I didn't say so; but we have had two remarkably narrow escapes to-day."

"I wish I could get dry," remarked Jack. "It is rather monotonous being wet all the time."

"It strikes me there is something in this."

"What do you mean?"

"These two things could not have happened by accident," said Harry.

"Why couldn't they?"

"It does not stand to reason. We have an enemy who has done this."

"Nonsense!" laughed Jack.

"All right; you wait and see."

Jack shrugged his shoulders.

"Who wants to injure me?" he demanded.

"It isn't you."

"Who then?"

"Me. My uncle, the Squire, is my enemy We have an unseen foe. You suffer because you are my friend."

"That won't frighten me," exclaimed Jack. "I shall stick to you all the more like a leech, or—or the gout."

Harry looked earnestly and sorrowfully at him.

"You had best cut my acquaintance," he said.

"I won't—that's flat!"

"You and your father are very good to me; but I do not want to involve you all in trouble, ruin—perhaps, death!"

Jack put his hand upon his friend's mouth.

"Will you stop it?" he answered. "If you don't I'll make you! We are friends, and nothing can separate us. Our fishing is all up for to-day. Let us have a chat with the poor miller, and go to the old spot for some refreshment."

"Do you mean the 'Cricketers'?"

"Certainly. Are you agreeable?"

"Yes," answered Harry, recovering from the gloom which had taken possession of him. "We've got the day out, and we may as well utilize it."

The miller was delighted to see them alive; his mill was now one mass of flames; the roof having fallen in. He was insured, so his loss would not be very great.

Still it was a great shock to him.

When he heard how they had made their escape from the imminent danger which had threatened them, he much admired their ready invention and courage.

"I thought you were done to a cinder," he said.

"How did the fire originate?" asked Jack.

"I had no fire. It must have been spontaneous combustion from the heat. You didn't do it, because you were up a-top, and I didn't do it, because I was having a nap below."

"It is a mystery, then."

"Completely so."

"Did you have any inflammable articles on the ground floor?" continued Jack. "Matches or oil?"

"Oil, certainly, for lubricating purposes. Nothing else," replied the miller.

Jack did not press him with any more questions. He expressed his sympathy for his misfortune, and wished him good-day.

A lot of people now began to arrive from the neighbouring farms.

Help was offered on all sides, but it was too late.

Jack and Harry, with thankful hearts, walked leisurely to the old inn, where they had so often enjoyed themselves.

When they entered the house, Corks, the landlord, was in the bar, and he welcomed them as old friends and customers.

"Glad to see you, gents," he exclaimed. "Want some pop? I have some in prime condition, I'll wager."

"We require a fine fowl, as quickly as you can get it ready. In the meantime, you can open your prime pop."

They were supplied with the ginger beer.

"I do hear that the mill's on fire," said Corks. "Have you seen anything of it?"

"Rather."

"Do tell us. Grain is a very worthy fellow, and an old friend of mine. I be main sorry for him."

Jack related all that had happened to himself and Harry, at which Corks marvelled greatly.

"It is a wonderful escape," he remarked. "I don't wonder you have given up fishing for the day."

Being rather unnerved, Jack said they should like to go into the parlour and wait for the fowl to be killed and cooked.

"You can't go in there, sir," replied the landlord.

"Why not, pray?" asked Jack.

"It is engaged."

"By whom?"

"The Squire's son. He is having a snack, with a small bottle of champagne, and waiting, he says, for someone to come along and give him news of the fire at the mill."

"Do you mean Squire Rawlings?" cried Jack, in surprise.

"Certainly," replied Corks. "Haven't you heard that he has adopted a young fellow as his son?"

"Not a word."

"I thought everybody knew that by this time. A very nice going fellow he is, though inclined to be a little uppish, and put on airs."

"I am the Squire's nephew," said Harry. "The son is a new idea to me altogether; but if he had a dozen, I do not suppose it would make any difference in his treatment of me."

The door of the parlour was open, and Charlie was standing on the threshold looking out.

"There he is," said Corks.

Jack and Harry turned their eyes in the direction indicated; but they did not recognise in Charlie Rawlings the young snake charmer, nor had they heard anything about the death of MacNab. Charlie, however, knew them again in a moment.

He had heard the narrative of their escape from the fire, and his face became pale with rage.

It seemed as if Harry bore a charmed life.

He did not want to make friends, or, in fact, have any conversation whatever with him, after what his father had told him.

Re-entering the room, he banged the door, and sat down at the open window to finish his wine.

He was very proud of his newly acquired position.

Not for all the wealth of the Indies would he have had his identity discovered with the boy snake-charmer.

MacNab was dead. Who could expose him? Still, he might be found out.

"Your parlour is public, isn't it?" said Jack to Corks.

"It's never been 'xactly private as I know of."

"What's to keep us out, then?"

"Only Squire Rawlings' son," replied Corks. "He told me he didn't want to be interrupted or interfered with by any common vulgar people, or he would not use my house again."

"That prohibition does not apply to us."

"By no means, sir; don't take it that way, for it was not meant," Corks hastened to reply.

Jack seemed annoyed that anyone should keep him out of the parlour; hitherto he had always been the favoured guest.

Who was this new-comer, that he should be a usurper?

"Well, gents, I'll go and kill the fowl. Say an hour-and-a-half, and it'll be ready."

With this remark the landlord called his little boy to sit in the bar while he was gone, and hurried away.

Jack Spencer expressed his annoyance at being kept out of the parlour.

"If he *is* the Squire's son," said he, "I don't see why he should monopolise the room."

"Nor I," replied Harry; "it's open to all."

"See how he banged the door! There is too much uppishness about it to suit me."

"Let's have him out," exclaimed Harry.

"Well, I won't say we will have him out of it," answered Jack; "but we will go in, anyhow, and sit down."

"That's the idea."

They did not feel at all afraid of the Squire's son; nor were they conscious of any breach of good manners in entering the room, which, as long as they had known it, they had always regarded as public.

Opening the door without going through the formality of knocking, they walked in.

"'YOU MUST PROVE HIS INNOCENCE,' CRIED THE GIPSY."

No. 6.

Charlie stared at them, and they returned the stare with interest.

"What do you fellows want in here?" he demanded.

"I should like to know how and why it is any business of yours?" Jack replied.

"I make it my business, as I wish to be alone," said Charlie.

"Go out into the fields, then, and stand behind a hedge like any other donkey."

"This is an impertinent intrusion, and I will thank you to vacate the premises, or you will compel me to use force to turn you out."

Jack and Harry each took a chair, and sat down.

As for Charlie, he had gone too far to retreat, unless he wanted to eat his own words.

Under the circumstances, it would have been peculiarly mortifying.

Yet he did not know which to attack first.

"Come on," said Harry, tantalisingly. "I am waiting to be ejected. Why don't you do it?"

"What are you waiting for?" asked Jack.

"I'll start on you, my fine fellow," retorted Charlie, singling out Harry, who was quite prepared for him.

He put his hand on Harry's coat collar, intending to run him to the door, and throw him into the passage.

Intention is one thing, however, and performance is another.

In a moment Harry swung himself round, and dealt Charlie a sledge-hammer like blow.

It sent him spinning towards Jack.

The latter was ready for him.

He had resolved to give him as hot a reception as possible.

Raising his foot, he favoured him with a kick in the region of his coat-tails, which made him bang his head against the wall.

Thoroughly discomfited, he fell in a heap to the floor.

With a rueful countenance he got up, looking as if he were more than half inclined to cry.

"How do you find yourself by this time?" inquired Jack.

"Want any more?" asked Harry. "There is plenty of it at the same shop."

"Always kept in stock," said Jack.

"Back numbers continually in print," continued Harry.

Charlie shook his head.

"I'm not of a greedy disposition, and I have had enough," he said. "You've got a fist like a leg of mutton, and you other fellow kick like a horse."

"It will teach you a lesson."

Charlie opened the door.

Looking at them with a scowl, he replied—

"It will teach me this lesson, to attack one only when another is not present. I'll have my revenge for this."

"You can't frighten us!" laughed Jack.

"I shall know you again."

"What a distinguished honour. I am sure we ought to feel highly flattered to think that so exalted a person will condescend to remember two such insignificant objects as ourselves."

"Do you think that clever?" sneered Charlie.

"It's good enough for you!"

"I'm a gentleman!"

"Are you?" said Jack. I declare I should never have known it if you hadn't told me."

Harry snatched up a loaf of bread and threw it at the Squire's son, giving him a painful knock.

Full of rage and fury, Charlie beat a hasty retreat.

He left them masters of the situation entirely. They laughed heartily at his confusion, little thinking that he had become their bitterest enemy. After dinner they returned to the school.

The news of their adventures at the mill had preceded them, and the masters and boys congratulated them on their escape.

Peeping Tom and Knowall Dick were profuse in assuring them that they were very glad no harm had come to them.

The hypocrites almost overdid their part.

"We know you hate and despise us!" said Peeping Tom; "but our hearts are full of thankfulness to think you were not drowned or burnt."

"I could shed tears of joy," cried Knowall Dick.

Jack and Harry thanked them, but they did not believe in their protestations.

In a short time they were to find out how hollow these assurances were.

CHAPTER XVII.

THE DEATH OF KENNEDY—AN AWKWARD FIX.

LITTLE Kennedy loved to get up in a secluded corner of the field, and lie down on the grass under a chestnut tree.

Here he would shut his eyes and dream strange dreams about the white-robed angels of the spirit world.

Melancholy seemed to have marked him for its own.

He was shy and retiring by nature; and even if Warner had not made a practice of constantly bullying him, he would have preferred to be alone in play hours.

The birds got to know him, for he always put some bread in his pocket for his little feathered friends, and an old sheep the doctor was fattening for Christmas would come and lie down by his side.

For him life ought to have been one long summer dream.

He was in his usual corner, one beautiful June morning, reading.

The boys were all down at the bottom of the field, devoting themselves to watching a match between the first and second cricket elevens.

Kennedy did not expect any interference, though he knew Warner was about.

The bully had sprained his ankle, and could not play in the match.

This had made him devote a good deal of his time to poor Kennedy, who had not led a happy life for the past week.

He would sooner have seen a black snake in his path, than have come across Warner.

He was fated to be interrupted by more than one person that morning.

The first to come near him was Harry Rawlings.

He carried a bat in one hand, and a cricket ball in the other.

On the ball he had written his name with pen and ink.

This turned out to be an important factor in the events that shortly followed.

"Hullo!" exclaimed Harry, "I thought I should find you in your sunny corner."

"It is very nice here. Will you sit down?" replied Kennedy.

"I haven't time," said Harry; "the elevens are playing. Jack's in the first, and he has sent me for his pads."

"Are you in?"

"No; I thought I should be. It is a shame. I am left out in the cold."

"Perhaps you will have better luck next time. I hope so," exclaimed Kennedy, smiling.

"Just mind my bat and ball, please," exclaimed Harry.

"With pleasure."

As Harry was about to move away, to execute his errand for Jack, he heard his name called.

"I say, Rawlings, aren't you nicely sold?"

About twenty yards off was a wall, which separated the doctor's private garden from the field.

He looked up.

On this wall were Peeping Tom and Knowall Dick.

"Confound you two chaps!" said Harry, "I'm blessed if you aren't like a regular Jack-in-the-box. You are here this minute, but nobody knows where you will spring up next."

"Sold again!" cried Knowall Dick.

"How am I?"

"Thought you would be in the second eleven, didn't you? But it didn't come off."

"I'll have *you* off if you don't vanish," said Harry.

He made a dash towards them, but they dropped on the garden side of the wall, and were seen no more.

"Hateful little brutes," added Harry, as he walked away.

When he was gone, Kennedy put down his book, and amused himself by throwing up the cricket ball and catching it.

While he was thus occupied, Warner happened to pass by.

He was going to look on at the match, but he could not resist the temptation of bullying the little fellow who had always been his victim.

"Ah," he exclaimed, "you look too comfortable! I shall have to stir you up a bit."

A deadening sensation took possession of Kennedy when he saw his tormentor.

His heart sank.

"Please let me alone," he replied. "I am not feeling very well to-day."

"Oh, there's always something the matter with you," answered Warner. "You want waking up, I tell you."

"Do go away."

"Not I. Shy that ball to me, and get on your pins, or I'll make you."

With a sigh, Kennedy reluctantly rose to his feet, and threw the ball to the tall bully.

"Now," continued Warner, "there is an old song called 'Wheel about, and turn about, and jump Jim Crow.' You've got to jump that. I shall throw this ball at you if you stop jumping 'Jim Crow.'"

"I'm not strong enough to keep on at that sort of thing," Kennedy replied.

"You'll have to. I'll whistle the tune for you, and clap my hands, as the nigger minstrels do."

"Do, please, go away. I am not equal to it. Don't be so hard on me."

"Will you do as I tell you?" shouted Warner, menacingly.

Seeing that there was no escape from his tyranny, Kennedy, much against his will, began to jump up and down.

He was ordered to kick up his feet, and throw up his arms.

These antics made him look very grotesque, and Warner laughed till his sides ached.

Reeking with perspiration in the hot sunshine, panting for breath, and quivering with exertion, the boy kept it up as long as he could.

At last a sudden vertigo seized him.

A mist swam before his eyes.

He reeled and fell.

"Get up!" shouted Warner. "No shamming."

"I can't," replied Kennedy, faintly.

"If you don't, I'll shy this ball at you."

"It doesn't matter much what you do."

"Oh, doesn't it? I'll soon let you know," cried Warner.

Kennedy tried to get on his feet, but the effort was an utter failure.

He sank on to his knees, and held up his hands. Warner raised his arm.

The cricket ball was in his hand.

"Have some mercy," said Kennedy, crying bitterly. "I haven't done anything to you."

"Oh, you canting, whining, whimpering little humbug."

"I'm not, Warner. I haven't the strength to go on."

"Will you dance 'Jim Crow?'"

"I would if I could. Have I not done my best? My strength is all gone. I feel as if I should faint."

"Nonsense! Look at the fellows playing cricket in the field. They cut about, bowling, batting, and fielding. Why can't you?"

"Because I'm delicate," replied Kennedy.

"Delicate!" exclaimed Warner. "Anyone would think you were a girl. Get up, I say, or I'll use you for a wicket, and bowl at you."

"Don't! Don't!"

"I will, by Jove! Look out! Mind your eye. Play!"

There was a look of piteous resignation upon Kennedy's pale face.

He shut his eyes, and made no effort to protect himself from the threatened attack.

Warner sent a swinging round-arm ball at him.

It struck the ground about a yard from Kennedy, bounded up, and hit him on the temple.

He fell full length on to the grass, as if he had been shot.

It was a terrible blow.

No cry—not even a sob escaped him.

"Ah, ah!" laughed Warner; "that ball was well put in. It took his middle stump. How's that, umpire?"

Kennedy did not move.

Suddenly an uneasy expression came over Warner's countenance.

The boy was so awfully still, that a vague fear took possession of him.

What made him so silent, so ghastly, so death-like? Why did he not scream with pain, as he usually did when he was hurt?

"Hang the little beggar! What's up with him?" muttered Warner.

He did not like it.

Could it be that he had gone too far?

"Is there anything wrong with him?" continued the bully. "No, no; he's doing this to spite me. Perhaps he is stunned, though. He'll come to directly. I wish I hadn't bowled so hard at him."

The expression of concern on Warner's face deepened.

Going to the boy, he noticed a terrible bruise on the temple, from which blood was flowing.

He knelt down and shook him.

"Wake up, old man," he said. "Speak to me. I didn't mean to do it."

No answer came from the livid lips.

"I'm awfully sorry, 'pon my word, Kennedy," he went on. "Don't lie there like that. Just pull yourself together, and I'll give you a shilling to spend."

The boy answered him not a word.

Warner was by this time deeply agitated. Beads of perspiration trembled on his brow, and his hands shook.

Undoing the little fellow's waistcoat, he put his hand on his heart.

All pulsation had stopped.

This was quite enough to show Warner that life was extinct.

He had not intended to kill him; but he was, in the eye of the law, no less a murderer, through bowling that unlucky ball.

"Good heaven! I've settled him at last," he said. "What shall I do?"

It was dangerous to stay there.

He slunk away with bowed head, and knees knocking together, as might have been the case with Cain, the first murderer, after he had foully slain his brother Abel.

There was one circumstance that kept his courage up.

As far as he knew, no one had seen him commit the fatal deed.

In this belief, however, he was entirely mistaken.

He had not gone far before he heard his name uttered.

"Warner!"

Looking up he saw the spies of the school sitting on the garden wall.

They had been there all the time watching the tragedy.

For a moment he was terrified.

His palsied lips at first refused to speak, but he roused himself by an effort.

"How long have you fellows been there?" he asked, trying to look unconcerned.

"Ever so long," replied Peeping Tom.

"Did you see—"

His tongue faltered.

"Everything," said Knowall Dick.

They both dropped off the wall, and came up to him.

"I—I did not mean to hit him so hard with the ball," stammered Warner. It was an accident."

Peeping Tom picked up the cricket ball, and looked at it.

"Harry Rawlings gave him the ball and the bat to mind," he exclaimed. "We heard him. He will be back directly. Look! here is his name on it."

"Put it back," said Warner hastily. "Put it where you found it."

"What for? When he comes to, he will know who hurt him and tell."

"He can't."

"Why not?" inquired Peeping Tom.

"Because he is dead. I have killed him, without meaning to do so. It is a sad thing; but can't we say it was Rawlings? Come down the field. Don't let us be seen talking here."

Peeping Tom replaced the ball, and he and Knowall Dick walked quickly away with Warner.

The idea he had suggested was one that found favour in their sight.

They wanted to ruin Rawlings, and here was an opportunity ready to their hand.

Talking earnestly, but in whispers, they went towards the spot where the cricket match was going on.

Scarcely had they disappeared, than a door in the wall opened, and Doctor Birch-often, arm-in-arm with Mr. Dobby, passed through.

"Some of the boys have been at my blackheart cherry-tree," remarked the head-master.

The culprits were Peeping Tom and Knowall Dick.

"That is plain enough," replied Mr. Dobby. "I can see that it has been considerably depleted of its fruit, sir."

All at once they came in sight of Kennedy.

"Dear me!" exclaimed Mr. Dobby, "whom have we here?"

"Kennedy, by the look of him. He seems to be taking it remarkably easy; but I have remarked that the boy is strange in his ways—quiet and retired. Call him."

Mr. Dobby did so, and receiving no answer, made an examination of him, which resulted in the discovery of the fact that he had ceased to breathe.

"The boy is dead," cried Mr. Dobby; "he has been killed. Ah, here is a ball. A name is written on it."

"Whose name?" asked the headmaster.

"Harry Rawlings! This is very serious," continued Mr. Dobby.

He turned the ball over, and scrutinised it carefully.

"There is blood on it," he went on. "Evidently this is the weapon with which the lad was killed."

"It is certainly proof presumptive, if not positive," replied the doctor.

Peeping Tom and Knowall Dick now came running up.

"Oh, sir; oh, Mr. Dobby," cried Tom, "Kennedy is dead! We thought you were looking on at the match, and have been searching all over the field for you."

"What do you know about it?" asked the doctor.

"We were on the wall, and saw Rawlings talking to Kennedy, and pitching the ball at him."

"Were they quarrelling?"

"I don't know, sir; though it looked like it. The ball hit Kennedy, and he fell to the ground."

"Rawlings must be sent for," said the doctor, gravely.

At this juncture, Harry was seen coming along with the pads of which he had been in search.

He was perfectly unconscious of anything having happened to Kennedy.

"Ah, here he is!" exclaimed Mr. Dobby.

Harry walked up, wondering at the grave expression of the master's face.

"What have you been doing to Kennedy?" demanded the doctor.

"I, sir? Nothing," replied Harry. "What is the matter with him?"

"He has been struck on the side of the head with a cricket ball, which has your name on it. The blow killed him, and Harris and Wilkins say they saw you throw the ball."

Harry was inexpressibly shocked at this statement.

He could scarcely realise that he had heard aright.

"I certainly gave him the ball," he said, "and asked him to mind it; but I did not hit him with it—that I swear."

"These two boys declare you did."

"Then they are guilty of deliberate falsehood. They do not like me, and would hatch up any false charge against me. It is a wicked plot, sir."

Harry spoke quickly and with indignation.

"I am very sorry if I am acting under a wrong impression," answered the doctor, "but the case must be investigated by the police. It may be only manslaughter. it may be murder, or it may be that you are innocent."

"I am, indeed, sir."

"That must be decided by a jury. It is very deplorable. However, I shall at once send for the police, and you will go into the schoolroom, and there await their arrival."

Harry was completely dumfounded.

"I never had a quarrel with Kennedy in my life," he cried. "I always was his friend, and took his part."

"It may be so. Mark me, I do not say it is not."

"Won't you take my word, sir?" pleaded Harry.

"Impossible under the suspicious nature of the circumstances, and the evidence of Harris and Wilkins."

"They would be glad to hang me."

"Why so?"

"I don't know. They have always hated me."

"That is nonsense; it must be your fancy. If you did commit the crime, you are an infamous wretch, and well deserve the harshest punishment of the law. Go!"

The doctor waved his hand imperiously.

Almost broken-hearted at this sudden misfortune, Harry staggered off like a drunken man to the schoolroom.

It was deserted.

Looking out of the window he saw the doctor and Mr. Dobby bear the lifeless body of Kennedy into the house.

Then he noticed Mr. Dobby walk down the road.

Doubtless he was gone for the constables who were to arrest him.

Harry sat down and hastily scribbled a few lines to his friend, Jack Spencer.

His head was in a whirl; he was seized with a sudden panic, which made him lose his presence of mind.

All he knew was that he wanted to get away somewhere—anywhere, in fact, away from the school.

He felt that he could not stand the disgrace of being handcuffed and marched off to the station-house before his companions.

He was utterly unable to bear the strain of being accused of this terrible crime.

Of what would his consciousness of innocence avail him, when the spies were ready to give lying evidence against him?

Looking out of the window again, with a hunted, scared look on his livid face, he noticed that the game of cricket was suspended. The boys had broken up into knots, and were talking earnestly.

Clearly they had heard the dreadful news, and were discussing it.

No doubt Peeping Tom and Knowall Dick had carried the intelligence to them.

The doctor had not placed a guard upon him, thinking that he would not dare to attempt escape.

Therefore it was easy enough to quit the schoolroom and proceed along the passage to the back door.

Tuffins was in his den cleaning knives for dinner, and had not heard anything about the tragedy which had taken place.

Handing him the letter he had scrawled, in a nervous style, Harry asked him to give it to Spencer.

"He's down the field," said Tuffins, "why dont you go to him yourself?"

"I'm not well, and I'm going for a walk," Harry replied.

"All right; he shall have it. You do look bad."

"Yes; I am very ill."

Saying this in a hollow, sepulchral tone, he hastened into the yard, got into one of the meadows, and ran like a hare across the country.

In a few minutes he was lost to sight.

That there would be a hue and cry after him, he was sure.

His brain was burning like fire.

Had he not run away, he would have gone mad.

Yet it cannot be denied he was guilty of a very foolish act.

He should have stood his ground, and faced the charge like a man.

By running away he lent countenance to the weighty accusation which hung over his head.

It was, in reality, the worst thing he could do, for everyone would say that a guilty conscience induced him to fly.

We must leave him for a time that we may relate what took place at the school subsequent to his departure.

It was quite half-an-hour before Mr. Dobby, hot and dusty from his exertions, returned with a constable.

When these two and the doctor went to look for Harry, of course, they discovered that the bird had flown.

He was hunted for everywhere without avail, and the constable said that all they could do would be to issue an alarm, giving his description.

Most likely he would be captured in a few days.

Tuffins was still at work, when Miss Martha, much agitated, called him into the kitchen.

"Yes, ma'am. What is it?" he asked.

"Have you seen anything of Rawlings?" she replied.

"More than half-an-hour ago he gave me this note for Master Spencer, and walked into the yard, saying he was ill. He did look bad, too."

"No wonder."

"What's he done?" inquired Tuffins.

"Murder! That's what it is. He has killed Kennedy with a cricket ball. The police are in the house. Oh, dear, I am half dead with the shock. It is awful to think that such a thing could occur in a well-regulated, highly respectable academy like ours. I shall never get over it. I know I shan't."

"Lor'," ejaculated Tuffins, "I shouldn't have thought it."

"The school is ruined."

"Don't say that, ma'am. Accidents will happen."

"See what a name we shall get," continued Miss Martha. "Still waters run deep. I always thought that boy was a villain under the surface, and now it's come out."

"He is the last I should have suspected."

"Don't take his part. You are as bad as he is."

"What am I to do with this note?" asked Tuffins.

"Take it to the doctor. I will not touch it. Perhaps you have had something to do with it? I think it odd that you should be the last to see the horrid criminal."

"Come, that's a nice thing to say," cried Tuffins, indignantly.

"If I were the policeman, I'd lock you up on suspicion," replied Miss Martha. "Go to the doctor with that mysterious letter. It may throw some light on the awful subject."

Tuffins was glad enough to get away from her.

"Ain't she a nice old treat?" he muttered, as he went.

He found Doctor Birchoften, Mr. Dobby, and the constable by themselves in the schoolroom.

They were gravely discussing the precipitate flight of Harry.

"It looks very black against him," remarked the officer of the law.

"Very," answered the doctor. "If his conscience acquitted him, he would not have fled."

"I will leave no stone unturned to find him," continued the policeman.

The doctor noticed Tuffins at the door.

"What do you want?" he asked.

"Master Rawlings, some little time back, gave me a note for Master Spencer, sir."

"Oh, he did, eh?"

"He said he felt ill, and was going for a walk."

"Did he say anything else?"

"That's all, sir. I've only just heard about the murder from Miss Martha, or I would have brought you the note before."

"Hand it over!" exclaimed Doctor Birchoften. "This is important. It may give us a clue. Spencer is his great friend."

He looked pleased, so did the policeman, so did Mr. Dobby.

They all three felt as if they were on the eve of some great discovery.

"I will read it aloud," continued the doctor.

He adjusted his spectacles for that purpose.

"My dear Jack," wrote Harry, "somebody has killed little Kennedy. Unfortunately, I am accused of the crime; but I know no more of it than you do. The spies, Harris and Wilkins, have been hatching up lies against me. I am half mad, and cannot stay here. Just these few lines before I run away. Where I am going I do not know. Heaven help me! Try and prove my innocence. Of course, you know I could not have done such a thing. Good-bye. We may never meet again."

"Humph! there is not much in that," was the doctor's comment.

"Nothing at all," observed Mr. Dobby. "He can deliver it to Spencer."

"Very well, sir," replied Tuffins, to whom the letter was given back.

Making his usual bow, the page left the room, and the deliberations of the principals continued for a little while, after which the constable departed to send out to scour the country for Harry.

A good many of the boys had come back from the field into the playground.

Jack was among the number.

He was pacing up and down, looking up anxiously at the schoolroom windows.

Tuffins came to him, and silently handed him the note. He read it eagerly.

"He gave it me just afore he bolted," explained Tuffins. "The doctor's seen it."

"It is a bad business," sighed Jack. "I can't understand it."

"'IF I HAD A PISTOL, I WOULD SHOOT YOU LIKE A DOG!' CRIED CHARLEY."

"I'll never believe he did it," cried Tuffins; "he wasn't that kind of chap."

"Harris and Wilkins say they saw him throw the ball."

"Oh, they'd say anything," replied Tuffins, contemptuously.

"So they would."

"I wouldn't believe them on their hoath. Me and Master Rawlings was always the best of friends. Many a sixpence he's give me."

"Ah, he was a good fellow!" exclaimed Jack. "I never met one I liked better."

"I 'ope as 'ow he won't go and make away with hisself!" continued Tuffins.

He always dropped his h's when he was excited, and mangled his mother tongue.

"There is no telling. It is awful to have an accusation like this brought against you. Besides, we were both of us so fond of poor Kennedy."

Tuffins winked his eye knowingly.

"There is one who wasn't, though," he observed.

"Who's that?"

"You know as well as I do."

"Warner?"

"That's the chap; he was for hever-lasting a-bullying of Kennedy. It was a case of the wolf and the lamb."

"True; he couldn't let him alone," said Jack.

"The spies, as you calls them, is pretty thick with Warner."

"I know it."

"Look at 'em now, a-walking up and down together."

He pointed to the old wood-shed, and, sure enough, Warner was pacing the yard, with Peeping Tom on one side of him, and Knowall Dick on the other.

"That's odd. I must watch Warner," Jack said. "I wish this affair had never happened. I shall miss Harry."

"Do you think the police will catch him?"

"Heaven only knows! He is in the toils. Perhaps it will be best for him to get right away; but he has no friends—no money to speak of. What will he do alone in the world?"

"Well, I must go and lay the cloth for dinner. This I do say, I wish him luck," exclaimed Tuffins.

"We must clear his character. Will you help me?"

"Like a bird."

"Keep your eyes and ears open. Watch the spies."

"I will."

"Watch Warner, as a cat does a mouse."

"I'll do it."

"I feel confident we will prove Harry's innocence yet," added Jack.

How it was to be done, though, he had not the remotest idea.

He could only trust to the chapter of accidents.

That Harry was the victim of a foul and villainous plot he did not doubt for a moment.

When Tuffins left him he continued to walk up and down, unable to think of anything but the all-engrossing tragedy.

Peeping Tom and Knowall Dick left Warner, and came towards him.

News spreads fast in a school, and somehow they had heard that Harry had run away rather than face the magistrate.

"Rather a sad affair this!" exclaimed Tom, with a look of consummate impudence.

"Don't address your remarks to me," replied Jack.

He felt that he could not bear to speak to either of them just then, on account of the way in which he thought they had treated his unhappy friend.

They grinned at him.

Nothing annoyed him or provoked him so much as this grimace of theirs.

"Lost your chum, haven't you?" said Knowall Dick.

"Hold your tongue, and leave me," answered Jack.

"I feel sorry for you, Spencer. It is hard to lose a friend," cried Peeping Tom.

"Will you stop it?"

"I should feel very melancholy without Dick."

"Hold your noise, will you?"

"If Tom was gone, I should be inconsolable," said Dick.

"I'm in no humour for chaff," replied Jack.

"So I should think. Kennedy was a nice little fellow. What did Rawlings kill him for?"

Jack clenched his hands angrily, and faced the two spies.

"Look here!" he exclaimed. "I am upset, and I'm not going to be bear-baited by you. If you say another word, I will knock you down."

They retreated a few paces to get out of his reach.

"Harry Rawlings must have hit him pretty hard with that cricket-b " remarked Peeping Tom.

"It was a mean thing to do," said Knowall Dick.

He was always a kind of echo to Tom.

Their remarks stung Jack as if they were the bite of a mosquito or the sting of a wasp.

"Will you stop it?" asked Jack.

"I'd choose a better friend than a murderer," answered Tom.

" Fancy being a boy killer!" said Dick.

Jack controlled his temper with great difficulty.

" Chaff away my lads," he said, with a bitter smile. " I have got your measure down to a fine point."

" And what are you going to do?" asked Peeping Tom.

" Foil you yet."

" How?"

" I'll find out all your plotting. Harry Rawlings did not kill little Kennedy. It suits your purpose to say so; but beware! I am on your track."

" Are you?" asked Peeping Tom, with a sneer.

" It makes me feel awfully bad," laughed Knowall Dick.

" Laugh away, you cowardly hounds."

" Ha, ha!"

" Ho, ho!"

" I'll hunt you down now, or when I'm a man!" exclaimed Jack; " so beware!"

With these prophetic words, he put his hands into his pockets, and strode away.

He was terribly in earnest in what he had said, and our sequel will prove how he kept his word.

CHAPTER XVIII.

STINGWELL HALL C.C. VERSUS CLARE CHAMPIONS C.C.—A DISCOVERY.

A WEEK elapsed, and nothing was heard or seen of Harry Rawlings.

The detectives were utterly baffled in their efforts to find him, and his fate remained an impenetrable mystery.

Kennedy's friends came and took the body away for burial.

The sad affair soon ceased to be talked about.

The great event of the half arrived.

This was the annual match between the eleven of the Stingwell Hall Cricket Club and an eleven of Clare, the townspeople calling themselves the Clare Champions Cricket Club.

The match always took place in the spacious and beautiful park of Lord Stonehaven.

His lordship kindly sent wagonettes to convey all the boys to his park, and never failed to give them a good dinner and plenty of refreshments.

He was a great lover of the game of cricket.

All that he could do to encourage it he did.

Doctor Birchoften's pupils looked forward to this outing with the greatest eagerness.

Jack was in the eleven, which Clayton, the captain, had got together with all the care of which he was capable.

Precisely at half-past nine the breaks and wagonettes drove up to the school, and the boys, with loud cheers, got in.

Tuffins, as an extra hand to wait at table, was allowed to accompany them, and a carriage was set apart for the doctor and his assistant masters.

The drive to Lord Stonehaven's park was a delightful one, the day being bright, sunshiny, and everything that could be desired.

A splendid wicket had been prepared, and at eleven o'clock play commenced.

Clayton won the toss, and elected to send his men in first.

Jack, and a very careful batsman, named Turner, went to the wickets, and prepared to do their best.

The Stingwell Hall boys knew that they would have to face excellent bowling and fielding, so they were all determined to play well for the honour of the school.

It was a pretty sight in that magnificently wooded park, with its old oaks, elms, and chestnuts, to see the tents and the spectators.

Jack drove the first ball for four, amid loud cheers.

Presently Turner was bowled, and went out for a duck.

This was bad, but another man went in, and between him and Jack, the score was rapidly hit up.

Jack made several sixes.

Loud cries arose of " Well played, Spencer!" and in half-an-hour the first fifty was registered on the telegraph board.

Never had Jack felt so fit, or in such good form.

The second man was now bowled, leg before wicket; a third came in, who was a hard hitter.

Then the century was hoisted.

One hundred for two wickets, and the cheers arose again.

With careful play the score rose to a hundred and fifty, and the bowling was changed.

The captain of the Clare Champions did not at all like the state of the game.

It happened that the new bowler was a slow one.

He delivered tantalising lobbs and half

volleys, which puzzled Jack, who was used to swift round hand.

With the score at hundred and ninety, a lobb rolled into his middle stump.

He had tried to block it, and missed.

Amidst deafening cheering, Jack retired to the pavilion, having put together a hundred and thirty-one.

His reception was tremendous.

Lord Stonehaven and Doctor Birchóften shook him by the hand; he was clapped on the back by his overjoyed chums, till his breath was taken away.

To avoid all this congratulation and noisy demonstration, he slipped on his jacket, and went into the refreshment booth to get a drink.

Tuffins was standing at the counter eating tarts.

He was very red about his fat face, and breathed with difficulty.

"What are you up to, you incorrigible young gorger?" asked Jack, as he helped himself to a glass of dry sherry.

"Ain't this prime," replied Tuffins. "Tarts, cakes and buns, any quantity, unlimited supply, and you can tuck in all you want, and nothing to pay for it. Oh my, ain't it spiffing!"

"You will have a fit of apoplexy."

"No appleplexy for me." I don't want any in mine. Don't I wish there was a cricket match every day in the year!"

"Did you see my play?" inquired Jack.

"Yes, I did. Very fine play it was, too— soo-perb. I've hollered myself 'orse a-cheering you. Didn't you 'ear me?"

"How could I distinguish your voice when the boys were like a pack of hounds giving tongue in pursuit of a fox."

"That's kerrect. Oh, dear," sighed Tuffins, "what a pity it is I can't eat any more."

"You gormandising little wretch!" laughed Jack.

"If I don't take a walk I shall bu'st. You chap behind the bar, give us some ginger-pop to wash it down."

The attendant quickly supplied his wants.

"Long life to Lord Stonehaven," added Tuffins. "I wish there was more like him. He's got a 'art he has."

"Where are you going for your walk?" queried Jack.

"Into the wood, where it is nice and shady. No 'ot sun for me."

"I've a good mind to go with you. The fellows make such a fuss with me. I want to get out of it, and I reckon our men won't be all out for at least an hour."

"Not they. Clayton hasn't been in yet. Come with me and have your fortune told," said Tuffins.

"What?"

"There's gipsies in the wood, I've been told; in fact, there is mostly always gipsies in Lord Stonehaven's wood. His lordship likes and encourages them. I mean to have a bob's worth of the footure and chance it."

Jack smiled. He was not superstitious, nor did he believe in fortune-telling; but it seemed as though Fate urged him on.

Jack would not be wanted on the field for some time.

"A fool and his money are soon parted," he replied. "However, I'll go with you, just for the fun of the thing."

"We are out for enjoyment, and I mean to have a day, I can tell you," said Tuffins, struggling for breath.

"You are blowing like a porpoise, Tuffy. Beware!" answered Jack, solemnly.

"I'd like to die of tarts, cakes, and buns."

"Would you?"

"Rather. That's the kind of death I want. Come along; let us go and consult the wizard of the wood. I am just dying to know what will happen to me in the misty footure."

They quitted the tent, and walked towards the wood, which was of large extent, and might justly have been described as a forest, owing to its wealth of old trees.

Though they did not remark it, the spies of the school saw them go off.

"What's up now?" said Peeping Tom. "Spencer and Tuffins together!"

"That means something," replied Knowall Dick.

"I am very much interested in the match, but I think we ought to be in the know," Tom continued.

"Oh! certainly. Couldn't be out of that for anything—not for worlds. Wouldn't think of it."

"Shall we follow them?"

"Yes," grinned Dick. "If we didn't, I shouldn't sleep all night."

"Nor should I. The unsolved mystery would haunt me."

"You see," continued Knowall Dick, "Jack Spencer is in the eleven, and he would not quit the field unless he had some special object in view."

"Very special."

"That is precisely my idea. We have settled his friend Rawlings, and I should like to perform on him."

"So should I, dearly; but we must not let them see us. Spencer hits hard, and it is too hot to-day for a thrashing."

"It would tire me out," replied Dick. "Besides, when you've been bruised, roughed and tumbled about, and generally sat upon, it spoils all the fun."

"You are right," said Tom. "I'm not volunteering for that kind of thing."

"We'll follow him, though."

"To the end."

Jack and Tuffins were just entering the wood when the spies of the school started after them.

Very cool and shady was it under the trees, and Jack thoroughly enjoyed it after his exertions in the cricket-field.

Tuffins had been there before, for he was a great hand at birdnesting in the spring, and blackberrying in the autumn, as well as nutting.

There were few good spots for that sort of amusement for miles round that he did not know.

He knew where the gipsies were in the habit of camping.

It struck him, however, when he came to reflect, that there could not be many about at that particular time.

If there had been, the cricket match would have attracted them.

He had not seen one.

After a short walk under the trees, they came to a secluded spot.

There was a good deal of sandstone hereabouts, and they saw in a large block an opening, as if to a cave.

The rock was covered with honeysuckle and ivy, which made it look very pretty and picturesque. Tuffins stopped short.

"This is the place where I saw the old woman, in the spring!" he exclaimed. "I believe she lives in that cave. She came out as I was looking for a nest in that little hawthorn tree over there, and asked if I would have my fortune told."

"Did you dip into futurity on that occasion?"

"No. The old hag came upon me so unawares, that I was badly scared."

"What did she say?"

"Just this—'You will come again, young man, to me, as the needle goes to the loadstone. We shall meet again ere long.'"

"Perhaps she has gone away?" replied Jack.

"We will soon see."

"How?"

"She told me, before I went away, that if I wanted her, I was to come outside the cave and clap my hand three times," said Tuffins.

"You had better try the experiment."

"That is what I mean to do, though I should never have been able to pluck up enough courage to come here by myself."

"Advance and summon the witch."

"Stick close to me, Master Jack," replied Tuffins, nervously.

"All right."

They went to the entrance to the cave, which was just large enough to allow a man of average height to go in without stooping.

It was quite dark inside.

They could see nothing.

Tuffins clapped his hands loudly three times.

As the echo died away, a woman, whose back was bent, and face wrinkled with age, made her appearance.

She was leaning on a stick.

A more repulsive-looking hag cannot be imagined.

Her long white hair hung over her shoulders; her eyes were dull and bleared, and her skin was dark as mahogany.

She had on a ragged cotton skirt, and over her shoulders a faded red cloak.

"You have summoned me," she said, in a wheezing, creaky voice. "Who are you, and what do you want?"

Tuffins nudged Jack's elbow.

"You speak to her," he whispered.

Jack nodded.

"We are boys from Stingwell Hall," he exclaimed, "and we want our fortunes told. What is your charge?"

"Simply what you choose to give," replied the gipsy. "The poor Zingari asks for nothing. She lives upon the generosity of those who consult her for the sake of her art."

Jack presented her with a shilling, and Tuffins did the same, after which she looked at the palms of their hands.

"I will begin with you," she exclaimed to the page; "for to you I have not much to say. You will always have one friend—namely, yourself; for you love yourself better than anyone else loves you."

"There is some truth in that," remarked Jack.

"You will never marry," continued the gipsy; "nor will you ever make a name in the world, because the line of life is cut short prematurely, and you will die before you are twenty."

"Oh, lor'! what of?" cried Tuffins, aghast.

"Too much eating."

"Here's a bob's worth of footure," said the page, dolefully. "I wish I'd never invested in it."

"Was it not your desire to draw aside the veil?"

"Bother the wale; I don't like it. I like tarts."

Jack pushed him on one side to take his turn.

After poring over the lines in his palm, the sybil spoke—

"You will live to a good old age," she said, "and die honoured and respected by everyone, amidst troops of friends."

Tuffins uttered an angry growl.

"Why didn't you say that to me?" he muttered.

"Peace!" cried the gipsy. "You, my young friend, will cross water. You must beware of firearms. A young lady will love you, and you will return her affection."

"What am I thinking about now?" asked Jack.

"An absent friend to whom you are deeply attached."

"How and where is he, mother, at this present moment."

"Safe, though not happy, owing to a false and cruel charge which is hanging over his head," replied the gipsy.

"Shall I see him again?"

"Yes."

"When may I expect to do so?"

"Before long; but you must prove his innocence first—that is your task. He is unable to do it."

"Can you tell me any more?"

"I have done. Good-day. It is not permitted me to say any more. Remember the words of the poor gitana."

Uttering this in a solemn tone, the old woman tottered to the cave, and, plunging into the darkness, vanished.

Both the boys were much impressed with her predictions and remarks.

"Oh! didn't she give me a character," observed Tuffins. "She reckoned me up as if she had seen my death certificate. It don't matter, though. If I've got to go early, I must, for I sha'n't leave off eating."

Jack scarcely listened to him.

"I can't help thinking of what she said about my absent friend. That is very extraordinary. She must have meant Harry. That was no hap-hazard hit or misobservation!" he exclaimed.

"You've got to cross water," Tuffins said.

"That's nothing. Everybody travels in these days. Besides, I could do that if I only crossed the river by the aid of the bridge."

"And beware of firearms."

"I believe the tellers usually put that warning into a fortune. But how should she know about Harry Rawlings? That is what is puzzling me."

Suddenly Tuffins saw a nest in a bush which was growing on the top of the cave.

"I must be going," said Jack. "Suppose our eleven gets disposed of in a hurry, and we have to field out?"

"Wait a minute while I get that nest," cried Tuffins.

"Look sharp, then," said Jack, impatiently.

Tuffins was determined to have the nest and carry it home as a trophy, to do which he had to climb up the side of the cave.

This was not a very difficult achievement.

Jack watched him go up, clinging here and there to a branch, saw him reach the summit, and then, to his utter astonishment, saw something else.

He disappeared!

To all appearances he sank through the earth as if he had been engulfed in a quicksand or a quagmire.

Jack could not make it out, and to ascertain the nature of what he feared was a dangerous accident, he also ascended the rock.

He was particularly careful to be very cautious in his movements, lest he might share a similar fate.

When he got to the top, he saw a large hole or fissure in the stone, which, like a shaft, descended into the cave.

The cause of the disappearance of the fat page was now apparent.

He had fallen down the hole.

Jack bent his head over the chasm and listened.

Groans and the sound of voices reached him, but indistinctly.

He could not hear what was said so as to be able to understand.

Unwilling to abandon the unlucky Tuffins to his fate, whatever it might be, he descended the rock.

His intention was to venture into the cave, whether he incurred the displeasure of the gipsy or not.

When he reached the entrance, he found that the passage wound in a devious manner, for he knocked his head against a projecting ledge.

Extending his hands, he groped his way along, and after proceeding about twenty yards, saw rays of light.

This relieved his anxiety, and he pushed on boldly until he came to a spacious vaulted chamber.

It had evidently been carved in the sandstone by the cunning hand of Nature.

A hole in the top admitted air and light.

By the aid of the latter he saw three people in the cave, which, with the exception of two three-legged stools and a table, was destitute of furniture.

The gipsy woman was standing up; a boy was bending over Tuffins, who was apparently in great pain.

"He has broken his arm," exclaimed the boy.

"Hush!" said the gipsy, "a stranger comes."

The boy looked up, and his eyes met those of Jack.

"Great heaven!" cried the latter, "it is Harry Rawlings."

Harry, for it was he, went up to Jack, and shook him by the hand in a hearty manner.

"Yes, old friend," he said, "you have found me."

"How came you here?"

"I owe my life to this good woman," replied Harry. "When I ran away from school, with that hateful charge over me, I wandered into this wood. For two days and nights I was without food or shelter. I laid myself down to die. She found me. I told her my pitiful story, and she brought me here."

"Oh, Harry, I am so glad to have met you," said Jack; "you will be safe in this place."

"Ella, that is her name, knew you from my description when you came to have your fortune told. I had half a mind to come and speak to you, when Tuffins fell down. What shall we do with him? He has broken his arm."

"He can walk. I will take him back to the park. He must see a doctor, and have the bone set."

With a little coaxing Tuffins was induced to get up, and sit on a stool.

His arm was very painful, and he was bruised about the head and face.

"Oh dear," he moaned, "I wish I had never been borned."

"Don't be a coward!" said Jack; "you will soon be all right."

"To think I should be such a hass to fall down that 'ole."

"It can't be helped. You must make the best of it. Can you walk to the field? I really must go back."

"No I can't, and that's flat," said Tuffins. "I feel as if all the stuffing was knocked out of me. You go and fall down that there death-trap, and see if *you* will feel like walking back to the park."

"Not I, thank you. I always avoid a bad example."

"I will see him a little way through the wood," exclaimed Harry, "when he feels a bit better."

"Be careful," replied Jack.

"Trust me. Has anything transpired at the school?"

"Nothing. Kennedy's friends took him away and buried him. There is a warrant out for your arrest—that is all."

"What do the boys say about the affair?"

"They all say you must have done it. Tuffins and I are your only friends; but don't fret. Your innocence is bound to be proved before long."

"Thank you for saying that," exclaimed Harry, whose pale face lighted up with a faint smile.

"I'll come and see you every time I can get out," Jack went on.

"Can I trust Tuffins?"

"With your life," replied the page. "I'll never say a word to betray you."

"He's right enough," cried Jack; "I'll answer for him. Excuse me, Harry, but I must go. I'm playing in the annual match against the Clare Champions."

"And ain't he made a topping score!" said Tuffins, repressing a groan.

"I'm glad to hear that—very glad."

Jack gave all the money he had in his pocket to Ella, the gipsy.

"For you and Harry," he remarked.

Then he shook hands with his chum, and hastened away, fearful lest his services might be required before he got back to the cricket field.

As he left the cave he did not see Peeping Tom and Knowall Dick.

They were hiding behind two trees.

But they saw him, and danger threatened his friend.

CHAPTER XIX.

THE ATTEMPTED ARREST.

HARRY RAWLINGS did not exactly like the idea of leaving the safe seclusion of the gipsy's cave, but he felt that he must see Tuffins through the wood.

Accordingly, after putting the page's arm in a sling, he started off with him.

"Be not rash," said Ella.

"I will not go far, mother," replied Harry. "He requires a little support until he can get to the confines of the wood, then he will not find it so difficult to meet with a doctor."

"Take care that you are not seen. Your schoolfellows are in the park."

"What of that?"

"They all know you, and the warrant for your arrest——"

"Bah! I am not a child," interrupted

Harry. "In half-an-hour I will be back. It is kind of you to warn me, but I know my way about, although I am under a cloud for the present."

"Heaven watch over and preserve you," replied Ella.

Harry gave her a glance full of gratitude.

"It may be in my power to make it up to you some day," he exclaimed.

Tuffins put his arm in that of Harry, and they quitted the cave.

As a matter of course, they were observed by the spies.

"Well, I never did!" said Peeping Tom. "This is wonderful! We have discovered Harry Rawlings' hiding-place."

"What shall we do?" asked Knowall Dick.

"Follow him. It won't do to lose sight of him."

"He is sure to come back."

"Do you think so?"

"Certainly," replied Dick. "Don't you see that Tuffins has hurt himself, and the other one is helping him along?"

"Then you advise waiting here?"

"I do."

"All right," said Tom. "Keep close. I am so glad we have made this immense discovery. The doctor shall know about it before long, and if we don't have Master Harry in prison this day, it won't be our fault."

He rubbed his hands with glee, and Dick grinned with delight.

They waited in silence for about an hour, when Harry returned, having assisted Tuffins to the edge of the wood.

He would have liked to witness the cricket match, but he did not dare to go any farther, lest he might be perceived.

The cheers, which were continually arising, were borne to his ears.

Tuffins had expressed his intention of going into the town at once, to get his broken arm set.

The spies saw Harry re-enter the cave, whereupon they started for the park.

"Our fox has gone to his den," remarked Peeping Tom.

"Yes we've treed our coon, as the Yankees say," replied Knowall Dick.

They lost no time in getting back to the spot where the sport was proceeding.

Stingwell Hall was out for a capital score of nearly three hundred, and the Clare Champions had gone to the wicket.

Jack was bowling.

In the scoring tent the spies found Doctor Birchoften.

"Oh sir," exclaimed Peeping Tom, " such a discovery!"

"We keep our eyes open," said Knowall Dick.

The doctor smiled at their excitement.

"What is it?" he asked. "Speak out! You are raising my curiosity."

"We know where Harry Rawlings is hiding, sir," replied Tom.

"Indeed! That is great news. I thought he would not long evade the meshes of the law!" cried the doctor. "Where is he?"

"In a gipsy's cave in the wood."

"How did you know?"

"We followed Jack Spencer and Tuffins, who went to see him."

"Ha! Spencer is his friend. We could not expect him to betray him," answered the doctor. "Now let me see. There is a policeman here to keep order. The best way to act will be to have him arrest Rawlings without delay."

"We will guide him to the spot," said Peeping Tom.

"You are good boys, and shall have your reward."

"Thank you, sir."

"I will accompany you, and assist in the capture of the murderer. Is it far?"

"Oh, no, sir," replied Tom.

"Then come with me. The ends of justice shall be served. The blood of Kennedy calls aloud for vengeance. He who sheds man's blood, by man shall his blood be shed. That is the universal law, and has existed from time immemorial," said the doctor, sententiously.

During the conversation they had approached the policeman, whose name was Atkins.

He had been actively concerned in prosecuting inquiries for Harry, and was much annoyed at being unable to find him.

It wounded his professional pride.

"Ah, Atkins, good-morning," said the doctor. "I have something for you to do."

"I am ready, sir," replied the policeman. "It is hot work standing here. I think we shall have a storm."

The aspect of the sky bore out his words.

The wind had dropped, and it was very sultry and oppressive.

Clouds were drifting up on the verge of the horizon.

"A thunderstorm would not do any harm," remarked the doctor, "for I have heard the boys say the wicket is very hard."

"Hard as iron, sir, or old nails. See how the ball jumps. There's a topper. It went clean over the wicket-keeper's head. But what is it you've got for me, sir? Nothing wrong, I hope?"

"We have found the hiding-place of the boy-murderer!"

"SLABBER CAUGHT JACK BY THE COLLAR, AND DRAGGED HIM UP."

"Young Rawlings?" queried the policeman.

"The same. He is concealed in a gipsy's cave in the wood."

At this news the policeman slapped his thigh, and uttered a prolonged whistle.

"Bless me," he exclaimed, "if I haven't been everywhere, except there."

"Do you know the gipsy?"

"I've known her for years. She got three months for fortune-telling two years ago, and now she regularly lives in an old sandstone cave."

"How does she live?"

"Oh, people go to her and give her money to reveal the future. They take her food, too. She's an old creature, named Ella. There's no harm in her that I know of. All the gipsy tribe tell fortunes."

"Pretend to, you mean?" cried the doctor, "It is all nonsense, Atkins."

The policeman shook his head, and a very grave expression came over his face.

"I don't know, sir," he answered. "My father had his fortune told, and I had mine. The teller said that he would die of water, and I should die of fire."

"Well?"

"Sure enough the old man did get drowned in the river."

"But you are not dead yet," laughed the doctor.

"I've got it on my mind though, sir; but we'll drop the matter, with your kind permission."

"Atkins, my opinion of you is that you are a—a—shall I say, donkey?"

"If you like, sir. You are welcome to your opinion, so am I to mine. I stick to my belief that I shall die by fire."

"Stuff! Nonsense! I won't listen to it."

"Why did my father die by water?" persisted Atkins.

"Accident, I suppose. But come, let us make this arrest without any further delay," said Doctor Birchoften.

"At your service, sir," was the reply.

She spies of the school were in readiness to lead the way. They were in hot haste to effect the arrest of Harry.

It was a task congenial to their malicious natures.

The doctor spoke a few words to Mr. Dobby, telling him of the matter in hand, and requesting him to explain his absence to Lord Stonehaven.

As they entered the wood all was calm. Not a leaf stirred. The heat was almost intolerable.

There could be little doubt that a fearful storm was threatening.

Even the birds perched on the branches of the trees, and refused to flit about.

A short walk brought the party to the cave.

Ella, the gipsy, was outside busily engaged in cooking.

She had lighted a fire, and suspended a pot from an iron tripod.

From the pot rose a savory smell of stewing rabbits and onions.

Harry, however, was not to be seen.

When she saw the constable, she started and turned pale.

"You know me?" exclaimed Atkins. "I have had you in custody."

"Yes," replied Ella, "the poor Zingara has suffered, because of her art in foretelling events; but if you interfere with me again, I will put my malediction on you!"

The policeman looked troubled at this threat.

"I wish I had not come on this duty," he said.

"Listen not to the miserable cheat!" cried Doctor Birchoften. "She is but a common impostor! Are you her dupe?"

"No, sir; I'm no dupe," rejoined the man, adding, "Now, my good woman, I want to come to business."

"Proceed."

"You have a boy, who is accused of murder, concealed in your cave. Produce him promptly."

"It is false!"

"I shall have to search for him."

The gipsy's eyes flashed.

She placed herself in front of the entrance to the cavern.

"I live here," she exclaimed, "by the kind permission of Lord Stonehaven, and you have no right in my cave."

"We are in pursuit of a criminal."

"Where is your search-warrant? Show me that!"

"I have not got it with me," answered Atkins.

"Go and get it. My cave is my castle. The law gives you no power to enter it without a search-warrant, and I refuse my permission."

"That is correct enough," said Atkins; "but we know the boy is inside. Give him up to save further trouble."

"I will not allow you to enter. You shall pass over my body first. As for the boy you speak of, I know nothing about him."

Ella's one object was to gain time.

She was well aware that, owing to the acoustic properties of the cave, Harry could hear all that was going on.

It was her hope that he would climb up to the hole in the top, through which Tuffins had fallen, and make his escape.

He could hide in the wood till night fell, and then return for shelter.

Doctor Birchoften began to lose his patience.

"I am the head-master of the school where this boy was a pupil," he cried; "and if you determine to frustrate the ends of justice, we must use force against you."

"Dare to do it at your peril!" she replied.

"I will take the consequences on my own shoulders. Atkins, do your duty. I order you to enter the cave."

"Beware!" cried the gipsy. "Sudden death is near!"

"Pay no heed to her rubbish. Thrust her on one side and enter," exclaimed the doctor.

Atkins, with evident reluctance, advanced to do as he was commanded.

He siezed the old woman by the arm, and forcibly removed her.

At this treatment her features became convulsed with rage.

"Scoundrel!" she cried; "have you no respect for grey hairs, and helpless old age? Beware, the malediction!"

He was about to enter the cave, but he paused on the threshold.

"I am only doing my duty," he said.

"You shall not die in your bed," answered Ella. "Your days are not long in the land, and when you die it will be by fire!"

Atkins staggered as if shot.

"There it is again!" he stammered.

Doctor Birchoften pushed his way past him.

"Weak fool! he said; "I will arrest the boy without your aid."

He disappeared in the cave.

At the same moment Peeping Tom uttered a loud cry.

"Look out!" he shouted.

"What for?" asked Atkins, who was beginning to recover himself.

"Rawlings is on the top of the cave. He will get away if you don't mind."

It was true.

Harry had heard what was taking place, and, with great difficulty, had succeeded in climbing up the shaft.

Peeping Tom's eyes had, unfortunately, seen him.

Nothing escaped his vision.

Sliding down the side of the cave, Harry hoped to be able to get away and conceal himself from his enemies in the intricacies of the wood.

In this expectation he was sadly mistaken.

Atkins was after him with all the speed of a sleuthound.

An exciting chase ensued.

Rumblings of thunder, ominous of the coming storm, were heard.

Forked lightning rent the sky

Before Harry had gone a hundred yards, he stumbled over the root of a tree, and fell heavily to the ground.

With a shout of triumph the policeman was about to seize him, when a most extraordinary event occurred.

A flash of lightning struck the man, and he fell dead to the ground.

The spies of the school were struck with awe; their faces blanched, and their legs trembled.

Doctor Birchoften had emerged from the cave, and, with the gipsy, was a witness of the awful event.

"This is dreadful!" he muttered; but his words were drowned in the loud thunderclap which followed the death-dealing flash.

"It was to be his fate," said Ella. "I predicted his father's death, and his own end."

"You!"

"Yes; and I could tell you yours if——"

"Silence, witch!" interrupted the doctor; "the prisoner is escaping! Hi, Harris! hi, Wilkins! stop him!"

The two spies had been too paralysed to move.

Roused by the schoolmaster's voice, they made a movement towards Harry, who had got up.

The lightning had not injured him at all, though he was horrified at the sudden death of Atkins.

He saw his opportunity, and he did not mean to neglect it.

As soon as he rose to his feet, Peeping Tom and Knowall Dick rushed upon him.

Harry saw that he would have to fight for his liberty, and, perhaps, his life.

It was no time to stand upon ceremony.

He took up a stone, which he saw lying at his feet, and threw it at Tom.

It hit him on the forehead, making him stagger like a drunken man.

"Come on," cried Harry to Knowall Dick; "I'm ready for you!"

"Not for me," replied Dick, turning to run.

A stout stick of wood presented itself to Harry's view, and, picking it up, he dealt Knowall Dick a blow on the head which made him see stars.

Then he went boldly up to Ella, still holding the stick in his hand.

He took her hand in his, and raised it to his lips.

A tender, loving kiss was imprinted on it, just such a kiss as a son would give his mother.

"Heaven bless you!" he exclaimed, "I shall never forget your kindness."

"Go, my boy," replied the gipsy. "This is no place for you since you have been betrayed. Remember what I have told you!"

Doctor Birchoften extended his hand, and tried to grasp Harry by the collar.

"I think I have something to say in this matter," he exclaimed, angrily. "You are my prisoner."

"Don't make any mistake," replied Harry, raising his stick.

"Do you dare to resist my authority, rascal?"

"Yes, sir. I am innocent of the charge brought against me, and I am not going to surrender myself."

"You must."

"Touch me, and you will repent it bitterly."

"What! Am I to be defied by a boy?" cried the doctor, whose wrath was increasing every moment.

"Stand on one side," answered Harry.

The doctor advanced.

"Back, or take the consequences."

Unfortunately for himself, the irascible and self-important schoolmaster would not accept the advice.

He laid his hand on Harry, and was felled to the ground with a blow from the stick.

It stunned him for a few seconds, and Harry was enabled to effect his escape.

The spies did not attempt to interfere with him.

They had had enough of that kind of thing to last them for one day, at all events.

CHAPTER XX.

HAUNTED.

DAYS passed by after the cricket match, in which the schoolboys were victorious, but nothing was heard of Harry Rawlings.

The gipsy's cave was carefully watched.

He did not return there.

The mystery respecting him was deeper and more impenetrable than before.

Meanwhile, the author of all the mischief, Warner, the brutal bully, who had done Kennedy to death, began to recover his courage.

He had been very despondent for some time.

There was a horrible dread in his mind that his sin would come home to him.

Peeping Tom and Knowall Dick were a source of worry to him, because, knowing he was in their power, they made him pay for their silence.

First, they came upon him for money.

When his stock of silver was gone, they made him give up his cricket bats, books, pocket-knife, and any other little article of commerce that they could sell in the town.

At last they sucked him dry.

Meeting him in the yard one morning, they called him into the woodshed, which, as we know, was their favourite place for talking privately.

On this occasion, however, they were not so private as they imagined.

Pranks had got well.

That is to say, he was well enough to walk about by the aid of a crutch.

Jack was very kind to the boy, having quite forgiven him for his conduct, for it was not in Jack's disposition to bear malice.

Pranks was sitting down on some faggots in a shady corner, having gone inside to get out of the heat, which was oppressive.

No one noticed him.

"What do you want with me?" asked Warner, impatiently.

"We want some money," replied Tom.

"Can't get on without it," said Knowall Dick.

"You have drained me dry. I haven't a thing left. You have even got my pocket-knife."

"Can't help that," answered Tom.

"No business of ours," said Dick. "You've got to part, or—"

"Yes," chimed in Tom, "or—"

They looked at him in a very significant manner.

Pranks heard all this, and made a note of it, wondering why the spies of the school should hold the whip-hand over Warner.

As a rule, the bully did not care for anybody.

He had proudly called himself the "Cock of the School;" yet here he was, the abject slave of Peeping Tom and Knowall Dick.

It was a thing that Pranks could not understand.

On no account would he have revealed his presence, so he shrank back into the corner and listened, quietly as a mouse.

"If you don't give us something, we'll tell all we know about you," continued Tom.

"Bound to do it," put in Dick.

"You'll drive me mad," replied Warner. "I never saw two such little vampires."

"Should the truth be known—" said Tom.

"Stop!" interrupted Warner. "I cannot stand it. Wait a couple of days."

"What for?"

"I will write to my mother. She always sends me something."

"Very well, we will wait; only don't forget us. One word to Jack Spencer about Kennedy—"

"For goodness sake, be quiet," again interrupted Warner. "Somebody might hear you."

"Give me that watch you are wearing," replied Peeping Tom.

"Yes; we could sell it down the town. That will do," said Knowall Dick.

It was a present from Warner's mother on his birthday.

He did not like to part with it.

But he durst not refuse, and reluctantly he gave it them.

Pranks was more astonished than ever.

There was a hidden secret. It concerned Harry Rawlings, for Kennedy's name had been mentioned.

He resolved to tell Jack what he had overheard.

After giving up the watch, Warner went away, and the spies of the school followed him, chuckling at their success.

They had played well upon his fears.

When Pranks was alone, he got up from his place of concealment, and walked into the field.

He knew Jack was down there, because he had seen him carry his bat in that direction.

Not far had he gone before he encountered Spencer returning.

"How are you?" exclaimed Jack, in his cheery way. "Glad to see you about again."

"Oh, I am getting on nicely, thank you," replied Pranks.

"You look rather serious. Is there anything up?"

"I want to tell you something about your chum. You know I played rather a shabby trick about the MS.?"

"Yes. Don't talk about that," cried Jack. "It is forgotten and forgiven. Let bygones be bygones."

"It is very kind of you to say so."

"Can you find poor Harry Rawlings, or do anything in the world to clear his character?"

"I think I can," replied Pranks.

This rejoinder greatly surprised Jack, who had almost abandoned hope in Harry's case.

He told Pranks to speak plainly, and listened to his tale with a certain amount of pleasure.

The conduct of the spies, the behaviour of Warner, his giving up his watch, all pointed to one conclusion.

Warner had killed Kennedy, Peeping Tom and Knowall Dick were aware of the fact, and together they had thrown the blame of the deed upon Rawlings.

"What do you make of it?" asked Pranks.

"There is something in it, my boy," replied Jack, "and I am glad you have told me."

"Don't you think Warner did it?"

"Of course. He was always bullying poor little Kennedy, whose life was a misery and a burden to him for that very reason."

"Everybody in the school knows that," said Pranks.

"The question is, how are we to prove it?" Jack added, in some perplexity.

"We must act on his fears and on his superstitions," replied Pranks. "I know Warner better than you do. We used to be chums before last Christmas, when we quarrelled over a knife he took from me, and then I became friendly with Wildash."

"Why don't you come to the point?" Jack interrupted, impatiently.

Pranks was a great chatterer, and a very discursive talker; but he restrained his propensity to ramble.

"My idea is just this," he exclaimed: "let us haunt him."

"Haunt him?" repeated Jack.

"Yes."

"How can that be done?"

"Easy enough," said Pranks. "My father is a sculptor and modeller, and he has taught me to make masks, faces, plaster of Paris casts, and all that sort of thing."

"What of that?" asked Jack, who did not yet grasp his meaning.

"If you have a photo of little Kennedy, I will make some masks exactly like him, and we will put them on, and give the brute Warner such a scare that his conscience will betray him."

"Agreed!" exclaimed Jack. "If we could make him confess, it would be a great thing, though I despair of seeing Harry again."

"Why so?" inquired Pranks.

"I fancy he has gone to sea. But to return to our subject. You really think Warner is easily frightened?"

"I know it. Didn't I tell you I was his chum?"

"Come with me into the schoolroom," said Jack. "In my locker I have a photo of Kennedy, which he gave me a few weeks before his death."

"Hurrah! that's capital. Let me have it, and I will soon make the masks."

They went into the schoolroom, and the photograph was produced.

"I shall have to do the ghost business," Jack remarked, "as you are lame."

"True. I forgot that. A ghost on a crutch would be out of the order of supernatural things," replied Pranks, laughing.

It was arranged that he should make one mask, and have it ready by the following day, which was Saturday.

This was always a half-holiday.

By accident, Jack heard Warner say that he should go fishing in the afternoon of the next day.

He determined that his first attempt at haunting should be made on that occasion.

Warner had no intimate friend. As a rule, he went alone when he took his amusement.

Jack wanted only the mask and a sheet; the latter article he intended to take from his bed.

The mask was duly completed by Pranks before dinner on Saturday, and putting it and the sheet in a little hand-bag, Jack started for the river.

He had previously seen Warner go out with his rod and line.

There was no doubt as to his finding him.

There was a favourite spot for fishing near the roadside inn which flourished under the able management of Mr. Corks.

It was to this spot that Jack Spencer directed his steps, guessing that Warner would select it for his amusement.

Nor was he mistaken in his conjecture; for when he got to the bridge, he saw the tall bully busily engaged in pulling out the fish.

So intent was Warner upon his pleasant occupation, that he had eyes for nothing else.

He did not see Jack's figure cross the bridge, and pass along the opposite side of the stream.

Nor did he notice him slip behind the thick trunk of a large tree almost facing him, and undo his bag.

All this was lost on the intent angler, who, when not unhooking a fine perch, was watching his float.

The sun had become obscured, and drifting clouds denoted rain before long.

Jack was by no means a bad mimic, and he had all the morning been trying to imitate Kennedy's voice, which he recollected perfectly.

Putting on the sheet, he adjusted the mask (which was very life-like), put on his cap, and emerging from behind the tree, stood in front of the lone fisherman.

The latter nearly landed a fish, but it was a big one, and contrived to slip from the hook and escape.

An exclamation of disappointment, mingled with anger, broke from Warner.

"Hang the luck!" he muttered. "I wouldn't have lost him for a pension."

Jack thought this was a good opportunity to attract his attention.

"Ha, ha, ha!" he laughed, in sepulchral tones.

Warner instantly looked up to see whence the sound proceeded.

All the blood left his face, which was convulsed with a nameless horror.

The apparition unhinged him altogether, for he had been for some time the prey of an accusing conscience.

His nights had been sleepless; his days were days of unrest, and his nerves were thoroughly shaken.

"Who are you?" he stammered, as well as his chattering teeth would permit him. "And what do you want with me?"

"I am the spirit of Kennedy, and have come to haunt you," replied Jack.

Warner's hand trembled so much that his fishing-rod fell from his grasp into the river.

"You will be haunted by me," continued Jack, "until you confess your crime."

Warner sank on his knees.

"Spare me!" he moaned.

"No; it cannot be. Another is suffering for your offence. Justice must be done. Confess."

He stretched out his hand in a threatening manner.

Overcome with dread, Warner covered his face with his hands.

For fully a minute he remained as if stunned.

When the feeling of abject terror passed off, he removed his hands, and looked up.

The ghost of Kennedy was gone.

Jack had packed up the mask and the sheet, and, with his bag, had regained the high road, making his way to the old inn parlour.

He sat down highly pleased with the result of his experiment.

It was reasonable to hope that in time his stratagem would be successful.

Yet even if it were, how was he to find his friend?

How lonely the parlour seemed without Harry. Many happy hours and much fun had they had there in their holiday time.

He felt very dull and miserable when thinking of his chum.

While he was plunged in a brown study and the prey of a melancholy he could not drive away, Corks came into the room.

Under his arm he carried a quaintly carved oak cabinet, about two feet in height, and one in width.

It was black with age.

He put it on the table, and greeted Jack kindly.

"Ha, Master Spencer," he exclaimed, "I didn't know as you was here, or I'd have been in sooner. You look down a bit."

"I miss my chum, Harry Rawlings," answered Jack.

"Ah! that was a sad affair; but I don't believe he did it," said Corks.

"No more than you did."

"Right will triumph in the end, sir."

"I hope so; it won't be my fault if it does not. I'm a true friend, whatever else I may be."

"It's a zigzag world," mused Corks; "we all have our ups and downs. Talking of Harry reminds me of the young Squire, as they call him—Charlie his name is."

"What of him?"

"He's going the pace, he is."

"How so?" asked Jack.

"Why, he's made friends with Lord Stonehaven's son, who is home on leave. A lieutenant in the navy he is, and the fastest young rip out. He drinks like a fish, and gambles all the time."

"A bad companion."

"You may well say that. The Honourable Hugh Charteris—that is the title and name of Lord Stonehaven's son—knows a trick or two."

"His father is not rich, I have heard," said Jack.

"No, sir. He's very good-hearted, though, and gives away a lot to the poor, so he can't afford to supply his son's extravagances. The Honourable Hugh has been winning largely from Charlie Rawlings."

"How do you know?"

"Only this morning he came to me—Charlie, I mean—and borrowed five pounds. His father gives him an allowance, but that's all gone, and he can't get any more till next week."

"You're a man of the world," exclaimed Jack, "and it isn't for me to dictate to you, but don't you think you will lose your money?"

"Not me," replied Corks.

"What precaution did you take?"

"I got security in the shape of this old cabinet," returned the landlord.

"Indeed! You are more alert than I gave you credit for being. Where did it come from?"

"Up at the Hall. He told me his father, the Squire, said he might have it if he wanted it."

Corks opened the cabinet, which had several shelves and drawers.

All these Jack, with boyish curiosity, examined.

They were empty.

"Perhaps a hundred years ago," he remarked, "some lady kept her jewels and love-letters in this."

"Very likely, sir," said the landlord. "I must be going now. Is there anything you want?"

Jack ordered some refreshment. This was supplied him, and he left alone.

A desire to look at the cabinet again seized him.

He sat down in front of it.

CHAPTER XXI.

THE OLD OAK CABINET—THE SECRET DRAWER.

IN a listless way Jack handled the cabinet, turned it on its side, on its back, weighed it, looked at the carving, and wondered what it had been used for.

Probably it was an heirloom in the Rawlings family, which was one of the oldest in the county.

And now a young spendthrift was making use of it for a trifle to get money to supply his vices.

Suddenly a drawer shot out of the bottom piece, which had seemed to be a block of solid oak.

He had put his finger inadvertently upon a spring, which had revealed a secret drawer. In it was a document, folded as lawyers fold deeds, and tied with a red tape.

It did not look old, and had no musty smell about it, which it would have had if it had been there a long time.

Taking it out of its repository, Jack turned it over, and was greatly surprised to read the writing upon it.

This was as follows—

"The last will and testament of Ernest Rawlings.

"James Venables, Solicitor, Lincoln's Inn Fields, London."

Here was a discovery!

Perhaps it might be of the utmost use to his friend Harry. Everybody had said there was, or ought to be, a will in his favour. Was this it?

Tremblingly he slipped the will into his

"SLABBER GLIDED UP TO HER WITH ALL THE STEALTHINESS OF A SNAKE."

pocket, and pushed the drawer back into its place.

No one had witnessed the finding of the document, and the secret so far was safe in his own keeping.

He had no friendly feeling towards Squire Rawlings.

It would rejoice him to the bottom of his heart to turn him out of the property, and instal his chum Harry in its possession.

For a moment he was in doubt how to act, but he soon made up his mind to do what every sensible boy should when he finds himself in a difficulty.

This was to consult his father.

The farm was not very far off.

Accordingly he left the inn, and cut across the fields.

Naturally he was in a state of some excitement.

If the will was of any value, Charlie had, to gratify his extravagance, thrown away his fortune.

When he reached the farm, Mr. and Mrs. Spencer and Marian were just sitting down to dinner. They were delighted to see him, though somewhat astonished.

After kissing his mother and sister, and shaking hands with his father, he exclaimed—

"Don't look frightened; there is nothing wrong."

"I don't expect there ever will be with you," replied Mr. Spencer. "You have been brought up in the right way. Sit down and have some dinner."

"Can I speak to you privately, father?" asked Jack.

"Your father has no secrets from me," said his mother.

"And it is a shame to keep one from your sister," observed Marian.

"All right," answered Jack; "I'll tell you all what I have got to say after dinner. It is too bad to spoil this leg of mutton I see before me. Cut away, father, my little affair will keep."

The dinner proceeded, and the conversation naturally turned upon Harry Rawlings, and the death of Kennedy.

Marian felt Harry's absence greatly.

Everybody at the table expressed confidence in his innocence.

"I should like to see Harry cleared," exclaimed Mr. Spencer, "and master of the Hall, for we have no reason to like the Squire."

"What has he been doing?" inquired Jack.

"Since my horse beat his, he has given me notice to quit the farm at the end of my tenancy."

"When is that?"

"Three months' time, and where to go I don't know. I have spent a heap of money on this farm, and improved it; but there is no clause in my lease giving me compensation for improvement. By leaving I shall be a heavy loser."

"He's a scoundrel!" Jack said, indignantly.

"I wish that I could foil him," replied the farmer, bitterly.

Jack smiled.

"Perhaps you may," he remarked, "with my help."

Everyone stared at him as if he had taken leave of his senses.

Drawing the will he had found in the secret drawer of the old oak cabinet from his pocket, he threw it on the table.

"Look at that father," he cried.

"What is it?" inquired the farmer.

"It is the business that brought me here," Jack replied. "Read it and give me your candid opinion upon its contents. I have only looked at the endorsement on the outside."

Mr. Spencer unfastened the red tape, and carefully perused the document.

It seemed to interest him greatly.

"Have you shown this to anybody else?" he inquired.

"No," rejoined Jack; "I brought it straight to you."

"Where did you find it?"

Jack related precisely how it had come into his possession.

"Well," said his father, with a smile of deep satisfaction, "all that I can tell you is, that you have discovered the missing will that people have been talking about."

"Is it indeed so?" asked Jack. "I scarcely dared to hope for so much as that."

"The Squire will have to step down from his lofty position and go out of the property, which is undoubtedly Harry's. I will go to London to-morrow to see the solicitor who drew the will, and inform him of the facts of this remarkable case."

"Are you sure of it, father?"

"As positive as that I am sitting at this table and just going to drink this glass of ale."

Jack looked immensely gratified.

"Then I have done something for my friend, after all," he said.

"Undoubtedly you have. We will prove in a week whose the estate is. The Squire won't ride the high horse any more. I congratulate you, Jack, my boy. Harry shall have his own."

Marian looked up with a sigh.

"Father," she remarked, "haven't you allowed your enthusiasm at this discovery, the importance of which I do not underrate for a moment, to carry you too far?"

"How is that?" demanded the farmer.

"You seem to forget that poor Harry has a criminal charge hanging over his head, and also that he cannot be found."

"He will turn up when he is advertised for."

"If he does he will be arrested in connection with this unfortunate affair of Kennedy."

Mr. Spencer's face assumed a blank expression.

"I had forgotten that," he said.

"If there is no claimant for the estate, we can't disturb the Squire," continued Marian.

"Then I have had all my labour, or luck, or whatever you like to call it, in vain," observed Jack.

"I believe we shall never see him again," exclaimed Mrs. Spencer. "Harry was a very high-spirited boy, and he could not face undeserved shame and calumny."

"Anyhow," exclaimed the farmer, decisively, "I will go to the lawyer to-morrow and have the will proved. Ha, ha! that will stir the Squire up as if he had a nest of hornets round his ears. I hope the best about Harry, but, dang me, if I don't make his uncle repent what he has done."

Jack suggested to his father that, whatever he did, it would be best to keep it a profound secret for the present.

When the proper time came—strike!

Lay the mine, and, at a fitting opportunity, fire the train and have the explosion.

In this view the farmer entirely concurred, and Jack went back to school in high spirits.

It was something to know that Squire Rawlings was a forger and an impostor.

If Harry could only be proved innocent of Kennedy's death and found, a villain would be thwarted, and an honest man have his own.

CHAPTER XXII.

THE CONFESSION.

WHEN Warner recovered from his attack of fright sufficiently to remove his hands from his face and look up, he was trembling like a leaf.

The shock of the supposed apparition of Kennedy had made him as weak as a child.

Throwing himself on the grass by the side of the fish he had caught, he gasped for breath.

A violent palpitation of the heart seized him, and he fainted dead away, turning on his face.

It chanced that Peeping Tom and Knowall Dick were prowling along the bank of the river.

The spies of the school had not found out anything lately to report to Mr. Dobby.

They felt rather low-spirited in consequence.

Not a boy in the school had been birched for a week, and they thought that either the school was getting too good, or they were not so clever as they used to be in finding out things.

"Hullo!" cried Peeping Tom, espying Warner; "what's this?"

He did not recognise who it was.

"What a lovely lot of fish—over a dozen and a-half," said Knowall Dick.

"Beauties," replied Tom.

"It strikes me we are in luck," exclaimed Dick. "The fellow is asleep. Let's take his fish."

"I'm game, if you are," said Tom.

"Right."

Dick ran to a willow tree, and broke down a switch to string the fish on.

Meanwhile Peeping Tom felt he must have a look at the fisherman.

He could not have rested if he had not done so.

Warner's breathing was difficult and stentorious. He laboured frightfully in drawing his breath.

This alarmed Peeping Tom.

"Hold on!" he cried; "there is something wrong with this chap. I believe he is in a fit."

"What has that to do with us?" asked Dick.

"He might give us something if we bring him to."

"We might get into trouble if he dies. Let him alone."

"No; I am going to turn him over."

"More fool you! We shall lose the fish, if nothing worse happens."

Peeping Tom, however, was not to be denied.

He stooped over the prostrate body, and turned it over, which afforded Warner some relief; for he had been stricken with an epileptic fit, and if he had not been moved, he would have died.

"Bless me!" cried Peeping Tom. "Come here, Dick."

Dick was stringing up the fish, which he meant to have for supper if he could get the cook in a good-enough humour to prepare them.

"Let me alone," he replied; "I'm busy. Can't you see?"

"It's Warner!"

Dick let the fish drop on hearing this.

"What!" he exclaimed, in accents of astonishment. "Warner? Never!"

"Fact, as I live," answered Peeping Tom. "Scoop up some water into your cap, and dash it in his face while I hold his head up on my knee."

"Is he so bad?"

"He's dying, I think."

Knowall Dick did not hesitate to do as he was told; he got some water, which, in a short time, revived the fallen bully.

He sat up and looked wildly towards the other side of the river.

"Is it gone?" he asked, shivering as if with the ague.

"What?" asked Tom.

"The ghost of Kennedy. I am haunted. It stood opposite me as I was fishing, and told me to confess, or it would never leave me. Oh, it was awful!"

Blankly the spies looked at one another.

It was easy to see that they thought Warner had suddenly become demented.

"You must have been dreaming," replied Dick.

"No, no; I saw it distinctly. Never shall I forget that face."

"Don't give way to such fancies."

"I can't stand it," exclaimed Warner. "If I see it again I shall go mad. Whatever comes of it, I must confess."

The spies did not like the aspect the affair was taking.

It would make it very serious for them.

"Don't split upon us," said Tom.

"I will not mention your names. You helped me all you could," Warner replied.

"Too much. If you make a fool of yourself by confessing, we are sure to get in for it."

"Oh, dear," groaned Dick. "I wish we hadn't said anything. Everything was going on so well. We have been to see Squire Rawlings, and when we told him what we had done in the matter, he gave us five pounds apiece."

"I must confess, to relieve my mind," persisted Warner. "If I don't, the ghost will come again; it told me so."

"It is jolly awkward," mused Tom. "We stated we saw Harry throw the ball, and if you say you did it, we shall be birched pretty severely."

"Perhaps expelled," said Dick.

Warner rose, shaking like a leaf.

He walked away like one dazed, leaving the spies in no very amiable frame of mind.

They were sure of a flogging at the heavy hand of the doctor, if nothing worse ensued.

The pitiable expression of their faces was a complete study.

Warner's awakening of conscience was thorough. He did not falter for a moment in his set purpose.

He was determined to make a full confession, and take the consequences, whatever they might be.

When he reached the school, he heard the merry voices of the light-hearted boys in the playground, and they sent a chill to his heart.

Never more would he be able to join in their innocent diversions.

There was a foul sin-blot on his soul, and he would have to expiate his crime.

When he came out of prison his father would probably send him to a foreign land, where nothing was known of his antecedents.

With bowed head and deathly white face, he knocked at the doctor's study door.

"Come in," said Doctor Birchoften, who, in company with Mr. Dobby, was engaged in correcting some Latin exercises.

The culprit entered sadly, but terribly in earnest.

"Please, sir," began Warner, "I want to confess."

"What have you been doing?"

"It was I who accidentally killed Kennedy, while I was bullying. I am very sorry for it, and I cannot bear the strain of silence any longer."

The doctor and Mr. Dobby were amazed at this declaration.

"Heaven bless me! Is this true?" asked the doctor.

"Harris and Wilkins stated that they saw Rawlings do the deed," suggested Mr. Dobby.

"They must have been mistaken, sir. It was I," exclaimed Warner.

"Or they told a deliberate falsehood," replied the doctor, adding, "You have allowed an innocent boy to lie under suspicion, which greatly aggravates your offence. No one knows what has become of the unfortunate fellow. Dear me! it makes the deplorable affair sadder than ever."

"I can only repeat that I did it, sir," said Warner.

"You are fully aware that you will have to be tried for this?"

"Quite so. I did not mean to injure him."

"Yet you threw the ball, and are old enough to know the danger of such an act. What were you doing?"

"Bullying him, as I was in the habit of doing."

"It amounts, then, to a charge of manslaughter. Mr. Dobby!"

"Sir," replied the second master.

"I have a painful duty to perform. You must acquaint the police."

"At once!"

"Warner will remain here with me until you return."

"Very well, sir."

Mr. Dobby promptly withdrew, and Warner saw that his doom was sealed.

His fate depended on the finding of the jury, and the merciful consideration of the judge before whom the case would come.

Yet he felt he would rather have it so than face the ghost again.

"Take a chair," said the doctor, when they were alone. "You look very ill. Will you take a glass of wine?"

"No, thank you," answered Warner, sitting down.

"This crime has preyed upon your mind. It is curious that you should confess, after all the time that has elapsed."

"I have not had a moment's peace since; and—and——"

He paused abruptly.

"What? Go on."

"To-day I saw Kennedy's ghost. It spoke and threatened to haunt me till I gave myself up. Oh, sir, I could not bear it."

"Some hallucination, I suspect."

"Not at all. It was his spirit. My head is clear enough on that point."

"Strange!" said the doctor. "Yet I cannot believe in your ghost."

"I wish I could not," Warner answered, "It was so clear, so life-life, though draped in white. The voice was the same."

"Then it was not remorse that was gnawing at your heart, it is fear that has driven you to this course?"

Warner made no answer.

Doctor Birchoften went on writing, and nothing more was said until Mr. Dobby reappeared, accompanied by a constable.

He had been made acquainted with the facts as they walked along, and was prepared to take the prisoner to the lock-up.

"This is the boy!" exclaimed Mr. Dobby.

The policeman produced a pair of handcuffs.

"I do not think there is any necessity to inflict that degradation, constable," said the Doctor.

"We have to take precautions," was the reply.

"He is not a desperate criminal, and will go quietly enough."

"Excuse me; it is our rule, sir, in murder and felony cases."

Warner held out his hands.

The tears came into his eyes as he did so.

His face, hitherto so pale, became flushed with shame. The steel bracelets quickly encircled his wrists.

"Good-bye, sir," said Warner, in a broken voice. "Good-bye, Mr. Dobby."

"I cannot say that you have my sympathy," answered the doctor, "for you have behaved very badly, and brought my school into disrepute. Nevertheless, I am sorry for you."

"Seek consolation and pardon from above," exclaimed Mr. Dobby.

Grasping Warner roughly by the arm, the constable led him away.

He was taken out through the front door.

This spared him the additional disgrace of being seen by the boys, who were trooping in to dinner.

"Mr. Dobby," said the doctor, "bring Harris and Wilkins to me. They have spoken falsely, and I shall punish them."

"They richly deserve it, sir," replied the second master.

"And they shall have all that they have merited."

"Anything else, sir?"

"I am upset by this occurrence to-day, and shall not come into dinner. Will you be good enough to make a brief speech to the boys, and inform them of the facts that have come to light?"

"With the greatest of pleasure, sir," responded Mr. Dobby.

When the usher was gone, Doctor Birchoften unlocked a cabinet, and took from it two new birches, with long handles.

He swished them through the air and smiled.

The music they made seemed to please him hugely.

In a few minutes the two spies arrived, looking very dejected.

"You boys," exclaimed the doctor, "have done Rawlings a great wrong, why or wherefore, I know not. Warner has confessed that he was the culprit."

"Please, sir," replied Peeping Tom, "we made a mistake for once."

"I cannot help that."

"It looked like Rawlings, and his name was on the ball. We saw the affair from a distance."

"When Kennedy fell, the boy who killed him ran away," said Knowall Dick.

"You told a different story before. Prepare for punishment!" cried the doctor.

Reluctantly the spies removed their jackets, and in a short time howls and yells proceeded from the study.

These were interspersed with cries for mercy, and lasted a long while.

The spies had got their just reward.

They did not forget that interview with their head-master for many a day.

Meanwhile Mr. Dobby was haranguing the boys, who were all seated at the table in the dining-room.

He told them that Warner had made a full confession that he, and he alone, had caused the death of Kennedy.

A policeman had removed him from the school to prison to await his trial.

He asked them to think well of the unfortunate Harry Rawlings.

This announcement fell like a thunderclap on the boys.

Jack Spencer was very jubilant, for he had not expected his ruse to be so soon successful.

He and Pranks exchanged glances.

Rising in his seat, Jack waved his hand.

"Hurrah! Three cheers for Harry Rawlings!" he cried.

The boys responded in a hearty manner, for they were generous enough to see their error, and do justice.

But what good would this do Harry now?

Where was he?

What had become of him?

That was the mystery which no one there could fathom.

CHAPTER XXIII.

PRIDE HAS A FALL.

WE must return for a while to Charlie, who had quite forgotten that he had ever been a snake-charmer and a vagabond stroller from fair to fair.

He was a young gentleman now, and held his head high.

The Squire was very proud of him, and highly approved of the friendship he had established with the Honourable Hugh Charteris.

His intimacy with the son of Lord Stonehaven was something to talk about.

The day after Warner had made himself a martyr for conscience sake, Squire Rawlings and his promising son were seated at breakfast.

When they had finished the repast, a servant announced a boy from the school.

"Show him in, and close the door," said the Squire.

In a minute Peeping Tom entered.

He was asked to take a seat, which he did.

"Have you breakfasted, my little man?" asked the Squire.

"Well, I have and I haven't," replied the spy. "I've had some weak tea and some bread and scrape, but I could do with some of that stuff on your table. Running over here has made me hungry."

"You have some news for me?"

"Very important."

"Eat first, and talk afterwards. Hospitality is the first law," answered the Squire.

"Will you have some tongue, ham, spring chicken, cold duck, honey in the comb, muffins, buttered toast?—tea or coffee?"

Peeping Tom nodded his head violently, and his mouth opened.

"All that," he rejoined.

"All?"

"Yes, sir, thank you; I can fill the bill. I had nothing yesterday but brimstone and treacle."

"How was that, my boy?"

"I got birched, and Miss Martha, the housekeeper, attended to me according to the rules and regulations."

"Oh, I see. You were put on punishment diet. What for?"

"I'll tell you when I have had some of what you mentioned," replied Peeping Tom.

Charlie, obedient to a sign from his father, waited upon him, and Peeping Tom made a more luxurious breakfast than he had ever done in his life.

The Squire thought he was never going to stop.

Not that he cared how much he ate, but he was anxious to hear his news.

Having a guilty mind he was always anxious, expectant, and ill at ease.

At last Peeping Tom laid down his knife and fork, and drew a long breath.

"That's worth living for," he said. "It beats the record."

"To what do you allude?"

"The breakfast you have given me. I should like to live with you; but now to my business. Warner has confessed."

The Squire looked troubled.

"Do you mean that he has exculpated my nephew?" he demanded.

"Yes, sir. Harry Rawlings' character is cleared."

"Then he can come back when he likes?"

"Exactly."

"What has become of Warner?"

"He is taken to prison to stand his trial for the murder!"

"How could he have done such an act of self-destruction?" asked the Squire.

"He said he saw a ghost, but I reckon he got weak-minded; anyhow, I and my friend Dick got the jolliest hiding from the doctor any boys ever had. If these chairs hadn't got soft cushions, I couldn't sit down. I thought it best to come over and tell you."

The Squire thanked him, made him a present, and asked him to let him know all the news regularly.

If Harry came back he was to run over instantly.

Peeping Tom took his leave, and Charlie and his father discussed the new phase of the affair.

"I had hoped that we were rid of that wretched boy for ever," said the Squire.

"It is not likely he will turn up now," replied Charlie.

"I feel he is destined to be our ruin."

"Why?"

"I can't tell you the reason. It is a presentiment, and mine never deceive me. I can always tell when trouble is brewing."

"Nonsense, father! You give way to idle fancies."

"I hope I do."

"Such thoughts do not find a place in my mind," laughed Charlie. "I mean to enjoy myself while I am young. To-day I have an appointment with the Honourable Hugh Charteris. We are going for a drive."

"He is a very desirable acquaintance," replied the Squire. "Cultivate him. I wish you to mix with the first families in the county."

"Why not? Nobody knows what I was."

"Take care they never do."

"I could only be found out by meeting some of the fair people. Most of the boys I used to play with have seen the marks on my arm. They could identify me easily enough."

"You are not likely to come in contact with them."

"Not I," said Charlie, haughtily. "Do you think I would mix with such scum?"

"You have no proper pride, and no sense of discretion if you do."

"Trust me."

"Where do you meet Charteris?" asked the Squire.

"He is going with the dog-cart to the inn kept by Corks. I am to be picked up there, and, after a drive, he is to take me to the Hall to lunch."

"Very good. Do you want any money?"

"I could manage with a few pounds."

The Squire opened his purse.

"There are five for you," he exclaimed. "Always remember to behave like a gentleman. I hope you will enjoy yourself."

"Thank you, father," replied Charlie.

He put on a deer-stalker hat, and, whistling merrily, left the house, expecting to have a good time.

He was destined to be bitterly chagrined, ere he returned home.

It would have been better for him if he had not gone out.

His way to the inn lay across some fields past Farmer Spencer's homestead.

Whistling for want of thought, he neared the house, when he suddenly caught sight of Marian, who was plucking some wild roses from a hedge.

Charlie thought he had never seen such a sweet girl before.

He looked again, and being irresistibly attracted, determined to speak to her.

This was a very bold and impudent proceeding on his part, for she was a perfect stranger to him.

Rude though it was, he could not help it.

The temptation was not to be resisted, for it was a case of love at first sight.

"Good-morning, my dear," he exclaimed.

For the first time she became aware of his presence, so intent had she been on her wild flowers.

A hot flush mantled her neck and face.

"I have not the pleasure of knowing you," she replied.

"You shall have, if you like," he went on.

"Indeed! I am much obliged to you, but I have no wish."

"At least, condescend to tell me who you are."

"Farmer Spencer's daughter. My name is Marian."

"Well, my little Marian, will you be my sweetheart?" he demanded, with all the assumption of a man.

"How dare you talk to me in that way?" she cried, angrily.

The hot flush that mantled her face deepened.

"Really, you must excuse the liberty I take," said Charlie, "but you are such a nice girl that I cannot help it. It is the homage I pay to beauty."

"Go away at once, or—"

"Don't get vexed. Give me a kiss."

He approached Marian, who retreated towards a stile.

"If you come a step farther, I'll call my father," she said.

"Bah! what do I care for him? I am going to have a kiss, my pretty Marian."

"You shall not."

"I will, at all risks and hazards."

Ere she could put her foot on the stile, he caught her by the waist.

Slipping his arm round her slender form,

he drew her towards him, and imprinted a kiss on her lips.

At this audacious act, Marian gave vent to a loud shriek.

Mr. Spencer happened to be working in his garden on the other side of the wall.

He threw down his spade and listened.

"Help! help!" cried Marian.

He recognised his daughter's voice.

Filled with alarm for her safety, he rushed to the stile, and vaulted over it.

"One more," Charlie was saying to the half-fainting girl; "one more kiss."

The farmer did not stop to ask any questions.

He was one of the rough and ready sort.

It was a blow first with him, and a word afterwards, in a case of this kind.

Clenching his hand, he knocked Charlie down.

Marian leant against the stile for support, she was so overcome and agitated.

"Take that, you hound," cried Spencer; "that will teach you not to insult a respectable girl again."

Charlie got up, having rather confused ideas of things in general.

"You have assaulted me," he remarked.

"Didn't you insult my girl? Answer me that."

"I only gave her a kiss. There's no harm in that."

"Isn't there? How were you brought up?"

"Better than you, my good man," sneered Charlie. "I am the son of Squire Rawlings, and you shall answer for this."

The farmer chuckled quietly to himself.

"What! Be you that?" he exclaimed.

"My father is a magistrate, and one of the most influential men in the county. I am an intimate friend of the Honourable Hugh Charteris, son of Lord Stonehaven—"

"Any more of it?"

"I should think you have heard enough to convince you that I am in a position to have you severely dealt with."

"Go on."

"And I will, too, if you do not instantly apologise for the blow you have given me," continued Charlie.

He was in a great passion, and thought that his bombastic talk would make an impression on the farmer.

But it did not in the least.

Quite the contrary.

He made a rush for Charlie, and before that young gentleman could escape, he grasped him by the collar of his coat, and in spite of his struggles, dragged him to a neighbouring ash tree.

It did not take him long to tear down a long, lithe bough.

"I say," cried Charlie, in alarm, "what does this mean?"

"I'm going to give you a hiding, my fine fellow," replied the farmer.

"Didn't I warn you just now what would happen to you?"

"I'm taking all risks."

"You common fellow, do you forget I am a gentleman?" persisted Charlie.

"Why don't you behave as one?"

"Touch me at your peril! If I had a pistol, I would shoot you like a dog!"

Charlie's further utterance was stopped by a vigorous application of the ash stick to his back and legs.

In vain he threatened, begged, kicked, and swore.

Spencer, for more than one reason, had made up his mind to give him a sound thrashing, and he did.

While this was going on, Marian retreated to the house, glad enough to get away from her tormentor.

At length the farmer relinquished his hold of Charlie, who fell on the grass, writhing with pain.

"Go home, and tell your father what I have done," he said, "and what it was for."

Charlie made no reply. All the pluck was taken out of him; but he gave Spencer a horribly vindictive look.

With a contemptuous glance, the farmer walked away, and disappeared over the stile.

The young squire, as he wanted everyone to call him, had a face convulsed with rage.

It was intolerable that a simple farmer should beat him as if he were a disobedient hound.

His dignity was terribly outraged, and, what was worse for the moment, he was aching and stinging all over.

Seizing a stone, he ran to the stile, determined to have revenge if he could.

One thing he entirely forgot, and that was that he richly deserved all he had got as he was the offender in the first instance

The farmer had resumed his work in the garden.

Charlie threw the stone at him, and being a fair shot, succeeded in striking him on the cheek.

A deep gash was inflicted, from which the blood flowed freely.

"Ah, ah!" cried Charlie, "that fetched you?"

"You vicious young whelp!" replied the farmer.

"That's me. You've got it now. How do you like it?"

"If I get hold of you, I'll make you pay for this."

"'I—I THINK I'VE EATEN SOMETHING THAT HAS DISAGREED WITH ME,' STAMMERED CHARLEY."

"Come and try. I've got another stone. If you want any more, you can have it."

The farmer put his hand to his cheek, and withdrew it covered with blood.

"You and your father shall suffer for this!" he exclaimed. "You are a brood of vipers!"

"Thank you. what do you call yourself!" asked Charlie.

"I'm an honest man, and never committed forgery!"

"Who has done so?"

"You go and tell your father what I say. Forgery! Do you hear?—forgery!" shouted Spencer.

He forgot his resolution to keep quiet about the will. Charlie's conduct had exasperated him.

The solicitor to whom he had gone in London had told him that the will which Jack had discovered was a genuine one, and that Squire Rawlings would undoubtedly be turned out of the property.

He went further than that, saying that he would institute criminal proceedings.

"You don't know what you are talking about!" exclaimed Charlie.

"Wait and see," replied Spencer.

"I have no further time to waste on you now. We are partly square, but I have not done with you. That scar on your cheek will last you for a few weeks."

With these words, Charlie walked hurriedly away, for he saw the farmer coming towards him.

As he proceeded on his way he almost forgot the thrashing he had received in thinking of Marian.

"By jove!" he mutterred, "she is a pretty girl. Just taken my fancy. I must see her again, in spite of her brute of a father."

When he reached the inn, he saw the Honourable Hugh Charteris's dog-cart standing outside.

A groom, in a handsome livery, top-boots, and a hat with a cockade on it, was at the horse's head. He respectfully touched his hat as he saw Charlie.

"Master inside, Sam?" enquired the latter.

"Yes, sir; been here half-an-hour," was the reply.

Charley entered the passage and walked into the old parlour, where he saw Charteris comfortably seated, smoking a cigar, and drinking champagne.

"You are a nice fellow, I must say!" cried the son of Lord Stonehaven, "to keep a man waiting like this. If you can't keep an appointment, why don't you say so?"

The Honourable Hugh was fond of talking in this high-handed manner.

He fancied it gave him a superior, gentlemanly tone.

Though he made a friend of Charlie, he always let him know and feel that he was his superior.

"I beg to apologise. Really I couldn't help it," replied Charlie.

"Hang it all, you don't suppose standing in the sun will improve my horse. I hate kicking my heels with nothing to do but popping corks."

"It was all through a girl—"

Charteris smiled and waved his hand.

"Oh, that's all right," he exclaimed. "If there is a woman in the case, I will say no more about it. We all know what they are."

"I should have been here an hour earlier if—"

"That will do. It is bad form to keep a man waiting, but I accept your explanation. Will you imbibe?"

"Thank you, yes. I am warm and thirsty."

"Help yourself. The wine isn't so bad, but the worst of this forsaken hole is, there is no ice," said Charteris.

Charlie poured out a tumbler of wine—the Honourable Hugh said that was the only way to drink champagne—and drank.

"I had a row with the girl's father," he remarked, "and——"

"More fool you," again interrupted Charteris; "you should never quarrel with a girl's father. Did he set the dog on you?"

"Worse than that."

"Serve you right. Always make friends with the father if you want to make love to a girl. Does he smoke? buy him a box of cigars. Does he drink? send him a dozen of whiskey. But come, drink up. The mare is fit to-day, and I want to get on the road."

They went out, got into the trap, the groom sprang up behind, and away they went at a spanking pace.

There was a soft breeze blowing, and the motion was very exhilarating on such a hot enervating day.

"She was a deuced fine girl," began Charlie.

"Oh, bother the girl!" cried Charteris. "Can't you talk about something else? A lover's talk is never interesting. We sailors fall in love at every port we touch at."

"You are not in a very good temper to-day," said Charlie.

A caravan was discovered right in front of them as they turned the corner of the road.

The horse jibbed at the sight of it, and swerved half across the road.

Charteris had the greatest difficulty in holding her

"Whoa mare," he cried, as she pulled hard. "Want to bolt, do you? What's the matter? I thought you knew who your master was?"

This admonition had no effect upon the mare, who put back her ears, and fairly ran away.

"Show your nasty temper!" continued Charteris. "We've got a fair field and no favour. Go it, my beauty; we will see who will get tired first."

He gave her a couple of stinging cuts with the whip.

The mare accepted the challenge, and went like the wind.

Unfortunately for the Honourable Hugh, he had no control over the horse as he reached the caravan.

The consequence was that the wheels of the two vehicles caught, the van lost one wheel, and fell on its side, while the dog-cart was totally upset.

"Capsized, by jingo!" was all the Honourable Hugh had time to say, before he flew up in the air, and caught hold of the branch of a tree.

Charlie was sent spinning into a dry ditch.

His head knocked against the bank, and he was stunned for awhile.

The groom had seen the probability of the collision, and, with a discretion peculiar to gentlemen's servants, had dropped from his seat before it happened.

Shafts were broken, and the dog-cart was shattered to pieces.

The horse walked to the side, and stood there shivering.

Sam, the groom, however, did not pay any attention to the animal.

His master was hanging a good twelve feet above the road.

"Hang it all, Sam!" he shouted, "I can't hold on much longer!"

"I'm coming, sir."

"It's time you were."

Sam stood under the bough, and the Honourable Hugh dropped into his arms, alighting on the ground unhurt.

"By jingo!" said Charteris, using his favourite phrase, "that was a narrow squeak!"

"Close shave, sir."

"Is the mare all right?"

"Yes, sir,"

"All's well, then?"

A tall, dark-complexioned man, dressed in a shabby suit of clothes, had approached them unperceived.

"No, it ain't, guv'nor," he said; "it's all wrong, unless someone pays me for the damage done to my wan."

Charteris turned round, and looked scorn-fully at him.

"Your what?" he asked.

"My wan. That 'ere thing ower there, wot you knocked the wheel off of."

"Who are you?"

"The registered proprietor. Name of Slabber. I'm Slabber, I am. That's my wan. You've broke it. I want immediate compensation, or your card, so as I can take proceedings; but I daresay we can arrange things if we talk 'em hover hamiable."

Charteris looked at the van.

It certainly had the name of Slabber written on the side, and under it were the words—"Proprietor of the Living Skeleton. Warranted to be the Thinnest Man in the World!"

"I have certainly done you some damage, Mr. Slabber," said Charteris; "and, of course, I am willing to pay for it."

"You're a gentleman—every inch of you," was the reply.

"I'm the son of Lord Stonehaven, and—"

"Bless his heart! he is the friend of the poor gipsy and the stroller," broke in Slabber. "Many a time have I camped in his woods."

"Well," continued Charteris, "have your van repaired. Estimate the damage, and send in the bill to me. Will that suit you?"

"Perfectly, my lord."

"It's my father who is the peer, not I."

"Never mind, you will be some day," said Slabber.

At this moment the door of the van opened, and the most deplorable-looking specimen of humanity crawled out.

He was six feet in height, and almost as thin as a hop-pole; his black clothes seemed to hang upon him; his eyes were deeply sunk, and his skin was in wrinkles on his face.

This was Tibbits, the Living Skeleton, and well he deserved the name.

"What's up, guv'nor?" he asked, plaintively.

"Case of smash," replied Slabber. "We shall have to get a blacksmith before we can proceed with the wan."

"I thought as how it was an earthquake, and was afraid to come out," moaned the skeleton.

Slabber pointed with pride to him.

"That's the chap as I makes my money out of, my lord," he exclaimed. "Look at him; there's no deception. He's the genuine article."

"He most decidedly is," replied Charteris.

"Only walks about on two legs to save funeral expenses."

"How do you keep him so thin—starve him?"

"Not me," said Slabber. "He's an awful big eater. You should see him put the food away; but he's naturally one to fret, and I give him two doses of winegar a day—that's the secret. Winegar's the stuff what does it. Let him get fat, if he dares."

"I wouldn't be so base as to try when you're so good a master," remarked Tibbits.

"You dare, that's all!"

"Not for the universal world, guv'nor. I know myself better than that."

"He means it, my lord," exclaimed Slabber. "The chap's got a good 'art, I'll say that for him. We've been on the road together for years."

"And I 'opes as how we shall continner for many more," replied Tibbits.

Slabber shook his head.

"No, my boy," he said, mournfully, "you ain't going to live for ever. Skelingtons never does. They ain't long lived, my lord. The winegar's a strain on their constitooshuns."

"How old is he now?" asked Charteris.

"Twenty-four come Christmas. They generally pops off at thirty; but I'll give him a first-class funeral."

"Thank you, guv'nor; you're werry generous," sighed Tibbits, "and I'm grateful."

He wiped away a tear.

Suddenly Charteris recollected that he had seen nothing of Charlie.

"Sam!" he cried.

"Yes, my lord," replied the groom.

"Where is Mr. Rawlings?"

"Last I saw of him, sir, he was flying across the road towards that ditch, as if he was anxious to get there in a hurry."

"It is very bad form of me; I had entirely forgotten him. We must look him up. I hope he isn't hurt," said the Honourable Hugh.

Charlie was lying on his back with his eyes closed, still insensible.

All crossed over to see what assistance they could render.

"He seems in a bad way," remarked Charteris.

"We must undo his collar, so as to let him get his breath. Here, topboots," said Slabber.

"Who are you a-calling out of his name?" asked the groom.

"Don't fluster yourself, topboots, 'Old 'is 'ed hup, while I undress him a bit."

Sam partially raised Charlie, and Slabber took off his coat and vest, then his necktie and collar.

"I fancy I've seen that face before," remarked the showman.

The living skeleton peered over his shoulder.

"I'd a'most swear to it," he said.

"Who would you take him to be?" asked Slabber.

"Him as used to travel with MacNab, who was shot at the Hall here by Squire Rawlings for an attempted burglary one night. The papers was full of it at the time; it was all the talk."

"The young snake-charmer?"

"That's the one, guv'nor," replied Tibbits.

The Honourable Hugh Charteris laughed.

"My good fellow, this gentleman is Squire Rawlings' son," he observed.

"We can't both be mistook," answered Slabber; "I never forget a face."

"It is impossible."

"There is one way of telling," exclaimed the skeleton.

"What's that, skelington?" inquired Slabber.

"The boy snake-charmer was tattooed on his arm—faith, hope, and charity it was. There's the cross for the first, the hanker for the second, and a 'art for the third."

"Are you sure?"

"Certain. We've bathed together, and I've seen the tattoo marks hover and hover ag'in."

"Let us turn up his sleeve for the fun of the thing," said Slabber; "I 'ate to be beat. You ain't no objection, my lord?"

"Not I," replied Charteris. "It is not a very gentlemanly thing to do, and he might not like it—that's all."

"But he's insensible and won't know."

"Go ahead," said Charteris, carelessly. "If what you allege is true, he is a fraud, and ought to be exposed."

"P'r'aps the Squire adopted him after shooting old MacNab, out of a kind of remorse for the poor orphing."

"It may be so."

Slabber unfastened Charlie's cuff, and turned up the sleeve of his right arm.

Everyone uttered a cry of surprise.

There were the marks just as the living skeleton had described them.

At this juncture Charlie opened his eyes, drew a deep breath, and looked around him.

His eyes rested on Charteris, then on Tibbits, and Slabber. A shudder ran through his frame.

"Where am I?" he gasped.

"Among old friends," replied Slabber, "if you ain't too proud to recognise them?"

"What do you mean?"

"I'm Slabber, and that's Tibbits, the skelington. You ran into our wan and took the wheel off—that's 'ow we came to meet. I ain't seen you since the night of the races, when old MacNab got shot. You was snake-charming then."

Again a shudder convulsed Charlie.

"You have made a mistake, my friend," he said. "I never saw you before in my life!"

"You know that's not true."

"It is!" replied Charlie, emphatically.

"What about the marks on your arm, eh?"

Charlie looked at his naked arm; he became deathly pale, and, with difficulty, staggered to his feet, when he hastily pulled down his shirt-sleeve.

"Ridiculous nonsense!" he exclaimed, with a forced laugh, as he put on his vest and coat with a nervous eagerness. "You don't believe these poor fools, Charteris?"

"I cannot help doing so," was the frigid reply.

"What do—do you think?" stammered Charlie.

"Simply that you were a van boy, and for some reason Mr. Rawlings has adopted you. I can't help it; but our acquaintance must cease."

"Don't say that."

"I can't have a low-born cad for my friend! Good-bye. When we meet again I will thank you not to speak to me!" exclaimed Hugh.

Telling Sam to drag the remains of the dog-cart to the hedge by the roadside, and lead the horse home, Charteris walked away without saying another word to anybody.

Charlie felt as if he could die with shame and vexation at this unexpected incident.

His new-born pride had, indeed, suffered a severe fall.

CHAPTER XXIV.

THE SPIES COME ON THE SCENE AS USUAL.

SCARCELY had Sam, the groom, led the horse away, leaving Charlie alone with Slabber and Tibbits, than Peeping Tom and Knowall Dick came along the road.

They saw there had been a carriage accident, and they also recognised Charlie.

In a moment they darted through a gap in the hedge and were secure from observation.

"They didn't see us," remarked Tom.

"No. We dodged them very neatly," answered Dick. "I wonder what's up."

"We must find out."

"Of course. What do you think?"

"A travelling caravan has been run into. The young Squire, as Corks calls him, has probably done it. He is trying to square the van fellow. Let us get a little nearer and listen."

"That is the idea," said Peeping Tom.

The knack they had of coming on the scene of an adventure was very remarkable.

They selected a spot in the hedge-bottom where they could sit down, look into the road, and hear everything that was said.

"This is pleasant," observed Peeping Tom.

"Very," replied Knowall Dick. "This little corner was made for us. Isn't the young Squire in a wax, by the look of him?"

"Fearful. Something has brushed his feathers the wrong way."

"Hold your noise; He is speaking," whispered Dick, who quivered with curiosity to find out what was going on.

In fact, Charlie was in a very bad temper.

There was no need, he thought, for any further concealment now.

The Honourable Hugh had gone away, after cutting him in the most decidedly cool manner.

This hurt Charlie, because he felt sure that Charteris was not at all likely to keep silent for his sake.

Everybody would get to know that he had been a strolling player, lower than a caravan clown.

His indignation was principally directed against Tibbits.

"What did you want to say I'd been a snake-charmer for?" he demanded, fiercely.

"I didn't mean any harm by it," replied the skeleton. "Wasn't we mates? An't we played together, and shared our bit o' wittles when times was 'ard with us?"

"What of that?"

"I thought you'd be glad to see me."

"You need not have proved that I had the marks on my arm."

"Has it done you such a lot o' hurt?" asked Tibbits.

"I was passing as a gentleman, and you've knocked me out of good society, that is all," replied Charlie, bitterly.

"Then I'm sorry; there's my hand on it."

The skeleton extended his attenuated palm.

"I don't want your hand," said Charlie, "My name," he added, "will be a bye-word and a reproach. I shall be looked down upon and scouted, all through you."

Slabber touched Charlie on the shoulder.

"Let me put my spoke in this 'ere wheel," he exclaimed. "Tibbits is a poor 'armless creechur, and didn't know your haltered position."

"He's done the mischief, though," replied Charlie.

"Hinnercently."

"What does that matter when it's done? I shan't be able to show myself among decent people again."

"If that's so, as the skelington's the cause of it, I'll make you a hoffer," cried Slabber.

"What of?"

"A birth in the wan."

Charlie looked at him with ineffable scorn.

"No, thank you," he exclaimed. "I have done with that life for ever!"

"P'r'aps you may change your mind," continued Slabber. "There's many a gentleman whose gone on the road out of pure love for the stroller's perfession."

"I tell you, I have done with it."

"Think it over. You used to like the life. I never seed you unless you was as merry as a sandboy, whether the biz was good or bad."

"Don't waste your breath," responded Charlie, with infinite disdain. My father is a gentleman of wealth and position."

Slabber whistled.

"Oh, if that's the game," he said, "I don't wonder at you turning up your nose at fairing; but how did he come to adopt you?"

"I'm his lawful son, I tell you."

"Really?"

"MacNab stole me when I was a child."

"Well, of course, you know best," replied the showman, with an incredulous smile. "It's a queer story though; but look here, my wan wheel's off. I shall have to go back to the Inn as old Corks keeps; his back yard will be our repairing dock, where we shall stay for some days till we get our bill for damages paid by Lord Stonehaven's son."

"What has that to do with me?"

"Nothing much. Only if you should decide on j'ining us, I'll stand your friend."

"You have ruined me!" said Charlie. "In these parts, at all events. I shall have to go where the people don't know me."

"It is unfortunate, if you are really the squire's son," remarked Tibbits.

"You know I am," cried Charlie, wildly. "Haven't I told you so, you idiot?"

The living skeleton fell back in alarm.

"Don't hit me," he said. "If you did, the consequences might be werry serious."

"Drop it," said Slabber, with a voice of authority. "I won't have no quarrelling. There's a bottle of beer in the wan, Tibbits, also a bit of cold 'am and bread."

"Yes, guv'nor."

"Take it to the 'edge. We'll refresh ourselves a bit. You won't be above eating something with us, just for the sake of the old times we have had together, eh, Charlie?"

Charlie had no inclination to depart; his head ached from the effects of his accident; his mind was upset at his exposure, and he took a seat in a shady spot, partaking of what the showman was able to give him.

Thinking that they had heard all they were likely to hear of any importance, the spies retraced their steps, got through the gap, and walked up the road towards the van as if they were unconscious of anyone being there.

Peeping Tom and Knowall Dick had ascertained that Charlie was an impostor.

He was identified with the boy snake-charmer, and that was enough for them.

As they approached the spot where the little party was picnicing, Peeping Tom uttered a cry of pretended surprise.

"Hullo!" he said; "here's a free show—the living skeleton on view for nothing."

"Yes," added Knowall Dick; "and if I'm not greatly mistaken, the other's Charlie, the boy snake-charmer, with his sunday clothes on."

Charlie looked up, and recognised the school boys who had called on his father about Harry Rawlings.

He flushed deeply, and gnawed his lip.

"Another show-up," he muttered. "This is a little bit more of it. What shall I do?"

"You have seen him at the Squire's?" said Tom.

"And at the fair, too," replied Dick.

"Right," exclaimed Tibbits, whose thick head could not keep him from making mistakes. "He was a snake-charmer, but the Squire's adopted him; still he ain't above associating with his old friends."

Charlie felt that he was thoroughly exposed now, and it would be impossible for him to remain with any comfort in the county.

To let Peeping Tom and Knowall Dick learn any secret was as bad as advertising it in a newspaper.

Seeing the chagrin, which he could not suppress, Tom said—

"We do not want to tell about what you were."

"Not we; it isn't our style or custom." added Dick. "We know how to hold our tongues."

"Everybody says that of us."

"We're models," Dick continued.

"Masterpieces, you may say," supplemented Tom.

"Always provided we are paid for it," remarked Dick. "Now, a couple of sovs., divided between my friend and me, would seal our mouths, and nobody would ever hear from us about the snake-charming."

Charlie took the hint. He gave each a pound, which they pocketed with great glee, and noticing that Slabber's supply of beer was nearly exhausted, as well as his bread and meat, the "young squire" handed him ten shillings to go and get a further supply from the inn.

The showman departed with an alacrity he always exhibited when there was anything to eat or drink.

It was the hottest part of the day. Charlie was comfortably seated in a shady spot partly concealed from the road by hawthorn and blackberry bushes. He was considerably shaken and annoyed. Rest was what he wanted for the present. Various ideas were floating about in his mind.

The more he thought of Marian Spencer, the more he felt she was necessary to his happiness, and the more determined he was to get her from her home for himself.

He had heard the Squire say that he had a yacht at Harwich.

Perhaps if he asked for permission to use this vessel, it would not be refused him.

During the absence of Slabber, he indulged in all sorts of wild fancies.

At length the worthy showman returned, and spread out a fresh feast, to which Tom and Dick were invited.

"This is what I call comfortable," remarked Slabber. "I wouldn't give up the road for a palace. There's much enjoyment in life in a wan, ain't there, Tib?"

"You bet, guv'nor," replied the skeleton. "I'm that happy sometimes, I can't 'old myself. It's this kind of feeling—bu'st I must, or die."

"Ah! he's a playful creechur, like a kitten, though he don't look like it," soliloquised Slabber.

"Where are you going when you quit these parts?" asked Charlie.

"Harwich," answered the showman. "It's a flourishing town. The people are well-to-do. They eats well, and drinks a sight of beer; that fattens them. Now, by contrast, a skelington always goes well in a town of stout people."

"Don't go till you have seen me again."

"Why?"

"It may be worth your while," said Charlie, with a look which enjoined silence for the present.

At this moment the form of Jack Spencer was seen coming along at a quick pace.

He walked direct towards the little party.

At length he stopped short, and looking at Charlie, he exclaimed—

"I suppose, from the description I have had of you, that you are Charles Rawlings?"

"What's that to do with you?" demanded Charlie.

"Don't try and squirm out of it, Master Snake-charmer," replied Jack. "I don't wonder that you are ashamed of yourself, trying to get into society under false pretences."

"What do you mean, sir?"

"I have just met the Honourable Hugh Charteris, and he has given me a full account of you, telling me in what society I was likely to find you."

"Cannot I choose my own company? As for that, two of your schoolfellows are with me," said Charlie.

"Just having a little picnic," remarked Peeping Tom.

"Sit down and join us," observed Knowall Dick.

"Not I," replied Jack, disdainfully. "I would not break bread with such as you. You are the two worst boys in the school, and my enemies."

Slabber rose to his feet.

"Look here!" he exclaimed. "I don't know who you are, but—"

"That's just my case," said Charlie. "Who is he, and why does he come here to bully me?"

"Precisely," continued Slabber. "I reckon it will be carried by a hunanimous wote that the 'armony of the meeting shall not be disturbed. If a thrower-hout is required, I'm a wolunteer in that sense."

Jack looked fiercely at Charlie, and clenched his hands.

"I am Jack Spencer, whose family lives at the farm up yonder," he exclaimed.

Charlie's countenance fell.

"Do you know me now?" Jack added. "Come out here, and stand up before me like a man."

There was no movement about Charlie.

"I challenge you!" cried Jack. "Are you coming?"

"No, thank you," answered Charlie. "I much prefer remaining where I am. It is too hot to fight."

"Coward."

"Possibly."

"Villain, as well as coward," shouted Jack.

"Call me what you like," drawled Charlie, satisfied that Slabber would take his part. "Pass the malt liquor, Tibbits, and make yourself useful."

"'GET UP LIKE A MAN, AND FIGHT IT OUT!' CRIED HARRY."

He knew that by some means Jack had heard of the insult he had put upon his sister Marian.

That was why Jack had come to search for him, full of wrath.

The fact was that Jack had run over to the farm from the school to hear if there was any news from the lawyer about the will.

He had found Marian in tears, and his father growling on account of the blow he had received from the stone.

They told him all about the young Squire's conduct, and pointed out the road he had gone.

That was enough for Jack.

He followed up the trail until he ran his quarry to earth, and now that he had done so, the cowardly passiveness of Charlie made him more angry than ever.

"If you don't come out," said Jack, "I shall be under the painful necessity of dragging you forward."

"What for?" asked Charlie.

"You know well enough. I have been home, and I find you have grossly insulted my sister."

"I admit I kissed the girl—that is all," replied Charlie, in the most aggravating manner.

"Is that not enough?"

"I'll do it again when I get a chance."

Jack made one spring; it resembled that of a panther or jaguar, for he went for the throat of his prey, and seized it, intending to drag him into the road, and there castigate him.

Fortunately for Charlie, the stalwart Slabber was close at hand.

He caught Jack by the collar, and dragged him up.

"Now then, Shadder," he cried, "ready with that bit of rope?"

"Right you are, guv'nor," replied the skeleton.

In spite of Jack's struggles, Slabber held him tightly, so that he could not get at Charlie.

Tibbits, having been previously instructed, was prepared with some rope, with which he tied Jack's hands firmly behind him.

Then Slabber marched the young fellow into the road, and there left him, powerless to do anything to his foes.

The skeleton smiled admiringly.

"How beautifully the guv'nor does it," he remarked. "So clever, and yet so considerate."

"Young man," said Slabber, addressing Jack, "if I was you, I'd make tracks for home."

"That is good advice," observed Charlie; "his dear sister might miss him."

Jack trembled with impotent rage.

"I'll be revenged for this," he exclaimed. "Don't think that because I cannot do anything now, I shall forget."

"My good fellow," replied Charlie, who grew brave when he saw he was safe, "whatever you may feel disposed to do, is a matter of the most perfect indifference to me."

"You say so now. Wait."

This was all that Jack felt disposed to say. He would have to walk to the inn to get his hands unbound. This he did; but he had scarcely started before he had to look round.

The spies were clapping their hands loudly.

"Ah, ah!" laughed Tom. "See the conquering hero bolts. It's a good riddance. What did you come here to kick up a row for?"

"He's gone away with his tail between his legs, like a dog that isn't wanted," said Dick.

"All right, my hearties," exclaimed Jack, "I'll attend to you before long. You think you have got the grip of me now, and so you have; but it will not be always so."

"Go on," replied Tom; "we are tired of you. Can't you see you have got yourself disliked?"

Jack paid no further attention to their taunts; he walked quickly away towards the inn.

He looked somewhat ridiculous, for his cap had fallen off.

Loud shouts of laughter followed him, making his ears tingle.

We will leave Slabber and his merry little party to follow Jack to the inn.

When he reached its hospitable portals, he found a cart standing outside covered with a netting.

Inside were half-a dozen fine pigs, which Lardner, the butcher, had just bought, and was conveying to his shop.

Being a thirsty soul, and, moreover, a very old friend of Corks', he had stopped to rest awhile, water his horse, and have some beer.

Jack walked into the parlour, and Corks presently made his appearance.

"Give me your hand, Master Spencer," he exclaimed.

"I can't," replied Jack.

"How's that?"

"I'm tied up. Cut the cord, please."

"So you are! Who's been having a lark with you? They've had you this time. It is generally the other way."

"Never mind, my turn will come," replied Jack, smiling, as Corks liberated him. "I have to thank young Harris and Wilkins for this."

"They were here just now, and said they were coming back again."

"I'll wait for them. Don't say I am here."

"Right, sir. I understand."

The landlord's attention was drawn to something on the table. It was two pairs of new handcuffs. The polished steel glistened like silver in the sunlight.

"I'm blessed," he exclaimed, "if Nobes, the police superintendent, who was here just now, hasn't left his bracelets here!"

"I'll take them into the town for him," answered Jack. "By the way, I see Lardner, the butcher, has his cart outside. Where is he?"

"Asleep in the arbour outside. He's been pig-buying, and has had an extra glass over the deal."

"Let him alone. I have an idea," Jack said, as his eyes twinkled merrily.

He ordered some light refreshment, and Corks left him.

Jack put the handcuffs in his pocket, and hid himself behind the door to await the return of Peeping Tom and Knowall Dick.

He had not long to remain in suspense.

In a short time the spies entered the room, choking with laughter.

They sat down in blissful ignorance of Jack's presence.

"I say," cried Tom, "what a spree we had with Spencer. Didn't he look a fool as he marched up the road?"

"Don't," said Dick, "I shall burst if you keep on. My sides ache already.

"He thinks he can play all the practical jokes, but we had him this time. It is all the more delightful, too, because I hate him so."

"Such fellows as he want taking down a peg or two sometimes. Ah, ah!" laughed Knowall Dick.

"You're right. Ho, ho!" roared Peeping Tom.

At this moment Jack deemed it expedient to let them become aware of the fact of his presence. He stepped forth from his place of concealment.

"Fellows like *you* want taking down occasionally," he exclaimed.

Had a thunderbolt fallen in their midst, the spies could not have been more amazed.

The laughter died away upon their lips.

They looked blankly at Jack, who quickly closed the door to prevent any attempt at escape being successful.

Fairly enough they were driven into a corner.

"Who would have thought of seeing you here?" said Tom.

"Quite an unexpected pleasure," stammered Dick.

Jack produced a pair of handcuffs.

"Come here, Tommy," he cried, "I want you. It seems as if you were a little too playful."

"Oh, no. I feel quite sad and low-spirited, I can assure you, on my word of honour," was the reply.

"Come here, I tell you, or you will be sorry for it."

With great reluctance Peeping Tom approached his tormentor who seized his wrists and slipped the irons on them.

They closed with a snap.

Only the police-superintendent could open them, with his private key.

"Now, Dick, it is your turn," continued Jack.

Knowall Dick made a rush to the window, which was partly open, hoping to get out that way.

But Jack was after him like a flash, and knocked him against the wall.

"Would you?" he exclaimed, as he slipped the handcuffs on him, with all the skill of an experienced detective. "That is what I call unkind of you. Why should you run away from your best friend?"

"I don't see any friendship in this," replied Dick.

"You want correcting. 'Spare the rod and spoil the child,' don't you know."

"What's your intention?" asked Tom.

"Lardner's cart is outside, with pigs in it. I'm going to put you with the swine. The prodigal son once herded with them, and you will do the same."

"Put us with a dirty lot of pigs!"

"Yes. 'Birds of a feather fly together.' How do you like the prospect."

"Not at all. I call it a shame."

"Come with me," said Jack, taking each by the collar and pushing them through the doorway.

They were unable to resist. Very crestfallen, they were conducted to the cart.

Jack undid the netting on the top, and with some difficulty hoisted the spies up, one after the other.

"Lie down with your relations," he added, "or you will taste the whip."

The pigs made a terrible squeaking and grunting as the boys took their places by their sides.

It was very warm. An unsavoury smell arose, but the spies had to put up with their disagreeable surroundings.

The netting was made fast again.

Handcuffed as they were, it was impossible for the boys to get out, though their legs were free.

"I'll pay you for this, Jack Spencer," said Peeping Tom, grating his teeth.

"As soon as you like, dear boy," replied

Jack, pleasantly. "We know there is no love lost between us; it is open war, only I happen to score this time."

"I should like to—to have your—your life!" cried Knowall Dick, furiously. "Pah! what a smell there is!"

"Not all eau-de-cologne, is it Dickey?" asked Jack.

"It's enough to kill one."

"Won't Lardner think he has got two funny pigs when he comes to unload!"

"You ought to be punished for this," said Peeping Tom. "It is an outrage, and against the law."

"Is it? I didn't know you were a lawyer before. Isn't it a spree—ha, ha! Why don't you laugh, Tommy? You were full of it just now."

"I'm half stifled. My clothes will be utterly ruined."

"You won't fancy pork again for some time to come. Good-bye for the present. I am going to wake Lardner up. We shall meet again."

"This is beyond a joke."

"I never intended it for one. All I want is to take you down a peg, as you flattered yourselves you had done me."

With these words, Jack left them, proceeding to the arbour, where he found the butcher, who had just roused himself.

"Hey! Master Spencer, is that you?" he cried. "Gi'e me your hond. I ha' been pig buying. Your father traded one off to me. I be a bit sleepy, and ha' had forty winks; but I maun be getting on t' road now."

"I'm going into the village. Will you give me a lift?" asked Jack.

"Wi' all the pleasure in life, my lad."

"I'll stand the beer."

"Well said. I be half-muzzy now and want a livener. Coom on."

Lardner led the way to the bar, and requisitioned more beer from Corks, who did not know the trick that Jack had played on the spies.

"Have you seen the gentlemen you were expecting, sir?" he enquired.

Jack went close to him, and whispered in his ear—

"Go and look in the cart outside."

Corks nodded, and immediately vanished.

When he came back, his fat sides were shaking with laughter, which he had some difficulty in controlling.

"You've got some very fine pigs in your cart, neighbour," he remarked.

"None better in the country," answered Lardner. "I'm going to kill to-morrow. Shall I send you a leg or a loin?"

"You can, if you like."

"I'll be off now. The missis will be waiting dinner, and that makes her plaguey cross. She do lead me a life if I be late."

Finishing his mug of beer, Lardner led the way to the cart, and got on the driving-board, Jack taking a place by his side.

The butcher was not as clear in his head as he could have wished to be.

"Do 'ee take the reins, lad," he said.

"Had not you better drive?" asked Jack.

"No. Take the lines, I tell 'ee. My head be that bad, what wi' the sun and the drink, I shall like enough drive thee into a ditch."

Jack complied with his request, and started the old horse with a crack of the whip.

The butcher's head nodded, first on one side, then on the other.

As soon as the cart began to move, the pigs began to squeak and roll about, causing Peeping Tom and Knowall Dick an infinity of annoyance.

They were sitting down as far away as they could get from their four-footed companions.

The jolting sent a pig on to the knees of each, then when they came to a newly-made bit of road, the pigs knocked against their faces, and otherwise incommoded their fellow-travellers.

"Help!" shouted Peeping Tom. "I can't stand this."

"Let me out!" yelled Knowall Dick.

"Grunt, grunt! Squeak, squeak!" went the pigs.

"Police! Help!" continued Tom.

"Heaven above!" yelled Dick. "Stop the cart!"

"Help! help!"

"Police! police!"

Jack grinned, but said nothing, as he drove over the stones.

The noise reached Lardner's sleepy head, but he did not recognise anything human in it.

"What a plaguey noise them there pigs do make, to be sure," he remarked.

"The pig is usuallly a noisy animal when on his travels," Jack replied.

"Drat 'em! Lend Oi the whip."

Jack gave it him, and poking the butt through the netting, he hit out right and left.

Peeping Tom got a cut on the face, and Knowall Dick received a heavy blow on the mouth.

They rolled over on to their backs, lying at full length, and then had several pokes in the ribs.

This taught them to be cautious, and they ceased making a noise.

"Quiet now," chuckled Lardner. "I thought I'd learn 'em. Drive on."

The remainder of the journey, which was not more than a mile, was performed in comparative silence.

Lardner's shop was half-way up the little town, but at the entrance of the latter, Jack gave the reins to the butcher.

"I shall have to leave you here," he said.

"Good-day," replied Lardner. "Thank you. for driving."

He drove on as Jack alighted, but the latter did not lose sight of him. He ran after the cart, and as the man drove into his yard, Jack went to the back wall and climbed up a tree.

Here he could see without being seen.

He anticipated some fine sport.

Lardner was met by his assistant, who held the horse while he got down.

"Have you done well, master?" enquired the man.

"Ah! you'll say so when you see," was the reply. "Let down the back-board, and lift 'em out."

The man did so, and took up a fine pig, which he deposited on the ground.

Another followed, and then he got hold of Peeping Tom by the foot.

He gave it a jerk, which nearly dislocated his ancle.

Tom kicked out, and struck him under the chin.

"Oh, aw," he cried, "this be a rummy kind of a pig, master!"

"Hand him out, you fool!" replied Lardner.

"Not me!"

"Afraid of a pig, are you? Get out! I'll soon see what's the matter."

"It ain't no pig," said the man. "I never heard of a pig that could kick a man till his teeth chattered!"

"Hold your noise, or I'll make you!"

"It's the truth, master."

Lardner was enraged at the man's obstinacy.

Without waiting to verify the truth of the fellow's statement, he gave him a blow on the head.

This sent him rolling into the horse-trough.

"That settles you!" he cried. "I never did see such a i'jot. Never!"

He went to the tail of the cart, and plunged his hand in, laying hold of something.

"Now, then," he added, "out you come!"

He got Knowall Dick's foot in his hand this time, and Dick, following the tactics of Tom, kicked out. The butcher recoiled.

"Blow it!" he gasped, "the chap's right after all. These be most extr'o'nary kind o' pigs!"

Jack saw and heard all from his coign of vantage in the elder tree.

He nearly died of laughing.

It was all he could do to hold on to a bough to prevent his falling off.

"Turn it up!" cried Tom. "What are you pulling me about for?"

"My leg's nearly out of joint," said Dick.

The butcher's hair stood on end.

The man had got out of the horse-trough, and came up to his master's side, trembling.

"You didn't treat me right!" he exclaimed; "but I'll forgive that, though I might have the law on you; but there's some funny business a-going on in this cart."

"I'm sure," replied Lardner.

"Let us come out quietly," cried Peeping Tom.

"We don't want to hurt anybody," added Knowall Dick.

The butcher felt as if he could fall to the ground.

He caught his man by the hand.

"Oh, Lord," he groaned, "bless us and save us! Forgive me, Bob; I'd no call to hit you, mate."

"Don't say no more, master. You didn't know what it was till you'd tackled 'em."

"Talking pigs!"

"Talking imps o' darkness, master—that's what they be!"

"What shall we do?" asked Lardner. "Send for the police, and have 'em locked up, or get my shot-gun and kill 'em right off?"

"Shoot 'em—that's what I'd do. They don't lock pigs up, talk or no talk."

"Get the gun, then. Hurry up!"

At this awful threat, which meant death and destruction, Peeping Tom and Knowall Dick began to bestir themselves.

They wriggled to the edge of the cart, and dropped down as well as they could with their manacled hands.

"It's all right," said Tom.

"Don't fluster yourself," added Dick, "I will explain all."

They were very warm and very dirty.

Lardner rubbed his eyes, and stared as if he had seen a ghost, and so did his man.

"Be you boys from the school?" he asked. "And how did you come in my cart along wi' the pigs, hey? That's what I want to know."

"We were put in by Jack Spencer," replied Tom.

"Why didn't you get oot ag'in?"

Both held up their hands.

"Because we were handcuffed," said Dick; "and when we shouted, you knocked us about with the butt-end of the whip."

The butcher shook his head gravely,

"That won't do!" he exclaimed. "It's my opinion that you are escaped convicts, reformatory boys, or desperate malefactors of some sort."

"How dare you insult us in that way?"

"Get out of my yard; I don't want to have aught to do wi' 'ee."

"Can't you let us stop here while you send for the police and have these handcuffs taken off?"

"I'll not be mixed up wi' you at all. Clear out, or I'll know the reason why," returned the irate butcher.

"Listen to reason," said Peeping Tom.

"You will repent this hasty conduct," observed Knowall Dick.

"Not much I won't. Bob, gi'e Oi my whip."

"That will I do wi' pleasure, master," rejoined the man. "They be two bad eggs or they wouldn't ride wi' t' swoine and kick Oi under t' chin."

He handed Lardner the whip, and the spies were chased out of the yard.

As they could not run very fast with their hands fastened together, they received several sharp, stinging cuts.

Their yells of pain filled the air.

At last they got outside, and the gate was banged to, and barred behind them.

They halted under the tree, in the branches of which Jack was concealed.

"Here's a go," whined Tom.

"We'll have to go to the police-station," said Dick; "and perhaps they will keep us till they have sent to the school and made enquiries."

"Spencer has got the better of us this time. I wouldn't care if I wasn't handcuffed. It is the disgrace of going through the town I don't like."

"I call it a dirty trick to play anybody. If Spencer was here, I'd kick him."

"So would I."

Jack slid down the tree, and stood before them.

"I am at your service, gentlemen," he exclaimed, in the blandest and most polite accents.

It was a day of surprises for the spies.

"Get us out of this scrape," said Peeping Tom. "We have been cuffed and whipped."

"And nearly suffocated," put in Dick.

"We shall be late for school," added Tom.

"Doesn't it serve you right?" asked Jack. "Why are you always prying into other peoples' business, and poking your noses into what does not concern you?"

"It is all an accident. We don't try to do it."

"You did not try to do anything to poor Harry Rawlings. Oh, no! Two innocent ones, you are. But what can I do for you?"

"Send a policeman here to take these wretched things off our wrists. We will wait under the tree."

"All right. But, I say."

"What now?"

"You fellows want a bath," said Jack, putting his handkerchief to his nose.

He left them looking very shamefaced and miserable.

Just as he turned the corner, he met the constable on duty, who knew him, through having worked on his father's farm before he entered the force.

"Have you heard the news, sir," asked the policeman.

"No. What is it?"

"Master Warner, your schoolfellow, who killed the boy with the cricket-ball, has been tried to-day."

"Indeed! What did he get?"

"The jury found him guilty, but recommended him to mercy."

"That is lucky for him. I'd have inflicted the severest penalty allowable upon him," replied Jack.

He felt rather embittered against Warner, on his friend Harry's account.

"I think there is a little affair for you. back of Lardner's house," exclaimed Jack, "I saw two dirty, disreputable boys lurking under the elder tree."

"What were they like, sir?"

"They had escaped from somewhere, as they had handcuffs on."

"This is serious," remarked the policeman. "I heard there had been a break out at the reformatory. I had best go and take them. There's a reward and I may get promoted."

"Go at once," said Jack; "it may be a chance that only comes once in a lifetime."

"Thank 'ee, Master Jack. You always was a good sort. Give my duty to your father when you see him."

Jack nodded, and walked away to hide himself in a door-porch to see the fun, while the policeman went to effect his capture.

He crept very gingerly round the corner, and pounced upon the spies.

"Oh! you young varmints!" he exclaimed, "I've cotched you this time, have I?"

"What do you mean?" asked Peeping Tom, angrily.

"Don't put on that face to me. I see what you are, and you'll have to come along to the station."

In vain they expostulated.

They were dragged off ignominiously through the main street, amid the derisive jeers of the people who came out of their houses to look.

The fact of their being handcuffed was enough to pre-suppose their guilt, and their dirty, dilapidated condition increased the suspicion, that, though young, they were criminals of the deepest dye.

It happened that the superintendent was out.

Their explanations were not listened to, and they were thrust into a close cell to await his return. Jack went back to school, smiling.

He thought that he had been sufficiently revenged for all they had done to him.

CHAPTER XXV.

THE YOUNG SQUIRE'S PLOT.

WHEN Charlie quitted his roving friends, he went straight back to the Hall in an unamiable state of mind.

He at once told his father what had happened, and the squire was as deeply pained at the news as he was himself.

"My career, as a gentleman, is cut short here through this," said Charlie.

"Would you like to go to college?" asked Mr. Rawlings.

"No; the story of my having been a strolling snake-charmer will get about. It will follow me there."

"It is very annoying," said the Squire. "I would not have had it happen on any account."

"If I am taunted about it, I shall do something desperate!" cried Charlie.

"What is to be done?"

"Let me travel. I want to see the world. Have I not heard you say you have a yacht laid up at Harwich?"

"Yes," answered Mr. Rawlings; "the 'Cassandra,' five hundred tons burden. If I were to telegraph to Captain Williams, who is my skipper, he would get her ready for sea in a week."

"Can I have her for six months?"

"Yes. I will see about it at once. You shall have a reasonable amount of money, and I hope you will, while enjoying yourself, improve your mind by seeing foreign countries."

Charlie thanked his father very much for his generosity, and forgot his grief in the glorious prospect before him.

Captain Williams was communicated with, and undertook to have the "Cassandra's" stores and crew on board in seven days.

When this was settled, Charlie sought out Slabber at the inn.

The caravan was repaired, and the Honourable Hugh Charteris had paid the bill.

"Glad to see you," said the showman. "I am anxious to get on the road; but as you told me you wanted to speak to me, I waited."

"You will find it to your advantage," replied Charlie.

Seeing that the conversation was to be of a private nature, Slabber opened the door of the van.

"Come inside. We can talk there without being overheard," he observed.

"Where's the skeleton?" asked Charlie.

"He's been gorging and swilling. Since we have been here, he's sat in the bar, as a kind of free show, and the yokels have treated him. I saw him beginning to swell and put on flesh, so I dressed him up in three flannel shirts, and two great coats, and sent him for a ten-mile walk."

"What! in this melting weather?"

"Cert'n'y, to take his risin' flesh down, and I give him also a hextra dose of winegar."

"Such are the penalties of greatness," laughed Charlie. "I should not like to be a celebrity."

The van was neatly, but plainly, furnished.

"You see we are comfortable enough here," remarked Slabber, as he closed the door, and offered his visitor a chair.

"Don't I know it?" replied Charlie. "Haven't I lived on wheels? Wasn't the happiest part of my life spent in a van?"

"You'll come back to it. But what can I do for you?"

Charlie placed a ten-pound note on the table.

"Take that," he said; "you shall have another when you have done what I tell you."

"No killing, I hope? I draw the line at that," replied Slabber.

"Don't be alarmed. You are going to Harwich, so am I. My father has a yacht, called the 'Cassandra,' there. I intend to travel in her, but it is necessary that I should have a companion."

"I say, you ain't goin' to ask me for the loan of the skelington?" cried Slabber open-mouthed.

Charlie laughed, and assured him such was not the case.

"That's all right," added the showman. "You see, he's my bread and butter, and I couldn't afford to part with him."

"It is a female I want!" exclaimed Charlie.

Slabber grinned, and put his finger alongside his nose.

"And she don't want you," he answered. "I understand. You want me to conwey her in the wan to your yot."

"Clever man! you've read my thoughts!"

"Who is this 'ere hinteresting specimen of female 'umanity, if I may make so bold as to enquire?"

"The sister of that fellow who came to thrash me, when I was with you—Miss Marian Spencer—who lives up at the farm,"

"And you are going to carry her off?"

"You will have to do it for me. Get up to the farm in the evening, throw a cloth or a shawl over her head to drown her cries, and put her in the van. I will meet you at Harwich and see to the other details."

Charlie uttered this villainous proposal with the utmost coolness. Slabber, tempted by the money, promised to do his part of the business; and, leaving the van, they went into the public-house to seal the bargain with something stronger than water.

While they were enjoying themselves, the living skeleton returned, bathed in perspiration, and looking greatly fatigued.

"Here I am, guv'nor," he said; "that is, what's left of me."

"Take off your coats and jump on the scales," replied Slabber.

The scales were close by. Tibbits obeyed his instructions, and his proprietor carefully weighed him.

"Am I up to or, rather, down to the correct standard?" asked the skeleton.

"Exact," answered Slabber.

Charlie ascertained that Slabber expected to be at Harwich in five days, and undertook to meet him at the end of that time.

He then took his leave, perfectly satisfied with the arrangement he had made.

Slabber took the first opportunity of telling Tibbits that he was going to carry off a girl, who would be placed in the caravan, and must be closely guarded.

"I suppose it's all right, guv'nor?" said Tibbits.

"Of course it is. When we get to Harwich we shall be rid of her," rejoined the showman. "If she cries and pleads to you, don't listen to her."

"I'm rayther tender-hearted when it comes to the softer sex."

"You'll have to be 'ard, then."

"All right, guv'nor. You won't have no call to complain of me."

Slabber waited till the evening, when he put a cloth in his pocket and walked up to the farm.

Marian had been so thoroughly described to him by Charlie that when he saw her wandering under the trees in a meadow, he knew her at once.

It was an insufferably hot evening, and not a breath of air was stirring.

Marian had left the confinement of the house to see if she could get cool in the field.

All unsuspicious of evil, she strolled along, thinking of Harry, and wondering why, if he were alive, he did not write to her.

Overcome with heat and fatigue, she paused beneath the wide-spreading branches of a tree, and gave herself up to meditation.

The shades of night were falling.

"Oh, Harry!" she murmured, "would that I had you by my side."

Slabber glided up to her with all the stealthiness of a snake.

He got behind her, and suddenly dropped the cloth over her head.

She uttered a smothered shriek.

"Make no resistance!" he hissed in her ear, "and no harm will befall you."

"Mercy!" she cried, in broken accents.

Then she fell to the ground in a dead faint.

Taking her slender form in his strong arms, Slabber carried her in the growing darkness, unperceived, down the meadow.

"She's fainted!" he muttered. "All the better. I shan't have so much trouble with her—that's what I call good luck."

Marian knew nothing until she found herself on a bed in the van.

The showman had succeeded in conveying her into the yard and hiding her away, no one having seen him.

Tibbits was in the bar of the inn, talking to half-a-dozen rustics, who were spending their money freely.

The showman had removed the cloth from Marian's head. Her eyes were closed, and the long fair hair streamed in wavy masses over her neck and shoulders.

He had been busy making a gag, so that if she attempted to make a disturbance he could prevent her.

In half-an-hour he intended to hitch up his horse, and start on his journey; but he wanted her to come to first, and explain her position to her.

At last she opened her eyes, and looked in a frightened manner about her.

The parafin lamp hung on the side of the van, enabled her to see the rugged features of her captor.

They were totally unfamiliar to her.

"Where am I?" she asked, feebly.

"In a travelling caravan, miss," answered Slabber. "I am your friend. Don't be alarmed. If you keep quiet for a day or two, you will be all right."

"Why am I here? Oh, heaven! what are you going to do with me?" asked Marian.

"SHE ARRIVED IN TIME TO STRIKE THE COWARDLY ASSASSIN DOWN."

"That is a secret I can't—"

She uttered a loud cry.

Instantly Slabber forced the gag into her mouth.

"Will you?" he cried; "I'll soon stop that. Now, look here, I can't have any kick up. I'll have to tie your hands and feet. It's all your own fault for not keeping still."

He did as he had threatened, and poor Marian fainted a second time.

Slabber called Tibbits out of the bar; they put the horse between the shafts, and, with hearty good wishes from the rustics, started on the road which led to Harwich.

Tibbits had to sleep on the floor, but he was used to roughing it. Slabber was soon snoring; but as for Marian, to whom consciousness had returned, her feelings were too dreadful to allow her to close her eyes.

She could not imagine why she had been kidnapped in this cruel fashion.

Her brain reeled.

So cleverly had the abduction been performed, that no one had the slightest inkling of the fact.

Farmer Spencer, on missing his daughter, scoured the neighbourhood, but could gain no information respecting her.

CHAPTER XXVI.

JACK SPENCER IS SORELY TROUBLED—BREAKING UP FOR THE HOLIDAYS.

THE summer half at Doctor Birchoften's select academy for young gentlemen was nearly over.

Only a week remained to be spent in study before the boys broke up for the holidays.

The cricket eleven had distinguished itself by winning several important matches, and the boys felt deservedly proud of their school.

Only the death of Kennedy at the hands of Warner tempered the jubilation with some sadness.

Mr. and Mrs. Spencer were terribly upset and alarmed at the disappearance of their daughter.

They could not account for it, though they were suspicious of the young Squire, and when they ascertained that he had left the Hall, their suspicions increased.

The farmer made ceaseless enquiries and offered a large reward.

But no trace could be discovered of Marian.

They did not inform Jack of the dreadful fact, thinking that he would be home in a week. It would be quite time enough then.

He was destined, however, to hear of it in a very disagreeable manner.

After breakfast, he was in the yard waiting for ten o'clock school, talking to Pranks, whose leg was now quite strong again.

The other boys were in the field playing.

"I don't know how it is," remarked Jack, "but I feel awfully low-spirited to-day."

"I'm as lively as a cricket," replied Pranks. "Hurrah for the holidays!"

"It is a pity I can't feel like you."

"I am so jolly," continued Pranks, "that I know I shall do something to get into a row."

"Don't be so stupid."

"My dear fellow, I can't help it. I am bound to do something against the rules and regulations."

"If so, I sha'n't join you."

"Wait till you are asked. What I shall do, I can't tell, only you wait and see if I don't turn this school upside down before the day is out."

Jack was about to attempt to dissuade him, when the spies came up.

There was a gleam of malicious satisfaction on their sinister faces.

"Heard the news, Spencer?" asked Peeping Tom.

"Cut on with your news," answered Jack, curtly. "I don't want you sneaking about me when I am talking to a friend."

"Perhaps you don't want to hear what we have to say?" observed Knowall Dick.

"You have always got something to say about everybody."

"It's a wonder your father did not tell you."

Jack contracted his eyebrows angrily.

"What are you driving at?" Spencer demanded.

"Haven't you heard?"

"What?"

"About your sister Marian," replied Knowall Dick.

In a moment Jack was by his side, and had caught him by the arm.

"What have you to say about my sister?" he queried.

"I? Nothing. Only Dick and I have been in the town, and it is placarded all over with bills, offering fifty pounds reward to anyone who will give information as to where she is."

Jack let go his hold of Knowall Dick, and a faint feeling of horror came over him.

"I—I don't believe you," he stammered.

"Here's one of the bills," replied Peeping Tom. "Read it for yourself."

Mechanically, Jack took the bill from his hand.

A mist came into his eyes, and it was with difficulty that he could make out its contents. It ran as follows—

"£50 REWARD !

"WHEREAS, yesterday, MISS MARIAN SPENCER disappeared from her home, without any apparent cause or reason. The above sum will be paid by her father to anyone giving information which will lead to her recovery."

"There is no doubt about that, is there?" said Tom.

Not the slightest," replied Jack, "unless you have done it for a joke."

"Is it likely?"

"No; it is not. Some calamity must have happened. I shall go home at once. I cannot stay here till I know all about it."

"Can I do anything to help or serve you?" enquired Pranks.

"At roll-call, excuse me to the doctor for being absent—that is all," replied Jack.

His mind was in a whirl.

Off he went to the farm without saying another word to anybody.

Pranks was intensely disgusted with the spies.

"Aren't you fellows ashamed of yourselves?" he exclaimed. "If not you ought to be. You are always interfering in business that does not concern you."

"I don't see how you make that out," replied Peeping Tom.

"It is all very well to make accusations," remarked Knowall Dick. "I am sure we are innocence itself."

"Oh, yes," retorted Pranks, sarcastically. "Why did you upset Spencer with the news about his sister?"

"He had to know it sometime or another."

"If his father had wanted him to know, he would have told him."

"Who would have thought he'd have popped off like a champagne cork?" said Knowall Dick

"Be off yourself, or I'll kick you," threatened Pranks.

The spies retreated to a safe distance.

"You're a model," laughed Peeping Tom. "Don't excite yourself, or you might break your leg again."

"Keep out of mischief!" said Knowall Dick. "You are the worst boy in the school—a precious deal worse than we are."

Pranks made a dash at them, and they vanished into the field to find out something else if they could.

They left the gate open, and a young donkey, which had strayed from a neighbouring meadow, walked into the yard.

"Hullo!" smiled Pranks; "here's a new scholar come to school."

The donkey deliberately proceeded towards the schoolroom.

Tuffins, who had got over the injury he received in the wood when he fell into the gipsy's cave, was in the room dusting the masters' desks.

As Tuffins had not shut the door, there was nothing to prevent the donkey from going into the schoolroom, which it did, much to the delight of Pranks.

Quickly following up the animal, he entered the room, finding that Tuffins was fully alive to the situation.

"Two at a time's rather too much!" he exclaimed. "Ain't you rushing it a little bit?"

"It is more of a connection of yours than mine," rejoined Pranks.

"Oh, come now, draw it mild! Where did you find the neddy?"

"He came here of his own accord, as if he knew he would find a friend here.

"Drop it, can't you? My ears aren't so long as all that."

"We will keep him here now he has come," exclaimed Pranks. "The window behind the black-board is down; I will tie him up with the cord. It will be a lark when school begins."

Tuffins rubbed his hands approvingly.

Pranks pushed the donkey into the corner where the black-board stood, and secured the quadruped with the window cord.

A large white sheet covered the board when not in use, and this effectually concealed the animal.

Perhaps it was tired, and thought the schoolroom was a barn. At all events, it reclined on the floor and rested.

"Bootiful!" said Tuffins. "It's as good as a trained 'un. I believe it could do its A B C, and cypher up to ten."

"The doctor takes the first class in arithmetic to-day, when school opens, and begins with the black-board," observed Pranks, with a grin.

"Ain't there any other little delicate attention you could pay him?" asked Tuffins; "such as stuffing a pin in his chair."

"I've had him that way," replied Pranks, "and the old beggar is getting so cautious that he always feels the seat before he sits down."

"Couldn't you blow him up with gunpowder, by means of a slow combustion fuse?"

"I haven't got any powder handy"

"Isn't it possible to ease up a plank in the floor, so as to let him vanish from the festive scene?"

"That would take a long time. How are you getting along with Miss Martha?" Pranks enquired.

"It's very considerate of you to enquire," said Tuffins, "but I ain't no hesitation in sayin' that I should like to give her a dose of p'ison."

"Whatever for?"

"The way the hartful hold cat has treated me through my illness. When my arm was set, I was obliged to lie in bed for awhile. That was her opportunity. She'd got it in for me. Nothing but dry bread and grool did she let me 'ave. Look at me! I've wasted away to a shadder!"

"So you have. I did not notice it so much until you called my attention to it."

"I ain't 'arf the size I used to be. But do you know what cuts me to the 'art?"

"Can't tell for the life of me."

"I can't get enough to eat now I'm up and well."

"But you have four square meals a day," said Pranks.

"True, and what I cribs besides, when cook ain't lookin'; but it ain't enough, I tell you. There's a void to fill, a gulf to supply."

"What do you do, then?"

"I goes into the town whenever I have a chance, and draws some of my 'ard-earned money out of the savings bank, and spends it in food. Good-bye. Miss Martha's a-calling. All right, mem; I'm a kimming."

Saying this, Tuffins ran away to answer Miss Martha's noisy summons, and Pranks took a look at the donkey.

It was sleeping in the most contented manner.

Not wishing to be seen in the schoolroom by the spies or any other tell-tale, Pranks left it.

On the outside wall was a vine. It is needless to say that the boys did not allow many grapes to remain on it.

Pranks was attracted by the sound of humming and droning. Looking at the vine, he saw that a swarm of bees had settled on a branch. The demon of mischief was more than ordinarily rampart that day in him.

He took out his pocket-knife and cut away the branch, and placing his hat over the bees, carried them into the schoolroom, depositing them in the doctor's desk.

The lid was banged down, and the rude shock disturbed them, but they could not get out until the lid was raised again.

A second time Pranks vanished like a spectre, and played about until the bell rang.

The boys took their places, and the masters went to their desks.

Doctor Birchoften little knew what was in store for him.

The donkey was quietly slumbering.

The bees were not so quiet.

They wanted to get out, and hungered for revenge.

The doctor stepped to the black-board, with a bit of chalk in his hand, stately and solemn as usual.

"First class in arithmetic, stand up!" he cried.

The boys promptly rose in their places.

"I am going to see what you remember," he went on, "of the first book of Euclid, and will question you about the fifth proposition. That is usually called the *pons asinorum*. What does that mean, Clayton?"

"The bridge of asses, sir," was the reply.

"Why so called?"

"Because it is a very difficult problem, and many cannot understand it, or remember it, on account of its length.

"What kind of an angle is it?"

"The legs are of unequal length, sir."

"Come here. Draw it on the board, if you please, and tell us all about it," exclaimed the doctor.

Clayton left his seat, and the doctor drew the sheet away from the board, which action disturbed the donkey.

The latter rose to his feet.

Adjusting his glasses, Doctor Birchoften stared at the intruder.

"Hee-haw," brayed the donkey, loudly, as if favouring them with a friendly salutation "Hee-haw."

A titter ran through the school; the boys got on forms, the better to see what was going on.

In vain did Mr. Dobby and Mr. Caner order them to resume their seats.

"Mercy on us!" exclaimed the doctor; "it is a live ass! This is a grave breach of discipline. Who brought this here?"

There was a dead silence.

"I ask again," continued the doctor, in a voice of thunder, "who is responsible for the presence of this creature in the schoolroom?"

No one made any reply.

Pranks looked quite innocent.

Mr. Dobby came to the side of his chief, and, as if he recognised him as an old acquaintance, the donkey again gave vent to a loud hee-haw.

The boys were convulsed with laughter.

One in particular, by name Harkins, who was close to the doctor, nearly choked himself.

This excited the head-master's rage. He wanted a victim, and he had found one ready to his hand.

"Come forth," he cried, seizing the hapless Harkins by the arm.

"Please, sir," said Harkins, "I did not do it."

"Did I accuse you? It is for laughing in this grave crisis that I am going to punish you."

"I was laughing at the donkey, sir. It would make a cat laugh."

"You are not a cat. Mr. Dobby!"

"Sir," replied the usher.

"Oblige me by going to my desk and getting me my cane. After laughing shall come crying."

Mr. Dobby hastened to obey the command of the head-master. Harkins rubbed his eyes with his knuckles in anticipation of what was coming. The boys became grave, and the donkey went off to sleep again.

Looking towards the schoolroom door, Pranks was glad to see that it was left open on account of the heat.

He knew what was coming, and was determined to be one of the first to escape.

Opening the desk, Mr. Dobby put his hand in for the cane.

Instantly he withdrew it, uttering a howl of pain.

Then he began to beat the air wildly with his hands, for the bees were coming out in scores.

His first instinct was self-preservation. He ran frantically to the door, shouting for help. The bees followed him.

The little insects were very savage at the way in which they had been treated. They flew at the boys, stinging them on the hands and faces.

A deafening chorus of yells and howls arose. Doctor Birchoften was not spared.

Everybody ran for the door, tumbling over forms, and over one another.

The confusion was almost indescribable.

At length the room was empty. Even the donkey had broken away. The boys rushed into the field to escape the bees. Discipline was at an end. School was closed abruptly.

Mr. Dobby and the doctor ran into the kitchen to get a blue-bag for their stings, and were attended to by Miss Martha.

"How did it all happen?" inquired the latter.

"Someone brought a donkey into the school, and put a swarm of bees in my desk," replied the doctor. Woe betide him if I find him out!"

"The school is becoming awfully demoralised," said Miss Martha. "An example must be made, mark me!"

"I am always punishing somebody; but it seems to do no good."

"You are not half severe enough. I wish I had the management of the boys to-day. I would flog everyone in the school."

"That I cannot do. To punish all for the fault of one would not be fair."

"What are you going to do about it?"

"Really, I cannot tell. If the boy will not give himself up, what can I do?" asked the doctor in despair.

"I should make every boy write out a hundred lines each day until the culprit is discovered," suggested Mr. Dobby.

"Send for Harris and Wilkins; they will spy for us. Very little escapes those two boys," said Miss Martha.

"I will adopt both your suggestions."

Mr. Dobby was despatched to inform the boys of the punishment. Tuffins was sent for Peeping Tom and Knowall Dick, to receive their instructions.

Of course there was no more school that morning, but the imposition of a hundred lines prevented any idea of play.

Great was the indignation of the innocent, who thought that the guilty party ought to give himself up.

This, however, Pranks had not the least intention of doing.

There was only seven days to the end of the half, and he thought it would not hurt his schoolfellows to write out the lines each day till the expiration of that short time.

The spies came into the kitchen, with their caps in their hands.

"Ah, Wilkins and Harris!" said Doctor Birchoften. "You must help us in the hour of need."

"Certainly sir," replied Peeping Tom.

"Often have you rendered signal service to your masters on former occasions."

"It has been our pride and pleasure to do so, sir."

"Very well said. The French adopt the *mouchard* or spy system in their schools, why should not we? Now, have you any idea who played this asinine trick on us to-day?"

"No, sir. We did not see or hear anything to excite our suspicions."

"Hold on!" cried Knowall Dick. "We came upon Spencer and Pranks in close conversation, and they ordered us off."

"There may be something in that. Watch those two. Five shillings for each of you, if you find out the delinquent," said the doctor.

"And the prize at Christmas for assiduity and obedience to your superiors," put in Mr. Dobby.

"And two slices of plum-cake of my own making, now," exclaimed Miss Martha, who presented each with a big piece.

"Thank you all kindly," replied Peeping Tom.

"We're treated so well here," said Knowall Dick, "that I shall feel sad when I have to go home."

"It's a blessed thing to have such friends and to be thought so much of," added Peeping Tom. "This school is a little heaven below."

"We always try to do our duty," observed Dick.

Miss Martha held up her hands in admiration.

"What good boys! they redeem the rest. It is beautiful to hear them talk!" she exclaimed.

"You shed a ray of pure light over the academy, miss," said Peeping Tom. "Without your fostering care, where should we be?"

"Ah! where, indeed?" sighed Knowall Dick. "I long for Sunday to come, to see you look so saint-like in church."

"Go away, you silly boys," answered Miss Martha, much delighted with this fulsome praise; "yet, stay a moment while I find another piece of cake for you."

They were glad to get away, for they were choking with suppressed laughter.

One side of the doctor's face was getting like a football or a balloon, while Mr. Dobby's nose was assuming alarming proportions.

"There will be no school until the afternoon," said the doctor, "and the lines need not be shown up before supper."

"That will give these two plenty of time to make enquiries," responded Mr. Dobby.

"You talk about supper," observed Miss Martha, tossing her head. "I would not give the boys any at all, and for dinner they should have only bread and water."

"It will not do to starve them, my dear?" replied the head-master.

"Why not, pray?"

"The parents would not like it, and we must study the parents or they will take their boys away, which will cause us to suffer in the matter of income."

Peeping Tom and Knowall Dick did not stay to listen to a discussion which was not intended for their ears.

Discreetly withdrawing, munching the extra piece of cake with which they had been favoured, they sought their old lair, the wood-shed.

Getting out of the almost perpendicular rays of the sun, they sat down in a shady corner.

Their faces beamed with smiles, for they felt highly honoured at the compliment which Doctor Birchoften had paid them.

"We are in luck," remarked Tom. "A prize at Christmas is something to look forward to."

"It is, indeed," replied Dick. "Didn't we lay it on thick to Miss Martha? But as you say, our luck is in. If we only find out who played the tricks this morning, we shall be in higher favour than ever."

"Towards the end of the half," said Tom, "I have noticed that lots of fellows will break out who never dream of such a thing before."

Suddenly Dick pulled Tom by the arm.

"Keep quiet," he whispered; "Pranks and Spencer have just met, and are coming this way."

"Can they see us?" asked Tom, shrinking back.

"I think not. No; they have stopped close by; their backs are turned towards us. Listen!"

Jack had been to the farm. An interview with his father confirmed his worst fears, and he was told about the mysterious disappearance of his sister Marian.

Her fate was an impenetrable secret at present.

"Well, old fellow," said Pranks, who was trying to extract the sting of a bee from the back of his hand by the aid of a small key, "how goes it?"

"Very badly," replied Jack. "My sister is nowhere to be found. My mother is ill in bed, and my father is nearly distracted."

"Had she got a sweetheart? I don't want to be rude; but—"

"Only Harry Rawlings, who is always as welcome as the flowers in May at our house."

"What is the meaning of it?" continued Pranks. "If anybody's head is to be punched, you can depend on me."

"Oh, I'd do the punching!" replied Jack, "if I could only find out the proper person. I hope she has met with no accident. Perhaps it will turn out all right; but it makes me miserable. I can't rest. Don't let me worry you with my troubles. It is selfish. How is it you are out of school so soon? Did you make an excuse for me? What is the matter with your hand?"

"Don't bombard me with questions," answered Pranks. "We have had no school; I, therefore, made no excuse. A bee stung me."

"Nasty things, if you provoke them," said Jack.

"So the masters and a good many of the boys think. Ha, ha! I cannot help laughing. Excuse me. I know you feel bad; but, I say, you should have been here when the doctor opened school this morning."

"Have you been up to your tricks?"

"I don't mind admitting to you that I have. I saw a donkey wander into the yard; the temptation to drive him into the school was irresistible. After that I found a swarm of bees, and I put them in the doctor's desk."

"You young sinner!" cried Jack.

"Judge of the great man's surprise and delight," continued Pranks, "when, as he was about to solve the fifth problem, the Jerusalem pony started up with a Jubilee kind of asinine hurrah!"

"I should have liked to see the effect," replied Jack.

"Oh! but the lark was, when the bees were let out. There was a stampede then. I got off better than some. The doctor has given the whole school a hundred lines every day."

At this juncture the spies emerged from their place of concealment, and to the consternation of Pranks, took up a position in front of him.

"You hateful little sneaks!" he cried, "what are you doing here?"

"We have heard all you have had to say," replied Peeping Tom.

"Come now, what did I say?"

"You confessed to playing the tricks in the school this morning."

"How dare you say that?" exclaimed Pranks, trying to brazen it out.

"My dear fellow," replied Knowall Dick, "we make it our business to find out everything."

"You fellows ought to be smothered," cried Jack. "I call you a disgrace to the school."

Tom and Dick were bold. They did not agree with this sweeping accusation, and they felt it incumbent upon them to protest.

"How about Pranks?" queried Peeping Tom. "He made the disturbance. If anyone is a disgrace, he is."

During the whole of this conversation, Pranks was getting his blood up.

It was clear that the spies knew that he was the author of the mischief.

There was a certainty of punishment, so he resolved to have some little satisfaction in giving the spies something on their own private account.

"I'll let you have it!" he shouted, as he drove them into the corner from which they had emerged.

They could not escape.

"You cowardly wretches!" Pranks went on. "You dastardly hounds! I'll make you pay dearly for this."

The spies called upon Jack to protect them. This, however, he refused to do.

Pranks let out with his right, then with his left, and knocked both Tom and Dick down on the flat of their backs.

When they were down, they would not get up again. Crawling on their hands and knees, they got past Pranks, with a kick or two, and ran off.

"Let them alone," said Jack. "It isn't worth while to put yourself in a passion about them."

"They have done me all the harm they can. I will defy them to do any more," replied Pranks.

"You are in for it."

"Yes, I see that. What shall I do? You know, I am going to leave at the end of this half."

"I did not know until you told me," said Jack.

"Oh! I thought I had told you. If I were to run away, my father, who is awfully strict, would send me back. You ought to advise me; it is through you I got into this scrape."

"Through me? It is scarcely fair to say that. I told you this morning not to play any tricks."

"So you did. That is true."

"How could I help those wretched spies listening to what you confided to me?"

"Right again. Forgive me; I am hasty. Cannot you suggest some way out of the fix?" said Pranks, in a deploring tone of voice.

Jack thought a moment.

"I hardly like to make the proposition," he replied; "but you can come with me and help me find my sister."

Pranks seized him gratefully by the hand.

"I will do it," he cried, "and take all risks. Wherever you go, I will follow, and work for you like a brick."

"Come along, then. We will leave our things here. When we get to my home, the governor will give me some money."

"I am ready," said Pranks, hope dawning in his breast once more.

Before they had time to move, Doctor Birchoften and Mr. Dobby made their appearance in the yard.

They advanced to the boys, and seized them unexpectedly by the arms.

"What is this for, sir?" asked Jack of the doctor, whose prisoner he was, Mr. Dobby having grappled Pranks.

"You are the accomplice of this mischievous boy Pranks. I shall put you both in the strong-room, and deal with you to-morrow."

"It is not fair. I have not done anything."

"I am the best judge of that," was the cold answer.

They had not expected this attack, but it was too late to resist now, and in spite of their protestations, they were dragged away and locked up in durance vile.

When the door of the bare, miserable room was closed upon them, and the key grated in the lock, the prisoners thought they were unobserved.

"MARIAN HASTENED ACROSS THE PLANK."

In reality they were not.

Acting always on the spy system, Doctor Birchoften had constructed a "Judas hole," as it used to be called in the old Bastile days.

That is to say, a hole had been made in the wall by removing some bricks, the aperture was thinly covered with paper, and everyone in the adjoining chamber could hear all that was said in the strong-room.

The doctor divested himself of his boots, put on a pair of list slippers, and gliding into the outer apartment sat on a chair, inclining his head so that his ear was close to the Judas hole.

"This is what I call a thorough shame!" exclaimed Pranks. "I suppose we shall be kept on short commons for twenty-four hours, and then be thrashed."

"It was not my fault," replied Jack. "You acted as my friend throughout. I thank you for it, but I am afraid that will not help you much."

"What did you want to play the fool for?"

"I can't help it sometimes. If I get a chance, I'll—I'll do something desperate. Set the house on fire, for instance."

"And burn the boys in their beds! That isn't a nice thing to threaten," said Jack.

"It's the old man I want to tackle. Tell me what I can do to get square with him."

"Nothing at all. You were in the wrong. Let him alone. You don't come to school to do as you like."

"But I must do something, and I will. I'll blow him up with gunpowder."

At this awful threat, the doctor nearly jumped off his chair.

"The vicious wretch!" he muttered. "Spencer is not to blame."

"Don't talk to me any more," cried Jack. "I like a lark as well as anybody, but I can't stand vindictiveness."

"All right. I don't want your assistance," snapped Pranks. "I will do my business my own way, without any help. If the old man thrashes me to-morrow, I'll be revenged on him, you see if I am not."

"It is very foolish to say so. Don't keep on worrying me with your petty spite. I have enough on my mind."

"I can't help your sister being missing."

"Who said you could?" cried Jack, angrily. "Say no more, or I'll punch your head."

There was a dead silence after this. The doctor waited a quarter of an hour to hear something more.

As they did not speak, he went away, satisfied that Jack had nothing to do with the disturbance in the schoolroom.

At dinner-time Jack was liberated. He thought better about running away, and resolved to trust to his father's exertions to find Marian, for, after all, it was little he could do.

Pranks was kept in the strong-room until the following day, when he had one of those private interviews with the doctor in the study, which the boys found so disagreeable.

His schoolfellows did not applaud him for what he had done; too many of them had been stung by the bees.

The time for breaking up came at last, and with songs and shouts, the boys went to their homes for the holidays.

When Jack got to the farm, he asked his father if he had received any news of Marian.

"None at all," replied Mr. Spencer, sorrowfully.

"Have you any clue?" Jack continued.

"I have not."

Jack's heart sank. His mother was still very ill from the shock of her daughter's disappearance. The farm seemed desolate. Marian had been the presiding good genius. Without her, all seemed a blank.

CHAPTER XXVII.

MARIAN'S ADVENTURES.

THE yacht "Cassandra" was the prettiest, tautest, and best appointed vessel lying in Harwich Harbour.

Her captain, Hugh Williams, was a middle-aged, bronzed, weather-beaten Welshman; and his mate was a rum-drinking, tobacco-chewing old Norfolkman, named Porter, who, however, when sober, was an excellent seaman.

It was evening. The sea was calm; no breeze stirred the water; innumerable stars of unusual brilliancy studded the sky; the air was soft and balmy, and if the wind stirred on the morrow, it would be capital weather for a cruise.

Williams and Porter were in the cabin; the boat had gone to the landing to meet the young Squire, who had sent word that he would come on board that night after dark.

"So we are in commission again?" exclaimed the captain. "My instructions inform me that we are bound for the coast of Spain.

"No better ground for pleasuring," replied Porter, "if we except the Mediterranean. How old is this youngster who is coming aboard?"

"Seventeen, I am told. Old enough to have his own way, and wreck the ship if he is allowed to be master."

"Which he won't be so long as you are on deck," replied Porter, with a laugh.

"Not much," answered the captain. "I always resent any interference with my command. The responsibility is mine, and I will have a free hand. Suppose we ring for the steward's mate, and have a bottle of fiz to drink success to the voyage before the cub comes and turns us out of these pleasant quarters?"

"With all my heart. The best of this kind of service is that there is always plenty of wine, beer, and spirits knocking about, and no questions asked."

"You will have to keep sober, my man," exclaimed the captain.

"What for?" asked the mate.

"There is a lady coming on board. I have had special orders to fit up a state-room with every accommodation for her."

"Bah!" said the mate, "to the bottom of the sea with the petticoats! I hate them."

"You didn't always, if report speaks true; but I don't think this one is likely to be very exacting. She is a cousin of young Mr. Rawlings, so he informs me, and of rather weak intellect. He is taking her to sea for the benefit of her health. She has hysterical fits sometimes, and we are to take no notice of her ravings, because she is subject to serious delusions."

"It seems to me that the ship will become a floating lunatic asylum!" growled Porter.

"No matter so long as we get our pay."

Captain Williams touched the gong. The steward sent his mate to answer the summons.

The mate quickly made his appearance. He appeared to be a young man about twenty-four years of age, short in stature, thin and pale, with a sad expression in his eyes.

He had whiskers of a dark brown colour, the same as his hair; but his chin was closely shaved.

"Bring a bottle of champagne," cried the captain. "Stay! you're a new hand, I reckon. I haven't seen your face before that I know of."

"Yes, sir; the steward shipped me this morning," was the reply. "The last man you had was drowned a month ago."

"Ah, I recollect. Have you ever been to sea before?"

"This is my first voyage, sir. I left home to better myself, and will try to do the best I can."

"You look as if you had been up to something wrong!" said Porter, with a rough laugh. "What's your name?"

"Tom," replied the steward's mate, reddening like a girl.

"Let him alone," exclaimed Captain Williams. "If he tries anything suspicious on here, I'll land him to shift for himself at the first port we make."

"I have never done anything wrong, sir!"

"If you have, the police won't find you here. We can't expect a character with everyone we take aboard."

"I couldn't get a character, sir, because I have had no regular employment during the short time I have been in Harwich."

"What have you been up to?"

"Anything that I could get hold of to keep body and soul together."

"Loafing about the quay," said the captain. "Mind your P's and Q's. I've got a ready knack of using a rope's end."

"If you please——"

"That will do. Stow your jaw tackle!" interrupted the captain.

"Haul your wind, you lubber!" cried Porter.

"Don't you see that we can't stand any more of your chin music? Cut along and get the wine, or the young Squire will be aboard before we have time to drink it."

A splash of oars was heard at this juncture, and then a voice rang out clearly on the night air—

"Ship ahoy!"

"'Cassandra!'" replied the lookout man, as the gangway was lowered.

Charlie had arrived. He had met Slabber as appointed. The caravan was near the landing-place. Marian, who had been kept a close prisoner, was conducted to the boat in waiting, being warned that if she made the least noise she would be gagged instantly.

This threat had been constantly held over her. For three days, during which she was in the caravan, she had tasted scarcely a morsel of food.

Her strength was greatly reduced by starvation, fretting, and terror of what might be in store for her.

When she was placed in the boat, it was too dark for her to see Charlie's face. As she tottered up the gangway, the ship's lanterns did not avail her much.

She was in total ignorance of her captor's identity until she had descended the companion, and was given a seat in the well-lighted saloon.

Captain Williams had hastened on deck to receive the owner's son, who had greeted him briefly, saying he would see and speak to him presently.

Charlie, with a fiendish smile of triumph on his thin lips, closed the saloon door, and turned his face full towards his miserable captive.

Their eyes met, and she uttered a startled cry.

"You!" she gasped. "Am I in your power? Oh! why have you acted thus to one who never injured you?"

"Cheer up," replied Charlie. "I do not mean you any harm. You will like me when you know me; I'm not half a bad fellow, and I have plenty of money."

"Where are you going to take me?" she asked.

"To the shores of sunny Spain, amid the orange groves and the vineyards."

"With what object?"

"I expect you to love me. We will be married. You shall come back to be mistress of the Hall."

"That is an empty dream."

"I do not think so. You will change your mind."

"Never!" said Marian, emphatically. "Let me tell you at once, to save further complications, that I love already, and have plighted my troth."

"To whom?" demanded Charlie, grating his teeth.

"Your cousin, Harry Rawlings."

"Bah! he is a fugitive and an outcast."

"But his innocence of the foul charge brought against him has been proved. He will return."

"How? A beggar! Forget him. You must and shall love me. I will cast you into the sea sooner than you shall belong to anyone else."

She shook her head sadly.

"Then, if you have no mercy, I must die," she answered, with an air of resignation.

"We will talk again to-morrow," he said. "Your mind will be more at ease now you know all."

"My poor father, my mother, my brother Jack, what will they think?"

"I'll send them a telegram in a few days, from the first port we touch at; rest easy on that score. We sail at sunrise to-morrow."

He walked across the saloon.

Throwing open a door, he revealed a fairy-like bower, which had been arranged for her.

"See!" he added. "I have thought of you. Come here."

Marian dried her tears by an effort. Actuated by feminine curiosity, she advanced, and when she saw all the beautiful things, she could not restrain a cry of admiration.

"How lovely!" she murmured.

Charlie looked pleased at this admission.

"By Jove!" he exclaimed. "No one can say it is bad. I'm glad you like my taste.

"Now," he added, "I'll leave you to yourself for an hour or so, while I go on deck. Supper will be served then."

"Do not trouble on my account. I have no appetite, but I will change my dress," said Marian.

"That's right; make the best of it. Everything is for you. Do as you like. I'm awfully sorry you were so badly treated in that horrid caravan; but I could not help it. You had to be brought here somehow, and I could not be seen in it."

Marian saw that to refuse his gifts and hospitality would not improve her position.

When they arrived at a port, she fancied, if she could throw him off his guard, she might be able to get at a British Consul.

If she could only succeed in doing this, she could claim his protection.

Consequently, she determined to make her life as comfortable as was possible under the circumstances.

"I must have time to think," she said. "My brain is terribly upset. "If you will not speak to me of love for a week, I will treat you as a friend."

"Bravo! You are a sensible young lady. Let me see Cinderella transformed into the Princess when I come back," replied Charlie.

Kissing the tips of his fingers to her, he quitted the saloon.

Charlie was dressed in a yachting suit of blue serge, with gilt buttons.

He wore a black tie in a sailor's knot, a white straw hat, a heavy watch chain, and a diamond ring.

This he imagined was the correct style, and he felt perfectly satisfied with himself.

Of the sea he knew nothing at all, never having been on board a ship in his life before.

This fact he did not intend to reveal to Captain Williams, who was standing amidships scanning the horizon when he came on deck.

"What do you think of the weather, captain?" he asked, as he came alongside him.

"If those mare's tails, as we call the white streaks over yonder, mean anything," was the reply, "we shall have a stiff breeze spring up after midnight."

"All the better. I like a spanker. How many knots can we do, eh?"

"Ten before the wind, with all canvas spread. How do you think you will like the sea, sir?"

"Like it? Do you think I have never been to sea before?"

"Beg pardon, I wasn't aware of the fact," replied Williams.

"Don't distress yourself," said Charlie, who liked to look big. "I can knot, reef, and steer, as well as the most of you, and, if needs be, I can take in sail, and handle an egg-shell of a craft like this in the biggest storm going."

"Glad to hear it, sir. Ever sea-sick?"

"A little at first. I soon found my sea-legs, though," laughed Charlie, who thought rather lightly of the pangs of sea-sickness, because he had never experienced them.

At that moment a breeze sprang up.

The surface of the water in the harbour was covered with ripples, and it was clear that, out in the open, they would have a good wind.

"We can weigh now, sir, if it is agreeable to you," said the captain.

"Have we got to be weighed before we can start?" inquired Charlie.

"Bless your innocent eyes!" replied the captain. "Ahem! I beg pardon. I alluded to weighing anchor."

"What does that matter? Set sail at once my good fellow. I don't care about the weight of the anchor."

"It means hoisting it up. I thought you knew—"

"Hang it all! why don't you say what you mean?" interrupted Charlie, angrily.

"You're all at sea, sir, I'm afraid?"

"That's what I want to be. Go on, and do your duty. If we can start now, let us do so, by all means. I don't want to stop on this mud flat."

"We don't generally start on the poor man's holiday—"

"What's that?"

"Night; but as you have given the order, we will sail. I am well acquainted with the coast."

"That is enough. Let us see what you are made of and can do," cried Charlie.

Captain Williams called the mate, the crew were roused from the forecastle, and, with a merry song, began to raise the anchor.

When this was done, the sails were set, and the "Cassandra" sailed slowly but gracefully out of the harbour.

"She's as pretty as a child's toy duck swimming on a basin," remarked the captain, as she gave a cant to leewards.

Then she pitched and heaved.

A cross-chopping sea struck her, and she shivered from stem to stern, before she went over the next wave.

"Lov—lovely!" stammered Charlie, who felt a qualmish sensation.

"Aren't you well?" Captain Williams asked.

"I—I think I've eaten something that has disagreed with me. Salmon and cucumber, perhaps."

"Likely enough."

"I'll go—go and look at the water."

Saying this, Charlie, who began to feel very bad, rushed to windward.

"Not that I'm really ill," he muttered. "I'm an o-old sailor, you know, but I've got to fi-find my sea-legs."

The captain chuckled quietly to himself, knowing now that his young master had been boasting, and was nothing more than an unsophisticated landsman, after all.

For fully half-an-hour Charlie was in all the horrible throes of sea-sickness.

He could not speak.

When he attempted to move he lost his balance, and fell into the lee-scuppers, where he remained unable to get up.

Captain Williams saw him fall.

Beckoning to the mate, he said—

"The Squire ain't used to the sea. Hadn't you better give him a drop of brandy?"

"Let the lubber lie," replied Porter.

"No, no; it ain't respectful. We get our money out of him, and when he gets used to it he may pay us out in our own coin."

"That's true. What shall I do with him?"

"Give him a dose of soda and brandy," said the captain.

"And then?"

"Steer him straight to the saloon. He'll be all right on the floor, or on a lounge."

The mate obeyed these instructions to the letter. He procured some soda and brandy, which he made Charlie take, putting a little life into his limp form, and then carried him into the saloon.

Supper had been laid; the table groaned with delicate viands of all kinds, calculated to tempt the appetite of an epicure, but Charlie had no taste or wish for anything.

He staggered to a sofa, threw himself on it, and groaned.

"Hold up, sir," said the mate.

"Le-leave me," replied Charlie; "I shall be or-oright presently."

Porter smiled and withdrew.

When Charlie was left to himself, the steward's mate came into the saloon with half-a-dozen bottles of champagne in a silver ice-cooler, which he deposited on the floor.

His movements were noiseless.

Charlie, however, saw him and said—

"Who are you?"

"Steward's mate, sir—Tom. Supper is ready," was the reply.

"Hang this sea-sickness! I cannot eat anything. Give me another drink of brandy and soda, Tom."

"Yes, sir."

Tom took up a glass, poured out the spirit, uncorked the soda, mixed it, and was about to present it to the young Squire, when the door of Marian's state-room opened, and a rustle of silk announced her presence.

Tom turned, and caught sight of her face.

His own countenance became instantly clouded; he trembled violently, and in his agitation, dropped the glass.

"You clumsy fool, what are you doing?" cried Charlie.

Tom recovered himself by the exercise of great effort.

"Very sorry, sir," he replied. "The lady came in so unexpectedly, that it frightened me."

"Oh, has the lady left her room? You can go; but be on hand in case I ring for you."

Tom bowed, and casting a peculiar glance upon Marian, which she did not fail to notice, but could not account for, went away.

Marian went to Charlie's side.

"Are you not well?" she inquired.

"Far from it. I am harried by the fiend of sea-sickness," he answered. "Much as I should like to do the honours of the table, I cannot. You will have to excuse me, and eat your supper alone, if you feel equal to it, which I hope you do."

"Yes," she said; "the sea has not affected me. Some people are born good sailors, and, I suppose, I am one of them."

He looked at her, finding that she had dressed herself very prettily, and was charming.

"My poor head!" groaned Charlie. "I feel as I did when I first tried to smoke a pipe."

"Perhaps you will be better presently."

"Perhaps so, but you really must excuse me. I can just crawl into bed, and that is all."

Marian was delighted to get rid of him.

With a white face and tottering limbs, Charlie smiled in a sickly manner, and walked to a passage aft, which led to his cabin.

He shut the door, got into his berth with his clothes on, and fell asleep.

Marian had made up her mind to be bold and courageous. She sat down at the table, and helped herself to some chicken and ham.

She knew what champagne was; but opening a bottle of the sparkling wine was altogether beyond her capacity, so she struck the gong for the steward.

Tom promptly answered the summons.

"Open some wine, please," said Marian; "I have to sup alone, as Mr. Rawlings has retired very ill."

"Yes, miss," replied Tom, and something in the tone of his voice seemed to strike her as being familiar.

"Where do you come from?" asked Marian. "I know someone who talked just like you, so you need not think my question impertinent."

"Not far from Clare, in Suffolk, miss," he answered.

"Indeed! That is where I live. How strange! I have seen a face like yours; but, no—you are much older. Have you been long at sea"

"This is my first voyage, miss. Can I assist you to anything?"

Marian looked up abstractedly, and disregarded his question.

"What part of Clare did you say you came from?" she inquired.

"You mistake me, miss," replied the steward's mate. "I did not say I came from the town at all."

"But where did you live?" Marian demanded, impatiently.

"Hush, miss!" said Tom, putting his finger on his lips. "If the master was to hear me talking to you, he might not like it."

"I care not," she replied.

"No, I do not suppose you do," said the young steward, "or you would not have abandoned home and friends to come to sea with such a one as he."

He spoke with ill-concealed bitterness.

"What do you mean?" she demanded. "You know nothing, or—"

"I know you, Marian Spencer," interrupted Tom, "and if your brother Jack were here, he would not care to see you decked out like this, and travelling goodness knows where with young Squire Rawlings."

"My brother! Do you know him?"

"We are intimate friends."

"Who are you?"

"That is my secret, and will remain so."

"You are wrong in your conclusions. I am playing a part here. I have been abducted from my home. If you really know my brother, you will help me to escape when we touch land."

"How did you come here?"

"I was kidnapped one evening outside my father's farm, placed in a travelling showman's caravan, and brought here, gagged, helpless, and nearly starved," she replied.

"Then you have no feeling of affection for Mr. Rawlings?"

"None whatever. I may tell you more. His father is an impostor and a forger."

"Ha! how know you that?" cried the young man.

"My brother has discovered the real will. It is made in favour of Harry Rawlings, who has run away."

"The charge made against him is false."

"We know that now."

"Indeed!" said the steward. "Is Harry Rawlings' character cleared?"

He seemed to be labouring under great agitation, which he could not control.

"His innocence has been proved beyond a doubt," answered Marian.

"How so? The clouds were thick around him."

"They have rolled by. Warner has confessed that his hand alone killed Kennedy, and he has been sentenced to a term of imprisonment."

"Heaven be thanked!" cried the steward, fervently.

"When Harry returns, the solicitor to whom the will has been given, will proceed to eject the Squire," went on Marian.

"Do you still love Harry?" asked the steward's mate.

"With my heart. My love never faltered even when he was accused. If you are a friend of his, will you not tell me your name?"

For one moment he hesitated, looking nervously around him.

Then he exclaimed—

"Marian, I am Harry Rawlings."

The girl uttered a loud cry of surprise and delight.

"Hush, for heaven's sake!" said Harry.

"But your whiskers——"

"Are a disguise. See!"

He unbent the wires which fastened them over his ears, and tore them off.

Marian threw herself into his arms.

"My love—my own—found at last!" she murmured.

At this moment, a pale form appeared from the passage.

It was Charlie, who had been roused by the sound of their voices.

Basely playing the part of an eavesdropper, he had listened, and heard all.

His countenance was distorted with passion, which made him conquer his feeling of sickness.

Rushing forward, he struck Harry a blow in the face, which caused him to fall back.

Completely taken by surprise, Marian sank into a seat, faint with nervous apprehension.

Harry put himself on the defensive.

"How dare you come on board my ship in a disguise?" roared Charlie. "I know you, villain."

"And I know you," replied Harry. "We have met before. Have you forgotten that before my uncle, Squire Rawlings, took you up, you were the young snake charmer, the boy with the hump, a tramp actor, and a thief? Eh, do you recollect that?"

Charlie foamed at the mouth with rage.

"It is false!" he cried.

"Perhaps you will say the same of what this young lady has just told me—namely, that my uncle has no title to the property he usurps?" replied Harry. "Why, the Hall is mine. This yacht is mine. You and your father, if he is your father, are no better than paupers!"

At this declaration, Charlie grated his teeth savagely.

"You will have to prove that," he said; "and, perhaps, proceedings in a court of law may put a different complexion on the matter."

"You will soon know that I am the rightful heir."

"Bah! It is easy to invent a story like that. Possession is the thing. We are there, and we mean to stop. I am master on board this ship. You are in my power. I will swear that you came here disguised to rob me! You shall be put in irons!"

"Do you dare to threaten me in that way?" demanded Harry, fiercely.

"I shall not stop at threats. I shall act. We will soon see who is master, you or I."

There was a speaking tube in the saloon connecting with the deck cabin, which was allotted to the captain.

Putting his mouth to this, Charlie shouted—

"Captain Williams, I want your help at once. Come below.

"Your business will soon be settled, my fine fellow," he added. "The fact is, you know a little too much."

Harry saw the folly he had been guilty of, now it was too late.

He ought to have bided his time, and seized a fitting opportunity to reveal himself to Marian.

"You can call your men," said Harry; "but I will give you something to call them for. Miss Spencer is a witness that I do not attack you without provocation."

"Stand back, or you will rue it!" replied Charlie.

Marian got up, and stood between them.

"Do nothing rash, dear Harry," she begged.

"I will not be restrained," answered Harry. "My hands itch to return the blow that coward gave me!"

"Be calm, I——"

Harry pushed her gently on one side, and dealt Charlie several heavy blows, which he, in vain, endeavoured to counter.

At last he was fain to adopt the favourite device of a beaten man, and fall.

"I feel satisfied now that I have settled that popinjay, who is masquerading in colours that do not belong to him," exclaimed Harry.

"What have you done?" asked Marian, alarmed.

Charlie was bleeding from the nose and mouth. He had been badly knocked about, and would feel the effect of his antagonist's blows for some time to come.

"I have spoilt his beauty, if he has any, at all events," replied Harry.

Marian was terribly agitated.

In spite of all her efforts to the contrary, she burst into a fit of hysterical weeping.

Harry Rawlings stood over his fallen opponent, hoping he would get up again.

But Charlie knew better than to provoke a renewal of the combat which had resulted so disastrously for him.

"Get up like a man, and fight it out!" said Harry.

Before Charlie could make any reply, Captain Williams, accompanied by the mate, dashed into the saloon. They looked from one to the other in amazement.

"Seize him!" cried Charlie, raising himself on his elbow, and pointing to Harry.

The captain grasped the latter by the collar of his coat.

"What's up?" he asked. "This doesn't look like the same chap I saw before."

"It is the same," answered Charlie, "but he had false whiskers on; he has crept into the ship under a disguise to rob me, I believe."

"You know better," began Harry.

The captain struck him in the mouth.

"Hold your noise!" he interrupted; "this is rank mutiny! What do you mean by knocking our commodore about like this?"

Harry was silent, for he saw it was useless to try to explain matters to those who were evidently his enemies.

"Take him away!" yelled Charlie. "Lock him up! Iron him heavily!"

"Ay, sir; trust me," answered the captain.

"Do not listen to any rigmarole he may want to pour into your errs."

"Me listen to any sea lawyer?" cried Williams, indignantly. "Not me! I think I know myself better than that."

"When you have manacled him, come below and have supper with me, both of you."

Captain Williams and Porter thanked him for this invitation, for they had their appetites raised to famine pitch by the sight of the glorious feast spread out on the table.

Harry was dragged away.

He cast a significant, but, at the same time, imploring glance upon Marian.

It meant, "Watch over and succour me, if you get a chance."

She slightly inclined her head, and he knew that she understood his meaning.

Williams and Porter hurried him up to the dingy, evil-smelling den, which was to be his prison.

They were anxious to have their supper, and so lost no time. The boatswain could navigate the yacht during their absence.

When they were gone, Charlie looked at Marian with a malignant smile.

"It is rather annoying to be found out," he observed. "I am willing to believe that Harry Rawlings' coming here was pure accident; but you and he were plotting nicely when I interrupted you."

"You knew I loved him!" replied Marian; "and if you or your men injure him, you shall bitterly repent it!"

"No one will hurt him; but I was obliged to put him under restraint when he began knocking me about."

"Who provoked it?"

"Never mind. I understand all about the situation," said Charlie. "Harry's innocence has been proved. A will has been found, and your people are going to try to get my father and me out of the property."

"It is not legally yours. It belongs to Harry."

"If Harry was dead—I don't mean that I wish him any harm—but if he was gone, there would be no other claimant."

"He could settle it on whom he liked," said Marian.

"You are not his wife yet," retorted Charlie, angrily, "nor has Harry Rawlings got the property. Beware, both of you. Ha! here comes the captain and the mate."

"Entertain your mercenary ruffians by yourself. I will not sit in their company."

"Please yourself," replied Charlie, making a mock courtesy bow.

Marian retired, bestowing a glance on Charlie which made him feel very insignificant.

She did not intend, however, to close her eyes that night.

The suspicion that Harry's life was in danger had crept into her mind.

It was for her to watch over and protect him.

When the officers entered, Charlie begged them to make themselves at home.

In answer to his enquiries, they assured him that they had put Harry in irons, and locked the door, leaving the key in it.

"THE BOYS RAN FOR THEIR LIVES."

"That is right," said Charlie. "I believe the fellow is so desperate at being found out that he would commit suicide by throwing himself into the sea, if he could."

"If the door was open he might struggle to the side of the ship and do it, in spite of his irons," replied the mate.

"The steward is a friend of his. You do not suppose he would liberate him?"

"Not he. The man has turned in."

"I shall not prosecute him, because I have lost nothing," continued Charlie, "but I intend to put him on shore as soon as I can, and let him take his chance. It looks bad for a man to come on board in a disguise, and I could never trust him again."

"How did you find him out, sir?" inquired Captain Williams.

"Oh! simply enough. His false whiskers fell off, and when I asked for an explanation, he attacked me."

"The hardened young villain."

"If you two had not come to my rescue, I believe he would have killed me," replied Charlie. "Allow me to thank you, gentlemen, for your timely assistance, and pledge you in a glass of wine."

They stood up, and clinked their glasses merrily together. An hour passed very pleasantly; then the captain and mate retired to get a few hours' rest.

Charlie was very glad to get rid of them, for his mind was full of a dark and sinister idea.

For fully an hour he sat plunged in deep thought.

Harry was the thorn in his side—the only obstacle intervening between him and happiness, prosperity and fortune.

What would his father have counselled had he been by his side at that moment?

Death—sudden, cruel, remorseless!

"Yes," muttered Charlie, "to save ourselves, I must do it. His life shall be cut short, for if he lives, we shall be ruined and thwarted in every way."

He knew that the only way out of the difficulties with which he was environed was to kill Harry.

If he could reach the deck-house unperceived, steal into it and stab Harry to the heart, he could drag him to the side of the ship, and throw him overboard.

Who would be any the wiser?

Pale as death, with his lips grimly set together, he secreted a sharp knife in his pocket, and stole up the companion.

The officer of the watch was talking to the man at the wheel.

Gliding stealthily to the little hole into which Harry had been thrown, he crouched in the shadow for a moment to see if he was observed.

Finding that he was not, he unlocked the door and entered.

Harry was sitting in a cramped position, his back against the wall, unable to find solace in sleep.

He was ironed heavily, and therefore incapable of offering any resistance to his cowardly would-be assassin.

Seizing him by the throat, Charlie held up the knife, and, in a hoarse voice, hissed—

"Your hour has come! Prepare to die!"

Harry tried to speak, but was unable to do so, owing to the pressure on his throat.

A feeling of indescribable horror and despair took possession of him. His life hung, as it were, on a single thread.

CHAPTER XXVIII.

THE CAPTIVE BALLOON—TREACHERY OF THE TWO SPIES.

It was Bank Holiday, in the month of August, a few days after the beginning of the holidays at Doctor Birchoften's academy.

Tuffins, whose broken arm was now as strong as ever, was, after breakfast, in the yard, standing by the dustbin, with a scuttle and a sieve full of cinders, which he had to sift.

One of Miss Martha's pet economies, and she had many, was to sift the cinders to save the coal.

Instead of attending to his work, Tuffins was leaning against the wall, enjoying the magificent sunshine, and reading a handbill.

The latter set forth that "Monsieur Carde-rossi, the world-renowned æronaut from Paris, would display his famous Ballon Captif, or Captive Balloon, in Cork's field, a piece of land attached to the 'Cricketers, Inn,' near Clare."

Capable of holding twenty people, at a shilling a head, in the car, the balloon, secured to the ground by a stout rope, wound on a wooden reel, would go up every half-hour to a height of a thousand feet.

Monsieur Carderossi called his captive balloon the "Highflyer," and invited all the neighbourhood to come and see it.

"This reads like a real good thing," muttered Tuffins. "It's a novelty, too, and I should much like to take it in. Wonder whether the old dragon will let me go?"

It happened to be washing day with Miss Martha, who was very busy.

On these occasions her temper was anything but sweet, whatever it might be on other occasions.

She required some cinders for her copper fire.

"Tuffins!" she cried, in a shrill, shrewish voice, "whatever are you doing?"

"'It will ascend, for the first time, at twelve o'clock, and every half-hour afterwards until dark,'" replied Tuffins.

He was reading from Monsieur Carderossi's handbill.

"I don't know what you are talking about."

"'From Paris, St. Petersburg, Vienna, Berlin, and all the capitals of Europe. Only one shilling. Floating in the Empyrean. Positively a new sensation.'"

"Will you listen to me, sir?"

"'Positively no danger,'" continued the imperturbable Tuffins. "'Up in a balloon, boys! Up in a balloon! Come early!'"

"I want those cinders," shrieked Miss Martha. "How long are you going to be about it? Oh, you little wretch, if I could only get hold of you, I'd shake the life out of you!"

Tuffins turned, and surveyed her leisurely.

"Beg pardon, ma'am," he replied; "this being the holidays, I had forgotten that there was work to be done, and the weather is really so seductive, I thought of taking a day off."

"You dare!" Miss Martha shrieked.

"I did, indeed, ma'am."

"If you do, I will discharge you on the spot!"

This had happened so often, that the threat did not daunt Tuffins in the least.

"It's Bank Holiday, and everybody's gone out," he said. "I fancied you would be glad to get rid of me."

"Servants are not allowed holidays. Make haste with those cinders, or I'll rattle a clothes-prop over your fat back!" she rejoined.

"Ain't she a sweet duck?" mutttered Tuffins, as he agitated the sieve. "Oh, she's a daisy! I should like to have a lock of her hair, and wear it next my 'art."

In a short time he had the scuttle full of cinders, and went to the back door with them.

The ground was damp and muddy from rain, which had fallen during the night.

The clothes which Miss Martha had already hung out to dry, were the heavy things, such as sheets and tablecloths.

They looked as white as snow.

As Tuffins passed under the line, he gave the main prop a vicious kick.

It slipped, and down came the line, dragging all the clean clothes into the mud.

Tuffins put the scuttle outside the back door, and went into the fowl-house to look for eggs.

He had reasons of his own for not wanting to be seen for a few minutes.

Miss Martha was busily occupied in the arduous process of wringing a counterpane.

When she had finished, she looked out of the window.

"This is a heavy week's wash," she said. "I might have had a woman in, only it would have cost too much. Bother the boy! where is he? Oh—oh-h!"

The exclamation was caused by her suddenly perceiving that all her clean clothes were dragging in the mud.

"Heaven!" she cried, "the line's down. Whatever shall I do? All the morning's work is lost, and I was up at six. Where's that awful boy? I do believe he's done it out of spite, because I would not let him have a holiday."

Firmly grasping the copper-stick in her right hand, she ran to the door, full of vengeful feelings.

As a natural consequence of the scuttle being placed in her way, she fell over it.

With outstretched arms, she took a header into the mud, and mixed up the clothes in the most alarming manner with the cinders.

Tuffins watched this catastrophe from his place of concealment with considerable hilarity.

Emerging from the hen-house, he put on an air of sober concern.

"What are you a-trying to do, ma'am?" he asked. "This isn't the skating season."

Rising with difficulty, red-faced, and covered with mud, Miss Martha seized the clothes-prop.

"You imp!" she cried. "I have to thank you for this. I'll teach you to set traps for me."

Then she began to chase him round the yard, Tuffins having the best of it all through.

At last she stopped through sheer exhaustion.

"Oh," she exclaimed, bitterly, "if I could only get hold of you!"

"Which is a thing you're not likely to do. Is there anything you want from the village, ma'am?" he asked.

"Didn't I say you were not to go?"

"Can't help that; my name's Walker. It ain't often I get a day out. Expect me at tea-time, and mind the crumpets is well toasted."

With his hands in his pockets, he walked away, whistling a merry air.

Miss Martha was ready to cry with vexation, for all her work had to be done over again.

"I suppose I shall be decorated with the order of the sack as usual," muttered Tuffins.

This did not concern him greatly, as Miss Martha, as a rule, discharged him twice a week—sometimes oftener.

He wended his way towards Corks' field, and overtook the spies, who were lounging lazily in the same direction.

They did not live far off, their families being neighbours; and when anything was going on in the vicinity, they were sure to be present.

Tuffins took up a clod of earth, and playfully threw it at Peeping Tom, knocking off his round hat.

"I say, stop that!" cried Tom, turning sharply.

"It's only me," said Tuffins. "I'm a funny chap, and like to do things in my own way, out of the common like. Folks call me a little eccentric."

"If you do it again, you will get a thrashing. We are two to one."

"I can run faster than either of you, so let's be friends. I suppose you are going to see the balloon? So am I. When I got up this morning, I felt so glad I was alive that I made up my mind to take a holiday."

"Take it and go," replied Knowall Dick.

"What do you mean—a hinsult?"

"We don't want you. Page-boys are not fit company for us, are they, Tommy?"

"Not by a long shot," answered Peeping Tom. "We can't bemean ourselves by being seen in public in company with the hired slavey who waits on us at table."

"And cleans our boots," put in Dick.

Tuffins' eyes grew bigger; he stamped his foot on the ground, and clenched his hands.

There was mischief brewing, for the blood of Tuffins was up. It would soon be at boiling point.

"What am I?" he exclaimed. "Hired slavey? Not good enough? We'll soon see."

Squaring up suddenly to Peeping Tom, he gave him a blow which knocked him at full length into the ditch.

Knowall Dick attempted to run, but a vigorous kick sent him sprawling into a bed of nettles, from which he rolled, much stung.

Neither of the spies attempted to rise.

They looked at the page out of their little round eyes to see what he was going to do next.

"What's your opinion of things in general now?" he asked. "If you'd been civil, you wouldn't have got beat. Don't you think I'm good enough to go to Corks' field with the likes of you?"

"I didn't mean it," replied Peeping Tom. "It was only chaff to see what you would say."

"Pride's sure to have a fall," rejoined Tuffins.

"It was only a lark," said Knowall Dick. "'Pon honour, that's all."

"I don't like chaps who lark in that way."

"Your only fault, Tuffy, is, that you will lose your temper so soon. You're like a bottle of fiz, up in a moment."

"And you were down in a jiffy. Ha, ha! that's the difference between us."

"Let us get up," pleaded Peeping Tom.

"Who's stopping you? The page boy isn't," responded Tuffins, with unmistakable sarcastic emphasis.

"That's true; but if we were to rise without your permission, you might knock us down again."

"Aren't you 'cute? Ah, ah!"

"May we get up?"

"Not yet. You volunteered for a hiding, and you'll get it, unless you consent to my terms."

"Name them. What are they?" cried the spies, in a breath.

"Oh, aren't you anxious? Don't be too eager. You'll have to let me walk between you to Corks' field."

"Yes; no objection to that," said Tom.

"Proud of the honour," exclaimed Dick, although his looks belied his words.

"Wait a bit; that isn't all."

"What else?"

"I shall want a bit of lunch and some beer at your expense, and you'll have to treat me to the balloon. You may reckon I shall cost you a few shillings before I've done with you."

"Never mind," replied Peeping Tom; "we are not without money."

"It is a bargain," said Knowall Dick. "Come on."

Tuffins was satisfied. He put aside his resentment, and helped them to rise.

More than that, he brushed the dust off them with his cap.

It was a great mortification to the spies to have to give in like this.

As usual, they harboured revenge in their breasts.

All they waited for was an opportunity to gratify their base passion.

The remainder of the journey was performed without any incident. When they reached the field, they did not find so many people there as they expected. The balloon was moored a few feet from the ground.

As yet, no one had been adventurous enough to get into the car and go up.

Some were anxious to do so; but they wanted someone to go first.

Amongst those on the ground was Jack Spencer, alone, and looking very gloomy.

The farm was now like a house of mourning.

No news had been received of Marian, and the hearts of her relatives were heavy with grief.

The spies went to the Frenchman, who was standing near his balloon, and bought a shilling ticket for ascent.

This they gave to Tuffins, and presented him, at the same time, with half-a-crown to buy what he liked with.

"That will do, gentlemen," said Tuffins; "the page boy is grateful for your kindness."

"You only wanted our money!"

"That is all. As for you two fellows, I wouldn't find you. I wouldn't have you as a gift. Over there I see Jack Spencer."

"What of him?"

"His little finger is worth the pair of you two chaps!" replied Tuffins, scornfully.

Putting his hat on the back of his head in a jaunty manner, the page hastened to that part of the field where Jack was standing.

"How are you, Master Spencer?" asked Tuffins. "I've heard of your trouble. Anything new?"

"Absolutely nothing," replied Jack. "Thank you for your kind inquiries."

"That's bad! You look worried; but, depend upon it, it will all come right in time."

"Heaven grant it may! If my poor sister and Harry were here now, I should be perfectly happy."

"Drive dull care away."

"I can't. What I want is excitement of some kind. That is why I came here to-day."

"Why don't you go up in the balloon?" cried Tuffins. "I'm going."

"All right; that's a good suggestion. Let us be the first," said Jack.

"I suppose it is safe?" remarked Tuffins.

"No danger."

"There's a strong breeze blowing. If the rope was to break it would be a case of Jack up the orchard with us."

"The man has been exhibiting his balloon all over Europe," replied Jack, "and has never met with an accident. I'm not afraid."

"If you are not, why should I be?" observed Tuffins. "Shall we go to the mussoo and ask him to give us a start?"

"Yes," Jack replied. "I was going to eat my dinner first, but it doesn't matter."

"Eat it in the car."

"That will do just as well. It is in this basket. There is more than enough for four. I thought I should meet some friends, who would share it with me."

"Let me carry it," cried Tuffins, taking up the basket.

"It's jolly heavy," he added.

They approached M. Carderossi, who was becoming impatient because none of the yokels seemed disposed to ascend.

"There really ees no danger, my goot frens," he exclaimed. "Ze rope shall go up a certain height, zen she shall stop. When you shall vant to come down, I shall turn ze crank, and ze sing is done."

"How long do you allow us to remain up in the air?" asked Jack.

"One half of ze hour by my watch. Zen ze balloon shall return."

"Here's my shilling," replied Jack.

"I've got a ticket," said Tuffins.

"Two gentlemen are about to ascend," cried M. Carderossi. "*Ma foi!* ze great Montgolfier, who made ze first balloon zat evaire was, vould be proud of ze 'Highflyer,' vich I name mine. Who says next?"

There was no response on the part of the crowd.

"You are positive it is all right, old man?" asked Tuffins. "'Cos I'm a little nervous."

"I have, in Berleen, take up ze emperor and all ze grand dukes wis perfek safety," answered M. Carderossi.

"Never had your balloon run away from you?"

"Nevaire, sare."

"That settles it," said Jack. "We will get in. Don't keep us waiting longer than you can help."

They went up a small pair of steps and entered the car, where they sat down.

Tuffins took care not to neglect the basket containing the provisions.

When they were seated, M. Carderossi told his assistant to turn the handle of the crank, and let out the rope.

Gradually the balloon began to ascend.

The spectators broke into a loud cheer.

"She go oop roight enow," said one rustic.

"Oi'll be in t' next carful," remarked another. "There be no danger. Dang me, if I doan't ha' a shillun's worth."

"Same here!" cried a third. "We'll keep t' ball a-rolling!"

The shouts and exclamations roused the two spies, who were imbibing ginger-beer in the parlour of the inn.

"What's up?" asked Peeping Tom.

"The balloon, I expect," replied Knowall Dick.

"Let's go and see all about it. No doubt Tuffins is having his shilling's worth. I wish the thing would break loose, and carry him into infinite space."

They quitted the room, and when they reached the field, saw that the balloon was far above their heads.

It swayed about a good deal, but could not escape from its fastenings.

The rope was attached to a bar of iron fixed firmly in a deep hole dug in the earth.

Stones and heavy weights were placed on the top of this, and above was the wooden roller, around which the rope was coiled.

This apparatus was hidden from public view by a wooden shed.

Having sent the balloon up, the assistant opened the door of his shed, and came out.

The assistant was also the orator of the show.

He had a telescope on a stand, and exclaimed—

"Those in the car now look, to the naked eye, like birds in the air. Have a closer view, ladies and gentlemen, for one penny."

Knowall Dick handed him the required coin, and put his eye to the lens.

"Penny a peep," continued the assistant— "only one penny a peep."

When Dick had taken a good look, he rejoined Tom, and other people coming up to have a pennyworth through the telescope, the assistant was kept fully occupied.

"Who do you think is up with Tuffins?" asked Dick.

"Anyone we know?" replied Tom.

"Jack Spencer. They've got some provisions, and are enjoying their dear selves."

A demoniac look crossed Peeping Tom's face.

"I say," he whispered, hoarsely, "it strikes me we might kill two birds with one stone."

"How?"

"I've got my knife with me."

"What then?"

"You watch the assistant, and I'll steal into the shed and cut and hack the rope so that it is bound to break in this wind."

"You daren't do it," said Dick, half frightened.

"Wait and see."

"What will become of them?"

"I don't care so long as I never see them again. No one will suspect us."

"I—I wouldn't do it," stammered Knowall Dick; "we might be found out."

"Bah! People will be sure to say that the rope was frayed, and broke from a constant strain. Keep dark. Leave it to me."

Peeping Tom slipped into the shed without being perceived by anyone.

Going to the roller, he drew his knife, and hacked away at the rope, cutting through several strands,

Beads of perspiration stood on his brow, and he trembled violently in every limb.

Outside, the orator was crying—

"In ten minutes the magnificent balloon will descend. Let me collect your shillings. You see it is perfectly safe."

When he had finished his foul work, Peeping Tom rejoined his companion, and they moved away together.

"Have you done it?" asked Knowall Dick.

"Thoroughly. Wait a minute or two, and you will see something," replied Peeping Tom.

No one had seen him commit the detestable act, and he felt perfectly at his ease.

He even had the coolness to light a cigarette.

"I like to do an ememy an ill turn," remarked Knowall Dick.

"So do I; it is glorious," laughed Tom.

The wind was rising, blowing from the west, and veering occasionally to the north.

Suddenly a furious blast shook the trees in the field.

The balloon careened, and the rope quivered.

In a moment, like a flash of lightning, the balloon shot up into the sky.

"*Mon Dieu!*" yelled the Frenchman, "ze rope has parted!"

A cry of terror broke from the assembled spectators.

Like an arrow from a bow, the balloon ascended.

"By Jove! you've done it," whispered Knowall Dick.

"Not a word," replied Tommy; "somebody might hear you."

M. Carderossi threw himself on the ground and tore his hair.

"Oh! I vas ruin!" he exclaimed. "Never more sal I see my goot balloon! *Diable!* I vas ruin!"

In less than ten minutes the balloon was out of sight.

CHAPTER XXIX.

UP IN THE AIR.

WHEN the balloon had become stationary at the extremity of the rope, Jack and Tuffins experienced a new sensation.

They looked over the side of the car, and the people below seemed to be dwarfed.

All around them was a magnificent expanse of country, through which the little river wound and twisted like a silver thread.

The air was so strong and keen that it nearly took their breath away, and the balloon rocked so much that it made them giddy.

"How do you like it?" asked Jack.

"Not over much," replied Tuffins. "I'd rather have three shies for a penny at the cocoanuts."

"Oh! I think it is grand," said Jack.

"How about that bit of dinner?" enquired Tuffins, who had no sentiment of poetry in his composition.

"Open the basket and help yourself, you're welcome. I want to enjoy the scenery," answered Jack.

Tuffins was not slow to avail himself of the opportunity, and was soon engaged in the pleasant pastime of eating and drinking.

The minutes passed very quickly.

All at once Jack felt a peculiar motion, and heard a hoarse roar.

He sat down in the car by the side of Tuffins, who was already taking his ease, with the leg of a fowl in one hand, and a bottle of beer in the other.

"What's the row?" asked Tuffins. "Had enough of the view and come to your oats? There's plenty left."

"Something's wrong," replied Jack.

"Oh, lor'! don't say that!"

"Look for yourself."

Tuffins did so, and peering over the side of the car, perceived that the people below resembled dots.

There could be no doubt that the rope had broken, and that they were drifting into space.

"Here's a pretty go," gasped Tuffins. "Oh, heaven! what will become of us?"

Jack made no reply. He had not the slightest knowledge of ballooning. What would become of them he could not tell.

In a short time they were among the clouds, the fleecy folds of which enveloped them.

When it became evident beyond the possibility of doubt that the balloon was freed from its moorings and cast adrift, Tuffins became the prey of an indescribable terror.

His face blanched, his lips were livid, and he trembled in every limb.

Not so Jack.

He saw the imminence of the danger, but he did not lose his head for a moment, though the balloon had shot up with startling velocity.

In an incredibly short time they had risen above the banks of clouds. The rope, which was long and heavy, acted as ballast, and having attained this elevation, they did not rise any higher, but were swept along by a southerly current.

The sun was shining on the masses of fleecy clouds, and they seemed to be in a new world.

Tuffins crouched in a corner of the car, his eyes starting, his hands clasped together, and his teeth chattering.

Jack was engaged in studying the balloon, to see if he could find out how to let the gas out.

Unless he could do that, he knew very well he could not descend.

All he was able to see was a network of ropes, which attached the car to the aeriel machine.

There was no particular one that he noticed which would open the valve.

"We are in for it!" he exclaimed, at last. "In spite of what the Frenchman said, the accident has happened."

"Oh, heaven help us!" groaned Tuffins. "What shall we do? I'm frightened almost to death. Can't you get us down to earth again?"

"If I could let the gas out—"

"Do it," cried Tuffins, eagerly. "Oh! why did I come out this morning? This is a punishment for disobedience. If I can only touch the ground again, I will always do what I am told. It is awful to be up in the air like this."

"At present there is no danger."

"There is—there must be. Don't try to deceive me like that."

"We are not rising now," continued Jack; "we are drifting southwards, as well as I can judge."

"Suppose the lightning came out of a cloud and struck us, or the car ropes broke. Try and descend, I feel my brain giving way."

"Unfortunately, I cannot."

"You lie!" screamed Tuffins, savagely. "If you like you can, but you will not."

"Indeed I don't know how to do it," protested Jack.

"'WHAT HA' YOU BEEN UP TO?' SHOUTED THE MILLER."

The speech and manner of Tuffins somewhat alarmed him.

He really looked as if the sudden shock was driving him out of his senses.

"I'll make you," continued Tuffins. "This is a plot against my life, but I will not die without a struggle."

He got up from his recumbent position, glaring like a tiger at Jack, who was leaning against the side of the car.

Its wicker framework came up to his shoulders, so there was no danger of falling out.

But he might be thrown over.

"Sit still, for heaven's sake!" exclaimed Jack. "What is the matter with you?"

"I'm mad—mad, dangerously mad!" replied Tuffins.

There could be no doubt about it now.

"Will you have reason?" continued Jack. "Don't touch me, if you do you will repent it."

Tuffins was not dismayed by Jack's threatening action, or loud tone of voice.

He viciously seized his companion by the legs, with the evident idea of throwing him into space.

"Ha, ha!" he laughed, demoniacally. "Now I've got you. We will soon see who is best man."

Jack fell on the top of him, grasping him by the throat.

Then began a fearful struggle for the mastery.

Filled with extraordinary strength, the page fought desperately.

More than once he nearly succeeded in hurling his companion from the car.

Jack was growing exhausted.

In their conflict they had overturned the provision basket, and the bottles of beer rolled out.

Getting hold of one, Jack forced his antagonist back, and, striking him with it, broke it over his head.

This ended the encounter, for Tuffins fell, stunned, at his feet.

It was indeed lucky that Jack had been able to find a weapon.

Long years afterwards, he remembered that terrible combat up in the air, amid the vast and awful solitude.

Though Tuffins was bleeding from the head, he was not much injured, and there was every chance of his speedy recovery.

When he came to, he would probably renew the contest.

To render him powerless for further harm, Jack determined to bind his hands.

In order to do this, it was necessary to get some cord.

Looking up, he saw a string hanging loosely.

He took hold of it and pulled it towards him to cut a piece off with his pocket-knife.

No sooner had he done so than he was conscious of a smell of gas.

At the same moment the balloon began to descend into the clouds.

He uttered a cry of joy.

By the merest accident he had discovered the string attached to the valve.

Keeping hold of it, he soon sank beneath the clouds, and looked out to see the earth once more.

What was his surprise to find that he was over the sea.

Beneath him rolled a vast expanse of ocean, on the surface of which he could distinguish sailing vessels and steamers, the latter throwing off long lines of black, trailing smoke.

He shut up the valve, as it was idle to dream of descending into the sea.

This would be to court certain death by drowning.

Safer by far was he in the balloon, sailing through the air.

As far as he could form any conjecture, he was fast drifting over the English Channel towards the coast of France or Spain.

Most probably the former.

Just as he was about to cut off a bit of the cord which he thought he could afford to spare, Tuffins sprang up.

Climbing up to the edge of the car, he sat on it, holding on by one of the suspensory strands.

"You villain!" he yelled. "It was your thought to kill me when I was struck down by that cowardly blow, but I will live to thwart you."

His cap had fallen off, and the wind blew his hair about, making him look wild, weird, and unearthly.

"I have no animosity against you," answered Jack. "Why should you think so?"

The idea was firmly rooted in Tuffins' mind that Jack was plotting to kill him.

Nothing could eradicate it.

"You are vile enough for anything," replied the page. "I have known you as my enemy for a long time."

"You are mistaken."

"No! but I will foil you. Look! down I go."

Before Jack could stop him he let go his hold of the rope, and swinging his legs over the car, plunged into space.

Horror-stricken, Jack leaned over the side, and peered down.

Over and over the mad boy turned, until he seemed no bigger than a bird.

After that, he looked a mere dot.

Then he disappeared from Jack's view altogether.

Jack felt it was useless to hope ever to see him again.

Faint and sick at the fearful nature of this totally unlooked-for catastrophe, he sank back in the car.

He was for the time completely unnerved.

At length he recovered himself and looked out.

The balloon was still travelling over the sea, which sparkled in the sun's rays.

He looked at his watch.

It was five o'clock, and he calculated that he had been up in the air about three hours, as it was nearly two when the machine broke away from Corks' field.

It seemed a much longer time to him; he could have believed that he had been up a whole day.

Feeling faint he sat down again, and ate some fowl and ham, with an appetite sharpened by the keenness of the air.

Some beer from a bottle helped to revive him, and raise his spirits a little.

When Tuffins had jumped out to his doom, it was like losing so much ballast, and Jack had let out more gas to equalise the weight.

Knowing now how to regulate it, he let it sink very low to see where he was.

Still he was over the sea, with no sign of land in any direction.

Some sailors in a ship shouted to him, and fired off guns and pistols.

He waved his hand in recognition of their salute, but being fearful lest one of their shots might hit the balloon and wreck it, he threw out ballast and ascended again.

Towards six o'clock he had the great satisfaction of seeing land.

Soon a large city was spread out before his eyes. He passed by it to the southward, and went inland.

Below were large tracts of land laid out as vineyards.

By this he knew he was either in France or Spain.

He had experienced enough of ballooning, and determined to descend to earth as quickly as he conveniently could.

To do this he wanted to see some trees, so that he could throw out the iron grapnel and hold on.

At length he approached a wood. Immediately he allowed the gas to escape, and the balloon sank nearly to the tops of the trees.

There was scarcely any wind blowing, which was fortunate for him.

Casting out the anchor, he had the satisfaction of seeing it catch on to a stout limb of a sturdy tree.

With a tremendous jerk the balloon came to a standstill.

In the car he had found a rope ladder, which had two hooks to attach it to the wickerwork.

Making it fast he cast it down, and was pleased to see that it came to within a foot of the ground.

He had the precaution, when he descended, to take his basket of food and the knife with him.

If he should find himself amongst a churlish peasantry, the latter might prove of inestimable service to him.

He had a watch, rings, and money on his person, which might tempt to robbery and violence, if not murder.

Without any mishap he reached the ground, thanking his good fortune at having escaped so well from the dangers to which he had been exposed.

He had descended at the extremity of the wood, so that he would not have to walk far to get out of it.

About the table-land occupied by vineyards he noticed very few houses, and the city he had seen must be, he thought, a dozen miles off at least.

It was very warm, however, and if he chose to sleep in the wood that night he would be comfortable enough on a bed of moss.

Being hungry again, he sat down and paid attention to the chicken and ham, with the addition of a little more malt to wash it down.

"This climate is delightful," he muttered. "I sha'n't bother to move from this spot to-night. The ground is good enough to sleep on. To-morrow I will see about getting home."

Just then a couple of mosquitos attacked him.

"My stars!" he continued, "there is a swarm of gnats. How they do bite in this country."

He was destined to have no peace from these little pests, and though he tried to fall asleep, leaning his back against a tree, he was unable to do so.

The sun was declining, and the branches of the trees cast funereal shadows on the ground.

"If it wasn't for those beastly gnats," said Jack, "I could sleep like a top."

He knocked a dozen of the insects off his hands and face.

The setting sun was glistening through the branches, making patches of gold at his feet.

In spite of the stinging bites of the mosquitos, which continued to swarm around him, he fell into a doze.

Suddenly he was rudely awakened by loud shrieks, in a woman's voice.

Springing up, he said, confusedly—

"What's that? Am I dreaming?"

After a momentary pause, the cries were repeated.

"Help! help! for heaven's sake, help!"

It was clearly a woman in distress, and she was speaking in the English tongue.

Jack did not hesitate a moment.

He snatched up the knife he had used to cut his dinner, and rushed in the direction whence the sounds proceeded.

His heart was beating violently.

What could it mean?

Perhaps some fearful tragedy was being enacted. If he could only arrive in time, he might be able to save a human life.

CHAPTER XXX.

SAVED!—THE ESCAPE—PURSUIT.

WHEN attacked in the middle of the night by Charlie, Harry Rawlings gave himself up for lost.

So tight was the grip on his throat that he could not cry out, and, with a sickening sensation at his heart, he awaited death.

This, however, was averted.

Marian had been on the watch. She saw Charlie quit the saloon with the knife in his hand.

Dreading the worst, she followed him. On the deck she picked up a belaying pin, and armed with this weapon, she arrived in time to strike the cowardly assassin down.

Another moment and Harry would have been foully murdered.

Charlie was as insensible as a log, and did not move.

Bending over her sweetheart, Marian cried

"Am I in time? Oh! say that he has not injured you?"

Harry looked up gratefully into her eyes, in the pale starlight.

"I am all right, Marian," he replied, "thanks to you. How can I ever thank you sufficiently?"

He could only press her hand with his fingers on account of his being bound, but she felt the grateful pressure, and returned it.

"Your life is not safe while that villain lives," she cried. "When he comes to, he may kill you."

"Call the captain or the mate. They are Englishmen. I don't believe they would like to see me foully dealt with."

"You're right. I will do so. An appeal to them may help us."

"Tell them the truth," continued Harry. "At present they have only heard a tissue of lies."

"How?"

"He has said that I was a thief, which you know to be false."

"Of course. What else?"

"It was reported on board this ship that you are a relation of his, and out of your mind."

"The wretch!" cried Marian.

"If you made any disturbance, it was to be put down to your insanity. Any statements you made were not to be credited."

"Can such villainy be possible?"

"He is capable of anything bad. You are supposed to be insane; the doctors have recommended a sea voyage for you."

A heavy footstep was heard outside the caboose.

"Hullo! talking to yourself, prisoner?" exclaimed a rough voice.

It was that of Captain Williams.

Marian rose from her knees.

"Eh—what!" continued the captain, as she confronted him. "You here, miss?"

"Yes; and it is very lucky I came here, for Mr. Rawlings was trying to murder the steward," replied Marian.

"Is that the truth?"

"Look for yourself. I was in time to knock him on the head with a weapon I picked up."

The captain examined Charlie in a very careful and deliberate manner.

Then he looked up at Marian.

"What's this young chap to you, miss?" he asked, indicating Harry.

"My lover," replied Marian, boldly. "He is a cousin to the other one, and the real heir to the property."

"How did he come aboard the yacht?"

"By the merest accident."

"I don't understand the business," said the captain, shaking his head. "I was told you were mad."

"No more than you are."

"It's a strange yarn. I—"

"Let me explain it all. I have been abducted, and—"

Williams interrupted her in his turn.

"Enough said," he cried. "Go below, please. I'll carry the master down, and I'll be answerable for the life of the prisoner."

"You may take Mr. Rawlings below if

you like, but I shall stay here till daybreak," said Marian.

The fierce light of determination burned in her eyes.

"You will?"

"Yes; and I defy you and all your men to remove me."

"I admire your pluck, my lass, whether you are right or wrong. The whole thing is a mystery to me. If so be as you mean to stop here, well and good, I sha'n't say you nay, for I never raised my hand to a woman in my life, and never will."

"It is easy to see that you are a gentleman, but your employer is not."

"I owe him my obedience, miss. He pays me."

"Not to oppress those in distress," said Marian.

"No harm shall come to you, nor the steward chap either. Will that content you?"

"I ask no more."

"Stay you here, then. It's a serious affair, but it is not for the likes of me to interfere and be a judge."

"I don't ask you to be. I only claim protection."

"And you shall have it. Fair play is the motto of an Englishman," replied the captain, "and you shall have it."

"Thank you, captain," said Marian. "It may be in my power some day to return your kindness."

"I'm not asking for that, miss."

"Nevertheless, I shall not forget you."

"Won't you come below and leave the steward chap to my care?"

"I dare not."

"Do so, Marian," said Harry, who had not hitherto spoken. "Seek the rest you so much need. I am sure I shall be safe in Captain Williams' hands."

"If I could think so—"

"Look here, miss," cried the captain, "I'm a man of my word, and when I say a thing, money can't buy me."

"Will you protect him?"

"With my life. I swear it."

"Then I will retire in a few minutes," said Marian. "Take Mr. Rawlings below, attend to his injury, and come back for me."

Williams took Charlie up in his arms as if he had been a child, and carried him down the companion.

"It's a queer start," he muttered. "Blessed if I can make head or tail of it, but the young governor seems to be a bad egg."

When Marian was alone with Harry, she sank on her knees again and kissed his face.

"How shall we get out of this?" she murmured. "Thank heaven, you are saved; but what of the morrow?"

"We must trust to Williams," replied Harry. "He seems to be a genuine old salt. If I could only remove these irons with which they have bound me, we might make a bold bid for freedom, when we reach a port."

"Whither are we bound?"

"To Bordeaux, in the south of France, I understand."

"I will fly with you anywhere; but alas!" said Marian, "I have no money, and you are equally as poor as I. How can we return to England? Once there in the dear old home, we are amongst friends, and safe from persecution."

"Keep a stout heart; we will find a way out of the difficulty somehow."

As Harry spoke, a French boy, about fourteen years old, came by. He had been engaged by the captain, at Bordeaux, to wait upon him.

His name was Pierre.

The boy's life on board the yacht was not a happy one. he longed for his own sunny clime, with its olives, vineyards, and mulberries.

He had been engaged for a year, his time was nearly up, and he meant to quit the yacht when she came to France.

"Shall you want anything?" he asked, stopping and holding up his lantern.

"Is that you, Pierre?" replied Harry, who liked the boy from what he had seen of him.

"Yes; it's me. Can I do for you something?"

"Not now; but you told me, if I am not mistaken, that you live in Bordeaux?"

"Out of it. My fader and mudder live in the Mulberry Wood, ten miles out of ze city. Keep ze silkworm; gather fruit for ze patron—you know, ze master. Me going to see them. No more sea for Pierre."

"Have you had enough of it?"

"More'n me like. Capt'in too ready with ze rope's-end; mate too quick with ze boot toe."

"You won't get your wages if you don't serve your time."

"Me not care. Me go home; run away in night."

"I wish you would take this lady and me with you. We have rich friends in England, and will reward you."

"What you done to be shoved into this hole, eh?"

"Nothing at all. I am being ill-treated."

"Ah! you love this lady," said Pierre, sharply. "Gentleman who own yacht love her ze same, and he imprison you because she love you best."

"That is the truth. Will you help us?" asked Harry, hope rising in his breast.

"Yes; wait. When we in Bordeaux, me release you—you both come with me to wood all night."

He laughed, winked his eye knowingly, and walked on.

It was lucky for all concerned that he did so, for at that moment Captain Williams reappeared on deck.

He advanced rapidly towards them.

"The skipper is hurt worse than I thought he was," he exclaimed. "He'll have to lie abed all day to-morrow."

"What a blessing!" cried Marian.

"It was a nasty cut on the head you gave him. What with that and the knock-down blow the steward chap landed him, he looks a picture."

"Serves him right. All he gets he fully deserves."

"We won't enter into that, miss, with your permission," said the captain.

"But you ought to, if you have the instincts of a man," cried Marian.

"Belay that kind of talk."

"Perhaps you have a wife—children of your own; loving sons and daughters—"

Williams shook his head.

"A mother, sisters—"

"Not me. I'm a foundling, which is worse than being an orphan. I've no kith or kin; I don't belong to nobody, and nobody belongs to me, so you've missed your pitch this time, miss."

"I can only say I am sorry for you."

"Thank you. Don't work up any sentiment on my behalf; it ain't needed. Likewise, don't pump up no tears. I've got along all my life without relatives, and I don't want any; I stand alone. All I can say is, the young Squire employs me, and pays me; it's my living, and I am not going back on him."

"Then we have nothing to hope for from you?" said Harry.

"Nothing at all."

"If you stick to the young Squire, as you call him, you may find yourself in difficulties."

"Don't threaten me."

"I do, and I will. There is such a thing as law."

"Yes," added Captain Williams, "and you will find it out, my fine fellow. When we reach Bordeaux, you will be taken to the prefect of police, charged with robbery and assault."

"Did your employer tell you that?"

"Yes. After we have disposed of you," continued Williams, who had been paying more attention to the brandy bottle, while below, than was proper, "we shall slip our cable, and start for the Mediterranean. Marseilles will be our first point; then we shall cross to Algiers."

"Then you do not intend to prosecute me?"

"No. If we lock you up, we shall be satisfied to get rid of you."

"But it strikes me that Charlie Rawlings ought to be given to the police and punished, for endeavouring to murder me. In addition to that, he has abducted this young lady—"

"'Vast heaving," interrupted the captain. "I sail with the money. Stow your jaw tackle, or I'll treat you in a manner you won't like."

"Brute!" ejaculated Harry.

"Am I? I'll teach you to address me in a different manner from that."

As he said this, Williams kicked out, and striking Harry on the head with his heavy boot, rendered him senseless.

Marian uttered a loud shriek.

The captain seized her rudely by the arm.

"Stop that!" he exclaimed. "None of your fine games here. Come below with me."

"You are intoxicated, or you would not behave like this," she said.

"Intoxicated or sober, what's that got to do with you?"

"Just now you talked in a very different manner."

"I'm to be well paid for what I am going to do," replied the captain.

"More shame for you."

"'Vast heaving! I know very well which side my bread is buttered. Come with me to your state-room, and leave this swab of a steward's mate to himself."

Marian did not dare to resist.

He dragged her below, pushed her into her state-room, and banged the door behind her.

There was no mercy to be expected from him or Charlie, and as she tossed restlessly on her bed, she could find consolation only in thinking of the promise the boy Pierre had made her and Harry.

This was something to look forward to.

At length she fell into a sleep, from which she did not wake until ten in the morning.

The head steward had set breakfast, and when he brought in the tea, he informed her that she would have to take the meal alone, as Mr. Rawlings was not well enough to get up.

The favourable breeze continued.

Going on deck, after partaking of a slight repast, hoping to be able to speak a few words with Harry, she was ordered below by Captain Williams.

The insult made her face and neck crimson, but she curbed her resentment.

In solitude she passed the remainder of the day.

Several times Williams came to visit Charlie, who did not get up, and they held long conversations together.

What passed between them she could not hear.

In due time they came to the French shore.

It was evening when they entered the harbour of Bordeaux, and by the time Williams had been on shore and paid the harbour dues, it was nearly twelve o'clock.

Nothing could be done against Harry at that late time of night.

Marian sat up in the saloon, filled with anxiety, and unable to sleep.

The boy Pierre came in with refreshments.

He put his finger on his lips.

"Any news?" asked Marian, in a whisper.

"At two," he replied, in the same tone. "Be patient—wait! Pierre is your good friend."

Marian nodded and thanked him with a smile; for she saw that only by his aid could she and her lover escape from the toils which environed them.

She took up a book from a side table, and tried to read, but without success.

The lines ran into one another, and she could not remember one moment what she had read the last.

A clock, swinging like a pendulum from the ceiling, struck the hour of twelve.

Two hours to wait!

She had the strongest faith in the good will of Pierre. Anxiety, however, prevented her from eating or sleeping.

Since she had frustrated Charlie's attempt on Harry's life, she had not seen the villain, because he had been confined to his bed.

To her consternation, he suddenly walked out of his cabin, fully dressed.

He bowed to Marian, and sat down to the table, helping himself to some oysters.

"Will you join me?" he asked.

"No," she replied; "I do not care for the society of would-be assassins."

He looked up angrily, and his eyes flashed.

"What about yourself?" he said, savagely. "You did your best to kill me with that belaying-pin."

"Simply because you were about to take the life of your cousin."

"Whom you love?"

"I admit it," replied Marian. "When I compare him with you, he is an angel."

"And I?"

"A demon. I hate you. Further disguise is useless; I throw off the mask. Friendship even is impossible between us."

"Ha, ha!" laughed Charlie. "I like these heroics. The tragedy queen business suits you. Why did you not go on the stage?"

"Mock me as much as you will, it will not make me think better of you."

"To-morrow, you will be entirely in my power," said Charlie. "Your sweetheart will be in a police cell."

"With a false charge hanging over his head."

"No matter. I shall have got rid of him. We shall sail away, and I will make you marry me, or—"

He paused abruptly, as if ashamed of his vehemence.

"Go on," said Marian; "you cannot frighten me, with all your bombast."

"Death!" snarled Charlie. "You shall never live to marry another."

"How dare you talk to me like that?"

"Bah! I have the spirit of a man, even though I am young in years."

"And the mind of a fiend," said Marian. "I will not waste my breath in talking to you."

She turned her back haughtily upon him, and he proceeded to eat his supper in silence, which lasted for some time.

At length, Charlie spoke again.

"If you are so sulky that you will not eat or speak," he said, "why don't you retire?"

"Because I have no inclination for sleep. Surely I can please myself in so slight a matter!"

"I order you to retire to your state-room," he shouted. "Look at the clock. It is past one now. I believe you have some deep design in sitting up."

"Your orders I refuse to obey."

"Ah! you defy me, do you?" cried Charlie. "Well, we shall see."

He knew he was master on board the ship. Nobody would dream of interfering with him.

It was his determination to show his power, and make her feel it.

His head was rather weak, and he had consumed nearly a bottle of champagne.

Had this not been so, perhaps he would have acted otherwise.

Rising, he walked towards her, with rather an unsteady gait, and seized her by the arm.

"I said you should—hic—go to your room," he cried, "and, by Jove—hic—you shall."

"Take your hands off me," replied Marian, "or you will repeat your audacity."

"By George—hic," he continued, regarding her with undisguised admiration—"your a doosed fine girl, and no mistake. I can't help loving you, in spite of your temper."

" Will you unhand me, cowardly ruffian ? " asked Marian.

" Not unless you give me a kiss, and consent to be jolly—hic ! "

" I will die first," she replied, her anger being thoroughly roused. " Unhand me, I say."

" Not yet, my beauty. I like you all the better for kicking over the traces. You will go into your room, and stay there until I choose to let you out. I am master here. The key is outside the door, and you will be my prisoner."

Marian was not at all disposed to submit to this treatment. She struggled with her assailant, who, being the stronger, had the advantage. He pushed her inch by inch towards the door of her state-room.

But suddenly, his foot tripped over a mat, and he fell on his back inside the cabin.

This caused him to relinquish his grip of Marian.

Quick as lightning she banged the door to, and turned the key.

Charlie had been caught in his own trap, and was securely locked in.

That he did not intend to remain a prisoner, if he could help it, was speedily made apparent.

He began to shout and kick at the door as if he would break it down.

" Let me out, you jade, or you shall suffer for it," he screamed.

" Stay where you are till you know how to behave yourself," replied Marian.

Renewing his shouts and kicks, Charlie made a tremendous din.

Marian was nearly beside herself, not knowing what to do.

It was not yet two o'clock, the time at which Pierre had hinted he would be ready to help her.

In despair, she ran up to the deck to consult with Harry, whom she expected to find in his prison.

The door was open, and the starlight enabled her to look in.

To her surprise it was empty.

But she was somewhat reassured when she noted on the floor the irons with which Harry had been shackled.

If he had been given to the police or thrown overboard, his enemies would not have unironed him.

She looked in every direction for Pierre, but could see nothing of him. Only one sailor was to be seen on the deck; the others were either below, or had gone ashore, which was easily gained by means of a plank, extending from the ship to the side of the stone quay.

The noise made by Charlie was audible through the porthole of the cabin.

Fearful lest he should attract attention, she stood distracted, not knowing in what way to act for the best.

" Help ! help ! " vociferated Charlie. " Where are all the fellows ? Help ! Confound it ! I will discharge everybody ! "

While Marian was hesitating, she noticed a dark figure on the other side of the plank.

As well as she could make out, it was Pierre.

He evidently saw her, for he raised his arm as if beckoning her.

" Let me out ! " shouted Charlie. " I'm locked up like a rat in a trap. What the deuce are you all about ? "

Captain Williams was in his cabin asleep. The mate was ashore. Being roused by the noise, the captain got up and ran below.

There was no time to be lost now.

Marian hastened across the plank. When she had done so, she was confronted by Pierre.

Ha !" he exclaimed. " Why you delay so ? Ze time was most precious. Zey have miss some one on board."

" Where is Harry ? " asked Marian, whose first thought was of her sweetheart.

" Harree orright. Me got him in vaiting close by. Come."

" Where ? I am so frightened, I know not what to do."

" To my home, where the silkworms and the mulberries are—to my fader and my mudder. Do not waste time. Harree is near."

" I will trust you," she said, taking his hand.

Pierre led her across the street, then plunged into an alley, where it was as dark as pitch.

Fierce cries and loud shouts came from the yacht.

Captain Williams had liberated Charlie. The flight of Marian and the escape of Harry had been discovered.

The greatest confusion reigned aboard.

Lanterns flashed in all directions. A search was being made for the fugitives. A few yards up the alley was Harry, who had been previously released and placed there by Pierre, who had managed to secure the key of the prisoner's irons.

" Come with me," the French boy exclaimed. " One hang on each of my arms, so we not lose one anudder in ze dark."

" Let me be by Harry," replied Marian.

" Just as you like. I know ze vay. By gar, we lead Captain Williams one fine dance."

Harry was overjoyed to see Marian again, and to think that they had so far cleverly eluded Charlie.

"JACK POINTED TO GARNER'S RETREATING FIGURE, AND THEY GAVE CHASE."

They had no time to talk, however, as Pierre hurried them along, and impressed upon them the necessity of silence.

Having been born in Bordeaux, and brought up in its environs, Pierre could find his way through the mazy intracacies of the sailors' quarter, as well in the dark as in the broad noonday sun.

The cries on the quay soon died away.

But the fugitives were not so foolish as to think that Charlie Rawlings and Captain Williams had given up the chase.

They were sensible enough to know that the flight of Pierre would speedily be ascertained.

The finger of suspicion would point towards him, as being the friend of the lovers, and he would be hunted up.

This idea occurred very strongly to Harry.

When, at last, they got out of the city and reached the open country, Pierre left the main road, and proceeded along a path which led through a vineyard.

The moon had now risen, which rendered their progress more pleasant.

"Talk now," said Pierre. "Take things easy—orright—get ze wind back—walk slow."

"We shall never forget your kindness to us," replied Marian.

"He's a splendid fellow, and must come over to England with us," said Harry. "We will entertain him right royally."

"T'ank you, me not like England; me stop here," replied Pierre, who was a thorough son of his own soil. "England no goot."

"Yet you have befriended us, who are strangers to you."

"That nuzzer t'ing. Me like you, but not English ways. Me stay at home, t'ank you all ze same."

"Does Captain Williams know where you live?" enquired Harry, anxiously.

"Oh, yes," replied Pierre. "He drive over to my fader in ze wood before he engage me on ze ship."

"That's awkward. When you are missed, they will begin to suspect something."

"What for they follow and take you?" cried Pierre; "you done nothing."

"No. That is true enough. But we want to be on the safe side and get where they cannot discover us."

"If they find, we will fight—eh?"

"What with? I am unarmed."

Pierre put his hand into his pocket and produced two sharp-bladed knives, one of which he gave to Harry.

"We show fight," he added. "What you t'ink?"

"That will do," replied Harry. "I am not afraid of half-a-dozen now, but I feel sure they will track us before twenty-four hours have passed over our heads."

"That is my idea, too," said Marian. "If we go to your father's house, Pierre, we are sure to be discovered."

"No go then," answered Pierre. "Hide in wood."

"That will be better."

"Nice place in wood. Little caves—holes in ze ground. Me get food and water; you two hide."

"Capital!" cried Harry. "Our little friend Pierre has hit upon a way out of the difficulty. Let us press on and gain the wood he tells us of."

Continuing their walk, they reached the mulberry wood about an hour after daybreak.

All were thoroughly exhausted by the fatigue they had undergone, and when Pierre took them to a small cave in a secluded spot, well shaded by trees, and provided them with grass and dry moss to recline upon, afterwards giving them an abundance of mulberries, they were more than satisfied.

Still they were haunted by a terror. Charlie might discover them. If so, Harry would be dragged to prison as a thief, and Marian conveyed back to the ship as an escaped lunatic.

Like a wily villain, Charlie had laid his plans well.

"Sleep," said Pierre. "The heat of the day is coming; take your repose. I will go and watch."

"A thousand thanks, my friend," replied Harry. "But do you not stand in need of rest?"

"I am used to a sailor's life, and can do without sleep for some time. Me not care. I will watch round to protect you. If danger comes, I will not be far off. Put your faith in me."

His manner seemed so thoroughly genuine, that they dismissed all fear from their minds, and sank back on the beds that he had made for them.

In a short time they were wrapped in a sound slumber, which was what they had not enjoyed for a week.

Pierre went into the interior of the wood, where his father's house was situated, but he did not go in.

He climbed up a tree, and, crouched amidst the foliage, watched the entrance.

More than once he saw his mother and father go in and out. How he longed to reveal himself and embrace them!

Yet he durst not, for the pursuers might come at any time, and his presence at home would be a sure condemnation of his friends.

He had resolved to save them, if it were possible to do so.

Midday came, and no visitors arrived at the cottage.

Nevertheless, Pierre kept his post, for the danger was still imminent, and he could not think it would pass away until darkness fell upon the earth.

Silently and patiently he watched, as if he had been at the masthead of a ship.

His patience was at length rewarded, and in the manner he had all along expected.

It was about four o'clock, and the sun was declining, casting golden shadows over hill and vale.

At this time he observed three men arrive at the house.

They were Charlie Rawlings, Captain Williams, and Porter, the mate of the yacht "Cassandra."

The mother and father came out into the garden at their noisy summons.

They asked if their son Pierre had been there, and being answered in the negative, they declared that they would search the wood, as he had escaped from the ship with a young man and a woman, who were wanted by the police.

Pierre's parents were greatly distressed at this information, for they could not believe their son guilty of any wrong.

They protested with tears that they were convinced there was some mistake.

Pierre had heard and seen enough.

He slipped down the trunk of the tree and disappeared into the wood, anxious to apprise Harry and Marian of the new danger that awaited them.

All around seemed hushed in the peaceful serenity of a calm summer day.

Silently Pierre made his way to the spot where he had left the fugitives to recover from their fatigue and excitement.

He found them awake.

"Well, my friend," cried Harry, "what news have you for us? Is it good or bad? I hope not the latter, though your face is grave enough."

"Bad—ze worst!" replied Pierre.

"Ha! we are pursued!"

"Yes. Ze capitaine, ze mate, and our patron, you call Charlie, have been to my father's house."

"Have you seen them?" asked Marian, turning deathly pale.

"Ay, and heard them talk. They shall scour ze wood, that ees what they talk."

Harry looked very serious, and handled a thick stick he had cut down.

"We must get out of this!" he exclaimed. "It is a pity we did not go at once to the British consul. Heigho! it seems as if we were to have no peace, but I am not one to

yield easily. I shall fight to the last, if we are interfered with."

At this moment the loud barking of a dog was heard close at hand.

"What is the meaning of that?" inquired Harry.

"My dog—that Hugo," replied Pierre. "Me know him by him bark. They see him, let him loose, and say, 'Go find me this Pierre.'"

"By Jove! they will soon be on us."

"Hugo love me; he smell my track. Yes; ze enemy be here very quick time now. Look out."

Harry clenched his teeth.

"Go into the cave, Marian," he said; "we may baffle them yet."

"No," she replied, resolutely; "I will not leave your side. Would that I had a pistol, I would teach these men a lesson they would not forget in a hurry."

"For my sake, go and hide," he urged.

Again she refused, and with a sigh, Harry awaited the onslaught of his relentless foes.

They were not long in coming. First arrived the dog, which sprang instantly upon his young master, Pierre, covering him with caresses. Immediately afterwards, Captain Williams, Porter and Charlie appeared upon the scene.

"Nicely caught," exclaimed Charlie, with a sardonic grin.

Marian, faint and heartsick, clung to Harry, who glared defiantly at his cousin.

"By what right do you pursue us?" he demanded.

"I don't want to have anything to do with you," answered Charlie. "It is only Marian we have come after. Give her up quietly, and you and the French boy can go to Hong Kong or Jericho, for what I care."

"Never!"

"Then we shall have to make you."

"It is an outrage. You have no claim to control Miss Spencer's actions. If you lay a hand on her, I will strike you to the earth."

"Set on them," cried Charlie to his comrades. "You know our arrangement. Williams takes Harry; Porter, the boy; and I will look after the girl."

"Ay, ay. Come on," answered Williams.

He and Porter were armed with stout bludgeons.

Harry gently pushed Marian behind him, and calmly awaited the attack.

Like a coward, Charlie did not take any active part in the affray.

The captain found Harry a tougher antagonist than he expected, for he warded off the blows aimed at him, and returned them with interest.

Soon Williams was bleeding from the head, and smarting with pain.

Charlie now saw his opportunity, for Pierre was hotly engaged with Porter, whom he had twice slightly wounded with his knife.

Rushing forward, the youthful villain seized Marian by the arm, and began to drag her into the wood

She struggled desperately, uttering piercing shrieks the while.

Captain Williams, at this juncture, contrived to break down Harry's guard, and gave him a blow on the head which brought him to his knees.

He was preparing to repeat the blow and render him senseless, when a youth pushed aside some bushes, and bounded like a deer on to the spot.

"Coward!" he cried.

With a blow of his fist, he sent Williams staggering against a tree, and the captain rolled over stunned.

"Hurrah! that's one settled, now for the other," continued the newcomer.

He ran to Pierre's assistance, and Porter, seeing what had happened, abandoned the fight and took to his heels.

Marian was all this while screaming for help in the wood.

With a fierce cry, the youth sped to her aid.

"Stop that noise and come with me, or you'll rue it," said Charlie, savagely.

His back was turned to the rescuer, and without seeing whence it came, he received a terrific blow, which caused him to relinquish his hold of the maiden, and sent him staggering.

With a sob, Marian fell in a swoon on the grass.

Turning sharply, Charlie uttered a cry of astonishment.

"Jack Spencer!" he gasped.

"Yes, villain, it is I," replied Jack.

"Where did you come from at such a time?"

"From the clouds. Providence sent me to thwart your base designs."

Gnashing his teeth with rage, Charlie slunk away.

With characteristic pusillanimity, he left his companion to his fate.

By a strange accident, which could only be a fatality, Jack had descended in the mulberry wood at the very time his services were required.

Taking Marian in his arms, he carried her into the enclosure where the cave was.

Pierre, who was not much hurt, was attending to Harry, who had got on to his feet again.

"Harry!" ejaculated Jack.

"Jack!" replied Harry. "This is indeed extraordinary."

"No more to you than it is to me," rejoined Jack, putting down Marian's slender form.

"I am quite bewildered," added Harry.

"And well you may be. The villains are gone, that's one good thing, and now we can safely enter into explanations. Let me tell my story first."

"I am listening," said Harry, shaking him earnestly by the hand.

Then came mutual explanations, to which Marian listened. She was only frightened, and had quickly recovered. While the old friends were talking, Captain Williams came to himself, and, judging that discretion was the better part of valour, made his escape by crawling through some bushes.

The field was now clear.

Charlie Rawlings had been signally defeated.

That he would immediately renew the attack was doubtful, and Marian felt a great sense of relief.

She was immensely happy to think that she was free from persecution.

Both she and Harry were very sorry to hear of the dreadful end of poor Tuffins.

They had liked him greatly, for he was a kind, simple-hearted fellow who had few enemies.

"All's well that ends well," said Jack, "and all we have to do is to get home."

"How is that to be done?" asked Harry.

"We will go into the city of Bordeaux, and apply to the consul."

"Come to my house, gentlemen," exclaimed Pierre; "my people shall make you welcome."

"A thousand thanks," replied Jack, "but I must decline. We shall be safer in the city."

"As you please, monsieur; but to-night it ees late. You will be my guests, eh?"

"For one night, I have no objection."

Following Pierre, they all three walked to the house in the wood, the dog bounding before them, and barking joyously.

When they reached the house of Pierre's fat er and explained everything, they were v t hospitably received and entertained.

Every precaution was taken that night to guard against an attack.

Next morning they took leave of their kind friends, promising to send Pierre some money from England as a reward for his services, and went to Bordeaux.

The "Cassandra" had quitted the port during the night.

On application to the consul, they were

forwarded to their own country, arriving safely at the farm.

The joy of Mr. and Mrs. Spencer can be easily imagined. They had feared that they would never see either Jack or Marian again.

Harry was received as one of the family.

Mr. Spencer informed him that the solicitor who was acting on his behalf had served Squire Rawlings with a notice of ejectment, against which he had appealed.

This would necessitate an action at law to settle the question at issue and prove Harry's title.

The case could not be expected to come on for some months, as the vacation had just commenced.

The Squire could not win, but he evidently meant to fight to the bitter end.

On the very day of the young people's arrival at the farm, Mr. Rawlings discharged his servants, shut up the hall, and proceeded to the Continent, probably to join his hopeful son on board the yacht.

Together they could plot fresh mischief against Marian and Harry.

Nobody at the farm thought that they had heard the last of the villainous pair.

CHAPTER XXXI.

FUN IN THE HOLIDAYS—THE WILD BEAST SHOW.

THE news of Jack, Harry, and Marian's return home was soon noised about, and at the same time Warner was released from prison, the judge having recommended him to mercy, as the death of Kennedy was accidental, not premeditated.

Of course the spies of the school were among the first to hear the news.

Their disgust was very great, for in their wicked hearts they had hoped never to see or hear of Spencer and Rawlings again.

Peeping Tom's father was a butcher.

The father of Knowall Dick was a dairyman.

When at home the boys had to make themselves generally useful.

On the morning after Jack had come back, Tom was in the shop, attending to customers, when Warner came in.

"Have you heard the news?" he exclaimed. "Such a surprise! I never heard anything like it; my breath is nearly taken away!"

"I haven't been out, so what chance have I had of hearing anything?" replied Peeping Tom.

"It's quite marvellous!"

"What is it? I can't bear being kept in suspense."

"Just book a haunch for my people, and I will let you know all about it."

With trembling eagerness, Tom wrote down the order in the book.

"Now go ahead," he exclaimed.

"What will you say if I tell you that Jack Spencer has come back?"

"I won't believe you."

"It's a fact," said Warner; "I have seen him. The balloon came down in France."

"Where's Tuffins?"

"Dead. He went mad, and threw himself out. More than that, Jack found his sister Marian and Harry Rawlings."

"Go on!" cried Peeping Tom, playfully. "You're having a lark with me. Don't give it us all at once."

"It's true, 'pon honour, and it appears Harry is heir to the property. The squire's bolted, and——"

"Drop it. I don't like fairy tales," Tom interrupted.

"All right; ask anybody if it isn't so. Good-bye. I can't stay."

Warner nodded, and walked off, leaving Peeping Tom so astonished that he could only draw a deep breath and sit down on the block.

"Well," he muttered, "I'm completely flabbergasted, as they say. This beats all. I shall die if I don't go and tell Dick."

His father was at the back of the premises, and, opening a door, he cried—

"Father, will you come and mind the shop?"

"What's up now?" asked Mr. Harris.

"Mrs. Warner has sent for a leg of mutton," replied Tom, forgetting the exact nature of the order, "and I'm to take it down at once."

"All right; take it and go. Don't be all day gone, as you usually are. I want you here."

"I'll be back in an hour."

"Mind you are, or you'll catch it, my lad," said Mr. Harris.

"Then I sha'n't have to run after it," grinned Peeping Tom. "You won't see me again, though, till night. I'm off for the day."

He took off a hook a fine leg of mutton, and, wrapping it up in paper, started off.

Not for Mrs. Warner's, though.

His was a totally different destination.

He went as rapidly as he could to Mr. Wilkins' premises, which were situated at the top of the street.

The dairyman had milked three cows, and was engaged in setting the pail and stool to milk a fourth. Dick was by his side, thinking of Tom, and making up his mind to go and see him, as soon as he had a chance to get away.

At the entrance to the yard was a dog, which had an instinctive dislike to Tom.

When he saw Tom approaching, he growled, showing his teeth.

"You needn't hump your back at me," said Peeping Tom. "I like you about as much as you like me, you brute."

He took up a stone and threw it at him, hitting him on the ear. Towzer—that was his name—uttered an unearthly yell, and bolted into the cowshed.

He yelped so that he frightened the cow, which kicked the pail, sending the milk flying over Mr. Wilkins, who also recieved a blow from a hoof, which doubled him up.

Rolling on the straw, he cried—

"Dick! if you don't drown that dog, I'll be the death of you."

"Yes, father; I'll do it at once."

The delighted Dick, who would have given anything to get away, did not mean to drown the dog. A friend had offered him five shillings for it several times, and he resolved to sell it.

"Here, Towzer. Good boy. Come here, lad," he said.

Towzer allowed himself to be caught, and Dick conveyed him into the wood-shed, where he locked him in, putting the key in his pocket, and intending to attend to him at his leisure.

"He's right enough. I'll make a little out of him before I go to bed," he muttered. "But I wonder what made him act so mad like? It ain't like Towzer to act like that."

Peeping Tom had hidden behind the cow-shed, when he saw the disturbance that Towzer had made.

He feared that if he were seen, he would be blamed for making the mischief, and punished.

When Dick walked out of the yard, he was surprised to hear someone say, in a low voice, "Lul-ly-e-tee!"

This was the call they always used to make each one's presence known to the other.

Dick found his friend anxiously beckoning to him. As they met, they shook hands, and, without speaking a word, hurried down a lane, fringed on each side with trees, which led to Corks' tavern and field.

When they were at a distance which precluded the possibility of being seen or overheard, they sat down on a bank.

"Was it you who made the dog run into the shed?" asked Knowall Dick.

"Yes; I threw a stone at him," replied Peeping Tom.

"I might have known as much. Anyhow, I have got a day off through it."

"Have you heard about Jack Spencer?" asked Tom.

"Not I. Have they found the body?"

"He's alive!"

"The deuce! Let's hear all about it."

Peeping Tom told him the startling intelligence he had received from Warner.

Dick could scarcely believe it.

"Does Spencer suspect us?" he enquired.

"No more than the Frenchman did; if so, it would be a pretty kettle of fish."

"It's a nuisance, those fellows coming back; they will be on to us worse than ever," said Knowall Dick.

"We can hold our own against them," replied Tom.

"But I hate them so."

"All the more fun in paying them out," said Tom, biting his lip. "It is annoying; I don't like it; yet I do not seem to care much."

"We won't leave them alone."

"Is it likely?"

"We'll be thorns in their sides, eh?"

"And prick them, too," replied Peeping Tom. "They shall have a nice reception."

"Mind they don't give us one," said Knowall Dick. "I say, didn't father look comical, as he went jigging about, covered with milk, to avoid the hoofs of that old cow?"

"I didn't see much of it, and wasn't in the humour to laugh."

"What are you going to do?" inquired Dick, "and what is that you have got under your arm?"

"A leg of mutton, ordered for Bully Warner's mother. I feel like making a day of it," answered Tom.

"I say, here's an idea," cried Dick. "Suppose we go to old Corks', and have a feed. He dines at twelve, and anybody can dine off his joint for a shilling. Mrs. Warner can wait for her leg of mutton. She dines late, and we can get to her house about three o'clock."

"Yes, I know; it is what Corks calls his ordinary. One shilling a head, much or little. It does not matter how much you eat, that's all you have to pay. If anyone has a good appetite, I suppose he relies on the sale of beer and spirits to supply the deficiency."

"He strikes a general average. Some

men are small eaters. No doubt it pays him."

"If it didn't, he wouldn't do it," said Tom.

"To-day," continued Knowall Dick, "I'm sharp set. I believe I could stow away about three pounds of meat, let alone vegetables."

"So could I," said Peeping Tom.

"Shall it be Corks' shilling ordinary, much or little, then?"

"Yes. Anything for a little 'divarshun,' as the Irishman said," replied Tom.

It was not a long walk to Corks'.

On their way they met some caravans belonging to a travelling menagerie of wild beasts.

On each gilded panel was written, in large letters, "Wuggles' World-renowned Wild Beast Show."

"Hullo!" cried Peeping Tom. "Something new on. I wonder why they have not billed the town."

"Perhaps," replied Knowall Dick, "they do not mean to stay."

"You mean, they are only resting?"

"Yes; they are on the road, I expect."

Several men were lounging about the caravans, and near the stables. The spies approached, and saw Corks talking to them.

"Good-day, gentlemen," exclaimed the genial host. "Glad to see you. Heard of Master Spencer's return, with his sister and Harry Rawlings?"

"That's stale news," answered Tom.

"It's so recent that I was not aware you knew of—"

"Tell us something we don't know," said Dick.

"Queen Anne's dead," continued Tom.

"The Dutch have taken Holland, and the income-tax has gone up a penny in the pound," cried Dick, sarcastically.

"Very clever young gentlemen, you are," replied Corks. "I do admire your talent, and no mistake."

"So you ought. Going to have a little tit-up in the way of a show?" inquired Peeping Tom.

"No. Mr. Wuggles is only resting. He'll start again, on his way to Cambridge, to-morrow at daybreak."

"That's a pity. I should like to see some wild beasts," cried Dick.

Neither he nor Tom had ever seen a menagerie, and their knowledge of natural history was consequently extremely limited.

They knew a horse, a cow, a cat, and a dog when they saw them, but that was about all.

"The lions, tigers, monkeys, and such like are in the vans," said Corks, "but the big beasts are in the stable. You can walk in for nothing, if you like."

"What are they?" asked Dick.

"The elephant, the giraffe, the camel, and the dromedary."

"Thank you. We'll have a peep free, gratis, for nothing; that's our style."

"Correct," laughed Corks.

"Haven't we always paid you?" said Peeping Tom, with pretended indignation.

"You are rather close with your money, and like to beat down prices, likewise to keep folks waiting. I've got a score against you now."

"Never mind; we'll square up some day," replied Tom. "Take this leg of mutton. Hang it up in your larder till we go away. It is for a customer of father's, so be careful of it."

Corks took it in his hand, and felt the weight of it.

"Prime leg," he remarked; "close on to ten pounds. I'll see to it."

"What have you got for your shilling feed to-day?" asked Tom. "We have an idea of partaking of your ordinary. Not that we are really hungry. Are we, Dick?"

"Far from it," replied Knowall Dick.

A peculiar smile crossed Corks' features, but it passed unnoticed by the spies.

"I've a leg of mutton," said the host; "singular coincidence, gentlemen. It will soon be ready, with greens and potatoes."

"Plenty to dine off it, I suppose."

"Only you two, unless someone else drops in. Mr. Wuggles and his men buy and cook their own victuals."

"That is splendid; but we sha'n't punish your leg much," replied Tom. "You'll be money in pocket with us, won't he, Dick?"

"That's a certainty."

"Very well, gents; go into the stable and see the elephant, the giraffe, the camel, and the dromedary."

Saying this, Corks went off with the leg of mutton.

The spies were delighted to think that they were going to get such a good dinner as they meant to eat, at so cheap a price.

They strolled into the stable.

No one was about. The great Wuggles, proprietor of the "World-renowned Wild Beast Show," was indulging in the pleasant pastime of angling.

His men were smoking, drinking, and idling in the yard or garden of the inn.

The four big animals were in separate stalls, munching the food that had been supplied to them by the attendants.

"I have read something about these creatures," said Knowall Dick, "though I have never seen them before. This beast

"TWO HANDFULS OF MR. DOBBY'S GLOSSY BLACK HAIR REWARDED HER PROWESS."

must be the cammomile, because he's only got one hump; and the next must be the drumandairy, because he's got two."

"You've got it wrong," replied Peeping Tom.

"How have I?"

"It's camel and dromedary; that's the way to pronounce it. You shouldn't call antediluvian things out of their names."

"Oh, you know a lot, you do," said Knowall Dick. "Perhaps the next one, with the long neck, isn't the araffe?"

"No, it isn't."

"Then it's the brafte."

"You silly ape, it's the giraffe."

"Call it the A B C raffe, or the whole alphabet raffe, if you like," cried Knowall Dick.

"You don't know anything," replied Peeping Tom.

"Well, we won't quarrel about it. Perhaps this next thing, with the trunk on him, isn't the bolifant?"

"Elephant, you mean."

"Shut up. I know as much about natural history as you do."

"Your history is very un-natural. Noah, in his ark, wouldn't have taken you for a clerk."

"You can call it what you like," said Dick, "I'm going to have a lark with the creature. He's big, but he's got no sense. Come over, you ugly-looking, ironclad cow."

The elephant turned and held up his trunk, expecting to receive a cake or a bun, as he usually did from admiring visitors.

Knowall Dick had a twopenny packet of tin-tacks in his pocket, and he generously presented them to the huge pachyderm.

The latter put them into his mouth, undid the paper, and tasted them to see if they were good.

He pricked his tongue as a natural consequence, also the roof of his mouth.

In a moment he ejected them, and made such a loud, trumpeting noise that the boys ran for their lives.

The elephant was after them.

He did not pursue Tom, but manifested his sense of injury by following Dick, whom he caught up close to a sycamore tree at the side of the yard.

Seizing him with his trunk, he whirled him round, and threw him into the air.

If he had fallen to the ground, he probably would have been killed, but by great good fortune he caught on to a branch of the tree, and holding fast, climbed along the bough to the trunk.

The keeper came up, and drove the elephant back to his stable.

"You chaps have been playing tricks with Caliph," said the man, "or he wouldn't act like that."

"My friend gave him some tin tacks," replied Tom, "and he didn't seem to relish them."

"If your friend is hurted, all I can say is, serve him right," continued the keeper. "The elephant's a very sagacious animal and never forgives a hinjury."

"Thank you, for that valuable information; I will make a note of it."

"In his native wilds he is harmless, and in captivity docile."

"Any more of it? I am thinking f writing a book on elephants, and am thankful for any new and interesting facts."

"Are you chaffing me? 'cos I won't stand that," said the man.

"Oh, dear no; wouldn't dream of such a thing. Don't he drink a bottle of whisky before breakfast?"

The keeper gave Peeping Tom a look of withering scorn, and turned contemptuously on his heel.

Tom ran under the tree to see what had become of Dick.

"Above! How are you?" he shouted.

"All right," was the reply, "only I don't know how to get down. The beast squeezed all the wind out of me. I didn't know where I was going to all of a hurry. Is the brute gone? I know he's a mark on me, and I wouldn't go near him again for a pension."

"The ground's clear; he's in the stable."

"Then here's for coming down somehow. Look out! Try and catch me if I drop," said Dick.

With some trouble, he dropped from bough to bough, and then slid down the trunk.

"I've come to the conclusion that I don't like elephants," added Dick, with a gruesome smile, "they are a fraud."

"When I saw you go up, I thought you were learning to fly. How did it feel?"

"It was a funny sensation. I don't want to experience it again, and the next time you find me fooling round a boliphant, you are at liberty to tell me of it, or an araffe, or a cammomile, or a drumandairy."

They strolled to the back door of the inn. A most appetising and savoury odour, which only a leg of mutton roasting can produce, was wafted towards them.

"Ah!" said Peeping Tom, sniffing, "that smells good. It's our dinner cooking."

"Never smelt anything so nice in my life," replied Knowall Dick. "Won't we peg into it, that's all! I fancy I see old Corks' face when he comes for our shillings."

"I vote we take a sharp walk up the

road; that will make us more hungry," said Tom.

"Agreed!"

They started off at a quick pace, and when they returned, the dinner was ready. It was served in the little parlour, smoking hot.

"Perfect pictur, gents!" exclaimed the landlord, setting down a jug of beer. "I hope as 'ow you'll enjoy it."

"Anyone else coming?" asked Tom.

"Not as I knows on, though some traveller might drop in. If so, I'll give him the j'int to cut off when you've done with it."

"Yes. Don't please disturb us till we have finished."

"Ring the bell, gents, when you've done. Don't 'ee stint yourselves," replied Corks, going away and shutting the door.

Tom took up the carving-knife and fork, and Dick began to help himself to vegetables.

They were soon eating like half-famished wolves, and enjoying it so much that they did not utter a word.

Dick soon emptied his plate, and held it out to be replenished.

For half-an-hour they kept on eating steadily, as if for a wager, and when at last they leant back in their chairs, filled to repletion, there was scarcely a couple of pounds of meat left on the bone.

"I'm forced to give in," cried Knowall Dick, "and I must let out a reef."

He unbuttoned his waistcoat, and breathed with greater ease.

"I must cry a go, too," exclaimed Peeping Tom. "What a tuck in we have had to be sure."

"I hope Corks won't be nasty over it. If he was to kick me out, full as I am, I should die."

"All I want is to go and lie under a hedge and go to sleep," continued Tom.

"Rattling good idea that. Ring the bell for Corks. I am almost too lazy to move."

Peeping Tom did as he was requested, and shortly Corks made his appearance, his benevolent countenance beaming.

He looked solemnly at the leg of mutton, which was a complete wreck.

"We have partaken rather freely," observed Peeping Tom.

"Rayther, to be sure," was the landlord's reply. "I generally reckon as a j'int like that will dine a dozen."

"How much have we to pay you? Nothing extra, I hope, because——"

"You don't owe me anything, gents," answered Corks, with a soft-soapy kind of smile.

"How's that?"

"I cooked your own leg for you, as you were in a hurry, and mine had not come from the butcher's—ha, ha! I won't charge you for the wegetables, nor the drop o' yale—he, he! The joke's worth more'n that."

The countenance of the spies fell—they were worth studying.

"I'll—I'll sue you for it," cried Tom. "It is a low, infamous trick."

"So is intending to eat a man out of house and home. Come, now, I can talk as well as you."

"I wonder you are not ashamed of yourself. Father gave me that leg of mutton to deliver to a customer. I shall catch it, and all on account of your trickery."

"We will never come to your house again," cried Dick.

"I sha'n't put up my shutters—ha, ha! The biter's bit this time."

Laughing loudly, Corks left them, and they were glad enough to slink out of the inn, cross the road, and lie down under the shelter of a hedge, which kept off the heat of the sun.

"Fancy being done like that! Isn't it a beastly shame?" remarked Tom.

"Hanged if I did not think there was something in the wind when the old humbug was so civil," replied Dick.

"I'll be revenged on him."

"Yes; we'll make him suffer for it."

At that moment, however, they were too sleepy to do anything in the matter, and pulling their caps over their faces, they soon dozed.

CHAPTER XXXII.

THE SPIES ARE SURPRISED, AND DO NOT ENJOY THEMSELVES SO MUCH AS THEY EXPECTED TO—REVENGE!

WHILE the spies were indulging in their after-dinner nap, it happened that Jack Spencer and Harry Rawlings strolled down to Corks' field.

Having heard from one of the farm hands that the wild beast show had halted there on the way to Cambridge, they were attracted by curiosity.

They thought they might get a look at the animals, and wile away an hour.

Corks received them very cordially.

"The sight of you does one good!" he exclaimed, addressing Jack. "When the rope was cut, and you and poor Tuffins went up——"

"Was it cut?" interrupted Jack, eagerly.

"I suppose you haven't heard that. The Frenchman showed it me; I saw the strands half severed by a knife."

"Then it wasn't an accident?"

"No; the hact was a malevolent one."

Harry looked at Jack significantly.

"My cousin Charlie again," he said. "Someone paid by him no doubt did it."

"Who else would?" replied Jack. "I have no enemies except him and Bully Warner."

"You forget."

"Whom or what?"

"Tom Harris and Dick Wilkins, the spies of the school."

"True. They like us both about as much as a certain personage, who shall be nameless, does holy water; but I can't believe they would be so base as to do a thing of that kind."

"That's you all over," said Harry.

"Why?"

"You're too good-natured. It isn't in you to believe ill of anyone until the thing is actually brought under your eyes and proved. Your heart's too big for this wicked world."

Corks burst into a laugh.

"Talking about Harris and Wilkins," he exclaimed, "reminds me that I have a story to tell you about them."

"Out with it," said Jack.

"A first-class story you will call it," replied Corks, who proceeded to relate the episode of the leg of mutton.

"Capital!" cried Jack.

"They've gone into the field across the road to sleep off the effects of it," said Corks. "I saw them go and pitch under the hedge near the stream."

"We will take a turn and interview them. Do they know we are back?"

"Oh, yes; what is it they don't know?"

"Get the quoits ready in the field. We shall be there presently."

"All right, sir. Mind the animals," said Corks. "There are lions, tigers, and bears."

"They won't interfere with us, I suppose, so long as we don't with them," answered Jack.

"I thought you might get looking in the vans while the men are getting their dinner."

"Not likely."

"Very well. I held it to be my duty to warn you."

Jack nodded carelessly. He passed out with Harry. In the road they met Mr. Grain, the miller, whose mill had been rebuilt. He had drawn up his waggon, which contained several large sacks of flour, at the side of the road, and was going to refresh himself.

"Glad to see you both here again," he exclaimed. "You two have some stirring adventures."

"We see a little life," rejoined Jack. "Are you busy again?"

"As usual. The insurance people rebuilt the mill. It be scorching hot to-day. I'm going to have a wet."

"Good-day, if we don't meet again."

Grain hastened in out of the sun, and Jack went with Harry to search for the spies.

In a very short time they found them snugly ensconced in a shady spot, snoring away.

"Look at them," cried Jack, "the gormandising little brutes! We sha'n't be proper members of society if we do not punish them."

"How will you do it?" inquired Harry. "Chase them down the meadow?"

"I have a better plan than that. Wait a bit. First of all, we will give them a taste of the old song, 'Uprouse ye then, my merry, merry men!'"

"What a lark it will be," laughed Harry.

Jack went to Peeping Tom and gave him a kick, which caused him to move uneasily.

"Leave off, Dick," he muttered; "I don't want any joking."

Then Jack treated Knowall Dick in a similar manner.

"Stop it," murmured Dick. "Don't act the fool, Tommy."

Jack and Harry could not help laughing.

"The cold water cure will be best for them," said Jack. "We will fill our hats at the stream, and dash the water in their faces."

It was soon done.

There was no resisting this experiment.

Directly they had done it, Jack and Harry crouched back against the hedge as closely as they could.

The spies jumped to their feet as if they had been galvanised, looking at each other in astonishment.

"What is it?" cried Peeping Tom. "Raining—thunderstorm?"

"Waterspout, I should say," replied Knowall Dick.

"No, it isn't; the sky is serene. You did it."

"I didn't; I'm as wet as you. My collar and shirt are sopping."

They gazed blankly around them.

Suddenly they saw Jack and Harry, who immediately stepped forth.

"What! Rawlings and Spencer?" exclaimed Tom, thinking to make a favourable impression. "This is one of your little jokes. Very well done. Welcome home."

"We were coming to congratulate you on your return," said Dick, taking his cue from his astute companion.

"Thank you; how kind you are," replied Jack. "It is so nice to have friends take an interest in one's welfare. I assure you we do in yours. Corks told us about your phenomenal dinner, and we came to seek you, fearful lest you might have an attack of apeplexy."

"It is very dangerous to lie down after a heavy dinner," put in Harry.

"No danger," said Tom. "I'm a little tight about the waist, that's all."

"Same with me," remarked Dick. "Nothing more. But I'm so pleased to see you both again."

"Thank you once more," Jack answered. "But, I say, you fellows, I am positive you have been eating too heartily."

"No, no, I assure you," protested Tom.

"Nothing more than usual," said Dick.

"You are red in the face. Dark circles are round your eyes. Exercise is what you require. You must move yourselves, or you will have a fit."

"Indeed you are mistaken."

"Not I. The symptoms are plain," continued Jack. "Now be advised and guided by me. Just outside the gate is the miller's waggon."

"I can see it through the fence," replied Tom.

"Of course you can. Well, he has in it a dozen sacks of flour. You two must drag them out, and pile them in the road. Harry and I will superintend the job, and if you don't work quick enough, we will stimulate you to exertion by means of a stick. No ill-feeling—all for the good of your health, you know."

Peeping Tom and Knowall Dick became rigid with despair for a moment.

Then they trembled with impotent rage.

While they were hesitating whether to comply or not, their tormentors cut a couple of sticks from the hedge.

"Don't delay," continued Jack, "your case is urgent. I'm a good doctor, and I am sure nothing but violent exercise, approaching to labour, will save your lives."

"That is evident," said Harry. "Poor fellows! it is rather lucky we found them in time."

"I've eaten too much to move sacks," whined Peeping Tom.

"It's downright cruelty to talk about it," cried Knowall Dick.

"Nonsense. Stir yourselves, or—"

The sticks were raised in a threatening manner, and reluctantly the spies walked to the waggon.

They resembled culprits going to execution.

Taking off their jackets and vests, they set to work. It was a sight to see them pushing and dragging the heavy sacks to the tail of the cart, and shoving them into the road.

How they gasped for breath, panted, sweated, and groaned under the boiling sun.

Jack stood on a wheel on one side, Harry on the other, and if they relaxed their efforts for a single instant, the spies got a cut with a stick.

About a quarter of an hour elapsed, and only two sacks remained to be tugged out.

"Mind the shop, Harry," said Jack. "I am going to send our men a drop of beer."

He winked as he spoke.

Harry took his meaning readily.

"All right," he answered. "I will see that they finish their work."

Jack walked into the inn, and found the miller eating some cold meat and bread.

"Excuse me, Mr. Grain," he said, "but did you tell Harris and Wilkins to unload your waggon?"

"Eh? Did I do what?" cried the miller.

He laid down his knife and fork in amazement.

Jack repeated what he had said.

"Unload ma waggon! Noa."

"They are throwing the sacks of flour into the road."

"Be that so? By Jarge! that mus' be attended to. Darn their hides, the young varmints, they won't play their schoolboy pranks on me."

He rose, and firmly grasped his whip, which he had placed in a corner.

"I thought it only right to tell you," supplemented Jack.

"You're a gentleman, every inch of you," said the miller; "I've always found you so. Won't Oi pay 'un."

"It's too bad."

"I call it a crying shame. Oh, if I don't lam' 'em, I'm not here."

Jack darted out and beckoned to Harry, who quitted the waggon and joined him, and with whom he slipped into the yard.

Faint with the hard work, Tom and Dick had dragged the last sack to the tail of the cart.

Tom gave it a shove, it fell, and so did he, on the top of it, and in trying to save himself, he caught hold of Dick, who sprawled on the top of him.

For the time, they were unable to move.

" Oh, dear ! I'm dead beat, and in a bath of perspiration," gasped Peeping Tom.

" I'm a rag. You might wring me, and hang me out on a line to dry," replied Knowall Dick.

" Every bone in my body aches," added Tom. "It's worse than the burning of Moscow. Oh, dear ! I feel all of a heap ; you might crumple me up ; and I've got the cramp, too."

" We'll have revenge for this," cried Dick. "I sha'n't be able to live unless I do."

" So will I, by Jingo ! I'm not a worm to be—"

Peeping Tom's little speech was cut short by the appearance of the miller on the scene.

Grain was furiously indignant, for Tom and Dick had never been favourites of his.

" Look here," he shouted, " what ha' you been up to ? This is a fine way to treat a man's goods."

Alarmed at his manner, they roused themselves, and got up.

" We were made to do it, Mr. Grain," replied Peeping Tom.

" Made !" answered the miller, with a sneer. "That's all my eye."

" Indeed we were. I'll swear that—"

" Oh, pshaw ! you swear to anything. I wun't listen to ye."

" But we—"

" See this 'ere whip ? If you don't plaguey soon put them sacks up ag'in where you found them, I'll warm you."

" We're too tired."

" Were you too tired to chuck 'em down ? Not you. That was for your own satisfaction. Now you will up with them, or I'll know the reason why."

" It is impossible."

" There's no sich a word in the English language, as the great Dook of Wellington once truly said. Up wi' em."

As the spies still hesitated, the miller raised his whip, and began to lash their backs.

" Run !" whispered Peeping Tom.

" Which way ?" asked Knowall Dick.

" Into the field. We can hide under the vans ; no one will think of looking for us there. Dart up the road when I whistle, and then we will double back."

They got hold of a sack, and, with infinite difficulty, pushed it up the back-board into the waggon.

" That's the way to do it," said the miller. " Put some elbow grease into it."

He relaxed his attention for a moment to look at the horses' nose-bags.

Suddenly Peeping Tom gave a low whistle, and started up the road, closely followed by Knowall Dick.

" Whoa !" cried the miller. " Stop 'em !"

The spies darted through a hedge, and were soon out of sight.

" Dang it !" added the miller. " They hev got the best of Oi, arter all."

Dodging round to the back of the inn, Tom and Dick reached the wild beast show, and crept, unperceived by anyone, under a caravan.

They were safe so far.

" We must get home as soon as we are rested," observed Tom. " My father is rather handy at using the cane."

" Pretty spectacles we shall look—no coats or vests, and you've lost the mutton. There will be a row about that."

" Oh, dear !" groaned Peeping Tom " it is all along of Spencer and Rawlings Things went on all right till they came back."

" There they are," said Knowall Dick.

He pointed to a piece of level ground, not more than thirty yards from the caravan under which they were concealed.

In a little arbour Jack and Harry deposited their coats and drank the refreshment Corks had put there for them, after which they began to play at quoits.

They laughed and talked as if they were amused at something or other.

No doubt they were making merry over the misfortunes which had overtaken the spies.

" Enjoying their dear selves at our expense," muttered Tom. " Gloating over our misery. Very nice, isn't it ?"

At that instant, a deep growl was heard directly over their heads.

This was followed by a scratching noise on the boards which composed the floor.

" Oh, dear !" cried Dick ; " it's one of the wild beasts trying to get at us."

" Don't be afraid ; he can't do it," replied Tom.

" None of the men are about. Inside the inn having dinner, I reckon. Wouldn't it be awkward if—"

He was interrupted by another deep growl of startling intensity.

" What kind of animal is it ?" asked Tom. " It's more of a growl than a roar."

Knowall Dick could not resist the temptation of finding out, and emerging from under the van, looked at the side of it, where he saw written, " American Black Bear."

He came back and told his friend of his discovery.

" I ain't so much afraid of a bear," cried Tom. " I thought it was lions or tigers.

What a spree it would be if we could let Mister Bear out, and start him for the quoit ground. Jack and Harry would have all their work cut out to master him."

"It might be done," muttered Dick, reflectively.

Looking up, on hearing the scratching again, he found that the bear's claws had made a hole through the flooring of the caravan.

It was not a very large aperture, scarcely big enough to put two fingers through, but still it was there.

"I say," he added, "the beggar is trying to break cover."

"So he is. Shall we help him and chance it?" said Peeping Tom, looking up.

"I'll work at it with my knife, if you like to lend a hand."

"I'll do my share. And look over there. The ladder is at the door of the loft over the stable, where the hay is kept. We can nip up there, and safely watch the proceedings below."

"Bravo! That will do."

They worked away with their pocket-knives to enlarge the aperture.

The bear was not idle, for, as if he knew that someone was helping him, he tore up the board with tooth and claw.

Soon the aperture was large enough for him to put his paw down.

Knowall Dick, full of the spirit of mischief, thrust the point of his knife into the fleshy part of the foot.

This caused the beast exquisite pain, and maddened him with passion against his unknown enemies.

He had sense enough to know that they were below, and, with a whining noise, he withdrew his wounded paw, and could be heard licking it.

When he had soothed his pain a little, he growled louder and more fiercely than ever, recommencing his digging operations.

With tooth and claw he speedily enlarged the hole.

It was palpable that in a very short time he would have made it big enough to drop through.

"I think it is about time to hook it," exclaimed Peeping Tom. "You stabbed him in a tender part, and he won't readily forgive you for it."

"What do bears do?" enquired Dick.

"Hug, bite, and scratch, go to sleep in caves in the winter, eat bees' honey in the summer, and make very good food for hunters when—"

"Bosh! I mean, are they dangerous? Will they kill a chap?"

"Like winking, so I've read."

"Then my name is Walker. Here's for the hayloft. I'm a volunteer for seclusion and security!" cried Dick.

They crawled from under the van, crossed the yard, and climbing up the ladder, got into the loft, from which they could see everything below, stretched out before them like a panorama.

As the large carnivora in the vans were not fed till four o'clock, they were beginning to get restless and noisy.

Impatient roars and growls resounded on all sides in a terrifying manner; but, thinking all safe, the keepers inside the inn were enjoying themselves, and took no notice of the noise made by the animals.

Spencer and Rawlings continued to play quoits, entirely unsuspicious that the ever-active spies had been getting up a benefit for their especial behoof.

It was one of those delightful summer afternoons when a man does not care to do much, and they played in a languid fashion, taking it easy, sipping their cooling drinks in the arbour, talking, sitting down occasionally, and not making a toil of pleasure.

"We shall have to think of going back to school in a week or two, and settle down to work," remarked Jack, as he sat upon a bench in the clematis-covered arbour.

"Yes," replied Harry, taking a seat by his side, and holding a couple of quoits in his hands.

"Let me see. We sha'n't have many changes this half. Pranks has left, Tuffins is dead, Kennedy ditto," said Jack, reflectively, "and Warner is let out of prison."

"We shall have him to contend with," answered Harry, "and the spies. I've got an idea we shall never shake them off as long as we live. Hullo! what the deuce is this?"

He was startled to see a big black bear standing at the entrance to the arbour, his nose pointing towards them, his eyes flashing dangerously.

They had been so absorbed in conversation that they did not notice his approach.

The animal got on his hind legs and sucked his wounded paw, standing in the threshold, so that egress was impossible.

Jack and Harry sat like two statues.

A more unwelcome visitor they never had in their lives.

"Don't move!" cried Jack at last, in a low voice. "Perhaps he won't attack us if we remain quiet."

"I think it's one of the tame, performing bears," replied Harry. "Shall I speak to it?"

"For heaven's sake, no! It has escaped."

The bear growled, and fixed his eyes on Harry.

"Go away, you brute!" cried the latter, losing his presence of mind; "if you don't I'll throw a quoit at you."

He rose and stretched out his arm.

At this threatening gesture, the bear stepped forward, and seized Harry with his paws.

Jack snatched a quoit from his friend's hand, and began to beat the bear over the head.

This timely interference prevented Bruin using his teeth, but he did not relax his hug.

Harry was too paralyzed with fear to do anything in his own behalf, and could only cry loudly for help.

It was a desperate situation, and became more serious every moment, for the blows Jack gave the animal did not seem to make any impression on his hard head.

The spies, from their lofty eminence, watched the encounter with the keenest interest.

"I'll bet on the bear," said Knowall Dick—"two to one on him."

"He's got Rawlings," replied Peeping Tom. "If he kills him the Squire will pay us well."

"Of course he will. Our luck is in."

"Bravo for the bear! Hug him tight!"

Suddenly a strolling organ-grinder stopped in front of the inn, and began to play.

As an old Italian melody floated plaintively on the still summer air, the bear let go his hold.

The tune was evidently familiar to him, and no wonder, for he had been a dancing bear, travelling with a Savoyard, at one period of his chequered career.

He retreated into the yard, and swayed his body to and fro in unison with the music.

Harry sank to the floor exhausted, panting for breath.

Jack bent over him, and fanned his pale face with his hat.

The organ-grinder changed the tune to the "Wearing of the Green," which made the bear dance.

"Confound that grinder!" said Peeping Tom; "he has foiled us."

"I'll never give an organ man a penny again as long as I live," cried Knowall Dick.

With difficulty, Jack assisted Harry to rise. He was trembling like a leaf.

"For goodness sake, pull yourself together," exclaimed Jack, "and let us get away."

"I shall be all right presently," replied Harry.

"Lean on me—so."

They quitted the arbour, and met the keepers coming out with some loungers in the bar to secure the bear.

It was only by chance that one of them, looking out, had seen he had got loose.

There was not much difficulty in getting him into his cage again, and a fresh plank was nailed over the hole.

A glass of wine revived Harry, and he soon began to laugh at the adventure, though he had really been within an ace of losing his life.

That he was indebted to the spies for this, he had no idea, nor had Jack, but they were apprised in a singular way of the plotting that was going on against them.

Among the customers who happened to be in the bar, and who went out to see the animal captured, was a man named Garner.

He was head bailiff to Squire Rawlings, much trusted by his master, and left with sole control of the Hall during his absence.

As he went out, he let a letter fall from his pocket, which Jack saw, and picked up.

He was going to call after him, when his eye fell on the address, which was, "Master Thomas Harris. To be delivered."

His second impulse was to put it in his pocket for the time, and he did so.

"What have you got?" asked Harry.

"Come towards home. When we are alone in the fields, I will tell you," replied Jack.

They walked into the fields, and wended their way back to the farm.

It was against Jack's principle to open a letter which was not addressed to him, but in this instance he was strongly tempted to do so.

Peeping Tom had worked them some mischief, and Squire Rawlings was the openly-avowed enemy of Harry.

He could not help feeling that there might be something in this mysterious letter of the utmost importance to them.

Stopping abruptly under a tree, where they were out of sight and hearing, he showed the envelope to Harry.

"Is that your uncle's handwriting?" he demanded.

"Yes," was the prompt reply; "I know it well. Why is he writing to Tom? Where did you get it?"

"I saw it drop out of Garner's pocket."

"The bailiff! That is strange. Garner dislikes me."

"Don't you think we are justified in opening it under the circumstances and mastering the contents?" asked Jack.

"It is scarcely the proper thing to do, but—" hesitated Harry.

"THE SQUIRE GRASPED HIM ROUGHLY BY THE WRIST."

No. 12.

"All is fair in war. The Squire has gone away, and he gives this letter to his bailiff to deliver—not to post, mind—to deliver to Tom Harris."

"It looks suspicious," replied Harry.

"I shall make bold to open it, and chance the consequences. It is not exactly honourable, still we must protect ourselves," said Jack.

"Do as you like."

"For your sake—for the sake of my only friend, I will open it, then. Here goes."

Without further parley, Jack tore open the envelope, and drew out the letter.

The missive was very brief, but its contents were significant, and only capable of one interpretation.

This was desperate and uncompromising hostility to Harry. It ran as follows—

"Mr. Rawlings to Thomas Harris:

"Remember what I have told you about Harry. Your reward is sure. Circumstances have induced me to go abroad, but I shall not be away long. Talk to Garner; he is in my confidence. If you have anything to communicate to me, write me, Poste Restante, Naples."

"What do you think of that?" asked Jack, as he finished reading the precious epistle to his chum.

"I have had a suspicion of it all along," replied Harry. "You see, I stand between my uncle and a fortune; naturally, being a bad man, he wants to get me out of the way, but he won't if I can help it."

"It is an infamous letter," said Jack, indignantly.

"What shall you do with it?"

"Keep it. If anything happens, we have it in black on white that the Squire is plotting against you."

"Would it be of any use to go to the police?" continued Harry.

"Not a bit; they could do nothing. We must fight the battle ourselves."

"I am afraid I shall never enjoy the property."

"Yes, you will. Right will triumph in the end."

"It does not always. Say nothing to your people about the letter. Marian would be very much upset if she knew it."

Jack promised compliance with his request, and they walked on.

That morning Jack had met Lord Stonehaven, and asked permission to have a day's rabbit shooting on his estate.

This was kindly given him, and he was told that he might bring a friend; consequently, he and Harry intended to avail themselves of the opportunity next day.

They had cleaned a couple of guns, and supplied themselves with powder and shot, for although they were not accomplished sportsmen, they hoped to have some fun.

What this day's pleasure would bring in its train, they did not anticipate.

If they had foreseen, perhaps they would rather have stayed at home, and let rabbits alone.

CHAPTER XXXIII.

THE MURDER IN THE WOOD.

MARIAN SPENCER was considerate enough to pack up an excellent lunch in a basket, which the boys agreed to carry by turns.

A shooting expedition is nothing unless the tired sportsmen can rest in a shady spot and refresh the inner man.

As it was only the middle of August, they could not touch the partridges or kill the pheasants, but there was an abundance of rabbits, and wood-pigeons were not scarce.

When a boy goes out shooting, he is perfectly satisfied so long as he kills something, if it is only a sparrow.

Jack and Harry started off in high spirits. After their recent troubles, they felt a higher capacity for enjoyment than usual.

When they reached the park, they turned to the right to go to a spinney, in which was a capital warren, where rabbits were always to be found.

Unsuspicious of danger, they chatted merrily and did not look about them, or they would have noticed three people lurking among the furze bushes and fern.

These were Garner, the steward of Squire Rawlings, and Peeping Tom and Knowall Dick.

What they were doing there was a mystery.

As the boys passed their place of concealment, they crouched low, evidently not wishing to be observed.

But they kept them well in view, and marked the direction in which they went.

When the warren was reached, Jack and Harry hid themselves behind some trees, and whenever a rabbit popped out of its hole, they shot at it.

Sometimes they hit and killed, more often they missed, but they enjoyed the amusement immensely for a couple of hours.

At the expiration of this time, they had a fair bag.

Tying the rabbits' legs together, they hung the animals over the branch of a tree to be out of the way of stoats and weasels, and as their shoulders ached with firing, began to think of lunch.

"Pretty good sport," remarked Jack. "We shall have better, though, in the afternoon, when the beggars come out to feed freely."

"We can't carry them all," replied Harry, "unless we borrow a wheelbarrow."

"Bother that!" cried Jack. "We are not pot-hunting, only amusing ourselves. The question of the hour—the burning question, I may say—is, where shall we lunch? I saw my sister pack up a cold shoulder of lamb, a fowl, and a knuckle of ham. It is about time these delicacies were attended to."

An idea suddenly struck Harry.

"I should like to see the old gipsy woman who was so kind to me when I was hunted about for that affair of poor Kennedy," he exclaimed. "Let us go to her cave."

"The witch's cave is a nice cool place to lunch," replied Jack. "It is well thought of. We will go there."

"It is not above a mile through the wood," continued Harry. "I will carry the basket, if you will take the guns."

"Agreed. That is a fair division of labour. I should like to see the old woman once more. I have a few shillings in my pocket, which she shall have. How did you find her out?"

"She found me," answered Harry. "When I ran away from school, I hid in the wood. For three days and nights I roughed it, living on berries. At last I was prostrated, and laid down to die. Ella saw me, took me to her cave, and brought me round. Heaven bless her for it."

"Do you believe she can tell fortunes?"

"She told me that I should come out of my troubles all right, but my career would be a chequered one, and the course of love would not be smooth."

"That is the usual patter with gipsies," laughed Jack.

"She also stated that the sands of her life were running out, and that I should be with her when she drew her last breath."

"That is singular, if true."

"When people live, as she does, in solitude, and grow old," said Harry, "perhaps they get an insight into the future. Who shall say?"

By this time, they had gained the wood, and plunged into its dark recesses.

The heat was intense, even under the trees. The guns and the basket were heavy, and they sat down to rest at the trunk of a large tree. All around them grew briers and underwood, forming a kind of bower which effectually concealed them from observation.

Suddenly they heard voices in their immediate vicinity.

"Hush!" whispered Jack. "Don't speak—don't move!"

He clutched Harry's arm tightly.

Both were silent as the grave.

"We've lost them," said one. "I know they came this way. It's a pity, for if young Harry Rawlings was found shot dead, everyone would say it was a gun accident."

"We should have to separate them first," replied another.

"That could be managed," exclaimed a third.

The voices were unmistakably those of Garner, Peeping Tom, and Knowall Dick.

Jack and Harry scarcely allowed themselves to breathe.

"I shall turn it up for to-day," exclaimed Peeping Tom.

"So shall I," said Knowall Dick. "It is too hot to go hunting all over the wood for them. We shall have lots of opportunities."

"Not me," rejoined Garner. "You two can go, if you like, I sha'n't. When I heard they were going shooting on his lordship's ground, I saw it was a chance, and I'm not going to give it up yet."

"Where are you going to find them, and how are you going to do it?" asked Tom.

"That is my business. If I do find them, and can get Harry by himself, it will be all right."

"Well, good-bye," said Tom; "we are off."

"Wish you luck," remarked Dick.

The spies now left Garner, and the confederates went in different directions.

It was evident that they had received private information of the movements of the two friends, and had followed them with an evil intention.

Garner's words pointed to murder.

"A narrow escape, so far," said Harry, when all was silent. "You must stick to me, old fellow. If we separate, I shall be killed."

"Garner wants to get the Squire's money," replied Jack; "and he is willing to run all risks for it. Yes; I will not leave you."

"If he meets us, he might shoot both."

"It is alarming to be persecuted in this

way," exclaimed Jack; "though it is only what I expected after reading that letter. Let us get to the gipsy's cave. Garner will scarcely think of looking for us there."

"By heaven! if he threatens me, I will shoot him," cried Harry, seizing his gun.

"Don't be hasty. Whatever we may be induced to do, must be done in self-defence," replied Jack.

Leaving their place of concealment, they pushed on to the cave. The gipsy was standing outside.

An owl, which she had tamed, was perched on her shoulder, and a couple of large toads hopped about at her feet.

When she saw Harry, her countenance brightened.

"I expected you would come," she exclaimed. "I have been present with you in my dreams. Your troubles are not yet over. Last night your star was obscured. There is danger in the air. I have had blood before my eyes all day."

"I know my danger," replied Harry, "and I am on my guard. Will you allow us to eat our lunch in your cavern? There is a man in this wood by whom we do not want to be seen."

"That must be the black snake I have seen in my sleep. Go in, and leave me to watch outside," said the gipsy.

"Do you know a man named Garner?" asked Jack.

"Yes. He was a gamekeeper once, and an enemy of the Zingari. He had me put in prison for trespass. My curse has rested on him ever since."

"That is the man we wish to avoid."

"Should he come, I will bar his entrance to the cave," replied Ella.

Jack carried the basket inside, followed by Harry, who carelessly left his loaded gun resting against a side of the cave, though Jack was thoughtful enough to take his with him.

Unpacking the basket, they sat down and began the meal, of which they stood in need by this time.

While they were engaged in this pleasant occupation, they forgot their former fear, and were anticipating another raid upon the rabbits in the cool of the evening.

The gipsy had not been on guard more than five minutes before a tall dark form emerged from under the trees.

To her surprise, she saw it was Garner.

"Ha!" he cried. "So you are still alive, you old witch!"

"Why should I not be," answered Ella, "while a wretch like you is allowed to cumber the earth?"

"Hold your peace. If you had your deserts, you would be hanged."

"That is a fate more likely to overtake you than me," said the old crone.

"It is false, hag!" exclaimed Garner, who became white with rage at her taunts. "If you anger me, I will make you dearly rue it."

"Touch me not. There is law in the land for the poor gipsy."

"Ha, ha!" laughed Garner, mockingly. "I would give you law, and prison law, too, if I was Lord Stonehaven."

"He is a humane man. Such as you and those you serve are no better than the brute beasts."

"Silence, I say," shouted Garner. "'Twas not my purpose, when I came here, to bandy words with you."

"Forsooth! may I not talk when spoken to?"

"You have a bitter tongue, witch, and give it too much licence."

"If you deem it so," replied Ella, "go your way and leave me in peace."

"I have a question to put to you," said Garner. "If you value a whole skin, you will answer truthfully."

"I am not given to lying."

"Well, well, that is as it may be. Some folks would be chary of believing you on your oath. Tell me this: Have you seen two boys, with guns, pass this way?"

"No, I have not," answered the gipsy, stoutly.

"Are you sure?"

"Have I not given you a good and sufficient answer?"

Unfortunately for her character for veracity, Garner happened to cast his eyes towards the cave.

The consequence was that the first thing he saw was Harry's gun.

"Why, you incarnate mother of lies!" he roared. "What do I see?"

For a moment the aged gipsy was disconcerted.

She, however, recovered her composure very quckly.

The crisis had come. She had to face it, and she proved herself equal to the occasion.

"You think you are very clever," she replied, forcing her wrinkled mouth into a smile, "but let me tell you that the gun you see was left here an hour ago by Lord Stonehaven himself."

"As if I could believe that."

"'Tis true. I expect his lordship back for it every minute. He left it, I tell you, in my charge while he walked to the tollgate. If he should catch you here, on his property, abusing and quarrelling with me, it will be the worse for you."

"I am neither seeking nor picking a quarrel with you, venomous jade that you are, but I will search your cave before I go farther," said Garner.

The corners of his mouth were drawn down with dogged obstinacy.

"What for?" demanded Ella, who was now on her mettle.

"Just for my own private satisfaction. I want to see if Harry Rawlings and his friend, Jack Spencer, are inside."

"You shall not do it."

"Who is to prevent me?" queried Garner.

"I will. Weak woman as I am, feeble with age, I will stop you. That cave is my house, given to me by Lord Stonehaven; it is as sacred to me as your home is to you. Dare to set a foot inside it, and beware of the consequences."

Garner laughed defiantly.

He made a side movement to the cave, his evident intention being to seize the gun.

The gipsy divined his purpose and frustrated it.

With remarkable quickness for one of her years, she darted forward, and grasping the gun, placed herself in front of the cave.

"Come, come!" cried Garner. "None of that. It won't do with me. I am going into that cave, if I have to walk over your body."

"That is the only means by which you will gain access," was the calm reply.

"Now I know that the boys are inside."

Ella pointed the gun at him as he advanced, hoping to terrify him.

Her attitude, however, determined though it was, had not the desired effect.

He was undaunted by her threats.

Owing to the peculiar formation of the cave, those within could not hear distinctly what was taking place outside.

Jack and Harry had satisfied their appetites, and were laughing and chatting as they drank some currant wine, which Marian had put up for them.

"Stand on one side!" exclaimed Garner.

"Not I," responded the gipsy. "Go away, or I'll fire."

"Will 'ee? It shall be in the air, then."

As he spoke, the man laid his hand upon the muzzle of the gun, and endeavoured to wrest it from Ella.

A fierce struggle took place between them for the possession of the weapon.

While this was going on, the trigger was pulled, and the muzzle being turned towards Ella, the shot entered her body.

With a deep groan, she pressed her hand to her heart, staggered for a moment, and sank to the ground.

It was speedily ensanguined with her blood.

"Perdition!" muttered Garner, between his teeth, "I meant to kill her. As soon as I got the muzzle her way, I pulled the trigger quick enough. But I must not be seen here."

He placed the gun where he had found it.

"No one has seen me," he added. "Dead men tell no tales, and she ain't likely to blab much, unless—"

He paused, and his ghastly pallor became intensified.

Perhaps he was thinking of the other world, and what the recording angel might have to place to his account.

He was about to walk off and slink away among the trees, like a guilty coward, when Jack and Harry rushed out of the cave.

They had been startled by the dull, sullen echo of the discharged gun which had penetrated the recess in which they were.

When they saw the dying gipsy—for Ella was at her last gasp—they were horrified.

"Who has done this?" asked Harry.

"Look yonder," replied Jack.

He pointed to Garner's retreating figure, and, actuated by one impulse, they gave chase.

Seeing that he was discovered, and that it was useless to try to avoid his quick-sighted pursuers, Garner stood at bay.

"What are you doing here?" demanded Jack. "Why are you running away, if you did not shoot that poor old woman?"

"I was passing through the wood. It is a short cut from Clare to Squire Rawlings'. I ran because I was late," replied Garner.

"Did you hear a shot fired?"

"Yes; and it's my opinion you fired it," continued Garner, growing bolder. "Looks to me like your gun, Master Harry, up yonder. If I'm asked about the matter, I'm bound to tell all I know, and it will go hard with you, or I am making a mistake all round."

Harry could scarcely restrain his rage at this insolent speech, and Jack was so angry that, without a word, he knocked the man down, and, with clenched hands, stood over his prostrate body.

"That's right!" cried Harry. "Don't let the scoundrel escape. We know enough about him already, and he must have shot the gipsy."

"We did not see him do that, though I have little doubt he is the murderer," said Jack.

Garner looked up into Jack's face.

"If you won't interfere with me, I won't with you!" he exclaimed. "We can each of us go to the police-station and tell his own story. Let the authorities believe which they like."

"Shall you say we did the murder?"

"Certainly; and you will accuse me of

it. Now let me go. That is the only way of settling it."

"Very well," replied Jack; "I have no objection, if Harry has not."

Harry nodded his head in token of assent.

"We will soon put the wretch where we can find him. His tale will not be listened to," he remarked.

Permitted by Jack to get up, Garner recovered his independent insolent air.

"Time will show," he replied. "No one saw me with the old woman or heard me speak to her."

"Be silent," cried Jack, in a tone of authority. "We know you, Garner. You were telling Harris and Wilkins just now that you were after us to shoot Rawlings, and say it was an accident."

"Who would believe that story? What reason have I for entertaining any ill-feeling towards the lad?"

Without a moment's hesitation, Jack produced the letter from the Squire, addressed to Peeping Tom, which he had found.

"You dropped this letter," he continued, "and I daresay you know the contents as well as I do."

"It is false. I—" began Garner.

"That will do. You are unmasked," Jack interrupted. "It is sufficient for you that we know your plans, and we will hang you for this day's work, if we can bring it home to you."

With a dejected air, Garner slunk away.

He clearly saw that it was useless to endeavour to brazen it out. The boys knew more than he had had the faintest idea of.

When he was gone, they returned to the cave, only to find the gipsy at the point of death.

She was unable to speak, and therefore could not tell them how the disaster happened.

Their pleasure was spoilt for that day. No more shooting could be indulged in. They hastened to the town, and gave information to the police.

Garner was at once searched for.

He was not to be found at his home.

All efforts to find him were ineffectual.

The general opinion was that he had fled the country.

The gipsy's death excited a great deal of sympathy, and as a verdict of guilty was returned at the inquest against Garner, he was execrated by all.

The holidays wore away rapidly after this event.

Early in September, the boys went back to Stingwell Hall, and put themselves once more under the care of Doctor Birchoften, Mr. Dobby, Miss Martha, and the other masters of the school.

CHAPTER XXXIV.

BACK AT SCHOOL—A DIFFERENCE OF OPINION—MR. DOBBY AND THE DOCTOR FIGHT IT OUT.

THE boys had been arriving all day. Miss Martha was dreadfully busy, because the task of receiving them fell upon her, and also the labour of seeing their boxes bestowed in the proper rooms.

Though she had not treated the lamented Tuffins with all the kindness and courtesy which he strove so hard to deserve, she bewailed his loss.

He had left a gap which she found it peremptorily necessary to fill up.

It happened that Tuffins' great enemy, the doctor's boy, whose name was Peter, had been discharged from his situation.

Peter had, by mistake, given an old woman solution of arsenic instead of tincture of rhubarb and nearly killed her.

Of course his employer dispensed at once with his services.

He then applied to Miss Martha for the place made vacant by the decease of poor Tuffins, and he got it, but he was not so pleased with the position as he thought he would be.

There was a good deal of work to be done. Miss Martha was capricious and arbitrary, priding herself on being what she called "thorough."

After working all day in receiving the young gentlemen and bestowing their luggage, Peter sat down to a well-earned cup of tea with Miss Martha, in the housekeeper's room, which was her special sanctum.

"They are all in," she said, looking at her list, on which she had checked off the names, "except one, and there is a difference of opinion about him."

"Who is that, miss?" inquired Peter.

"Warner. He has been in prison for killing Kennedy, by accident. Mercifully let off, he comes out before his time, and is naturally anxious to come back among his old schoolfellows."

"You can't blame him for that," said Peter.

"My brother (Doctor Birchoften) and I do not think he ought to be allowed to return. Mr. Dobby is of opinion he should."

"What are you going to do about it, miss?"

"We intend to put it to the vote."

"What vote?"

"That of the scholars in our school. If the majority vote for the readmission of Warner, he is to come in."

"If it's a minority, he stays out, I suppose?" observed Peter.

"Precisely."

"It will cause a split up, I reckon. If I had my way, it would be a minority. When a boy has been in gaol, he ought to be kept away from respectable lads, that's what I say."

"Religion teaches us to be merciful," said Miss Martha.

"They can't associate with felons, miss."

"Hold your tongue!" exclaimed Miss Martha, sharply. "You are not a schoolboy—only a servant."

"Ain't I got my feelings?"

"I have heard, Peter." continued Miss Martha, solemnly, "that Tuffins was your enemy. Now, if the poor fellow were to come back from the grave, would you not forgive him? Say the truth, now."

Peter put down a crumpet which he was just beginning to enjoy.

"No—I'm blowed if I would," he rejoined, stoutly; "that is—I beg your pardon, miss—I'm not one of the forgiving sort. If I had been a schoolfellow of that there Warner, who, from all accounts, was a regular bully, I would not like to have him back again."

"When I want your opinion, I will ask for it."

"I didn't mean any offence, miss."

"Finish your tea as quickly as you can, and go to the schoolroom."

"Yes, miss."

"Tell Harris and Wilkins I want to see them at once. Say it privately, so that no one overhears you."

Peter nearly choked himself in his haste to oblige his new mistress, with whom he wished to keep on good terms.

She had her reasons for sending for the spies, because Mr. Dobby had spoken very plainly about receiving Warner.

He had told Doctor Birchoften and herself that it would be an insult to the whole school, and he would not tolerate it.

Miss Martha wanted to know how public opinion was forming itself.

She caused Peter to place chairs for them at the table and retire, after which she poured them out some tea in her best china cups, assuring them that she was delighted to see them again.

"I am so fond of all the dear boys," she said, "that I feel as if I were a mother welcoming my sons."

"We are very happy here, ma'am," replied Peeping Tom.

"More so than we are at home," said Knowall Dick.

"It pleases me to hear you talk like that, because it shows me that my poor efforts to please are really appreciated. Have some of this jam?"

"Thank you, miss."

"Have you been amongst the dear boys since your arrival?" continued Miss Martha, in an insinuating manner.

"All through them for hours, miss," answered Peeping Tom. "Mr. Dobby has been making a speech in the playground."

"Really! that is disgraceful. I must tell my brother, the doctor, of that. What does he say?"

"I heard him talking to Clayton," cried Knowall Dick, "and saying that he would start a school of his own."

"Oh, the base creature!" said Miss Martha, holding up her hands in horror, not unmixed with amazement.

"He asked the boys to come with him if Warner was taken back."

"Hark to that, now."

"Some said they would, and others refused."

"It is worse than high treason, after the long years he has been with us, and the kindness he has received at our hands."

"He says that Squire Rawlings' Hall is to be let, and he can get it cheap. It is large, and would make a school big enough for one hundred boys."

"Oh, dear! Take away our pupils, would he?"

"Yes, ma'am, that's his intention, if the vote of the school is in favour of having Warner here again."

Miss Martha could scarcely restrain her resentment at the perfidious conduct of Mr. Dobby.

At one time she had fancied Mr. Dobby looked upon her with a favourable eye.

She had gone so far as to hope that she might one day become the cherished wife of Mr. Dobby.

"Treachery! ingratitude! heartlessness! that's what it is," she exclaimed. "ut his vile designs shall be frustrated. You are good boys. Glean all the news for me. How do you think the vote of the school will go?"

"'A NICE WATCH AND WARD YOU KEEP,' GROWLED MR. DOBBY."

"About half and half," replied Peeping Tom.

"More than that against Warner," said Knowall Dick.

"Do you think so?"

"Mr. Dobby, madam, will get a majority, and they will ask their parents to let them go to the new school at Squire Rawlings' Hall."

Miss Martha rose in great wrath.

"I must see my brother at once about this infamous intrigue," she exclaimed. "Dobby wants to ruin us."

"We will stay with you," continued Peeping Tom.

"Wouldn't leave on any account," said Knowall Dick.

"You are very good," said Miss Martha. "I will take care that you have some nice prizes at Christmas. The doctor's book is finished, and in the printer's hands. You shall each have a beautifully-bound copy. I always said you were the best boys in the school."

"We try to be."

"And you succeed. Go among the boys —talk to them. Try and influence their minds to vote for Warner."

"The voting is going on now," continued Peeping Tom. "Mr. Dobby has done all the mischief he can."

"It is infamous!"

With an angry toss of the head, the lady went away to seek her brother, who was in his private study.

In a few words, she told him of the tactics which Mr. Dobby was pursuing.

The doctor shared the indignation displayed by his sister, and no wonder. If the assistant-master took away nearly half his pupils to open a new school, it would be a very serious loss.

A long time must elapse before he could recover from the blow.

"I should not have suspected Dobby of such a bold stroke of villainy," remarked Doctor Birchoften; "he always seemed such a quiet, inoffensive creature, with no ambition beyond doing his work well."

"Still waters run deep."

"They do. I shall give him a bit of my mind. He will be here anon to tell me the result of the voting."

"Be firm with him."

"Had I not better offer him an increase of salary?"

"By no means. That would only encourage him in his base designs. Order him out of the house; crush him like a worm; trample on him; dismiss him without a character, and advertise him in the local paper."

"I will be guided by you, my dear," replied the doctor; "for, honestly, I do not feel very peaceably inclined."

A loud shouting was now heard coming from the direction of the schoolroom.

Again and again the boys hurrahed with the full force of their lungs.

It was evident that the voting was over.

Which way had it gone? That was the question.

Anxiously the doctor awaited the coming of Mr. Dobby, who he knew would hasten to bring him the intelligence.

Presently the usher made his appearance, with a red, flushed face.

It was impossible to doubt that he had been drinking. He had brought back with him a bottle of brandy, to which he had made frequent applications during the afternoon.

His walk was unsteady and his speech thick.

In a very disrespectful manner he sat down in the head-master's own particular arm-chair.

This was either a mark of singular forgetfulness, or a direct insult.

The doctor took it for the latter.

"What do you mean, sir, by this conduct?" he demanded, sternly.

"It's all right, old boy," replied Mr. Dobby, familiarly. "I have come to tell you that the voting is over."

"How did it result?"

"Majority of ten for the admission of Warner. You'll get your way. The assassin, for he is nothing else, is to come back."

"That shows a Christian spirit of forgiveness among the boys, and I am very pleased to hear it," said the doctor.

He breathed a sigh of relief, which was participated in by Miss Martha.

"Warner has suffered for what he did," observed the latter. "It is hard, for one fault, to be shunned by one's companions, and have a blighted career."

"His father wrote to me, I may state," added the doctor, "begging me to take him back. If I did not, he would have to send him to Australia."

"That is the proper place for such young criminals," cried Mr. Dobby.

"I am surprised to hear you speak like that. Have you none of the milk of human kindness in your heart?"

"Milk of humbug!" retorted the usher. "I tender you my resignation. In a week I shall leave you; that will give you time to get a successor."

"Very well," replied the doctor, mildly. "I was prepared for this, after what I have been told."

"What have you heard, may I ask?"

The doctor was burning to let the secret out and cover the usher with well-deserved confusion.

"That you intend to set up for yourself in the scholastic line," he said.

"Oh, indeed!"

"And take such of my pupils with you as you can induce to go to Squire Rawlings' Hall, a lease of which you expect to get, as the Squire has gone abroad."

Mr. Dobby looked rather shamefaced, but the brandy he had imbibed made him bold.

"It is time that I made a start in life," he answered. "Who is to blame me or prevent me doing so?"

"I do not complain of that; but my pupils, sir—my pupils—"

"Some of them refuse to consort with a boy who has been convicted and imprisoned for manslaughter," interrupted Mr. Dobby, "and they are to be honoured for their resolution."

"That is your view of the case; but it is not mine."

"They have petitioned me to take them with me.'

"Then you must have been tampering with them, soliciting their suffrages!" cried the doctor, "or how would they know you were going to make a start and open up a school at Squire Rawlings' Hall?"

"Answer that, you rogue!" exclaimed Miss Martha.

"Yes; I admit it."

"You knave!"

"Everyone for himself in these competitive times," continued Mr. Dobby. "I have been your poorly paid slave long enough. I have the names of fifteen boys on a paper in my pocket, who will apply to their parents to-morrow to place them with me. They will have none of Warner, your pet murderer. Perhaps the bully will kill another boy."

"How dare you talk like that?" asked Doctor Birchoften, trembling with anger.

"I dare do anything."

"Beware! You are trying to exasperate me."

"Bah!" cried Mr. Dobby, "I am not to be intimidated by you."

"Nor I by you, sir. This is my house. I have a good mind to put you out in the street to-night, and throw your box after you."

Mr. Dobby sprang to his feet, and turned up the cuffs of his coat-sleeves.

"Try it!" he shouted.

"I will."

"Come on. Try it!"

The doctor was a tall thin man, grey and elderly. He knew as much about fighting as a donkey does about conic sections or the cube root.

But his blood was up.

His assistant master had wounded him in his tenderest point. He was touching his pocket, when he tried to dismember his school.

Mr. Dobby was small in stature, and inclined to be corpulent. He was not yet forty. He was vigorous, strong, athletic, fond of cricket and football. His hair was black, and his eye flashed with the fire of youth.

In a bout of fisticuffs, Mr. Dobby had any amount of advantage over the doctor.

On this occasion, however, he was bemused with strong waters.

In other words, he had taken too much brandy, and not being used to that kind of thing, it had laid hold of him.

He had to catch on to the back of the arm-chair to steady himself.

He leant too heavily upon it.

Greatly to his consternation, it turned over, and, deprived of his hold, Mr. Dobby sat down.

He came on to the carpet with a resounding bump.

"Heaven bless me!" he exclaimed. "This is a very—hic—'stronary thing. Can't make it out."

The doctor looked sternly at him.

"Dobby!" he said with measured emphasis.

"Floor ain't level—something wrong."

"Dobby, look me in the face."

The usher did so, and the doctor then made use of these memorable words—

"Dobby, you are drunk!"

Miss Martha thoroughly endorsed this view of the case by nodding her head in a violent manner.

The accusation seemed to steady Mr. Dobby's nerves. Making a violent effort, he got on to his feet, and grasped the corner of the mantelpiece.

It was a baize-covered wooden shelf, only secured by two brass-headed nails.

On it were two valuable china vases, an ormolu clock, and some family photographs in plush frames.

Leaning too heavily upon it, his weight wrenched the nails out of the wall, and the shelf came down on the carpet.

Everything that had been on it was smashed up in one common ruin.

"Most 'stronary," cried Mr. Dobby. "Everything going wrong. Floor not level; shelf topheavy; very odd."

"You wretch!" cried Miss Martha, furiously, "you are doing this on purpose. Look at my beautiful vases, my clock, my— But you shall pay for it."

"Sue me for damage and see how much you will get."

"Adding insult to injury! Turn him out, or there will be a scene which it will be best for the boys not to hear of."

The doctor compressed his lips. He stepped forward and placed his hand on Mr. Dobby's shoulder.

"If you do not choose to go from this house of your own free will, after being told to go," he exclaimed, "it will be my imperative duty to put you out."

The usher looked him defiantly in the face.

"As I said before, try it, old chap!" he rejoined.

Never had Doctor Birchoften been spoken to in this manner. It roused his ire to fever heat.

With determination in his face, he pushed his assistant master towards the door.

"Hands off!" shouted Dobby.

"No. I insist upon your going at once," was the reply.

"There's a oner for you, then!" continued Mr. Dobby, striking him in the eye, and then giving him one in the chest.

"Oh! Oh! I'm killed!" cried the doctor.

He fell against the table, doubled up with pain.

The table was in two pieces, screwed together, it was loaded with pens, ink, paper, and books.

His weight made it collapse. He sank between the two leaves, covered with a weight of literature.

The ink surrounded his face like a black mask.

He kicked, struggled, and groaned, but he could not extricate himself.

"Ha! ha!" laughed the triumphant usher. "Turn me out, will you? I will go and put up at an inn; my luggage I can send for afterwards; but you shall never have the satisfaction of saying that you turned me out. No sir!"

"Help! help!" shouted the doctor. "I am dying!"

The usher had been reckoning without Miss Martha.

She had regarded him, while he was speaking, with the ferocity of a tigress.

Suddenly she sprang upon him, and scratched his face on each side.

He had little mutton chop whiskers. She seized them, and extracted two handfuls.

Then she caught hold of his glossy black hair, highly pomatumed, and scented with bergamot.

Two handfuls of this rewarded her prowess, and she would not have been satisfied with that, had not Mr. Dobby incontinently fled.

He thought, in his wild confusion, that the door was open, but it was shut.

His head went bang against it, and he sank to the floor stunned.

To add to his discomfiture, Miss Martha threw a couple of chairs and a mat or two over him.

These, however, were things which, for the time, did not affect him, as he was unconscious.

Miss Martha, attracted by her brother's moans and groans, went to his assistance.

She disentangled him from the *débris* and helped him into his chair.

He presented a strange picture, for the ink had disfigured him in such a way that he was scarcely recognisable.

"How are you?" asked Miss Martha. "Don't tell me you are hurt."

"I feel very bad. The wretch struck me twice. Has the rascal gone?" replied Doctor Birchoften.

"I was turning him out, when he knocked himself against the door; but we will soon have him out. It is you I am concerned about."

"Martha, my dear, we have cherished a snake."

"We have."

"There is no doubt that we have warmed a viper. Oh! how killing is ingratitude! That wretched man is endeavouring to ruin me."

Mr. Dobby had recovered from the knock he had given himself, and hearing these words, he raised himself upon his elbow.

If the doctor was a pitiable spectacle, the usher was worse. His face looked like that of a tattooed South Sea Islander.

"I *will* ruin you, too!" he cried. "Let me get out of this, and you shall see what I will do!"

"The villain has come to!" said Miss Martha. "If he does not get out, I will kill him."

She grasped the poker and advanced, full of fire and fury, towards the usher.

He saw her coming.

With a desperate effort, Mr. Dobby rose, jerked open the door, and rushed up the passage.

Unfortunately, he met Peter, who was carrying a tray of tea mugs to the school-room.

They encountered one another.

A terrible crash and smash ensued. Peter went down, and so did the usher on the top of him.

Miss Martha was after him, but in the half-light which prevailed in the passage, she did not know which was Mr. Dobby and which was Peter.

She dealt blows impartially with the

poker, and Peter got the worst of it, and howled terribly.

Taking advantage of this diversion, the usher got up again, and ran into the hall, seized the first hat he could get hold of, and left the school.

Peter continued to holloa.

"Oh, Lor'!" he cried, "what have I done to be treated in this way? I'd rather go back and be a doctor's boy, I would."

Miss Martha left off beating him.

"Aren't you Mr. Dobby?" she asked.

"No ma'am; I'm Peter," he replied; "and I ain't done nothing to be knocked about for."

"I am very sorry. I—I fancied it was that villain. Get up. I will give you a glass of wine."

"Pokering don't do a chap any good," whined Peter, who sat up, wiping his eyes with his knuckles.

"Say no more. I'll make it up to you."

"Mr. Dobby, he run ag'in' me. He's gone out of the front door. You ain't no call to hit me for him."

"Dear me," said Miss Martha, contemplating the damage. "Twenty-five splendid mugs broken!"

"My 'ed's broken as well?" whimpered Peter.

"And all through that Dobby!" she continued. "Oh, the wretch! the monster! Never mind. We shall survive his treachery. Our school has been founded a long time. Let me help you up; the boys will be wanting their teas."

She stooped to assist him to rise; he had been badly knocked about, and felt rather faint and dizzy.

At that juncture, a great noise arose in the schoolroom.

Boys seemed to be shouting, scuffling, and fighting with one another.

The door opened lower down the passage.

Mr. Caner, the third master, who, in the absence of the doctor and Mr. Dobby was always in charge, rushed out.

A shower of books followed him in his headlong flight.

Hisses, yells, and hoots pursued him.

As we have said, the passage was dimly lighted. He was going towards the doctor's study as fast as he could. He did not perceive Miss Martha bending over Peter.

Just as she had raised the new page-boy to his knees, Mr. Caner, who was short-sighted and wore glasses, fell over her.

She recoiled on Peter, and the three rolled over among the fragments of the mugs, clutching frantically at one another.

"Help!" cried Mr. Caner. "Confound it! what is this?"

"Lights! Help!" shouted Miss Martha. "It is a design to murder me."

"Oh, lor'," groaned Peter, who was at the bottom of the heap, "this is a little bit more of it. I don't like this place."

Hearing the hubbub, Doctor Birchoften roused himself from the torpor into which he had sunk after being assaulted by Mr. Dobby.

He was afflicted with spasmodic pains in the gastric region, and his right eye was rapidly closing up.

Holding the lamp, he came into the passage. The sight of Mr. Caner, his sister, and Peter struggling together, and the noise in the schoolroom bewildered him.

"What is the meaning of all this?" he asked. "Is it real, or am I mad or dreaming?"

Miss Martha heard her brother's voice. She stretched out her hand, and he helped her up.

Then Mr. Caner followed suit, Peter being the last to rise. A few words explained how the accident had arisen.

"I beg to apologise, ma'am, for not seeing you," said Mr. Caner, "but there is such a row going on in the schoolroom, and I was in such a hurry to consult you and ask your advice."

"Yes, I understand," interrupted Doctor Birchoften. "Go on."

At that moment, Mr. Caner caught sight of his employer's inky face.

"Dear me, you are black! It is the voice of my principal, but the countenance of a negro!" he exclaimed, in astonishment.

"I have to thank Mr. Dobby for this," replied the doctor. "We—we, to put it mildly, came into collision. He is going to open a school of his own. He wants to get my pupils."

"That is what I wanted to speak to you about, sir."

"Well, proceed."

"The boys have divided themselves into two parties, and are fighting."

"What are the two parties?"

"The Warnerites and the Dobbyites," answered Mr. Caner. "The latter are less numerous than the former, and if the riot is not stopped, they will be driven into the yard."

"If I understand you rightly, the Dobbyites will get the worst of it?"

"Yes, sir, unless the disturbance is quelled."

"Very well," said the doctor, complacently; "I do not think I shall interfere. What do you say, Martha?"

"I am quite of your opinion. When the Dobbyites are routed and forced to leave the schoolroom, we shall know our friends from our foes," she answered.

"That is good sage counsel."

"If Mr. Dobby has so undermined them that they are determined to leave us and go with him, let them go at once."

"So I should say; sooner the better," remarked Mr. Caner.

"They have no weapons, I suppose?" asked the doctor. "Nothing they can harm themselves with?"

"Only their fists and the books, sir."

"They shall fight it out. Come to my study, you and Miss Martha. We will there await the course of events."

Saying this, Doctor Birchoften led the way to his private room and produced a bottle of sherry.

Meanwhile the tumult in the schoolroom waxed louder and yet more loud.

"Peter," called Miss Martha.

"Yes, miss; I'm here," replied the page.

"Act as a scout. Watch the boys and come every few minutes to tell us how the battle is progressing—which side is winning, and which conquering—you know what I mean. Do this faithfully, and I will give you half-a-crown." ·

Peter held out his hand.

"What do you want?" she asked.

"The half-crown, please, miss. I've heard you've a bad memory."

Miss Martha could have boxed his ears for his impudence, but she restrained her inclination.

He received the money, and ran into the passage to watch the fight, so that he might make his report.

Looking in at the open door of the schoolroom, he saw the boys fighting, and throwing books at one another.

A heavy dictionary came in his direction, striking him on the shoulder.

"I say," he muttered, "what a lot of knowledge there must be in them there school books to make 'em hit so hard."

The boys who had voted for the expulsion of Warner, were led by Wildash and a third form fellow named Woosman.

They were less in number than the others, and had to give way before the onslaught of their foes.

This they did, step by step.

Harry and Jack had ranged themselves on the side of law and order—not because they had any regard for Warner, but they liked the school, they respected the doctor, and they did not want to go to Squire Rawlings' Hall with Mr. Dobby.

Clayton was at the head of the Warnerites,

At length he and his supporters succeeded in driving Wildash and Woosman, with their followers, into the yard.

The Dobbyites now scattered in all directions, while loud cheers arose from their foes, who locked the schoolroom door, so that they should not re-enter.

Peter ran to Miss Martha with the intelligence.

"Our side has beaten, miss," he cried. "Mr. Dobby's chaps are cutting away like mad."

Doctor Birchoften, Miss Martha, and Mr. Caner looked profoundly thankful.

The boys who objected to Warner, and had elected to follow Mr. Dobby's fortunes in his new school, were driven by the Warnerites into the field.

Here they took down branches from the trees to make sticks of, and presented a determined front.

Seeing that they were standing with their backs to the fence, evidently intending to renew the fight, Clayton halted his force.

He was in considerable doubt how to act.

Calling Jack to his side, he exclaimed—

"Will you run to the head-master and ask him what I am to do?"

"If they come back like lost sheep to the fold, there is sure to be a renewal of the disturbance," replied Jack. "We shall have no peace in the school."

He was about to start off and ask the advice of the doctor, when the gordian knot of the difficulty was cut unexpectedly.

Mr. Dobby suddenly made his appearance on the scene.

Woosman had despatched a messenger after him.

Seeing how the case stood, Mr. Dobby called Clayton to come to him.

"Do you wish to speak to me, sir?" asked Clayton.

"I simply wish you to convey a few words to Doctor Birchoften," replied Mr. Dobby. "Although not fully prepared for their reception, I shall march these boys at once to my new school. To-morrow I shall visit their parents, and send to this place for their boxes."

"We don't want them," retorted Clayton.

"No," sneered Dobby; "you have got the murderer—Warner. That is quite enough for you."

"You have been guilty of a mean trick."

"That is my business. I win my game—I laugh."

"That is rewarding Doctor Birchoften's kindness with base ingratitude. I did not think you capable of it, sir."

"Everyone for himself in these competitive times, as I remarked to Doctor Birchoften. If any other of your set like to come and join me, I shall be glad to receive them."

"I wish you joy of your new pupils."

"Why so?"

"They are the worst boys in the school."

Woosman stepped forward angrily.

"How about yourself and Warner?" he asked.

"I would rather have him for a chum than you."

"Take that, you cad!' cried Woosman.

He struck out, and hitting Clayton without any notice on the forehead, sent him to grass.

In a moment, Jack dexterously floored Woosman, which caused Wildash to come forward.

In vain Mr. Dobby held up his arms to avert the coming conflict.

Clayton was up again quickly.

The Stingwell Hall boys came to the front with a cheer, and rushed on those of Rawlings' Hall.

The Warnerites and the Dobbyites were soon engaged in a combat with fists and sticks.

Mr. Dobby was himself knocked down in the *mêlée* and trampled on.

"Hurrah!" cried Jack. "Give it the renegades! Do not spare them!"

"There's one for you?" Wildash exclaimed.

As he spoke, his stick descended on Jack's head, and he fell on his knees.

"And there's another for you!" shouted Harry.

In his turn, Wildash went down.

The scrimmage now became general.

"Down with the Dobbyites!" was heard on one side, while the rallying cry of the other party was "Down with the Warnerites!"

At length the superior numbers of the Stingwell Hall division prevailed.

Mr. Dobby saw the ranks of his supporters break, and scrambling to his feet, he led a headlong retreat.

Clayton did not think it worth while to pursue.

He called his men back, and returned to the school, proud of his victory.

The break up in the school was now complete.

Mr. Dobby had inflicted a severe blow upon the doctor.

Jack could not help thinking that the usher had some mysterious reason for acting in this way.

Nor was he mistaken.

As he was leaving the field of battle, he picked up a piece of a torn letter.

It was in the place where Mr. Dobby had been knocked down in the scuffle.

He would not have bestowed any attention upon it, or have taken the trouble to read it, if he had not seen the signature.

This was, "Simeon Rawlings."

It began with, "My dear Mr. Dobby," and went on to say, "you can have the Hall for a school and welcome, on a seven years' lease. All I shall stipulate for, is a bedroom when I visit Clare. My son Charlie will not reside there again, owing to the chance of his being arrested for his foolish escapade, in running off with Marian Spencer. You can take possession at once. I shall visit you shortly, as I have determined to take my nephew away from Doctor Birchoften's charge and place him under yours. He requires strict discipline and obedience. I think I can rely on you to enforce it. Wishing you every success in your new venture, "I am, yours faithfully,

"SIMEON RAWLINGS."

Jack whistled when he had concluded the reading of this epistle.

"What have you got there?" asked Harry.

"Something that concerns you."

"Let me have a look at it."

He took the letter which Jack handed him.

During its perusal his countenance fell.

"I felt sure my uncle was at work like a mole in the dark," he cried. "But can he do with me as he says he will?"

"I am afraid he can," answered Jack.

"How?"

"You see, he's your guardian. The law enables him to exercise control over you during your minority."

"But your father is kindly paying for me now," continued Harry. "If it had not been for your people, I should have been a homeless wanderer."

"That makes no difference. Your uncle can apply to the Court and get an order to take you away from Stingwell Hall, if you refuse to go willingly."

"I am glad we have seen the letter, for it gives us a clue to Dobby's conduct, and shows the relentless hatred of the Squire," added Harry; "but it makes my heart sink."

He clutched Jack's arm tightly.

A death-like expression crossed his handsome face.

"I feel, old boy," he went on, "that if I once get shut up as a scholar in Rawlings' Hall, I shall never—never come out alive."

"Why not run away?"

"Whither can I go? What can I do?"

"You ran away before, and no one could find you."

"Ah, Jack," replied Harry, "you do not know the misery of being friendless, penniless, homeless, and starving. I starved in the wood before Ella, the old gipsy, found me."

" Poor fellow," said Jack.

" You have always had plenty to eat, kind friends, and a good bed to lie upon."

" That is true, thank goodness."

" I starved in Harwich, and slept in any hole and corner."

" Perhaps my father would give you some money to go away with, or the lawyer who has your case would."

" That is a good idea."

"'You will come into the property soon, and—"

" If I live," put in Harry, with a melancholy smile.

" Of course you will. The lawyer will finance you. I will get leave to go to the farm to-morrow morning, and I can ask father to send you up to London to the lawyer."

" You will be my saviour, and I shall thank you all my life," cried Harry.

" Consider it as good as done."

" To-morrow morning the first thing? Delays are dangerous, you know."

" I will not fail," replied Jack.

They walked back to the school silently. Harry's heart was full. Several attempts had been made on his life.

Up to the present they had all failed.

But would every other attempt fail?

If he was once placed under Mr. Dobby's charge in the old Hall, he would be completely in the power of his uncle.

Mr. Dobby was the Squire's nominee. Having no capital, he would be completely beholden to the rich man.

A hundred petty persecutions could be resorted to, in order that Harry's spirit might be crushed.

Privations and tortures might be invented to make him break down and die.

Mr. Dobby would be obliged to render himself the servile and willing tool of Squire Rawlings.

After reading the letter Jack had found, it would be the height of folly for Harry to stay anywhere near Stingwell Hall.

Doctor Birchoften would be obliged to give him up on application, so would Farmer Spencer.

No matter how good their hearts were towards him or how kind their intentions for his welfare, they could not defy the law.

His guardian had the indisputable right to claim him.

All the other boys had got back to the school long before they reached the yard, and were in the house.

It was about tea-time, and they were growing hungry.

When they reached the woodshed, they saw a light under the door, and smoke coming out of the window.

The two spies were standing near, with their backs towards Jack and Harry.

" They are all in," said Peeping Tom. " We had best go, too, or we shall be suspected."

Jack seized Harry's arm.

They stood still and listened.

" Won't there be a flare-up directly," replied Knowall Dick.

" If you put enough paraffin oil on the wood."

" I emptied Peter's can. The doctor and everyone else will think that some of the Dobbyites have done it out of revenge. What a shine there will be! "

" Collar Dick," whispered Jack ; " I'll run in Master Tom."

Suddenly Peeping Tom found himself grasped by the neck, and Knowall Dick experienced a similar sensation.

" Not so fast! " cried Jack. " We know what you have done."

Oh, dear! " said Tom. " Who'd have thought you were behind us? But we didn't do it."

" Oh, no! " replied Jack, " you never do anything. Come with me to the doctor. You shall smart for this."

" I won't go."

" Yes, you will, Tommy. Come quietly, or I shall have to use the business end of my boot as a persuader. You will be birched for this, and get it hot, as the doctor is in a sweet temper."

" I'll run away to Mr. Dobby first," said Peeping Tom.

" So will I," chimed in Knowall Dick.

They began to struggle with all their might to get away, but their captors were too strong for them.

Kicking, and even biting, the spies were dragged into the passage, where Miss Martha was encountered.

" Whatever is the matter?" she enquired. " More fighting? Spencer! Rawlings! what are you doing to Harris and Wilkins? "

" They have set the woodshed on fire, ma'am," replied Jack.

" I won't—I can't believe it. They are such good boys."

" We heard them boasting of it. Look out of the door. You will see whether I am right or not.

Miss Martha did as she was directed.

The shed was now fully ablaze.

Luckily it was summer time, and there was only a small collection of faggots within the burning erection.

Had it been otherwise—that is to say, had it been winter instead of summer—a very serious fire would have arisen.

"HE MADE A RUSH UPON HARRY, BUT ALL THREE FELL UPON HIM WITH THEIR STICKS."

"Oh, dear," cried Miss Martha, "there is no end to our troubles to-day. Mr. Dobby has gone off with the boys, I am told, and now we are in danger of being burnt out."

"Shall I take the culprits to the doctor, ma'am?" asked Jack.

"Not now. He is too upset. I am just going to make him a cup of tea. His nerves are in a dreadful state. Let them go. It shall be inquired into to-morrow."

"They threaten to run away and join Mr. Dobby."

The spies turned up the whites of their eyes in a lachrymose manner.

"As if we would dream of such a thing!" said Peeping Tom.

"How could we be so mad as to leave such a splendid school?" cried Knowall Dick.

"And such a sweet home!" added Tom.

"And such a dear lady as Miss Martha," supplemented Dick.

The two hypocrites squeezed out a tear each like a couple of crocodiles.

"There must be a mistake," said Miss Martha. "I am deeply affected by their words. They quite touch me. Release them, please."

It went very much against the grain with Jack and Harry to do so, but they complied with the order.

It was easy to see they did it with an ill grace.

As soon as they were free, Peeping Tom and Knowall Dick ran to the door which led into the yard.

They had the audacity to put their fingers to their noses in token of supreme contempt and derision.

"What do you mean by this?" exclaimed Martha. "Harris and Wilkins, I am ashamed of you. Leave off those antics. Go into the dining-room at once, and have your tea with the rest."

"Here's off," replied Peeping Tom.

"We won't stay here any longer," answered Knowall Dick.

"Have you taken leave of your senses?"

"No more stale bread for me. Mr. Dobby has promised us an unlimited supply of new bread and the best Aylesbury butter, and coffee for breakfast, and meat for supper. The new school's a land flowing with milk and honey," said Tom.

"Wouldn't we be flats to stay here, when Mr. Dobby is not going to use the birch or the cane?" remarked Dick.

"Oh, you bad boys! How I have been deceived in you! Your parents shall hear of it."

"Put the fire out; it might spread," added Tom, jeeringly.

"Mr. Dobby is going to take the boys at half-price," observed Dick. "He is going to cut rates, so as to ruin you and old Birchy."

Miss Martha could not bear these taunts.

She was afraid that what the spies said was only too true.

Grasping a mop which stood in the passage, she ran after the spies.

Nimbly they eluded her, and rushed away into the field.

It was clearly their intention to throw in their lot with Mr. Dobby, and become prominent ornaments of his new academy.

By this time the fire had done its worst.

The roof of the shed had fallen in. The walls being of brick, offered no fuel for the flames, and all that could be seen was dense smoke arising from the smouldering embers.

"There is no danger now," said Jack; "not a breath of air is stirring. All will be out in half-an-hour."

"Peter shall throw a few buckets of water over the shed directly," replied Miss Martha. "Oh, those boys! How one can be deceived!"

"They are a bad lot, ma'am. I'm glad they have gone," said Harry.

"Dear me! How will it all end? My brother is dreadfully agitated. Mr. Caner is with him. Go to your tea, and preserve order as well as you can. Oh, those wretched double-faced boys!"

Jack and Harry assured her that they would do all they could to make things go well in the dining-room, and left her lamenting.

Of course the boys did as they liked that evening. It was the first of the half, and, as a rule, only the short holiday tasks that had been given out were enquired for.

Neither the doctor nor Miss Martha appeared. Mr. Caner came in at tea-time, and saw the boys into the schoolroom afterwards.

Then he left them to their own devices until bed-time.

On the following morning, lessons began. Doctor Birchoften made no allusion to what had occurred, he and Mr. Caner managing the work very well without Mr. Dobby.

Jack had no difficulty in obtaining leave to run over to the farm to see his father.

Mr. Spencer was greatly surprised at seeing his son, and more so when he heard the strange news he had to tell him.

"I can see through a brick wall or a milestone, my lad," exclaimed the honest farmer, "as far as most folks, and I can tell, with half an eye, who is at the bottom of all these doings."

"Squire Rawlings?"

"Exactly. Young Harry stands between him and the property."

"That is clear."

"He will stop at nothing to get him out of the way, and that is why he has induced this Dobby to start a rival school."

"Can he claim Harry?" asked Jack, anxiously.

"No doubt. The Court will give him the authority of a guardian over his ward."

"Then I did quite right in coming to tell you?"

"If you had not, they would have had the boy under their thumb—the Squire and Dobby," replied Mr. Spencer.

"What will you do with him?"

"He can't stop in these parts, that's certain sure. I'll write a letter for him to take up to the London lawyer who has got his case in hand. He will see him put in a place of safety."

"He will want a couple of sovereigns for expenses."

"You shall have them. Start him off at once. Let him go by the one o'clock train. Say nothing to anybody; keep your own counsel. Do not even speak to Doctor Birchoften," said the farmer.

"I will be as silent as the grave," answered Jack. "Harry is like a brother to me, and I would do anything for him."

"So would I. If he escapes the traps and pitfalls that are laid for him, he will become a rich man before long."

"It isn't that, father, I like him for," Jack hastened to exclaim.

"No, no; I am aware of that. We don't want a rich son-in-law, but your mother and I love the lad."

"Shall I say anything to mother and Marian?"

"Not a syllable. Least said, soonest mended," replied the farmer. "They haven't seen you yet. When you go into the house, tell them you've come after some books or something."

"Am I to stay at the school, father?"

"Yes. You can't do better. You are getting a good education, which is everything in these days. In time, I will try to send you to college."

Saying this, the farmer entered the house with his son, wrote the letter introducing Harry to the London lawyer, and gave it, together with two sovereigns, to Jack.

"That will settle the business," he remarked.

Harry put the letter and the money in his pocket, and managed to get away without being seen by his mother or Marian, who were in the dairy.

Mr. Spencer accompanied Jack to the garden gate.

"If the Squire is a villain," he observed, "that fellow Dobby is another."

"If he isn't, Mr. Rawlings will soon make him one," replied Jack.

"Yes. Some men will do anything for money. The reason a good many don't commit crimes is, they haven't the opportunity and the inducement. Good-bye, my son. Stick to your lessons."

"I will, father. I'll try to be a credit to you," answered Jack, cheerily. "You sha'n't spend your money on me for nothing."

With a heart relieved of some of its care on his friend's behalf, Jack hastened back to Stingwell Hall.

When he arrived there, school was just over, and the boys were out in the field. Cricket bats and balls were put away till next year.

It being winter half, football was the order of the day.

Harry was anxiously awaiting his friend's coming, standing by the ruins of the wood-shed, which Peeping Tom and Knowall Dick had burnt down on the previous night.

He had written a brief letter to Doctor Birchoften in anticipation of going away, which he intended to post in the town.

In it he stated that circumstances had arisen of a private nature, which necessitated his going away for a time.

This step he took in entire concurrence with the opinions and wishes of his friends.

He expressed his great regret at being compelled to leave the school, even for a short while, and declared he should look forward to a speedy reunion with his companions.

When Jack came up, he exclaimed—

"What luck?"

"It is all right," answered Jack. "Here's your money, and here is the letter which the governor has written for you."

"I go to the address on the envelope? It is in Bedford Row, London, W.C."

"That is correct. Heaven bless you, old fellow. May you live long and prosper, as the man says in the play," replied Jack.

Harry wrung his friend's hand, and, with difficulty repressing his tears, walked hurriedly away.

He was parting from all his old associations to go among strangers.

The trees had put on their rich autumnal tints, and the birds sang merrily in the still balmy air.

He, however, had no thoughts for the beauties of Nature, and pursued his way with bowed head and tear-dimmed eyes.

It was now half-past twelve. Having previously consulted the time-table, he knew that there was a train to London at one o'clock.

Consequently he quickened his pace, after examining his watch, and hurried to catch it, as he did not want to be seen waiting on the platform until another train came in. If Squire Rawlings heard that he had gone to London, it would give him a clue to his whereabouts.

CHAPTER XXXV.

THE PLOT THICKENS—SQUIRE RAWLINGS AT WORK—THE HIDDEN HAND.

AFTER taking his ticket, Harry looked at the station clock. He had ten minutes only to wait before the arrival of the express by which he was going to travel.

His heart fluttered a little, for he had no particular liking for the step which dire necessity had obliged him to take.

He was the only passenger that morning. The porter, who was named Timmins, knew him, and spoke.

"Good-day, Master Harry!" exclaimed Timmins. "I thought schoolboys was all back again at Stingwell Hall."

"So they are, but I'm going a little journey," answered Harry.

"Be 'ee going far?"

"Oh, no."

"I do hear there has been a tit-up atween the doctor and Mr. Dobby. Be it true?"

"Yes. Mr. Dobby has opened on his own account, and taken some of the boys with him," said Harry.

"Eh! but that be bad for the doctor," replied Timmins.

Further conversation was cut short by the approach of the down train from London, which was due five minutes before the up one.

The porter had to cross the line to attend to it, and left Harry to himself, for which relief he felt thankful.

He knew not why, but he felt like a hunted hare, and longed to get into the train.

Once in the carriage, whirling away to the great city at express speed, and he would be safe.

A vague fear of coming evil had taken hold of him.

He was a prey to the demon of unrest.

Slowly the down train steamed into the station. There was a grating sound of brakes being put on.

Then it came to a standstill.

In half-a-minute it went on again, leaving a gentleman behind.

Timmins took up his portmanteau, put it on his shoulder in porter fashion, and the solitary passenger crossed over.

Being engrossed with his own thoughts, Harry took no notice of him, but, turning his back, walked on a little way, nervously awaiting the arrival of the train.

He heard footsteps behind him.

Suddenly he reversed his walk, and came face to face with the traveller who had just arrived.

He uttered a cry of mingled surprise and alarm.

It was his uncle, Squire Rawlings, whom he had thought to be hundreds of miles away—at Naples or somewhere in the Mediterranean.

A sarcastic smile curled the corners of his lips.

"Uncle!" gasped Harry, turning white as a sheet, and trembling like a bird, under the fascinating gaze of a snake.

"How did you hear that I was coming home by this train?" asked the Squire.

"I—I did not know," stammered Harry.

"Nonsense. Mr. Dobby must have told you. Do not be delicate about it. I telegraphed to him, and of course he informed you of my expected arrival. It is kind, thoughtful, and I may say very considerate of you."

Here he took Harry's unwilling hand and shook it with mock cordiality.

"My dear nephew," he added, "I am so glad to see you. Come into the office. We can talk better there."

The porter had put down the portmanteau and was looking along the line.

The up train had been signalled.

"I have not seen Mr. Dobby since last night," said Harry.

He was in a terrible dilemma, and did not know what to do.

This unlucky meeting had disconcerted all his well-laid plans.

"How is that? Has Dobby gone from Stingwell Hall?" asked Mr. Rawlings.

"Last night he left for your house, which he said he had leased from you for a school, and he took a number of the boys with him."

"I hope he will get on. He deserves to, for being bold and brave enough to strike out for himself. But come into the booking-office."

"I would rather not."

"Eh—what?"

"Not now, thank you. I am going a short journey by the train that is just due."

"You had better wait for the next. We have not seen each other for a long time," answered the Squire. "Really, my dear nephew, you must postpone this excursion, for of course it can be nothing more than that."

"I regret to say I cannot put it off."

The train was now seen; in a minute it would be in the station.

Had Harry lost his chance?

The Squire no doubt saw that he was trying to make his escape, for he grasped him roughly by the wrist and dragged him into the booking-office.

Forcing him into a seat, he stood over him without releasing his hold.

"I am sorry to have to use violence," he exclaimed, "but your conduct is so extraordinary that I fear you have taken leave of your senses."

"How dare you do this?" demanded Harry, indignantly.

"Am I not your guardian?" was the cold reply.

The porter put his head in at the door.

"London train. Make haste if you are going on, Master Harry," he cried.

Harry jumped up and tried to wrest himself free, but the effort was in vain.

His uncle held him in a vice-like grip.

"Help! help!" shouted Harry

"You shall not go. I am master over you," said the Squire.

"Release me! Help!"

The station-master had gone to dinner. The booking-clerk saw what was going on, but did not consider it any business of his to interfere. The porter was seeing to the train.

The puff-puff of the engine, and the shrill whistle, warned Harry that he was left behind.

His attempt to escape was frustrated.

All at once the door was pushed open, and the burly form of Farmer Spencer appeared.

He looked first at Harry, then he turned his gaze, with a withering scorn, on Mr. Rawlings.

"Was it you holloaing for help, my lad?" he asked.

"Yes," replied Harry, faintly.

"Dang me, if I didn't think so. I was driving by the station with a couple of pigs for butcher Harris, when I heard the hubbub. What is the man a-doing of to you?"

"I was going by the train that has just left. My uncle met me here and stopped me."

"That's it, eh, Squire?" exclaimed the farmer.

"I do not deny it," replied Mr. Rawlings.

"What right have you got to stop the boy? You haven't taken much interest in him lately. This is a sudden freak. What is the meaning of it? I've been paying for Harry and keeping him."

"Your interest in him is easily understood. You think he will come into money and you are anxious to get him for a husband for your daughter."

The honest farmer's face crimsoned with rage at this insinuation.

"If the law wouldn't call it assault, I'd strike you," he said: "but I'll keep my temper, if I can. Don't push me too far, that's all."

"This boy is my nephew," exclaimed Mr. Rawlings. "He has no other relative."

"You have shown him a lot of kindness, I must say."

"Allow me to continue. I find my dear nephew running away from school, and—"

"Did you place him there," interrupted Spencer.

"I will not argue that point with you. My dear nephew will come with me."

"Show me your authority."

"Here it is. I always like to do things legally."

So saying, the Squire produced from an inner pocket of his coat a paper, duly signed by a magistrate.

This empowered him to take his nephew wherever he found him, from whoever detained him, and do with him as he thought best.

In fact, it gave him entire control over the boy as his legally constituted guardian and protector.

The farmer read it carefully.

"What are you going to do with him?"

"That is my business," answered the Squire. "One thing I may tell you: I shall take especial care that he does not see you or any member of your family."

"Tell me where he is going."

"That I absolutely refuse to do, and you cannot make me."

Harry seized the farmer's horny hand.

"Mr. Spencer," he cried, "will you not protect me?"

"I'll do anything for 'ee, lad, but I mustn't break the law."

"He is going to take me to Mr. Dobby's."

"How did you know that?"

"From a secret source," replied Harry. "It is all arranged between them. I believe the sole reason of Mr. Dobby being allowed to get the Hall for a school, is to put me there, so that I may be done to death by inches."

"They daren't kill you. Keep a stout heart, I'll be on the watch," said the farmer. "And as for that paper-faced villain, I'd like to punch his yed, dang me, if I wouldn't. There now."

Spencer clenched his hand and shook it at the Squire, who drew Harry to the door.

The scene had lasted long enough.

He wanted to end it without any further recrimination or altercation.

There was always a fly waiting outside the station for the convenience of travellers.

Mr. Rawlings conducted his nephew to it, placed him inside, and then got in himself.

The porter put the portmanteau on the front seat, the driver was told to go to the Hall, and the fly drove off.

Spencer shouted after it—

"You villain! I will thwart you yet."

The Squire smiled in a sardonic manner, and took off his hat as if he were receiving a compliment.

Harry was the picture of despair. His courage had deserted him, for he knew that he was helpless in the hands of his persecutor.

"The country is very pleasant at this time of the year," observed the Squire.

"It may be to those who have the heart to enjoy it," replied Harry. "I have not."

"Why are you so cast down, my dear nephew?"

"Don't talk to me like that. I know you hate me, and I would rather have you say so openly."

"Indeed, you are mistaken. I feel that I have neglected you too much."

"All I want is to be let alone by you."

"If I ignored you, I should not be doing my duty. You are a poor friendless orphan. I will place you with Mr. Dobby. You shall be cared for, well educated, sent to college in time, and be brought up to one of the liberal professions."

"You know you do not mean it," said Harry.

Mr. Rawlings turned up the whites of his eyes.

"What a world this is!" he exclaimed. "I intend to do my duty by my dear nephew, and I get no thanks. Why is this?"

"Because it is all humbug!" cried Harry, plucking up a little.

"You should not say that. Will you not be amongst old schoolfellows, and have a good home? How fortunate it was I chanced to meet you. Where were you going, my dear boy?"

"I refuse to tell you."

"Perhaps I can guess. Was it not to that lawyer in London, who, I hear, has taken up what they call your case on some forged documents?"

"It is a true will," replied Harry.

"That is what people tell you for their own purposes. They wish to serve their own ends, that is all."

"You will find out in time whether that is so or not—"

"Ha! excuse me. What is that sticking out of your pocket?" cried the Squire. "A letter, eh?"

With a dexterous movement, he snatched the letter which Mr. Spencer had written from Harry's pocket, from the top of which it was protruding.

Harry tried to take it away from him.

In return, he received a blow on the head, which half stunned him for a few seconds.

"None of that!" cried the Squire. "As I told you before, I am your master until you become of age."

Then he tore open the envelope and read the letter.

"Very prettily contrived," he went on. "Your life is in danger through me, your farmer friend is good enough to say."

"So it is," answered Harry, recovering himself.

"He recommends the lawyer to look after you, and make you a ward in Chancery. Nice goings on behind my back."

"Take half the money, and give me the rest," cried Harry, desperately.

"You have none to give. I dispute the will. You are a pauper. But no more idle chatter. Here we are at the Hall."

The fly drew up at the mansion, and Harry saw a number of familiar faces at the windows of the drawing-room.

Mr. Dobby had, for the nonce, turned this into a schoolroom.

A servant opened the door, and the Squire, with Harry, were shown into the library.

Here Mr. Dobby was waiting to receive them.

"My dear sir," he exclaimed, "I am so glad to see you. Your telegraphic dispatch came to hand an hour ago. How is my young friend Harry, and how did you manage to bring him here so soon?"

"The misguided boy was at the railway station, about to levant to London, acting on the advice of his false friends," replied Mr. Rawlings.

"Dear me, how sad!"

"It was fortunate I met him. You will know how to look after his welfare."

"I will be like a father to him, sir, rely upon that," answered Mr. Dobby.

"He must be treated with all kindness, Mr. Dobby."

"With a mild severity, I apprehend, sir."

"Ahem ! he must be watched. What do you do with a boy who is inclined to run away ?" continued the Squire.

"I place him under supervision. Two boys must always be with him. I have two with me now who will just do."

"Who are they ?"

"Harris and Wilkins. You shall see them and judge for yourself. They shall be his inseparable companions, and even sleep in the same room with him."

"Good. That will do. For his own sake, the poor boy must be guarded."

"Quite so."

Harry groaned inwardly.

He did not dare, however, to make any remonstrance.

Mr. Dobby touched a bell, and desired the servant to request Peeping Tom and Knowall Dick to come to him.

The spies had only exchanged one school, where their contemptible nature was appreciated, for another where it was equally esteemed.

In a few minutes they made their appearance.

When they saw Harry and his uncle, they could not repress a grin of amused satisfaction.

"Harris and Wilkins," said Mr. Dobby, "you are, doubtless, pleased to see an old schoolfellow ?"

"Yes, sir," replied Peeping Tom.

"Delighted, I'm sure," answered Knowall Dick, putting his tongue in his cheek.

"His uncle," resumed Mr. Dobby, "who is also his sole guardian, has deemed it advisable for his good to place him under my care and tuition. It is suspected that he will try to run away. Why, I know not, but—"

"I shouldn't like to leave such a good home," broke in Tom.

"And such a kind gentleman as you, sir," said Dick.

"Thank you. Observe, Mr. Rawlings, how my pupils esteem me ; but to my purpose. You two will be careful never to let Master Rawlings out of your sight."

"No, sir."

"Neither by day nor by night. You will sleep in the same room, and you must lock the door and keep the key in your possession, Harris. If Master Rawlings should prove recalcitrant, you will at once report to me, and other measures will be taken," added Mr. Dobby.

Mr. Rawlings held out his hand.

"Good-bye, my dear nephew," he said. "Study hard and improve your mind. As you will not be allowed out of the grounds, I will give you no money, for you will not require any. It is a pleasure to me to think you will be happy here."

"And well cared for !" cried Mr. Dobby.

"Certainly. Pardon me for omitting that."

Harry refused to accept the proffered hand of his uncle.

"I have nothing to thank you for. Some day—" he began.

"Take him away," interrupted Mr. Dobby. "No insolence to parents or guardians can be allowed."

He pushed Harry out of the door, and the spies placed themselves on each side of him as he walked down the passage.

Young as he was when his father died, he remembered every room in the old house and every corridor as well as if he had left it only yesterday.

What associations it recalled !

"Here's an unexpected pleasure," said Peeping Tom. "Give us your flipper."

"It is more correct to say, tender us your beeswing," exclaimed Knowall Dick.

Harry looked angrily at them.

"Look here, you fellows !" he cried. "I won't stand cheek here any more than I did at the other school, so mind that."

"Oh, yes, you will," replied Tom.

"Why should I ?"

"Because you can't help yourself," said Tom.

"Circumstances alter cases," remarked Dick.

"Am I a helpless prisoner, then, to be insulted by you two ?"

"That's what it amounts to," replied Peeping Tom. "If you kick over the traces, we shall report it, and then I pity you."

"So do I. Mr. Dobby is not going to use the birch, but he keeps canes. Oh, my ! won't he make you cry *peccavi !*" said Dick.

"Never mind," continued Tom, philosophically. "Some are born into the world to suffer."

"Make your miserable life as happy as you can under the circs. ; it will be all the same a hundred years hence," advised Dick.

Harry sighed deeply.

He was sure that he was doomed to a course of systematic ill-treatment.

The Squire had brought him to Mr. Dobby's in order that either his health might break down by cruelty and starvation or he should be driven to take his own life.

In the schoolroom the boys were playing at baste the bear.

When Harry entered, accompanied by the spies, who were to be his companions inseparably night and day for the future, they ceased their play.

"Hurrah! Another recruit!" cried Woosman.

"It's Rawlings," said Wildash. "I thought he, of all others, could not have any real affection for bully Warner."

"He didn't come of his own free will," replied Peeping Tom.

"How is that?"

"His uncle brought him here for the sake of the discipline," grinned Knowall Dick."

"Oh, you know everything, you do," said Wildash, who liked Harry, and was inclined to be his friend.

"I tell you he is no friend of our party," continued Dick, "and I vote we make him our bear."

"Agreed!" cried Woosman. "Rawlings is bear."

"I don't want to play," said Harry.

"Why not?" "You must." "Aren't we good enough for you?" and similar remarks were heard on all sides.

"Too good, very likely," replied Harry. "I'm not saying anything against anybody, but I'm not in the humour to play bear. My head aches."

"We can't accept any excuse!" exclaimed Woosman.

"I shall not do it, I tell you."

Woosman regarded Harry with an angry spiteful glance.

"Let him alone, can't you," said Wildash. "He has only just come, and anyone can see with half an eye he is not well."

"Nonsense! He could fight well enough yesterday, when he helped to chase us out of the field," remarked Woosman.

"If anyone of you touches me now, I'll floor him!" cried Harry.

"Oh, if you are well enough to do that, you are quite up to playing bear," said Woosman with a laugh.

"Don't try me too far."

How do you like that?" Woosman rejoined, bringing his knotted handkerchief sharply down on Harry's back.

The response was as prompt as it was unexpected.

Striking out, Harry hit Woosman between the eyes, causing him to fall over a chair, and roll to the floor.

Running to the wall, Harry put his back against it, seized a cricket stump which was lying near, and brandished it threateningly.

There was a quiet, steady, defiant light in his eyes, and a resolute expression about the corners of his mouth.

"Come on, all of you!" he shouted.

At the same moment he heard a carriage door shut, followed by the sound of wheels, and he knew that his uncle had left the house.

There had been ample time, however, for him to give Mr. Dobby full instructions how to deal with his nephew.

It is important to bear in mind that Dobby had no money and was entirely dependent for success in his new venture on the assistance of the Squire.

To deserve this assistance, of course a man like Dobby would stoop to anything mean or disgraceful.

All his life it had been his ambition to become his own master, and now that he had climbed to the top of the ladder, he did not mean to sink into the unthankful position of an usher again.

Just as Woosman was staggering to his feet, pale with rage, Mr. Dobby entered the room.

He surveyed the scene with an angry snort.

"What! fighting! Who is the cause of this?" he demanded.

"Please, sir," replied Woosman, "I asked Rawlings to play at baste the bear, and he struck me."

"Oh, very well," said Mr. Dobby.

He walked resolutely up to Harry, who set his teeth firmly together, and prepared himself for what he felt was coming.

CHAPTER XXXVI.

THE SCHOOLBOY SLAVE—A TYRANT TASKMASTER—DESPAIR.

Raising his hand, Mr. Dobby exclaimed—

"Put that stump down."

"Certainly," replied Harry, "if you will protect me. I don't see why I should be obliged to play if I don't want to."

"Is that any reason why you should grievously assault one of your companions?"

"He struck me first."

Seeing that Harry was inclined to be obstinate, Mr. Dobby made a grab at the stump, and by the exercise of superior strength, wrenched it from his grasp.

He was now defenceless.

"Follow me, if you please," continued Mr. Dobby. "I will talk to you in private. You have not come here to do as you like."

"Nor have I to obey you in everything," retorted Harry.

"That remains to be seen," said Mr.

Dobby, with rising anger. "If you refuse to follow me, I will cane you before the whole school."

"Rather than you should make a brute of yourself, I will follow you. Lead on."

"Silence!"

"A school is not a gaol. Surely I can speak?"

"Not without my permission."

Wildash stepped forward.

"Please, sir," he exclaimed, "Rawlings stated that he had a headache, and—"

"What have you to do with the matter?" interrupted Mr. Dobby."

"I like fair play."

"Hold your tongue."

"Don't get yourself into trouble on my account," said Harry. "I can fight my own battle."

He saw that Wildash was inclined to take his part, and he divined that he would be ill-treated in consequence.

From this fate he generously wished to save him.

Mr. Dobby was losing patience. He seized Harry by the collar of his coat, and marched him up the room.

The spies of the school kept close at their heels.

When the passage was reached, Mr. Dobby conducted his captive to a gloomy-looking, vaulted, ill-lighted room, with brick walls whitewashed, in which the boots and knives, etc., were cleaned.

He had not been able to engage an odd boy, like Tuffins or Peter, yet, and a number of pairs of boots, together with a lot of knives and forks, were waiting for someone to attend to them.

This den was called the pantry.

Pushing Harry inside, Mr. Dobby exclaimed—

"Are you willing to apologise to Woosman for hitting him in the cowardly manner you did?"

"Decidedly not," answered Harry.

"Then this knife and shoe hole will be your quarters?"

"What do you mean?"

"To punish insubordination, as they do in public schools, the army, navy—everywhere, in fact, discipline is the first thing."

"I am at a loss to understand your meaning."

"Brickdust and blacking, my boy. As a punishment, you shall be the slave of the school."

"Never!" cried Harry.

"These boots, knives, and forks must be cleaned before you have anything to eat," replied Mr. Dobby.

"You have no right to make a slave of me. I am a gentleman as much as any other boy here. Why should I be compelled to do menial work?"

"If you do not, I shall cane you."

"That is no answer to my question."

"I allow no questioning. My will is law," said Mr. Dobby. "You are placed in my charge by your guardian, unreservedly."

"But I came here to learn," replied Harry, "not to clean boots."

The spies were standing at the entrance to the pantry.

"Harris!" exclaimed Mr. Dobby.

"Here, sir," replied Peeping Tom.

"You will be good enough to stay here and see that Rawlings thoroughly performs the task I have set him."

"Yes, sir."

"Have it well done. No superficial work —no scamping. If you have any complaint to make, send Wilkins to me, and I will stimulate the flagging energies of Master Rawlings. Hunger and the cane are excellent persuaders."

"You are a cruel tyrant, and nothing better than a hard taskmaster. It is a pity you cannot be the governor of a prison," said Harry, boldly.

His spirit was by no means crushed.

Paying no heed to him, Mr. Dobby left the pantry, and Harry was alone with the two spies, whom, of all others, he most disliked.

He knew very well that they would gloat over his humiliation.

They could not help taking a fierce delight in seeing him humbled to the dust, and obliged to do work to which he was never accustomed.

A few yards down the passage was the kitchen. From this issued a savoury smell of roasting pork, which assailed the nostrils of the three.

Harry had sullenly seated himself on a stool, with a dogged air.

"I say, Rawlings," cried Peeping Tom, "you had best wake up and do your work, or you won't get any food."

"That will make no difference to me," replied Harry.

"Don't you mean to do it?"

"No. I would rather die."

"Well, I must say that is foolish. You deserve to be punished, because you hit Woosman without any provocation."

"Hold your tongue, or I'll serve you as I did him."

"I'll give you ten minutes to think it over. If you don't start then, I shall go and tell Mr. Dobby."

"Just what I should expect of you," replied Harry.

Knowall Dick had gone into the kitchen,

and persuaded the cook to give him a sop in the pan.

He came back with this in his hand, looking as if he were enjoying it immensely.

"Give us a bit," said Peeping Tom.

"Not me," replied Knowall Dick. "Go and get one for yourself."

"Is it good?"

"Prime."

Peeping Tom could not resist the temptation. He was off like a shot.

No sooner had he disappeared, than Harry jumped up from the three-legged stool on which he was sitting.

With a cry of stifled rage he sprang upon Knowall Dick, seized him by the throat, and hurled him to the ground.

The shock stunned the spy.

He uttered no cry.

Harry saw his opportunity, and was determined to make one bold bid for victory.

He did not care whither he went so long as he got away from the hateful thraldom and captivity in which his uncle had placed him.

If it were to be his lot, he was willing to starve again in Harwich as he had done before, until he could get to sea.

Anywhere—anywhere out of the control of Mr. Dobby.

Bending over the prostrate form of Knowall Dick, he saw that he was insensible.

Peeping Tom was in the kitchen, ministering to his gastronomic proclivities.

Here was a chance which might not occur again.

Stealthily he glided into the passage, passed the kitchen unperceived, and made for the back door.

How familiar the old passage seemed to him! its windings and turnings coming back to his mind out of the dim, misty past.

Once in the stable yard he could get through a gate into the garden, and through that into a meadow which went down to the high road.

He had just reached the door, and was breathing inwardly a prayer of thankfulness, when a dark form stepped out of the shadow.

A heavy hand was laid upon his throat.

With a rude shock he was thrown upon his back, and a man's foot was placed on his breast.

Looking up with a startled air he beheld Mr. Dobby.

"I had expected this, young man, he exclaimed "and I laid in wait for you."

"Let me get up," said Harry.

"Not till I have tied your hands. Desperate diseases require desperate remedies, my fine fellow."

"I will give in."

"Of course you will," replied Mr. Dobby, stooping and passing a piece of cord, with which he had supplied himself, round Harry's wrists.

"You are a man and I am only a boy."

"You want to fly too high. I must clip your wings. That will do. Get up now, if you like."

Harry did so, and looked very crestfallen.

Again he had been frustrated in his attempt to get away, and he felt that surely luck must be against him.

Taking the end of the cord in his hand, Mr. Dobby led his discomfited captive back to the gloomy, dirty, prison-like pantry.

There was an iron hook in the wall to which he fastened the cord, so that Harry was obliged to stand on his toes with his arms stretched upwards.

"Stay there," said Mr. Dobby, "until I am ready for you."

Peeping Tom, not being so successful as his friend, had been chased out of the kitchen by the cook, who began to think that the whole school was coming in for sops out of the pan.

He had found Knowall Dick lying on his back breathing heavily.

It made him wonder what had happened.

"A nice watch and ward you keep," growled Mr. Dobby. "If I had not been on the look-out he would have escaped."

"I only went away for a moment, sir," replied Tom. "Dick is hurt, I am afraid."

"If he is, it is your fault."

Knowall Dick, however, soon roused himself, and asked for a glass of water.

"Take him out to the sink or put him under the pump," said Mr. Dobby.

"Don't you want us any more, sir?" asked Peeping Tom.

"No. I can do better without you than I can with you by far."

"All right, sir."

With Tom's assistance Dick walked away, and Mr. Dobby went into the library for a cane.

Harry felt a kind of cold shiver pass through his frame.

He knew that something dreadful was going to happen to him.

Turning his head over his shoulder at the sound of Mr. Dobby's returning footsteps, he saw the cane and shuddered.

"What are you going to do?" he enquired.

"Punish you," was the curt reply.

"If you strike me I will summon you for an assault."

"Rubbish!" said Mr. Dobby. "If I gave you the chance to do so, no magistrate would listen to you."

"Beware! A day of reckoning will come. You are in league with my uncle. It is a conspiracy against me."

Mr. Dobby answered by swinging the cane in the air and bringing it down sharply over his shoulders.

Again and again he struck him cruelly all over the body.

Harry shouted for help, but none came.

To prevent his cries being heard, Mr. Dobby shut the door, and continued the chastisement.

He went on so long, evidently with a purpose, that Harry eventually fainted away.

His head hung over his shoulder, his face was as white as paper, and he scarcely breathed.

Alarmed at seeing this, Mr. Dobby released him.

Taking him in his arms, he laid him on the floor, undid the cord, and chafed his hands, but as this had no effect in reviving him, he threw some cold water in his face.

He was afraid that he had gone a little too far.

If he were to die through the severity of a beating, it would be a case of manslaughter.

"Rawlings," he said, in a frightened whisper, "wake up."

Harry only groaned.

"Thank heaven he is not dead—yet," muttered Mr. Dobby. "I'll leave him to come to. After I have given the boys their dinner I will visit him."

He placed a block of wood under Harry's head, and opened the door with a jerk.

To his surprise, as the door opened inwards, two boys fell at his feet.

They were Peeping Tom and Knowall Dick, who had been leaning against the door with their ears glued near the keyhole.

"How dare you spy upon me?" he asked, angrily.

Getting up with rueful countenances, they apologised for their conduct.

"Please, sir, we heard the howling and noise," said Tom, "and—and—"

"We really couldn't help it," chimed in Dick.

"Don't let me catch you at it again."

"No, sir; not me, sir," Dick hastened to say.

"Your word is law to me, sir," remarked Tom. "We always obey orders."

"Get out and don't bother me. Go away or—"

Mr. Dobby raised the cane menacingly.

The spies fled for their lives.

Then Mr. Dobby locked the door of the pantry, and put the key in his pocket, going into his library to reflect on what he had done.

Had he not been too hasty?

We must leave him to his thoughts while we accompany the spies to the schoolroom, where the boys were in a great state of excitement to know what was going on.

They had not been allowed out, as it was the first day at the new school, and Mr. Dobby had not had time to fix the limitations of a play-ground.

When the spies entered the room, the boys crowded round them.

"We heard a yelling!" exclaimed Woosman. "Who was it."

"The chief has been leathering Rawlings something awful," replied Peeping Tom.

"It will be some time before he gets over it," said Knowall Dick.

"Is he much hurt?" enquired Wildash, with a look of commiseration on his face.

"He can't move or speak," answered Peeping Tom.

"Serves him right," observed Woosman. "He didn't care how much he hurt me. I hate the cad."

"So say I," cried Peeping Tom.

"So say all of us!" echoed Knowall Dick.

"Where is he now?" asked Wildash. "I don't think he has been treated properly. If Mr. Dobby is going to start in this way, and treat all of us like this, his school won't last long."

Peeping Tom looked at him with a peculiar grin.

"If you talk like that," he answered, "someone will tell him what you say, and then there will be two victims instead of one."

"If so, you will be a sneak. Where is Rawlings?"

"In the pantry, and that's where he is likely to stay."

Wildash made no further remark. He went to the other end of the room, and no one took any notice of him.

When he found that he was unobserved, he slipped out, and gaining the passage, stole into the stable-yard.

The window of the pantry was made so as to look out on the yard, at the elevation of about four feet.

As Mr. Rawlings had sold his carriages and horses and dismissed all his servants, except the cook, who acted as housekeeper, and her husband, who was the gardener, there was no one about.

Going to the window, Wildash knocked his elbow against one of the panes of glass.

It broke instantly into a dozen pieces.

"Rawlings!" he exclaimed through the hole. "Are you there?"

He was answered by a faint groan.

"Harry," said Wildash.

"Who is it that calls?" asked the sufferer.

He was just beginning to recover from

the effects of what Mr. Dobby was pleased to term his wholesome discipline.

"Wildash, your friend," was the answer. "I have come to see how you are, and if I can do anything for you. I broke the window, and would come in if it were not for the iron bars; they are in the way."

Three iron bars, of considerable thickness, though somewhat rust-eaten with age, were stretched across the window.

The space between them was barely sufficient to allow an average-sized boy to pass his body through, and that was all.

"Thank you, for coming!" exclaimed Harry, sitting up. "That brute, Dobby, has nearly killed me. I am sure if I stay here he will do so."

"Then you must get away."

"How?"

"I have a file in my tool-box, and will bring it you. Work at the bars all night, and by morning you will be able to get out and make your escape."

"If I have the strength."

He got up on his feet, but tottered against the wall, uttering cries of pain the while.

Mr. Dobby had punished him cruelly.

"I've a bottle of port wine and some cold fowl and ham in the basket I brought from home. Will you accept of it?" enquired Wildash, kindly.

"Yes, and I thank you, old fellow, for your offer."

"It will give you strength for the night's work."

"Make haste, then, and do not let anyone see you there. If you are found talking to me, the spies of the school will be put on to watch. Dobby means to starve and ill-treat me till I die."

"It does not seem possible."

"My dear fellow, you don't understand the matter. I am the heir to a large property, and my uncle wishes me out of the way, so that all may be his."

"Ah! that alters the case," said Wildash.

"It is intended I should die, and Dobby is the paid agent; that I am sure of. Do what you said quickly, and heaven will reward you for being kind to a poor fellow situated as I am."

Wildash had sense enough not to prolong the interview. He saw the danger of remaining there, and he vanished from the window.

It did not take him long to obtain the articles he wanted, and he handed them to Harry through the broken window.

Uttering a few words of comfort, and recommending him to endure his pain as well as he could, Wildash again got away without being perceived.

This was a great point gained.

When alone, Harry made a capital dinner, for he was very hungry. What remained, he hid away, as he did the wine bottle, after breaking off the neck and drinking all he wanted.

The file he put in his pocket for use when darkness fell upon the earth.

Then he sat on some straw, with his back against the wall to rest himself, but he could not go to sleep for the pain he endured.

The dinner-bell rang soon afterwards, and a savoury smell of roast meat was wafted into his dungeon from the kitchen.

This would have tantalized him greatly, but for the meal he had had through the kindness of Wildash.

In about an hour's time, Mr. Dobby visited him.

He was anxious to see how he was progressing after the coercive treatment he had received.

"Not dead yet!" he exclaimed, coarsely.

"I soon shall be, or it won't be your fault," replied Harry.

"You shall have another dose to-morrow, my boy. What you had just now will last you for twenty-four hours. The best of a caning is, that the effect lasts—every bone in your body aches."

"If I die, my murder will be brought home to you, for there will be an inquest."

"Not necessarily," replied Mr. Dobby. "I will put you to bed, and send for the doctor when you are at your last gasp."

"Murderer!"

"The doctor will certify something or another. One thing I can tell you, and that is you shall not leave the place till you are dying. Think over that!" cried Mr. Dobby.

Darting a look of inhuman savageness upon his prisoner, the master closed the door and locked it again.

Fortunately he did not notice the broken window, or his suspicions would have been excited.

As it was, he knew the window was securely barred, and the possibility of escape did not occur to him for a moment.

When it grew dark, Harry, stiff and sore all over though he was, owing to the brutal treatment he had received, got up and began his work.

There was no moon, but the light of the stars enabled him to see what he was about.

He worked steadily on.

At last he was able to wrench the bars away.

His next task was to get through the window, which he did without difficulty.

He was free.

A sensation of unbounded delight took possession of him, and his blood coursed wildly through his veins.

All was still as the grave, for everyone in the new school was wrapt in a profound slumber. The dawn was breaking.

Every inch of the ground was known to him from childhood, and with ease he made his way through the shrubberies into the park.

His destination was Mr. Spencer's farm.

When he arrived at the farm, he discovered the farmer in the straw-yard, talking to Turmuts.

"Good-morning, sir," said Harry, smiling.

"Hey, lad, be that you?" cried Spencer. "Why, how the dickens did you manage to get away?"

"I broke out, although I was locked up," returned Harry, "and I have come to you to claim protection."

"I'll keep you here, as I would my own son, and defy anybody to touch you. Come in, my boy," said the farmer. "My lass Marian will be getting breakfast ready; we're early risers here."

Harry followed him into the kitchen, and was warmly greeted by Mrs. Spencer and Marian, who little expected to see him so soon, after what they had heard.

After breakfast, Mr. Spencer went again into the straw-yard, his wife repaired to the dairy, while Harry and Marian strolled into the garden to gather some peas for dinner, and talk over recent events.

Marian was filled with sympathy for him in his misfortunes.

"You shall never leave us again, Harry," she said, "until you come into your fortune and go to Cambridge. You can do without any more schooling."

"I have had enough of it for the present, anyhow," replied Harry. "All I want is to be near you."

"Don't come too close," she exclaimed, "or you will be kissing me next."

"Why shouldn't I?" queried Harry.

At this juncture a voice exclaimed—

"There he is!"

Both stopped short.

The voice came from the other side of the hedge.

Harry looked over, and, to his dismay, saw the spies of the school.

"Oh!" said Marian, "it is those horrid boys. Look out, Harry! Run into the house!"

"Wait a moment, darling," replied Harry, adding, "I say, you fellows, what are you doing trespassing there?"

"We are looking after you!" exclaimed Peeping Tom.

"You've run away from school," said Knowall Dick, "and we have been sent to find you out by Mr. Dobby."

"Thank you. Tell Mr. Dobby, if you please, that if he wants me, he can come

for me, and perhaps he will meet with a hot reception."

The spies saw they could do no good with Harry by themselves, so they made the best of their way back to the school.

Mr. Dobby was impatiently awaiting their return.

"Well," he asked, "have you found the truant?"

"Yes, sir," replied Peeping Tom, "we have seen him. He is at Mr. Spencer's farm."

"As I suspected."

"He says he will not come back, and defies you."

"Oh! oh!" laughed Mr. Dobby, "we will soon see about that. I shall have to talk law to the farmer. Tell Woosman to keep the boys in order till I return."

Out of breath, Mr. Dobby arrived at the farm, and saw the farmer, Harry, and the man, Turmuts, in the meadow.

"Hullo! you sir!" cried the farmer, loudly. "What is your business here?"

A bulldog behind him began to bark and show his teeth.

"You know what I want," replied Mr. Dobby.

"Clear off my ground," cried Spencer, "or we'll trounce you, and then set the dog on to you."

Mr. Dobby was convinced that he could not tackle such long odds, and so moved away.

"After 'im, Jowler!" cried the farmer.

Away flew Jowler, barking loudly, and away ran Mr. Dobby.

In the middle of the field was a cattle pond, one end of which was very deep.

He did not notice this, and the consequence was that he plunged in.

He could not swim a stroke.

When the others reached the pond Mr. Dobby had sunk for the third time.

Stripping off his boots and coat, Harry did not hesitate to dive for him, and after several attempts succeeded in finding him.

Spencer and Turmuts extended willing hands to drag the body to the bank, which was quickly done.

Every effort they could bestow to restore animation they made, but without success.

The man would never breathe again.

*　　*　　*　　*

A fortnight after the death of Mr. Dobby, a man dressed as a sailor, wearing a long black beard and whiskers, arrived at the farm.

He asked to see Mr. Spencer, and stated that his name was Ormsby. Marian showed him into the parlour and called her father, who at once went to his visitor.

"Mr. Spencer, if I'm not mistaken?" said

the stranger. "I've seen your picture scores of times, and ought to know your phiz."

"Where, may I ask ?"

"In Africa, on the West Coast."

The farmer was fairly astonished. In Africa! What could the man mean?

"You had a brother Robert who went to foreign parts years ago. You and he had a quarrel and parted bad friends, but he kept your picture, though," continued Ormsby.

"Yes, that's true. Robert went abroad —where I never knew. We did not correspond. I thought he was dead long ago."

"He's dead now— died six months ago, and it's about him and his affairs that I am here to-day."

"Bless me!" was all Spencer could say.

"It's business, and good biz., too, for you."

"Take a chair, Mr. Ormsby. I'm all of a flutter. You have recalled bygone days."

"Robert Spencer went as a sailor to the West Coast, and got in with a merchant there as his clerk; afterwards he became a trader himself. D'ye see?"

"I understand."

"Well, he prospered, and died worth a good bit of money and property."

"Glad to hear it, I am sure."

"So you ought to be," said Ormsby, "for he never married; he's left neither chick nor wife, and all his property is willed to you. His factory is worth a good bit, the stock is valuable, and there's money in the bank at Cape Coast Castle."

"Where's that?"

"On the West Coast of Africa."

"I ain't much of a hand at geography. Never was."

"Let me explain the situation to you," said Ormsby. "There are three countries adjoining one another: The Ivory Coast, the Gold Coast, and the Slave Coast. Our settlement is called Three Points, and is about fifty miles from Cape Coast Castle. We are on the Gold Coast, bear in mind. Your brother's factory is at Three Points. I know all about it, because I was his manager. With his last breath he ordered me to seek you and say that you were his sole heir."

"It would be a good opening for my son, I presume?"

"First-rate; nothing better—a large fortune in ten years."

"You must be my guest, Mr. Ormsby, for a time."

"Certainly, until you sail."

"I?" repeated Spencer.

"Oh, yes," said Ormsby. "You must go and take your son with you, and any friend he likes to invite. The 'Lapwing,' sailing

vessel, is now loading in the London Docks. She will sail in a fortnight. That is our vessel."

"Really, it is very sudden. But I must go and tell the missus and my daughter Marian and Harry this wonderful news."

"Who is Harry?" asked Ormsby, carelessly. "Your son?"

"No. Nephew of Squire Rawlings. I'm taking care of him. My son is at school. I'll send Harry up for Jack."

"I'll take a walk in the fields, if you don't mind."

"Do as you like, sir."

Full of excitement, Spencer ran into the kitchen, where his wife, Marian, and Harry were.

In a few words he told them of the good luck Mr. Ormsby had informed him of, and they were as much astonished as himself.

"Shall you really have to go to this place called Three Points, on the Gold Coast of Africa?" asked Mrs. Spencer.

"Certain sure," he replied. "If I don't attend to this windfall myself, I shall be cheated."

"No power on earth will induce *me to* go.'

"Enough said!" cried Spencer. "Thee and Turmuts shall stay at home and manage the farm. I want someone to look after it."

"I'll go, father!" exclaimed Marian.

"You shall come, if your mother will let you."

"Leave that to me. I'll persuade her."

Mrs. Spencer made no reply. Her tears fell fast. She saw herself left alone, and imagined all sorts of dreadful perils.

"Harry shall go, and Jack," continued the farmer, volubly. "It isn't much of a voyage. I'll wind up the concern, and if the boys don't like to stay and work the factory, we'll all be back in three or four months. I say, Harry, run up to the school and fetch Jack. He must see Mr. Ormsby and hear all about it for himself."

"All right, sir. I'll have have him here before dinner," replied Harry.

"Did you see Mr. Ormsby?"

"Yes; I saw him as he came up to the door."

When Harry reached the school, he readily obtained leave of absence for Jack.

Drawing him on one side, he imparted his news, at which he was highly pleased.

They walked down the field arm-in arm.

At the bottom they saw the two spies, who were talking to a man.

"Hullo!" cried Harry, "look at Peeping Tom and Knowall Dick with Mr. Ormsby!"

The three looked up when they heard Harry's exclamation.

"That is Jack Spencer, sir, for whom you were enquiring," exclaimed Peeping Tom.

Ormsby smiled, stepped foward, and extended his hand.

"How are you, my lad?" he cried. "I heard from your father you were at the school, and as I was out for a walk, I thought I would give you a look up, and tell you about your late uncle, though I suppose you have heard by this time. Meeting these two boys, your school-fellows, I stopped them, and asked where I should be likely to find you in the play hour."

He turned to the spies and waved his hand.

"Thank you. Good-day, young gentlemen," he added. "Now, Jack, I will go back to the farm with you. I imagine your friend is the Harry your father spoke of. I am glad to know you both."

When Jack and Harry were alone, after reaching the farm, the former said—

"Wasn't it rather singular that Mr. Ormsby should have been in conversation with the spies?"

"It does seem odd," replied Harry; "but he was asking for you."

"I don't half like it!" exclaimed Jack. "And do you know, I have a misty recollection of having seen a face like his somewhere."

"Impossible!"

"And the tone of his voice is equally familiar, though I can't place either."

"Fancy, my dear fellow."

"It may be. I hope it is," said Jack, thoughtfully.

A week passed, during which all the necessary preparations for departure were made.

One day, Jack was with Harry, at the old roadside inn, talking to Corks, the landlord.

To their surprise, Peeping Tom and Knowall Dick walked into the bar.

They were dressed in spick-and-span new midshipmen's clothes.

"Hullo!" cried Jack. "Are you going to a masquerade?"

"Oh, no; going to sea," answered Peeping Tom. "Do you imagine no one can go to sea but yourself?"

"Certainly not; but what makes you—"

"We are acquainted with Charlie Rawlings, my dear fellow," Tom interrupted. "He is on board his father's yacht at Naples, and, feeling he wanted the company of some old friends, about his own age, he has kindly sent for us. Good-day."

After this interview, the spies were seen no more. They had, it was said, gone to London to take steamer for Naples, where Mr. Rawlings' yacht was lying.

At length, the time for our friends' departure came. They all took an affectionate but cheerful farewell of Mrs. Spencer, and proceeded to London, when they went at once on board the ship "Lapwing," which was to sail next morning.

Mr. Ormsby introduced the captain, whose name was Wilcox, and the mate, Mr. Perry, but he did not allow any conversation to take place between them.

He had supper served in the saloon at ten o'clock, and, after that, proposed a game of cards, which passed the time pleasantly away until they turned into bed.

When they awoke, the next morning, they were below Gravesend, and fast nearing the Nore, favoured by wind and tide.

That night saw them in the English Channel, and in another twenty hours they were in the stormy waters of the broad Atlantic Ocean.

www.ingramcontent.com/pod-product-compliance
Lightning Source LLC
Chambersburg PA
CBHW080840250626
47161CB00009B/3129